NEW ORLEANS
MOURNING

NEW ORLEANS MOURNING

Julie Smith

A THOMAS DUNNE BOOK

ST. MARTIN'S PRESS · NEW YORK

Library of Congress Cataloging-in-Publication Data

Smith, Julie.
    New Orleans mourning / Julie Smith.
        p.   cm.
    "A Thomas Dunne book."
    ISBN (invalid) 0-312-03892-2
    I. Title.
PS3569.M537553N49   1990
813'.54—dc20
                                89-27051
                                CIP

First Edition

10 9 8 7 6 5 4 3 2 1

For Ann—a tour of the old neighborhood

A thousand thanks to Lieutenant Linda Buczek of the New Orleans Police Department and to Betsy Petersen, each of whom helped with a thousand details. More local lore came from Tom Petersen, Diane Angelico, Chris Wiltz, Betty Pearson, Sheila Bosworth, William Barlow, and a secret sleuth who must not be named. Dr. Patty Barnwell, Dr. Robert Harbaugh, Bob Celecia, and Philip Shelton were generous with technical advice in their areas. Heartfelt thanks to all of them and special, extra thanks to my literary agents, Vicky Bijur and Charlotte Sheedy.

PROLOGUE

In New Orleans, Carnival is nothing less than a season. It lasts thirty to sixty days and virtually consumes its celebrants, who in turn consume several oceans of inebriants. This exuberant annual escapade has its roots, as does almost every excess of high spirits, in pagan fertility rites.

Early on in Arcadia, to purify the soil, the priests painted themselves, the shepherds stripped naked, and the former chased the latter over the landscape, merrily lashing them with goatskin whips. But of course that was nothing compared with the Roman bacchanal that evolved from it. Naturally the church sought to end the hilarity. Just as naturally, it failed. Early quashing efforts only resulted in skylarks such as the medieval Feast of Fools, which included a mock mass and blasphemous impersonations of church officials.

Finally, in the spirit of compromise that has so often saved their bacon, the bishops offered instead their own celebration, neatly transforming a pagan debauch into a Christian one. It was first called *Carnelavare*, or "farewell to the flesh," because it preceded the forty Lenten days of fasting and penitence before Easter. But one must be sober to pronounce such a word, and so it became simply "Carnival."

The medieval custom of holding parades, masquerades, and revels in celebration of Carnival has been handed down in certain unruly cities—notably New Orleans, Rio de Janeiro, Nice, and Cologne. The two gentlemen who originally claimed Louisiana for France (Iberville and Bienville) got things rolling in that area one February night around the turn of the eighteenth century, when they camped on a small bayou and, overcome with homesickness, remembered that back in France the streets would be mobbed with revelers. They called the creek Bayou Mardi Gras, for "Fat Tuesday," the last-chance feast before the fast beginning Ash Wednesday.

The colony's settlers remembered also the customs of yore and declined, though far from home, to let the standards slip. In fact, they may have even raised them a bit, because in most cities Carnival lasts about a week. In New Orleans the season starts on January 6, making Mardi Gras Day itself the climactic moment of weeks of revels.

From time to time in New Orleans, by one early governor or another, Mardi Gras was banned as rowdy and dangerous. But it always popped up again, and always rowdier still. In 1857 people thought that it would die a natural death due to the high crime rate. In fact, that year's Mardi Gras was really the beginning of the frolic as we know it today. The Mistick Krewe of Comus paraded for the first time. This may have been the single most important event in the social history of the city.

Quite simply, Comus is the most elite and important of the city's krewes, or Carnival organizations, of which there must now be hundreds. Nowadays there are women's krewes, like Venus and Iris, black krewes, like Zulu, gay krewes, black gay krewes, krewes composed of suburban dentists, krewes that make fun of other krewes, krewes of every stripe, krewes from every stratum. But the important krewes are secret societies made up of male members of the crème de la crème. To get in, an aspirant may have to wait for someone to die. Then, of course, he must be voted upon and must be able to contribute substantial dues to pay for the annual ball and parade.

For the raison d'être of the krewes is to have a parade and a ball at Carnival. Eccentric as it may seem, they truly exist for no other purpose. (However, the membership of Comus, though theoretically unknown, also runs the Boston Club and therefore the city.)

Rex, the second most important krewe, is a different animal from Comus. Its membership is not secret and its focus is civic rather than social. Even a New Orleans newcomer might be asked to join if he had the right job, knew the right people, and worked hard for the good of the city. Despite such seeming common status compared with the rarefied circles of Comus, Momus, and Proteus, Rex himself, the civic leader selected each year as king of the krewe, is also king of Carnival. (He's very likely to be a member of Comus as well.)

The crown of Rex is the most coveted honor of New Orleans society. It's said that ex-Rexes tend to get carried away with their royal status. The one who had little crowns engraved on his stationery has gone down in history. Others simply rest on their laurels in the Rex Room at Antoine's, eating, drinking, and remembering.

The notion of Rex was invented in 1872, the greatest of all Mardi Gras. That was the year the city devoted its energies to impressing a visiting Romanoff so glamorous that in New York he'd caused near-riots and left the streets strewn with swooning women. The grand duke's favorite song, "If Ever I Cease to Love," became the theme song of Mardi Gras;

Mardi Gras was declared a legal holiday; and Mardi Gras got a king, all in the same year.

The first Rex, Louis Salomon, wore purple velvet embroidered with rhinestones and rode not a float but a horse. Though Salomon was a Jew, today no Jew can be Rex. This discrimination occurs because the monarch of mirth must now come from the Boston Club, which does not admit Jews, women, blacks, or anyone of any ethnic origin whose blood is not a vivid shade of azure. Originally just a group of guys who liked a card game called Boston, the club grew in numbers and exclusivity until it became the power hub of the city—solidly and absolutely committed to the preservation of the status quo.

Not only Rex but every krewe has a king, though in the fancy ones his identity is kept secret. Each king has his court of nubile young maidens as well—the season's debutantes and almost certainly the daughters of members. Far from being kept secret, the names and faces of the queens and maids are widely publicized, as there would be little point to the honor otherwise.

Naturally, the most important party of Mardi Gras Day (the Comus and Rex balls being scheduled for evening) is held at the Boston Club. The club being on Canal Street, which is right on the parade route, the Queen of Carnival and various other dignitaries (including the nearly forgotten wife of Rex himself) view the passing of Rex from a balcony draped in the purple, green, and gold of Carnival. From the thronged and frenzied street, the king toasts his queen.

Anticipating this moment could be an occasion of deepest boredom, but the inventive citizens of the City That Care Forgot are well practiced in the art of diversion.

THE BOSTON CLUB

1

Bitty would have to be propped up, and God knew what Henry would do. If Marcelle fell flat on her face that would be three grand screwups out of three. The least she could do was stay on her feet. She was the only one who gave a damn about Chauncey anyway. Except for Tolliver, maybe, and he wasn't even a St. Amant.

How many drinks were too many? She had had three, maybe four, and it was barely eleven o'clock. It would be almost another hour—nearly noon—before the parade passed and stopped so that her father could toast his youthful queen. She had to slow down—she wasn't supposed to be the

5

drunk in the family. Then again, it was Carnival. Who'd notice anyway?

Only everyone. Because all eyes were on the St. Amants today. In another hour and a half the population would be staring up at the balcony, where Rex's lovely family, to do their patriarch proud, must look like refugees from the '50s—even down to their hairdos and clothing. All three of them were wearing suits—son Henry, wife Bitty, daughter Marcelle. The wife and daughters of Rex always wore suits, just as Rex's queen was always a debutante of the season and the daughter of someone important. The queen—Brooke Youngblood this year, a Kappa at LSU—wore a suit as well.

Marcelle wondered if a woman would even be allowed on the balcony in a dress or pants. But the question wouldn't come up. You wouldn't make your debut in a black dress either.

Marcelle's suit was rose-and-black houndstooth checks with knee-brushing skirt and short, neat jacket. If she ever wore it again, she would shorten the skirt by at least two inches. Brooke Youngblood's skirt was box-pleated, and she wore her hair in a pageboy.

Being well into her twenties, Marcelle didn't have to go that far, but she'd had to smooth down her short dark hair. Normally she liked to look as if she'd had it styled sometime in the twentieth century; but today she wore no gel, no mousse, no spikes, no magenta rinse. She looked like Daddy's good little girl even if she wasn't, and everyone knew it.

Not, of course, that anyone cared. Certainly her mother didn't. Bitty cared about nothing that wasn't amber-colored and wet. As for Henry, he was a bigger slut than Marcelle. And Chauncey wouldn't even have noticed she'd grown up if she hadn't had a four-year-old son. He was forever ruffling her hair and buying her raspberry ice cream. When she was a kid he used to take her for walks and buy her cones. It was about the only pleasant memory of her childhood.

Marcelle's glass was still half full. For Chauncey's sake, she thought. For Chauncey she could make the drink last another hour.

It was absurdly quiet here. There was only the drone of conversation and the genteel clinking of glasses. You'd hardly know it was Mardi Gras at all, and indeed, in a way it wasn't. The Boston Club party was stultifyingly different from anything anyone else in the city was doing that day. There wasn't a soul in costume—unless you counted the two women from Mississippi in the clown outfits. Someone's guests.

And no one was rowdy, out-of-hand, or seemingly even drunk, though Marcelle suspected at least fifty percent had arrived with a blood alcohol content well above the legal driving limit. These were the sorts of people who held their liquor well and pretended their livers would last forever. Her grandfather, for instance. She'd never seen him drunk in her life, yet never seen him without a drink in hand, never kissed him without tasting bourbon. The old boy had been well pickled for the last forty years. Yet it didn't seem to interfere with his performance—he'd been bossing around most of the old coots currently juicing it up in these very dark-paneled rooms for most of his life. Too bad Bitty hadn't inherited his ability to remain standing while blotto.

Marcelle wondered where her grandfather was and hoped she wouldn't run into him. But he didn't walk that much anymore. Probably found a leather wing chair in which to sink and be surrounded by his sycophants. He'd be looking exactly like a toad on a leaf—enormous belly and chest, tiny legs, big ugly mottled head, and sharp, dangerous little eyes. No wonder Bitty had married someone so different—so handsome and gentle.

Oh, Chauncey, I hope Bitty or Henry doesn't wreck it for you. Or me, God knows. That's a distinct possibility. But what is there to do but drink? It's so dismal here.

Feeling defeated, Marcelle strolled to the bar and got her fourth drink of the morning. (If it wasn't her fifth.) In fact, she realized, this was a lovely room—not dismal at all. A kind of garden room. The rest of the club looked very much as she would imagine a men's club on James Street in London—dark wood, leather chairs, oriental rugs. Stately. Elegant. At the moment, full of forsythia and lovely spring flowers. The Boston Club was famous for the elaborate flower arrangements it always displayed at Mardi Gras. Marcelle almost smiled.

The ladies of Venus and the members of Endymion (880 strong) wore outlandish feather headdresses, but even these could barely hold a candle to the feather getups the Mardi Gras Indians conjured up. And the Indians were wildly out-flashed by the drag queens. But at the Boston Club, when they kicked out all the jams, that meant they had some flowers brought in.

Marcelle looked around her and wondered why she found the atmosphere so dismal. Maybe it *was* the clothes. To a man, the gentlemen wore dark suits—except for the ones on the reception committee, who wore full-dress morning clothes. The women's suits and silk dresses all looked as if they'd cost what Marcelle had paid for her car, and they were in punctiliously impeccable taste. But to Marcelle's mind, "frumpy" might have been a better description—nothing above the knees or very much below them.

It was middle-of-the-road city in these dark and hallowed halls. Neutral ground. That was what New Orleanians called the median strips that divided the streets. The phrase suddenly seemed a metaphor for what was wrong with the whole place—everybody trying to hold the neutral ground. You were supposed to look neutral, act neutral, pretend you were beige—when your whole family might be falling apart even though your father was King of Carnival. Suddenly it seemed funny. The drink was helping.

"That's more like it." It was Jo Jo Lawrence, all blond hair and football shoulders. He bumped against her slightly, dumping white wine all over her pink silk blouse. "Oh, Lord. I'm sorry." He dabbed at her with a paper napkin, lightly touching her breasts.

8

"It's okay." Marcelle brushed at her own chest. "It's white. It'll hardly show at all when it's dry." She raised her face to his. "What's more like it?"

"That little smile. I was watching you. Why so sad on Mardi Gras? Especially *this* one?"

"Mind your own business, okay, Jo Jo?"

"I heard your divorce is final."

Marcelle said nothing. Sometimes she wished she'd married Jo Jo. After Lionel's drunken rages, his vacant sweetness seemed a lot more appealing than it had in high school. She couldn't remember why she'd married Lionel anyway, or why she hadn't married Jo Jo. He hadn't asked her, she supposed. They'd been too young anyway. But he was the first boy she'd been to bed with—only it wasn't bed, exactly, it was the lakefront.

"How 'bout a kiss for Jo Jo? For old time's sake."

Why not? He was about the only man in town she hadn't kissed in the last six months. Why not Jo Jo? She lifted her face.

He kissed her gently, sweetly. Then he put both arms around her and kissed her for real. Right there in the Boston Club, in front of everybody. But did anybody notice? She'd be amazed if they did. Not a little thing like a kiss. Everyone kissed everyone at Carnival. No one would remember whom they'd kissed themselves, much less who else had kissed whom. You could go to church on Ash Wednesday and sit next to someone you'd done God knows what with and not even know it.

Jo Jo's body felt unexpectedly, familiarly good. Familiar and yet forbidden. Jo Jo was married now. But everyone was married, and that didn't seem to stop anyone else. Even her own father. It had never stopped Marcelle either.

It must be two weeks since I've been with a man—some kind of record for me.

Jo Jo was pushing her back toward the wall, toward the nearest doorway, his heavy body against hers, his breath redolent of Bloody Marys. I'm burning, she thought. I'm burning up. Her suit jacket was sticking to her, her corsage must be crushed.

I can't do this, it's crazy.

But lately she didn't seem to have much control. Oh, hell. She didn't want to be in this awful crowd anyway, with her mother and Henry and her fossil of a grandfather. They disgusted her.

Why shouldn't she fuck Jo Jo if she wanted to? Everything she did today she was doing for her father. Why shouldn't she do this one thing for herself? There would be time before the St. Amant moment of glory. (Plenty of time, if Jo Jo hadn't changed.) It was going to be a long, long day. She'd have her hands full in the next few hours. Why not take a moment first? It would help relax her. She wondered if Jo Jo had a rubber with him the way he always had in high school.

2

Henry was dead sober. So sober dead would have felt preferable. On the other hand, he was coked to the gills. He had to be, for the ordeal to come. But he felt as sick as if he'd been drinking martinis by the quart.

"Henry, ol' son, what's a ten?"

"A ten?"

"Like in the movie."

"Oh, a woman. I don't know."

"Four feet tall, flat head with a six-pack on it, and no teeth."

Much more in that vein and he was going to lose it. Too much meaningful colloquy with these upper-class twits and he might just bash heads, not merely fall on the floor. Falling on the floor was more Bitty's style anyway. And Marcelle's, when she got going. Passive resistance. The thought nearly made him laugh. When you got down to it, none of the three of them had been more passive than he had, given up more . . . no, that wasn't true. Bitty had. He wished he could make it up to her, somehow give her back what Chauncey had taken away.

Oh, Bitty, Bitty, Bitty, are you all right? Will you get through this? Where was she anyway?

He was wearing a suit and tie for her, a normal tie too, nothing flamboyant, nothing embarrassing. And how he would have loved to wear something really outrageous. Something to shock the pants off his father and all these Country Day graduates who were now budding bankers and lawyers and doctors.

Fortunately there weren't all that many young people in the place. Henry probably wouldn't have been there himself if his grandfather hadn't been who he was. Even his father's status as king for a day might not have gotten him in—men who weren't members weren't welcome at the Boston Club. But you simply didn't argue with Haygood Mayhew; you deferred to him and pretended the honor was all yours. The combined membership of the Boston, Pickwick, Bienville, and Louisiana clubs couldn't have kept Henry out of any place in the city if his grandfather wanted him there.

So much the worse, to Henry's way of thinking. He would have given all the doubloons of Rex to be anywhere else in the world today. But he was here for Bitty.

As it happened, Bitty, however, appeared to be doing great. She hadn't had a drink all day. Why this farce should matter to her he didn't know, but she'd pulled up her socks and carried on, like the heroine of some nineteenth-century English novel. Chauncey didn't deserve it, but maybe it would be a new beginning for her—maybe, ultimately, it would be worth it.

If he could just get away from this bunch of assholes—the extremely bored and jaded escorts of the queen's maids. He looked around for the only person he loved besides his mother. Where the hell was Tolliver when he needed him? *Life is tolerable only with Tolliver.* It was a line Tolliver had taught him when he was about two feet tall. When his parents were too much for him, Tolliver had picked him up and hugged him and kissed him and made him feel as if he had a real father, not just Chauncey.

And Henry had felt safe and loved. Tolliver was a tall man, though slight—not half the size of Chauncey, but big enough to feel like a dad. Henry thought he looked like Tolliver too—he thought of Chauncey and Marcelle as the dark ones, himself and Bitty and Tolliver as the light ones, the ones who were *really* a family.

He'd even asked his mother once if there'd been a mistake, if Tolliver were really his father. But she'd laughed and pointed out all his little resemblances to Chauncey—the round face, the strong, square jaw, the brown eyes—as opposed to Tolliver's long, elegant, almost lugubrious countenance with its watery, languid blue eyes. It was cruel, Henry had thought at the time. He'd wanted to believe Tolliver was his father.

Life is tolerable only with Tolliver. It was only recently that he'd realized how much truth there was in that bit of childhood nonsense.

Some dickhead from high school joined the knot of young men. "Henri! The man of the hour. How's it going, boy?"

"How's it going for you, Jack? I heard you're going out with a chawama."

"All the pussy I can eat, man. Say, how're you doin' anyway? Still working at Brennan's?"

"Uh-huh. Supporting my habit."

"I *heard* you were handin' out some pretty good shit."

"I meant my acting habit."

"Huh?" Jack looked blank. "Oh, yeah, forgot about that."

"It doesn't bring in the bucks like maritime law, I'm afraid."

"Say, you in anything now? Maybe I'll bring Doreen. I could get her to bring a friend, we could go out afterward, have a few—give you a chance to bone up on your yat."

"Not much call for yat in *Measure for Measure*."

"*Measure for. . . ?* Oh, yeah—that's what you're in. Hey, Shakespeare's not everything—maybe someone'll write a yat play someday. *Confederacy of Dunces!* Yeah! You can play Ignatius." Jack smiled, obviously extremely pleased at pulling off a literary allusion.

"Sure, Jack, bring Doreen. It'd be a pleasure to meet her."

Jack wasn't going to bring Doreen. Henry doubted he ever took her anywhere except to her corner bar to get her loosened up. And Jack wasn't coming to a little theater production of *Measure for Measure* either. Hell, if he were in Stratford-on-Avon, Jack wouldn't go to the theater. Unlike Henry's father. Chauncey went to the theater all the time— as long as the production was one in which Henry wasn't acting.

"Hey, man, you got any more of that coke?"

"I gave it all away. Sorry."

Jack shrugged. "Me too, man. Say, listen, you oughta try a chawama—good pussy, cheap date, no nervous breakdowns."

"Excuse me. I've got to find my mother."

Damn. Why had he said that? It sounded as if he meant he had to take care of her, to make sure she didn't get drunk enough to fall on her ass out on the reviewing stand. He was starting to lose it. What he had to do was get some fresh air. He couldn't take much more of this. Not even for Bitty. He had to steel himself for the interminable hours ahead.

3

"Bitty!"

She didn't turn around, probably hadn't heard.

Tolliver gave up and went upstairs to the men's room. He wet a paper towel, wrung it out, and held it to his forehead.

"Tolliver, you okay?"

He heard himself gasp—a loud "Aaahhhh!", almost a yell.

Dropping the paper towel, he caught a glimpse of his frightened face in the mirror. This was absurd; it was ridiculous. He turned around. The man who'd sneaked up was one of his customers, a man named Billy Ambrose.

"You startled me."

"Sorry." Billy gave him a winsome grin. "I didn't know I was that imposing. You okay? Headache or what?"

Tolliver tried for a smile that he suspected was more like a grimace and waved Billy into one of the stalls. "Fine," he whispered, knowing Billy couldn't hear him. He'd left his pills at home. Goddamn! Of all days to forget them. Worrying about Bitty was making him twitchy—even more so than he'd expected; and he'd known it was going to be a very difficult day indeed. He'd called out to her because he'd seen her stumble. He might have known. She'd been doing beautifully earlier, but how much could you expect of one human being? One very weak, unhappy, alcoholic human being who'd drawn hardly a sober breath in twenty years or more? But every now and then she cleaned up her act and was okay for a while.

No doubt it gave her liver a rest, but it was a long-term solution by no means. For years her family had been trying to get her to join AA, with no success. Bitty was afraid to give up drinking. Life held no pleasures for her now except the sweet haze of alcohol. Without it, she wouldn't want to live. And so, in a way, it was what was keeping her alive and they should all be glad of it. But it seemed that lately, for the past few weeks, she'd been worse than ever. Or was that his imagination?

Probably not. She was worried about today probably. He needed to get to her . . . to help her get through it. He knew she wanted to stay sober, and she was going to need a lot of support.

But he was useless with this nagging headache, this anxiety. He had to get out of here. He felt tired, dizzy, and spent.

Staggering himself, though hardly aware of it, Tolliver threaded his way to the street. God, he hated Carnival! He hated the masks and he hated the costumes and he hated the booze and the noise and the forced, desperate gaiety, and the pressure and the crowds and the revolting, no-holds-barred vulgarity of the thing. There was something else he hated this much—or someone. What was it? The hatred felt familiar, but he couldn't put his finger on it right now.

What had he thought he was doing, coming outside? The crowds were so thick you couldn't walk a step. But he had to get through them. He had to get home and get his pills, then there was something else he had to do . . . something to do with Bitty.

Yes. Now he remembered. He'd get the car and go home and get the pills and do what he'd planned to do, which was take care of Bitty. As always. He'd been doing it ever since he could remember, and today was an important day.

He wondered how Henry was. Would he get through the day okay? The thought of Henry—so young and vulnerable (though he thought himself so worldly)—made Tolliver suddenly warm and happy. If Bitty made it through the day okay, then Henry would be okay and maybe Tolliver would too. It was only that thought that was getting him through.

His head was beginning to clear. It felt better now. He had walked for a long time—very slowly. As a small boy he could remember holding his mother's hand, but not being able to see her. And that was on St. Charles, where things were tamer. The crowds were thickest here, right on Canal. Still, he didn't need to go fast. He was doing fine. He walked and walked and walked, it seemed. But the faces seemed familiar, the costumes too. The same feathers, the same sequins—or was every exhibitionist in town wearing a red-feathered cod-piece with silver-sequined suspenders? The same slave girl, the same top-hatted magician with the same ratty mechanical rabbit. Good Christ! The same teenage girl on the same balcony. The same crowd hollering, "Show your tits!" She had painted sunbursts on them.

How long had he been walking? He felt disoriented. Had he gotten his pills? His limbs felt stronger now, as if he'd walked off the twitchiness. His head hadn't hurt for a long time. Had he done what he'd set out to do? He must get back. He must start to find his way back.

Bitty would be wondering what had happened to him. Henry would be going nearly mad, trying to take care of her, wondering where Tolliver was. He stopped a man in a gorilla suit and asked directions.

4

Bitty smoothed makeup into the little bags beneath her eyes, then put on some eyeliner and mascara. Her hand was as steady as if she'd never had a drink in her life. She could hold it together when she wanted to, and she'd get through this day as easily as if she were as young and capable as Henry.

She'd stumbled on her way to the ladies' room and that worried her. People might think she was drunk. But so be it. That one little slip was all they were going to get to talk about. She'd been planning this day for six weeks, and she wasn't about to blow it now. She had even gone and bought herself a new plum-colored suit at Saks, where she couldn't bear shopping. But Gus Mayer and Godchaux's were gone now, and she had to have something new. Otherwise people really would have thought she'd gone to seed. She looked damn good in it too, unless she was much mistaken.

Her hair was as blonde as it had been on her wedding day, and her eyes were as clear—today anyway. Carefully, she washed her hands—very, very carefully. Anne-Marie De-lamore, who'd just gone into one of the stalls, had given her an odd look, as if wondering whether to stick around to pick her up when she fell. But no fear of that—absolutely none.

She simply felt the need for clean hands, that was all. Hadn't Anne-Marie ever seen anyone take her time?

She wondered vaguely where Marcelle and Henry and Tolliver were. But they weren't far, she was sure. Today was Chauncey's big day. Today he was Rex, the Monarch of Mirth, the King of Carnival, and the leading citizen of New Orleans. It was the climax of his whole life—the day he'd been working for ever since she'd met him. Just how hard he'd worked she hadn't learned till much later, and it was rather a bitter lesson, but today was undeniably Chauncey's day. All his little satellites—the beautiful family he was so proud of, the best friend who'd stuck with Bitty and Chauncey through some of the toughest times any family could possibly experience—they'd all be close.

She usually felt braver when she was drunk, but right now, stone sober, she felt exhilarated, as if she could do anything. She moved aside so Anne-Marie could wash her hands, then fumbled for her lipstick. She'd apply it slowly, carefully, so that Anne-Marie could see what a good little sober wife she was.

"Mrs. St. Amant? Is Bitty St. Amant in here?"

"Yes?"

It was Skip Langdon, not dressed at all properly for the party at the Boston Club. She looked like a heifer in that getup. Skip must be nearly six feet tall, and she'd been overweight all her life. "Mrs. St. Amant?"

"Yes? Skip, what is it?" She looked carefully at the younger woman's face, and she remembered what Skip was doing now—it wasn't a costume she was wearing. Skip looked so sad, so very sad, as if she could hardly bear to speak.

"Skippy—tell me. What is it?" Bitty knew her voice was coming out in a wail, but there was nothing she could do about it. She looked at Anne-Marie Delamore, who had turned paper-white. So Anne-Marie felt it too. Something was terribly, terribly wrong.

"Mrs. Delamore," said Skip, "could you excuse us please?" Bitty wouldn't be alone with her. No. She declined. Absolutely not. She would be with those she loved. Behind a scuttling Anne-Marie, she walked unsteadily out of the bathroom, through the anteroom with its pretty mantel, and back to the party.

THE MONARCH OF MIRTH

The quiet was deafening. Skip had forgotten that part, though she'd been here before on Mardi Gras—as Tricia Lattimore's guest, when they were both at McGehee's and nobody their age had invited them anywhere. She was at the Boston Club today for no other reason than that she knew these people, she was at home here—or so her brother officers imagined. True, her father had elbowed his way into Rex, but certainly not into this bastion of blue blood. And that didn't begin to tell the story. There was Skip's own peculiar identity crisis to reckon with. But Sergeant Pitre wouldn't know about that, and wouldn't care. She was handy, that was all. She'd been on the scene and no one else who had had been brave enough to beard the Brahmins in their lair.

*   *   *

Skip had been working parade routes, along with a third of the cops in the city, and she was scheduled for a twelve-hour shift like everyone else. The system really wasn't too bad. During Carnival a third of the department did their regular jobs from 6 A.M. to 6 P.M., a third took over from 6 P.M. to 6 A.M., and that freed everyone else for parade routes.

Skip's day had started with Zulu and a fight among three men and a woman. The woman's escort was obviously "from away," as New Orleanians put it. "Forget doubloons," Skip heard her tell him. "But if you catch a coconut, guard it with your life."

For once, Skip was standing with her back to the parade, watching the crowd, as regulations required. The speaker was a blonde woman wearing a UNO sweatshirt. Her friend had on a denim jacket. Skip's eye strayed over the crowd and a coconut thrown by a Zulu warrior whizzed over her shoulder. The man in the denim jacket, apparently impressed by his date's assessment of its value, jumped up, caught it, and cradled it in the crook of his arm like a football player catching a pass. "All r-i-i-ght!" Skip yelled. A few people clapped and hollered.

"Hey! Hey!" yelled the man with the coconut, and suddenly he was down. The crowd parted. Two well-dressed men were trying to wrestle away the coconut. Skip started toward them. "Okay, okay! Knock it off!"

The blonde glanced at her briefly, hesitating only a moment, and jumped on the pile, closing her teeth around the polo-shirted bicep of the topmost man. Skip paused, giving the three a chance to work out their differences. She stepped back to give the two ruffians room to run. Caught up in the spirit, she shouted: "A round of applause, ladies and gentlemen!" The crowd cheered, the blonde bowed, and her gentleman friend presented her with the well-earned coconut.

A satisfying morning. Unlike most of her peers, Skip liked working parade routes. It was a relief from having to make small talk with the likes of Marcelle St. Amant Gaudet, who had ice-blue chiffon behind the eyes.

It was a relief from a lot of things. She could remember the party at the Pontalba, where the host lowered a bucket from the balcony and shouted, "Alms for the rich." Unamused, his girlfriend tried to stop him, and he dragged her into the bathroom. There were some thumps and screams, then silence. Finally the host emerged carrying handfuls of frosted, permed, freshly cut hair, which he scattered among the guests.

The shorn girlfriend, apparently undaunted, spent the afternoon methodically seducing each male member of the host's family, racking up, by Skip's count, older brother, younger brother, and two cousins. She later told friends his father had been perfectly willing as well, but too drunk to get it up.

Even as a prepubescent hellion, Skip had liked the street at Carnival. Not Canal Street particularly, where the crowds were so thick people stood in the streets about an inch from the floats—literally smack up against them, so that if there was trouble the entire U.S. Army, much less the New Orleans Police Department, would be helpless. And where you couldn't even get your hands above your head to reach out for throws and where, if you were claustrophobic, you'd faint and be trampled to death because no way could you get your head between your knees.

What she liked was St. Charles Avenue, like Canal closed to traffic for the Rex Parade. But even here, famous as the site of "the family Mardi Gras," it could get rough. She'd forgotten how rough, how violent it could be, and she was relearning that morning. Yet in past years she'd given the cops as much trouble as certain drunk, foul-mouthed sorority types were giving her today.

The huddled masses stood several hundred deep on both sides of the avenue, some with ladders for their kids or themselves, some with toddlers on their shoulders, risking the kids'

lives, in her opinion—one bump and baby hit the pavement.
As a cop (instead of the dedicated troublemaker of old) she
was truly shocked at the way they pushed and shoved and
hollered for throws. They really did holler and beg—just like
the guidebooks said they did. It seemed to be proper Carnival etiquette for the hoi polloi. The aristocrats, (the male
ones anyway), grandly conveyed on floats, were supposed to
demonstrate their largess by casting trinkets into the crowds.
Little strings of beads, mostly, and Carnival doubloons.

She wondered how the knights and dukes of Rex decided
on whom to bestow the coveted gewgaws. Did they search
out the prettiest girls? The most flamboyant drag queens? The
least aggressive little kids? The recyclers, of course, those
who caught throws and rethrew them, bargained for nudity.
In the last few years it had become a fad in the Quarter for
women to take off their blouses for beads.

If Skip were on a float she would have insisted, she
thought, on rewarding those in the most amusing costumes.
Like that man across the street who'd apparently got himself
up as an Italian restaurant. He had a round, tablelike arrangement around his middle covered with a red-checked table-
cloth and topped with a plate of papier-mâché spaghetti and
an old wine bottle complete with colorful wax drippings. She
also liked the grasshopper with a little grasshopper kid just
about knee-high to him. If you were going to behave like an
idiot, which was the whole point of Carnival, you could at
least go all the way.

There were a lot of popes this year, as His Holiness had
earlier favored the city with a visit. Here and there was a
two-legged Dixie beer can, and the random screwball who
had sprayed himself gold or silver. Inevitably, there was a
film crew trying vainly to make some sort of visual sense of it
all. Skip wondered if the filmmakers would bother to record
the prodigious number of kids in fraternity sweatshirts carrying Hurricanes or beers—or even legal go-cups—and barfing
all over one another. The drinking age had recently been

raised to twenty-one, but the unofficial tall-enough-to-reach-the-bar rule was still very much in effect. And you could drink on the street as long as you didn't do it out of a bottle or glass, but on Mardi Gras who could enforce the go-cup law?

Skip was absolutely convinced that most of the damage done by Carnival drunks was perpetrated by the football and beer-bust crowd. She ought to know, having done quite a bit of it herself in her day. She was well aware of the legendary kinship between cops and criminals. It was only recently that she'd come over to the side of law and order.

A roar was gathering up the avenue. The sovereign float, the one bearing Rex himself, was approaching. The closer it came, the pushier people got. Skip knew this was the wrong time to let her attention stray—and all too well, she knew she wasn't supposed to turn her back to the crowd—but one of Rex's pages was calling her.

"Hey, Skip, whereyat, dawalin'?" Probably Tricia Lattimore's little brother, who was at the age where kids thought aping the yats was funny. She was dying to say hi. And that wasn't all—she had to get a look at one of her oldest acquaintances in his moment of glory. She turned around.

There he was—the King of Carnival, Rex himself, the Monarch of Mirth, all in gold and positively exuding noblesse oblige. Despite all the fancy sobriquets, he was known to his intimates as plain Chauncey St. Amant. He was a well-padded gentleman, like most New Orleanians of a certain age, and he was in his element playing Old King Cole the merry old soul. Skip hoped his arm wouldn't fall off from too much waving. She'd known him since her rubber pants days.

He looked up and waved at someone on one of the balconies. Automatically, Skip's gaze followed his. The float was just parallel to the balcony, one she knew well. Today it was draped with Mardi Gras bunting—purple, green, and gold. The single occupant standing on it was dressed as Dolly Parton in cowgirl finery.

Dolly had on her trademark curly wig, a red satin sequined blouse, blue satin skirt, fawn gloves, balloons in her bodice, and two-gun holster. She had on a white mask with eye shadow in three colors and sequined rouge spots. As Chauncey waved, she drew one of her six-shooters. She twirled the gun, clowning, and pointed it, leaning on the balcony. Not very amusing to a cop, but Chauncey was appreciative enough to throw her a doubloon. And then he fell off his throne.

The band in front of the float was playing "When the Saints Go Marching In," so Skip never heard the shot. All she knew was that one moment Chauncey was admiring Dolly and the next minute he was down on the floor of the float. Knowing instantly what had happened, Skip started to draw her own gun, but there wasn't a chance. She was pushed from all sides, had to fight to remain standing. One of the film-makers, determined to miss nothing, hit her on the side of the face with his camera. "Oh, God! Sorry. Are you hurt?"

"Shove it!"

"But did you see? Dolly . . ."

Her partner yelled, "Goddamnit, Langdon, quit acting like a broad!" She had time for one last look. Dolly was gone.

"It was Dolly!" she yelled back. "Dolly Parton!" But none of the other cops seemed to hear. Could she make a run for it? Get to the apartment house, intercept Dolly as she came out? Not a chance. You couldn't run two steps in that mess, couldn't walk, couldn't do anything but fight for your life. By now some of the other cops had their nightsticks drawn, and Skip knew she had to use hers too.

For a moment fear shivered through her body. This was a mob. Somebody was going to get hurt. And then anger replaced the fear. Goddamnit, these people were assholes. They were trying to kill her. Especially the self-important bastard with the camera. He was going to take her out, and ten little kids as well. Nightstick horizontal, she gave him a good shove and he had the gall to look surprised.

"Get back, dammit!"

He stared at her as if he hadn't heard. "But Dolly . . ."

"Back!"

The crowd closed in and he nearly lost his balance. Skip lost valuable seconds trying to keep him from going down. And then it was her against the mob. All she remembered afterward was pushing with all her strength, pushing till her arms hurt, for about a week and a half.

She later realized it had probably been no more than ten minutes. And then she was summoned to the float, where the Monarch of Mirth was laid out as if on a bier, his bloody mask beside him, a round hole in the royal temple.

Sergeant Pitre started to speak, but Skip interrupted. "Dolly Parton!" she blurted, causing her fellow cops to stare as if she were delirious.

She pulled herself together. "A woman dressed like Dolly Parton shot him. From that balcony."

As she pointed to the balcony, a second-story one on the river side of the avenue, she thought about the implications of its ownership—it was Tolliver Albert's. Albert was "Uncle Tolliver" to the St. Amant family and practically a member of it—Chauncey and Bitty's best friend. He was an antique dealer, a charming bachelor in his fifties much favored as an extra man at Uptown dinner parties. A social fixture. And yet someone dressed as Dolly Parton had stood on his balcony and shot Chauncey. "I saw it happen," she said.

"You saw the shooting?" Pitre's voice was belligerent, as if he weren't willing to bestow the exalted status of star witness on a rookie female.

Quickly, Skip sketched out what she'd seen. Pitre barked orders, dispatching other officers to the Dolly chase. "It's Tolliver Albert's place," said Skip. "He'll be at the Boston Club."

"Unless he's Dolly."

"The St. Amants'll be there too." Eventually the parade would have gone down Canal Street and stopped at the club, where the whole family would have been in the reviewing stand, and where Rex would have toasted his queen—if Chauncey hadn't been murdered. As it was, Mardi Gras was stopped in its tracks.

"I know where they'll be, Officer Post-deb. You're a friend of the family, right?"

Skip nodded, though she wasn't, really. She was just an old acquaintance, the daughter of their doctor, someone they probably thought of as often as they thought about their coatrack. True, she'd gone through McGehee's and Newcomb with Marcelle, had even been a bridesmaid at her brief marriage to Lionel Gaudet, but that was only because Lionel was her cousin. They weren't friends—Marcelle lived on her trust fund, lunching a lot and playing tennis; she interested Skip about as much as a stale beignet.

By now emergency vehicles were starting to arrive. Pitre held up a finger, commandeered one of the squad cars, and beckoned Skip to get in with him. "Come on. We're going to inform the next of kin."

Normally homicide would do that—they must have thought Pitre could get there faster than they could. Pitre was obviously too intimidated to go alone to a place where half the swells in New Orleans would be gathered. Skip was sure he meant her to do all the work, and she relished the idea. She had never fit in with the uptown crowd—at least not in her own mind—but Pitre didn't have to know that. After that post-deb remark, she was going to enjoy humiliating him by doing this job and doing it right. Even as she vowed revenge on Pitre, it came to her exactly what the job would entail; that Chauncey St. Amant was actually dead. She'd seen the murder, but she couldn't quite take in the dead part. This must be what shock is like, she thought—a kind of numbness that pushes tragedy out of your head.

The crowds on the parade route were thicker than Southern flattery, but Prytania, a block from St. Charles, was a ghost street. They turned onto it and flew. Skip was glad they were flying—she didn't want someone to phone the Boston Club and break the news urgently.

THE KING IS DEAD

Pitre rounded up the others while Skip went to the ladies' room to get Bitty. Bitty fled from her and stood still, once outside, staring wildly around as if disoriented. "I'll take you to the others," Skip said, and led her to the small third-floor room they'd been assigned. She tried to be fast, unobtrusive, but a hush fell as she walked through the crowd with Bitty St. Amant, elegant, fragile Bitty, Skip towering above her, the two of them looking like beauty and the beast.

Pitre, who'd taken off his hat, nodded at her. She called Bitty by her last name, as she had been taught—a girl whose daddy was from Mississippi wasn't on a first-name basis with parents of peers. "Mrs. St. Amant," she said, "I'm so sorry. Mr. St. Amant's been killed."

Skip could see that they were prepared for the worst.

When two cops turn up looking somber in the middle of a Carnival party, the best news one could expect would be a nonfatal accident. But being prepared didn't help.

Bitty and Marcelle wailed together in one high, desperate voice. Bitty fell, automatically it seemed, into Tolliver's arms. Skip saw his face twitch in pain and then she looked at Henry. She couldn't tell what she saw on his face, but if it was grief, it was mixed with something else—something a little like triumph, Skip thought. But Henry was a mean brat she'd never liked. Perhaps she was making it up.

Before she had time to ponder further, she was holding Marcelle, who was sobbing against her uniform. She seemed to have fallen as automatically on Skip as Bitty had fallen on Tolliver. Skip thought it odd that neither had chosen Henry. But then Bitty changed partners. She held Henry as if she were the daughter and he the father, shaking and holding tight to him. She seemed very small and thin in her plum-colored suit. Tears welled in Henry's eyes and escaped. Skip thought she might have been wrong about him.

Pitre withdrew. Skip didn't know how long she held Marcelle, who kept saying, "Daddy, Daddy," over and over, loud at first and then more softly, crying till she was cried out. When she stopped crying, Bitty did too, as if brought up short, and for a moment they all stared at one another. Then Pitre came in again with a couple of homicide detectives who'd just arrived. They were two of the department stars, Frank O'Rourke and Joe Tarantino.

Skip told the story of what she'd seen, in a small room the club lent them, and then Tarantino said, "Stay while we interview these people. You know them, don't you?"

"Yes." Everyone in the department seemed to know her life history.

"Maybe they'll feel more at ease with you here."

They called Tolliver in. He wasn't his handsome, dashing self. His skin was oatmeal, his posture a memory.

"Mr. Albert, did you leave the party at any time?"

"Of course not."

"Would you check and make sure you have the key to your apartment?"

Looking vague, as if the request hadn't registered, he pulled out a leather key case and showed his apartment key.

"Does anyone else have a key to your apartment?"

"My cleaning lady."

"Anyone else?"

Tolliver hesitated. "Why? What's this about?"

"Could you just answer the question please?"

"Mrs. St. Amant does."

"Did you see Mrs. St. Amant leave the party?"

"*What* is this about?"

"Did you, sir?"

"No!"

"Do you know anyone who was planning to dress as a cowgirl today? Or Dolly Parton?"

"No."

"Anyone who owns such a costume?"

"No."

"Do you own such a costume?"

"No. Why are you asking me these things?"

"Because, Mr. Albert, someone dressed as Dolly Parton shot Chauncey St. Amant from your balcony."

He already looked like a man who'd just lost his best friend. Now he turned from oatmeal to cream of wheat. He sagged against the chair back. "No. You're mistaken."

Tarantino raised an eyebrow at Skip.

She said, "I saw it. I know your house, Tolliver. It was your balcony."

"I live in an apartment. It couldn't have been mine."

"It was your apartment."

"Did anyone," he finally asked, "see Dolly coming out?"

Instead of answering, O'Rourke said, "Is there a back door?"

"Yes."

O'Rourke sighed in resignation: Dolly had probably slipped out the back.

After Tolliver, they invited Bitty in.

"You have a key to Mr. Albert's apartment?"

"I water the plants when Tolliver goes away," she said. "He takes buying trips. I've had a key for years."

She was so calm Skip thought she must be in shock.

"Mrs. St. Amant, do you have the key with you now?"

"Why are you asking these questions?"

"Did you leave the party at any time?"

She shook her head. Her lips pursed slightly, then straightened out, and Skip saw a muscle start to work in her jaw. "What's going on? Why do you want to know?"

"We'll tell you in a minute. Can you hang on for just a couple of questions more?" Tarantino's voice was soothing. Skip knew he was afraid she might go out of control before they found out where the key was.

Bitty nodded, her lips getting tighter.

"Where is the key now?"

"In my purse. I put it on a chair somewhere."

"Would you mind making sure it's still there?"

Bitty sent Skip to find the purse and rummaged through it for her key ring. "Here it is."

"How long has your purse been unattended?"

"A couple of hours, I guess."

"Who knew you had a key?"

"Why, everyone. I'm always having to water Tolliver's plants after lunch or something, and I usually say where I'm going."

They asked her the Dolly questions and then gave her the bad news about the balcony. The tight line of her lips broke. She screamed as she hadn't when they told her Chauncey was dead—a delayed reaction, Skip thought. The screams kept on, one after another, until they called Tolliver to hold her.

Marcelle's and Henry's interviews added little. Marcelle

had not left the party: Henry had gone out for some air—for about thirty minutes, maybe forty-five.

"I think," said O'Rourke, "that we ought to go to Mr. Albert's apartment and have a look."

They brought it up with Tolliver, who gulped and looked at Bitty. "I don't want to leave Mrs. St. Amant. Could someone else go with you?"

"Marcelle, you go," said Bitty. "Please." She took one of Henry's hands and held it. Apparently she wanted to be surrounded by the remaining men in her life.

Marcelle looked trapped. She said, "Skip, will you come?" Skip looked at O'Rourke and Tarantino. They nodded.

"Sure."

In the back seat of the dicks' car Marcelle turned to Skip and let tears once again come into her eyes, which seemed the size of small plates. Marcelle was a famous beauty. She had gotten the best genes from both parents—Chauncey's dark coloring and Bitty's Phidian profile. She'd married young and divorced early. She might not be Skip's favorite conversationalist, but for all her pampered existence, she was a gentle enough soul.

"Skippy, it's political, don't you think? My daddy had enemies. Mother used to warn him all the time. 'Chauncey, you shouldn't be so outspoken. There's a lot of nuts in the world.' She was right, I guess. It's got to be political, don't you think, Skippy?"

Skip didn't know whether Marcelle spoke for the benefit of the dicks or whether she just didn't mind talking in front of them. She said, "I just don't know," and wondered if it could be political.

For the first time she started to think of the difference Chauncey St. Amant's death would make in the political and cultural life of the city. It would be a huge loss. He had been a member of the Boston Club, which did not admit Jews, blacks, or women, but he had publicly spoken out against the club's policy. That might seem a small thing to outsiders, but in the circles in which Chauncey moved, it was radical. It would probably have been his undoing if he hadn't been the son-in-law of Haygood Mayhew. And that was just a tiny facet of his genuine commitment to civil rights.

He was president of the Carrollton Bank, which had one of the best affirmative action policies of any large corporation in the city. It had black and female vice presidents, and minorities in plenty of other executive spots. And he was a prominent liberal Democrat who had helped elect the current black mayor, Furman Soniat. Lately, though, there had been talk that he might run for office, possibly for the state senate, though Soniat was thinking of moving up himself.

He was also a jazz buff and one of the founders of the New Orleans Jazz and Heritage Festival. In addition, he had taken on several young musicians as his personal protégés, helping them find gigs and giving them what he called "artistic subsidies" when they needed them. Invariably his protégés had been black, and some of them had taken advantage of his generosity, spending the money on drugs and ending up in jail, which gave the racists in Chauncey's crowd ammunition against his liberal civic ideas—ammunition of the sort that is whispered rather than aired in the press. But a couple of unfortunate incidents hadn't stopped Chauncey on either front. He believed in civil rights and he believed in music, and he supported them. Not that he didn't also support the symphony (in the years when there had been one) and the museum—he believed in the arts, period—but because New Orleans jazz was largely performed by black people, his love of it had been lumped with what, even in the high-toned Boston Club, was still called "nigger-lovin'" (by its cruder members, anyway).

So Marcelle was right. He had lots of enemies. Racists and ultraconservatives who simply wanted to maintain the white male status quo. He'd had those for a long time. However, lately, as his political ambitions had come to the fore, he'd made enemies in his own political camp as well. Black politicians and ultraliberal whites who wanted to see Mayor Soniat in Baton Rouge had turned on him for attempting to split the liberal vote. He had political enemies, all right. But Skip wondered how any of them could get a key to Uncle Tolliver's apartment.

It was a famous apartment by New Orleans standards, having once been featured in *Architectural Digest*. It was slightly ornate for Skip's taste, but given her current spartan living conditions, she gasped with pleasure on seeing it again. It had the twelve-foot windows that opened from the floor, 14-foot ceilings, and anachronistic fireplaces of almost every building in New Orleans; perfect surroundings for the antiques Tolliver collected so lovingly.

He had painted the walls terra-cotta, a rich backdrop for the blue-and-white Chinese porcelains flanking an ormolu clock on the mantel. An American primitive hung over the collection. The rug was one of the quieter Chinese ones, the fabric on sofas and chairs, on the other hand, an assertive print that screamed Brunschwig & Fils.

Skip thought she would have killed for a mahogany desk she was sure must be Sheraton. But a very dark, simple, coffee table was obviously meant to be the center of attraction— the stage for Tolliver's most spectacular orchid performances. Smaller (though equally priceless-looking) tables were crowned with blooming orchids as well, but this one held a massive display of the plants Bitty watered, grown in a room in back that Tolliver had converted into a tiny greenhouse. The gun that must have killed Chauncey, an odd-looking old revolver, was lying beside a plain clay flowerpot.

In the middle of the elegant carpet was a tumble of clothes—a blonde curly wig, red satin shirt, blue satin skirt, gloves, mask, and D-cup bra with wadded-up rags that had given the balloon effect. A two-gun holster with one gun still in it had been flung onto a needlepoint footstool that jutted out at a funny angle in front of its chair. Dolly must have kicked it askew in her rush to undress.

The three of them had checked the place out, then called Marcelle inside to see if anything was missing. Looking at the pile, she made a little sound, as if she'd been jabbed in the solar plexus. "The clothes," she said. "You can trace the clothes, can't you? Surely whoever sold that outfit would remember."

They all moved closer and looked at the items, not touching. The wig could have come from Woolworth's. The other things looked cheap and sleazy. Probably the murderer had bought each item separately, and from some place that sold a lot of similar merchandise.

O'Rourke sighed. "We might have better luck with the guns."

They might indeed, Skip thought. She didn't know much about firearms, but these looked odd.

Skip moved out to the balcony. There were plants there— a Norfolk pine, jasmine, some smaller things. There was even a Christmas cactus in a clay wall sconce between the windows. Two old-fashioned wrought-iron chairs were grouped on either side of a damp, dirty circle on the floor. On one of the chairs sat a gardenia plant in a pot the size of the circle. Skip's stomach flip-flopped as she realized Dolly must have removed the pot so she could stand where she needed to to get the best shot.

The men left Skip with Marcelle while they looked around, came back to report that nothing had been disturbed. "Mrs. Gaudet, where can we drop you?"

"I'd like to go home to change please. Before I go to my mother's."

They took Skip back to police headquarters, questioned her for an hour, and left her exhausted. Exhausted and feeling cheated. She would have given anything to be O'Rourke or Tarantino today.

Lieutenant Duby called her in. "I've had a request from the chief."

Chief McDermott. Her dad was his doctor. Some said that was how she had gotten her job.

"He wants to use you as a sort of special investigator on this. You've been detailed to homicide for the rest of the week."

Skip clasped her hands in her lap, as her mother had taught her to do more than twenty years ago. She couldn't have heard what she thought she had. She said nothing.

"The chief wants you to go and do what Uptown girls do—do you understand?"

Skip did. They wanted her to spy.

"Cooperate with O'Rourke and Tarantino, okay? And report to me. Any questions?"

"Starting now?"

"Tomorrow."

She was still on parade routes. "I'd better get back to work."

"Langdon, what time did you report this morning?"

"Five o'clock."

"You're a casualty, officer. Go home."

Feeling only slightly guilty, she left his office, pondering the mysterious ways of Comus, Momus, and Proteus, the gods of Carnival. She'd become a cop to escape the Uptown crowd and now the very thing she'd hated most all her life— her tenuous place in it—was going to help her in her new life. She was going to do work hardly any rookie ever did, and all because she was an Uptown girl. Yet it wasn't for once because of her family's influence. Oddly, it was because of Skip herself; because she had expertise no other rookie had. The irony of it made her head spin.

Duby called her back. "You've got a phone call."

"Here?"

"Obviously here, officer. You're detailed here. Take it in homicide."

The detective bureau was divided into crimes against property and crimes against persons. You had to go through property crimes to get to the room homicide shared with robbery. It was roughly the size of an amphitheater and decorated with a single picture—a poster of a snake crawling on a naked woman. Homicide's desks were clustered neatly at one end of the room, robbery's at the other. There was no one at either end.

Shrugging, Skip chose a desk at random and asked for her call. "Officer Langdon? About time. This is Dolly."

It was a man's voice. Skip wondered how in hell she could get a trace when she was the only one in the whole place. No way that she knew of.

"I saw you," she said. "Did you see me?"

"You didn't see me, honey. I was shit-faced over at Maidie Blanc's."

Skip sighed and stopped worrying about the trace. "Cookie Lamoreaux. *Très amusant.*"

"Awful about Chauncey. I heard you saw it."

"Word travels fast."

"Actually, I had the inside track. I've got a houseguest saw it too. Old buddy from California here to do a film on Mardi Gras."

"Oh, that asshole."

"Hey, he speaks well of you. Says you saved his ass."

"He nearly cost me mine."

"He's got something for you."

"I've got something for him too."

"I'm putting him on, okay? I said I'd make the introductions."

"Hi," said a new voice, quite a pleasant one—a little businesslike, but a little friendly too. "This is Steve Steinman. I saw your name tag and Cookie said he knew you. Weird, huh? I didn't know it was such a small town."

"In some ways it's a village." (Some ways that she hated like tarantulas.)

"Thanks for helping me today."

"No problem. It's my job."

"Listen, I think I got film of the thing. I thought maybe you could tell me who to show it to. The names of the investigating officers."

Skip's ears started to ring. "You've got it on film? The murder?"

"I'm not sure yet. It's being developed. I won't get it till ten o'clock or so."

"Tonight?"

"Uh-huh. Should I just drop it by the cop shop?"

"It'll be a madhouse around here. Why don't you bring it by my house? I'll take it in first thing in the morning."

Sure. After she'd watched it six or eight times.

"Why not? Cookie says you're okay. Says you're the only cop in town he'd trust."

"He was drunk when he said that, right?"

"Guess so, come to think of it."

"That's Cookie."

She gave him her address.

THE NIGHT

1

Gratefully, after it was all over, Bitty took the pills Dr. Langdon offered. She had still not had a drink. The pills were enough for now; or they would have been if she hadn't had to wake up every time they wore off. When she woke, her chest and belly felt hollow, as if all her vital organs had been ripped out of her, as if all the booze and pills in the world couldn't fill such an emptiness. She cried until her head ached and her eyes burned. Yet there were more tears in her. That was all that was left there. No heart, no guts, certainly no liver. Just tears.

She knew how she'd feel in the morning—as if her body were a bell and someone had struck it, dooming her to shriek eternally. Shrieking sad, yet too sad to shriek. Immobile. Cold.

She took another pill and soon she felt warm and hardly any other way at all, not even hollow. Numbness, for a long time, had seemed better than life. She was numb now, and would be till morning—so numb she was able to allow herself certain thoughts. For the moment she could deal with them. Right now they didn't make her heart break, instead made her feel better, warmer, warmer even than the bed which a few moments ago had seemed her only comfort.

She was thinking about Chauncey, about how happy they were at first. She had quite literally never met a person like Chauncey in her entire life, and she would have done anything to make him happy—*had* done a number of things she never imagined she would. He was so dark and dashing—so protective. He made her feel safe, and she desperately needed that. There were reasons she needed a man like Chauncey. Reasons nobody knew except Bitty herself.

Oh, God, how had she gotten through today? And yet she had, because here she was lying in bed—her bed and hers alone ever since Chauncey had moved to the green guest room a few years ago. Yet thinking about that didn't make her cry now—not just at the moment. She kept getting distracted with thoughts about herself—proud thoughts about getting through it. Doing something no one could have imagined she could do. Chauncey certainly wouldn't have thought she could. Too bad he couldn't be here now to see her—to be amazed.

She would have a thought like that and then somehow a feeling or two would get through tiny cracks in the shell the drugs had built around her, and she would have a moment of utter despair.

But then it would go away. And she would be warm again, thinking once more about the early days. If she thought she was happy with Chauncey, she had no idea what having Henry would be like.

Tolliver had introduced her to Chauncey, hadn't he? It was vague in her mind now, but surely that was it. She'd known Tolliver all her life, and Chauncey was one of his fraternity brothers. A Deke—they'd been Dekes. Yes, it *was* Tolliver. She remembered it vividly, remembered seeing Chauncey towering over her, Tolliver dropping her hand, herself shaking Chauncey's. She felt something like an electric shock. Years later, she tried to tell her children about it, but they only laughed at her. Yet, for all the foolish romance of it, it was utterly genuine. In that moment, she had recognized her mate.

She could barely remember anything except Chauncey after that—dancing with him, eating crabs at the lake, kissing him, laughing, finally making love with him. It was ridiculous—her mind was like some stupid movie about a courtship. Literally all she remembered now were glowing romantic moments, lit always, always by Chauncey's brown eyes. His lovely, velvety eyes.

He was a senior and she a freshman when they met, and he didn't propose till that summer—after her freshman year. Good God, she'd thought her parents would croak. Not only was Chauncey a nobody from out by the lake, but Bitty was too young to marry; she must go to college and *then* get married and never use an iota of her education.

She offered her parents a deal—she'd finish her sophomore year and get married the next summer instead of right away. At first they argued about it, but her daddy (who'd always wanted a son) had taken a shine to Chauncey that wouldn't quit. In the end she had the most elegant wedding since Weezee Bettencourt's a good ten years earlier. And her daddy had practically adopted Chauncey, taking him into the bank and making him his protégé.

Then Henry was born, bald as a rock, wrinkled as a raisin, the prettiest thing Bitty had ever seen. People said he was ugly as a monkey (they thought she couldn't hear), but he had his daddy's gorgeous eyes and she didn't know why they couldn't see that. Would she ever forget the feeling of holding him against her breast—this rubbery, satiny invention of hers and Chauncey's? Even now, she could honestly say it was the crowning moment of her life. She'd had no idea how happy a child could make her.

She couldn't remember most of her labor. They said she nearly died, but then that was the sort of thing they did say in New Orleans. Maybe it was true and maybe it wasn't, all she knew was it was worth it and she'd do it a thousand more times if she thought she could get that feeling again.

But there was no going back. There never had been, never would be anything like having Henry. He needed her. He was the first being who ever needed her. And he loved her desperately—that was obvious from the start. They said babies weren't aware of very much outside themselves for a while, but it couldn't be true. Henry had wanted to make her happy. He was a perfect baby. Not near-perfect—perfect. He didn't cry, didn't fret, didn't complain, only ate and eliminated and slept and smiled. Their life together was sheer heaven—the sweetest, tenderest, gentlest thing she could ever imagine. She couldn't understand why Chauncey hated him so much.

And poor Henry never learned. He always thought that one day his father was going to be nice to him. When he was fifteen he asked Chauncey to teach him to drive. Pleased that his son was at last interested in some sort of self-sufficient activity, Chauncey readily agreed to have the first lesson on Saturday. When Saturday came, it was a beautiful day and Chauncey said casually, just as he picked up his keys, "Marcelle, want to go for a ride?"

Of course Marcelle did. What kid wouldn't? She was twelve then, and Daddy's little darling. She wore her hair in a single pigtail down her back, French-braided the way Estelle Villere had taught her. Her skin was the color of a praline, and just as smooth and clear. Her grades were A's. Her breasts were ripening apricots under her school sweaters.

Henry was as tall already as he was going to get, and so thin that when one kid called him a telephone pole, another said, "telephone wire's more like it." He was making C's and D's, and at the very height of his teenage acne attack. His hair tended to get greasy and his T-shirts were smelly. He spoke mostly in sneering monosyllables, but escalated to yelling fits if his feelings got hurt. Which happened absurdly often, he was so sensitive. He never made it through a day without lacerations of the spirit. Of course Chauncey wouldn't want to be alone in a car with him.

But when he asked Marcelle to go along, Bitty tried to intervene. "Don't you think this should be an experience just for you and Henry?"

"Why?"

"He's the one who's learning to drive."

"Marcelle can learn too."

"Marcelle, don't you have homework?"

"Mother! It's Saturday!"

"We'll all go, then. We'll make it a family occasion." Henry's eyes flickered with relief for only a second—a millisecond—but Bitty saw it and knew she had done the right thing. (Though she wasn't able to stop the coming disaster.)

They went out to the batture, in Audubon Park behind the zoo, and Henry took the wheel. "Don't grip it so tight, Henry. You aren't in a wrestling match. Loosen up!"

"Okay."

"Now stay in the middle of the lane. *The middle, goddamnit, the middle!* Shit, here comes a car!" Chauncey grabbed the wheel and would have pulled the car back to the right (though so far as Bitty could see, there was no danger at all), but Henry panicked and hit the brakes.

Both Henry and his dad hit their heads against the windshield. Bitty and Marcelle, in the back, were flung forward, and Marcelle hit her head on her brother's as his was thrown back on the bounce, cutting her lip with her tooth.

She squealed and blood ran down her chin.

Chauncey shouted, "Goddamnit, you little idiot! Can't you do anything right?"

And Henry, his face red with shame, said, "Just shut the fuck up, okay?" Whereupon Chauncey slapped him so hard his head flew back against the side window. It connected with a terrifying "whump."

Bitty threw her arms around his shoulders. "Darling, are you all right?"

Chauncey shouted, "A car's coming up behind us. Get out of the middle of the road. Get out of the middle of the road! Get out of the middle of the road!"

Bitty thought she'd go mad if he didn't shut up.

Henry accelerated, but the car leaped forward erratically. Again, Chauncey grabbed the wheel, and pulled it too far. The car ran off onto the shoulder. "*Now* see what you made me do!"

Henry's acne-mottled face was dead white, his bottom lip tight. Bitty knew he was biting it to keep the tears back. "God, Henry. Get out of this car. You stink to high heaven!"

It was true. The fear and stress were taking their toll, along with Henry's fifteen-year-old hormones. He certainly did stink, poor darling baby. Bitty wanted nothing so much as to hold him in her lap and rock him and sing him a lullaby.

He hurled himself out of the car and stood on the shoulder with his back to them, shaking. But he had forgotten to set the emergency brake and the car began to roll. "Shit!" Chauncey shouted, pulling it up. "Haven't you got the sense God gave you?"

Bitty said, "That's enough. Let's go home, Chauncey."

But Marcelle whined, "I want to try."

"Okay, baby," said Chauncey. "We're going to give you your chance, dollin'."

"Chauncey, no. Henry—"

"You don't think Marcelle should get a chance?"

What was she supposed to say in front of Marcelle? "I think it would really hurt Henry's feelings—"

"Henry! He had his chance. Come on, baby. You come on around."

Marcelle got out and Bitty made to follow. "I'll stay with Henry."

"No!"

Marcelle got in and closed the door. Chauncey said, "Let him stew in his own juices. The boy just doesn't *think*, that's all! Let's give him a chance, for once." He turned to Marcelle. "Now, dollin', turn the key gently . . ."

Marcelle took to driving as she had to reading, and finger painting, and piano lessons, and everything else she did. All she really needed to be told was the name of the ignition and accelerator, and brake—the rest seemed to come naturally. Smoothly, like a pro, eyes barely higher than the steering wheel, she maneuvered the car around the S curves and back again, while Henry sat on the shoulder, an outcast.

Bitty could have died, would certainly have cried, except she couldn't, just *couldn't*, in front of Chauncey and Marcelle. There was already enough strife in the family. She could make it okay till she got home and got herself a glass of wine or something.

On their second pass they noticed Henry was no longer sitting on the shoulder. Ahead, they could see his miserable hunched shoulders as he walked away from the spectacle of Marcelle the baby girl once again outshining him, the star of her own show after he'd once again been booed and hissed offstage.

Chauncey had Marcelle stop and change places with him. Driving like a maniac, truly endangering their lives, as Henry really hadn't, he whizzed down the road, came to a violent stop, leaped out and shouted, "Where do you think you're going, young man?"

Henry kept walking, didn't answer.

"You answer me when I speak to you!"

"Home!"

"You get in this car right now!"

For answer, Henry began to run. Chauncey chased him down, grabbed him by the arm, and marched him ceremoniously back to the car. He pushed him in like a cop getting tough with a felon.

Now he and Bitty were in the backseat together and she could feel the full blast of his humiliation. She blinked away tears and laid her hand gently on his leg. As she had known he would, he pushed it away and turned to stare out the window, but not before she caught the hunted, trapped-animal look in his eyes.

Chauncey thrashed him when they got home, on the excuse he had disobeyed and tried to run away, but she knew he didn't need an excuse. He was determined to beat up on his son, and that was all there was to it. It was the only time he'd ever done that, and she threatened to leave him if he ever did it again.

Afterward Henry left to walk the streets for hours (she later learned), finally ending up at Tolliver's. Like the good uncle he was, Tolliver listened to the story—or whatever tiny bits of it Henry's pride would let him tell (not much was Bitty's guess, but she also knew that Tolliver would have read between the lines).

In the end Tolliver had taught him to drive, and Chauncey had seemed grateful, thanking him for endangering his life and enduring "what no human being should have to."

2

Marcelle had put Andre to bed an hour ago and now Henry had gone up at last, after hours of draping his besotted self all over the parlor furniture, pretending to be alert in case Bitty needed anything. Bitty was out cold, having left Marcelle and Henry alone to cope with their father's death. Neither was strong enough, yet somehow they'd done it. Relatives came out of the woodwork, for one thing, and they'd done a lot of the heavy work of notifying other relatives and friends, planning a proper wake for the next day.

And when Marcelle got right down to it, Bitty herself was rather amazing. She had actually made the funeral arrangements before checking out for that never-never land she loved so well. And all without having a drink. Marcelle was dumbfounded at first, but when she thought back over the years she realized that her mother wasn't completely helpless. Indeed, to everyone's astonishment, she was absolutely at her best in a crisis.

Once over in Covington, Marcelle fell and ripped her leg open—not just a little cut, but a nasty laceration with puckered-up skin and blood flowing out like cranberry juice. Henry started screaming and wouldn't stop. Ma-Mère sat down and put her head between her knees. Chauncey raced around looking for a towel to stop the bleeding, running from one end of the house to the other, never finding it. Pathetic, drunken, incompetent Bitty simply tore down a curtain, tied up the wound, threw Marcelle into the car and drove her to the hospital before anyone noticed they were gone.

There were lots of incidents like that. When things were at their absolute worst, Bitty was a marvel of competence and efficiency. But if they were simply day-to-day, marginally awful, she was a vegetable. Chauncey was always touchingly protective of her, as if her illness, her addiction, were his fault, as if he could do something to bring her back to life.

Marcelle almost laughed. He'd had to die. Marcelle couldn't remember seeing her mother so alert in ten years or more. Chauncey wouldn't have been able to believe it, would have been falsely heartened—it wouldn't last, and Marcelle knew it earlier that day. It was over already.

But lately Chauncey had seemed to accept her condition. Marcelle guessed that's what you'd call it anyway. He'd obviously been making certain other arrangements for himself.

Finding herself about to burst into fresh tears at the thought, she went up to the bathroom to wash her face.

Then she went into her old bedroom, still decorated with her dolls and teddy bears, and changed into a short pink satin nightgown. She and Henry (and her son, Andre) were spending the night at their parents'—their *mother's*, she reminded herself and fought off more tears. She was here, but she didn't know what she could do for her mother. If Bitty called for something—water or another round of pills, perhaps—she was there. Meanwhile, she would have a drink herself—her first since Skip had brought the news.

Bourbon, perhaps. Something good and strong, because this was going to require a lot of help. She tossed one down, made herself another. And then she thought about the fact that she knew her father's murder wasn't political—the fact that she knew who the murderer was.

Should she tell Skip? Would any purpose truly be served by doing that?

3

Skip put on a pair of jeans and took a gin and tonic out to the balcony, dragging with her one of her two director's chairs. February and March were dicey in New Orleans, but it had been a warm day for Mardi Gras and tonight she was comfortable wearing only a sweater.

Still, no one else was doing any balcony sitting. Skip had come out because she wanted the sights and sounds of Carnival, the seasonal shouting and screeching along with the everyday raucousness from the piano bar at Lafitte's Blacksmith Shop. Sometimes she heard the music as she was falling asleep, and the next morning was awakened by children playing in the school yard across the street. Pleasant sounds to live with. And no matter how tiny her living space, who could feel poor who had a balcony?

Fortunate, she thought, that nearly everyone who lived in the Quarter did. Nearly everyone in the city, for that matter, who lived above the first floor. To sit on your own balcony, drink in hand, and stare at the lacy cast-iron galleries curving so gracefully round the flat-roofed buildings was enough to make your heart break, it was so beautiful.

It wasn't just one or two beautifully preserved eighteenth- or nineteenth-century structures that Skip could see. It was rows and rows of them, some carefully restored, some needing paint, some falling down, all (except maybe the Creole cottages) carved into little apartments like hers—not museums or monuments, just magnificent buildings for people to live in, as if suburbs didn't exist. Restoration had been sweeping the Quarter lately, and Skip didn't care much for it. The old buildings were being painted tasteful pastels that would have looked lovely in California, but here they just looked wimpy. New Orleans, like the Caribbean, cried out for robustness, even vulgarity, in Skip's view. She hated particularly the new fad of painting the lacy ironwork soft gray instead of the honest black it was meant to be.

On her street were two graceful old Creole cottages, one newly painted mauve and gray, the other an embarrassing pink with apple-green trim. The first looked like something a decorator who'd run out of ideas had dreamed up; the second fit in.

The man from the Quarter Master deli, dressed like a pirate, passed and waved. A white-coated vendor struggled down the street behind his crazy cart shaped like a hot dog, crying out for customers and making her, for some reason, think of Tennessee Williams. Surely Stanley and Stella and Blanche bought their dogs from these old guys.

She loved the Quarter as much as she hated the Garden District. It teemed with infinite variety and felt alive. Yet tonight she barely noticed her neighborhood. She was crying, and not for Chauncey either. For herself. It was Mardi Gras night and she had nowhere to go, no one to be with. True, she had to wait for Steve Steinman to bring the film, but that wasn't exactly the same as snuggling up with your sweetie.

The idea of even having a sweetie seemed so remote she couldn't imagine it. She wondered if she should go down to the Abbey and see Claude. But she couldn't stand the idea of braving the Carnival crowds, and besides, Toni might be there. Claude's wife. Claude was a yat with two semesters at Loyola, no future except maybe as bartender in a fancier joint, and no conversation except football and bigotry. And that was before you got to the married part. But he was big and liked his women big, and Skip didn't have anyone else. There probably *wasn't* anyone else for her.

She was an alien. A flying saucer had set down one day in her parents' State Street yard and abandoned her. Or so it seemed to her at times. Her father spent his time playing tennis and setting the bones of the rich and well-born. He was a member of Rex, but not of Comus, and this was his greatest disappointment. Her mother served on committees for charity balls. They seemed to care for only two things— social climbing and using her to promote their hobby. Surely they couldn't be her real parents. Surely real parents had at least a modicum of feeling for what a child actually is rather than only for what they want it to be.

In accordance with her parents' wishes, Skip went to McGehee's (though she was smart enough for Newman) and Miggy's dancing school in sixth grade, Icebreakers in seventh grade, Eight O'Clocks in eighth grade, and of course Valencia later on—never mind that she was too tall, too fat, too shy, too unpopular, and too confused about what it was all about. She even pledged Kappa at Newcomb, though that was her own doing and she should have realized by then that she no longer had to do everything her parents wanted. The realization came soon after, with a bang.

She made her debut. She could have been queen of a Carnival ball as well—her father belonged to Proteus as well as

Rex—but she drew the line there. Carnival queens were always someone's daughter, and she was sick and damn tired of being nobody but Dr. Langdon's daughter.

She agreed to make her debut for a very particular reason—it was possible, just possible that by doing this she might somehow learn to fit in. It certainly wasn't that she didn't want to. But from her earliest recollection she hadn't understood the rules. She got things mixed up. Not things like manners and etiquette, things with written-down rules. Those were easy. But she had no talent for conforming and couldn't seem to catch on to implied rules, social customs, fashions, fads, the what-is-done-when sorts of things southerners are usually born knowing.

For failing to conform she was ridiculed, lectured, even beaten. Yet no amount of correction had any effect, as she could never see the next problem coming. And so she had no way to win her parents' approval or the approval of her peers. She began to rebel at a very early age.

At five she was invited to a birthday party to which she didn't want to go. And so on the way home from kindergarten, she simply threw out the invitation. She hadn't yet been told the concept of R.S.V.P., yet on finding out about the invitation, her mother spanked her.

The unfairness of it being intolerable, Skip declined to tolerate it. She pulled one of the living-room lamps off its table just to watch its expensive base crack into shards. For this she was spanked again (this time with a hairbrush) and shut in her room for two days, during which she doggedly refrained from crying. (Years later she noticed that hardly anyone in New Orleans ever bothered with R.S.V.P. and caught on to the real reason for the spanking—the birthday girl was the daughter of people with whom her mother wished to curry favor.)

She'd been told her kindergarten teacher reported a change in her that year, a sadness that began to replace the high spirits of before. She did not retaliate for the two days of imprisonment—her revenges were sudden angry ones rather than planned attacks—but ever after she was acutely conscious of the unfairness of life on earth.

Which wasn't to say that the planet didn't have its pleasures, even for such a seeming outsider. Eating, for one. And later drinking, smoking, drugs, above all sex. The year she came out, Skip got pregnant. She wanted to keep the baby, but her mother noticed her clothes were getting snug, guessed the truth, and arranged an abortion.

After that she gave up. She flunked out of Newcomb, most of the time being too stoned or too drunk to go to class. (She was reading up, at the time, on Zelda Fitzgerald.)

LSU wouldn't take her after that, but Ole Miss would. They sent her there and she flunked out again. After that, she sold a little dope and used the proceeds to catch a plane to L.A., where, unable to compete with applicants who looked like starlets, she couldn't even get a job as a waitress. She ended up in San Francisco wearing her hair in spikes and riding a bike for Speedy's Messenger Service. On that unlikely job, she realized for the first time (and only after many months) that her size—her athletic build—was something in which she could take pleasure.

She began working out, lost her baby fat, and felt like Sheena of the jungle. She'd never lost that old sense of unfairness, though now it had evolved into what she thought of as a sense of justice. She saw a lot of crime as she went about her daily rounds and when one day she stopped a mugging as if by reflex, her life changed. She was headed down Fifth Street toward the *Examiner* when a teenage kid tried to shove an old lady to the pavement and take her purse. Before she knew she was doing it, Skip had her bike on the sidewalk, her body between the kid and the victim. That wasn't enough for her either—she "detained" the kid, as the cops said, till they got there.

After that she began to dream of being a cop. Literally to dream, at night, when her defenses were down. And then she daydreamed as well, and soon she was obsessed with it. She knew the place she had to do it was New Orleans. She was still very young and she wouldn't yet have put it this way (wouldn't understand it for years), but this was her final revenge against her parents and against the whole stinking crowd they ran with.

They would hate her for it. And yet how could they hate a responsible daughter on the side of law and order? They couldn't in good conscience—they'd have to hate themselves as well. It would be a perfect way of thumbing her nose at the whole damn social order. If she hadn't understood their rules, too bad—she was going to make some rules of her own.

She was only dimly aware of the revenge factor in her decision. On the surface she saw nothing but constructive value in it. She saw it as a way finally to fit into her hometown, to find out something about it besides the latest gossip in that tiny social group that had so puzzled Steve Steinman by its smallness. She saw it also as an adventure. She would go to neighborhoods she was barely aware of and truly meet the people, the real people, the yats and the ethnics. Best of all she would have power at last, in her own hometown. She would be someone other than Dr. Langdon's daughter.

She forgot the unfortunate fact that she wasn't going to fit in anywhere—certainly not with the old crowd and decidedly not with her fellow cops either. If she'd felt like an alien before, that was just practice for some of the deepest, truest loneliness she could ever have imagined.

In some ways she did have power. She truly loved her job, and liked—more than anyone could have told her—the sensation of being good at it. For the first time ever, she was accomplishing something, learning something, finding her existence worthwhile and exhilarating. Yet in her personal life she was utterly powerless.

Tricia Lattimore, who also hadn't fit in, was now a social worker in New York. Skip's only friend was Jimmy Dee Scoggin, her gay, fifty-year-old, hopelessly criminal lawyer landlord. (Unless you counted Tennessee Williams. Lately she'd been reading no one else, and Tennessee was helping her get through.) So was Jimmy Dee—partly with controlled substances and partly with outrageous anecdotes. At the moment Jimmy Dee was out with his usual coterie of young studs and amusingly aging drag queens. Which left Skip on her balcony, crying into her gin and tonic.

She was thinking of finding some nice, juicy worms to eat when the phone rang. "Skippy? It's Marcelle."

"Marcelle!" Of all people.

"Skippy, I'm so miserable. I know you haven't been with the police department very long, but I was just wondering—is there a Chinaman's chance you might work on Daddy's case?"

"Actually, I think there is. Is there something I can help you with?" She hoped she didn't sound too eager.

"I don't know." Marcelle started to cry. "It all seems so hopeless."

"You know I'll do everything I can for you."

"Skippy, can you tell me something? You saw Dolly, didn't you? What did she look like?"

"Look like? I'm not sure what you mean."

"I mean, I know she was *dressed* like Dolly Parton, but what did she *look* like?"

It was the same kind of question O'Rourke and Tarantino had asked her ad infinitum and ad nauseam. How tall was Dolly? Could she have been a man? Was she black or white? Thin or fat? Skip had no idea in hell. She thought Dolly had looked fairly tall and could possibly have been a man and she was pretty sure she wasn't fat, but with the balloon boobs, she couldn't be positive.

She didn't know the answer, but she also didn't quite understand why Marcelle was asking the question. "I really couldn't tell, Marcelle, but why do you ask? Did someone make a threat on your father's life?"

Marcelle gasped. Skip had had a few drinks, but there was no mistaking it. "No, of course not. I'm just so mad at the bastard, that's all. I want to *do* somethin' to him."

"Of course. That's only natural."

"Oh, Skippy, didn't you see anything? I just feel so helpless." She started sobbing in earnest.

"Now, Marcelle, don't cry. Don't cry and I'll tell you something good. Somebody got her on film. He's bringing the film over in half an hour. Maybe it'll help jog my memory. Maybe there was something I noticed but I just forgot."

"Do you think so? Do you really think so?"

She sounded so hopeful Skip was glad she had told her. Later, back on the balcony, she wondered if it had been wise. The film was police business after all, or soon would be. She made herself another drink.

She got bored on the balcony and went inside. Something perverse in her made her put on a Dolly Parton record. Forty-five minutes later she began to think Steinman wasn't coming. Another fifteen minutes and she was starting to get mad. She phoned Cookie Lamoreaux. Someone answered but couldn't hear her above the din. She wanted to go to bed.

Finally, when it was nearly midnight, her doorbell rang. She stepped onto the balcony. "Yes?"

"It's Steve Steinman."

He didn't sound like he had on the phone. Normally Skip would simply have buzzed him in, but something about his voice made her nervous. She went down for him, revolver in hand. The outside door was windowed and she could see that the young man outside was the same one she'd encountered at the parade. No one seemed to be with him.

She opened the door, gun at the ready. If possible, Steinman turned paler than he already was. "Oh, no." He sounded as if he'd lost his last friend, and Skip realized she probably didn't look the soul of hospitality.

Quickly, she put the .38 away. She was suddenly more alarmed than ever, but not about the possibility of armed intruders. Steinman was a big man, well over six feet and by her best guess, well over 200 pounds. At the moment he looked very ill. He stumbled over the threshold and into her arms. She had to brace herself to stay upright. "What is it? What happened?" She managed to get the door closed.

He put a hand to the back of his head. "Somebody hit me. Took the film."

Automatically, Skip's hand covered his, touching the lump on the back of his head. She winced. "Can you walk?"

"Let me sit for a minute. Could you get the projector? It's not mine—I had to rent one."

Whoever took the film had wanted only that. The rented projector was sitting unmolested outside her door. She lugged it in, settled Steinman on one of the worn, uncovered wooden stairs, and went up to get him a brandy and a couple of aspirin. For a while he just sat and breathed heavily. She was big, but not big enough to get this one upstairs. If he didn't recover soon, she would have to get help. Charity Hospital would be a madhouse. In fact, if she wanted medical attention tonight, she'd probably have to go to her father, who'd almost certainly be at home, the Rex Ball having been canceled due to the small matter of murder. But asking him for anything would require humbling herself and was therefore impossible.

If she'd been religious she'd have prayed, but she was far from believing in anything but her own determination. "Get better," she sighed, pleading with the filmmaker, but it came out more like a coo.

He managed a smile. "I am better. The brandy did it."

"Can you walk?" she asked for the second time.

"I think so. Shall we go up?"

He walked perfectly well, apparently being fairly far along toward recovery. Skip wondered what he'd been hit with. She showed him into her shabby studio, with its Goodwill hide-a-bed sofa now neatly tucked up for her guest, and just as well—when it was open, it nearly filled up the room.

Besides the sofa, Skip had a chest of drawers, a couple of small tables, and a large dracaena that was usually dusty but seemed to grow no matter what she did (or didn't do) to it. She would have liked a coffee table, but having to fold the sofa out made that impractical.

"No pictures," said Steinman.

"What?"

"You have nothing on your walls. I've never seen that before."

Skip flushed. She'd lived here nearly a year and hadn't had a single visitor except Jimmy Dee and company. "I haven't had time, I guess." She wondered what she wanted on her walls. She'd had heavy metal posters in San Francisco, but would they be suitable for a cop? Wasn't the whole idea a bit on the sinister side?

"What," said Steinman, "would a lady cop put on her walls?"

"Believe me, I'd be the last to know. Didn't Cookie tell you I'm no lady? What shall I get for your head? Something hot or something cold?"

"Damned if I know. How about some more brandy?"

When she'd gotten his drink and one for herself, she said, "What happened out there?"

He shrugged. "I've no idea, to tell you the truth. I was ringing your doorbell when someone hit me. I was only a few minutes late, so I think I must have been out quite awhile. When I came to, there was no film."

"Did you see anyone around before you rang the bell?"

"I didn't look."

"Who knew you were bringing it here?"

"Cookie. You. Everyone at Cookie's house. But they were probably all too drunk to mug a mouse, much less a man mountain."

Skip gave him a furtive once-over. Hardly a man mountain, she thought, but certainly a nice, tall round fellow with a pleasant demeanor and blue eyes behind a pair of spectacles that looked as if they grew on his face.

"Did you have it done at a lab? How about the lab people?"

"The guy's a friend of Cookie's—that's how I got him to work on Mardi Gras. I had to tell him what it was to get him to do it, and he did seem really eager—normally it would take overnight, but he did it fast, specially. In fact, he did it *really* fast because he wanted to get over to Cookie's bash. He got me to give him a ride over there afterward."

"So he couldn't have followed you."

"I don't see how."

"Wait a minute. This has got to be a print, right? Where's the original?"

He looked sheepish. "Do you know anything about film?"

"No."

"Well, you've hit on something there. Almost everybody these days uses color-negative film, which you do have to print. But if you're in film school, you scrounge for film. You knock on doors of production companies and beg for handouts, practically. You make deals and trades. And if somebody gives you a good price on it, you sometimes end up with color-reversal film instead of color-negative. A guy in a camera store gave me some for practically nothing, and that's what I was using today."

"I don't follow."

"You don't have to get a print."

"The original's all there was?"

"'Was' is right."

"Did you look at it before you brought it over?"

"Of course."

"And?"

"It was pretty amazing."

INTERLUDE

"Amazing how?"

"Perfect. Gorgeous."

"Move over, Zapruder."

Steinman flushed. "Sorry. I guess I sounded callous."

"A little. What's so perfect and gorgeous? What did you actually get?"

"Dolly pulling her gun, twirling her gun, and then by God, firing her goddamn gun. Unbelievable. Right there on film."

"Then what?"

He scowled. "Then nothing. Someone jostled me and I lost her. I got a back view when she turned around and then some bare wall. By the time I caught my balance, she was gone. Didn't get Rex falling either."

"Pity."

"Sorry again. Cookie says he's known the guy all his life. I guess you have too."

"You guess right. If I knew Chauncey I know Cookie and if Cookie knows me, he's got to have known Chauncey. There's only thirty of us in the whole town."

"Sounds like L.A."

"No place could be as bad as this. How's your head?"

"Getting better. Do you think we should call the cops?"

"You're forgetting something."

"No, I'm not. It's just that the average cop doesn't sit you down on her couch and give you brandy. Don't I have to make a formal report or anything?"

"Up to you. But I can't see the point, can you? The guy's gone."

"The film's evidence in a murder case. Shouldn't I let someone know about it?"

She shrugged. "I know about it. But listen, make the complaint if you want to. It just seems like hassle for you and a waste of time for everyone else."

"Now *you* sound callous."

"Hey, didn't I give you brandy? That's more than any other cop would do." She turned her palms up. "It's not that I'm callous. It's that everyone's overworked and they really can't do anything for you."

He didn't answer her.

"How about sleeping on it? Can we talk about it tomorrow?"

"Okay." He made no move to go.

Finally Skip said, "Oh, hell, it's Carnival. Let's have a Dixie. There's no more brandy."

Steinman smiled and Skip saw that he had a shy, sweet look when he did. For a moment it occurred to her that perhaps he found her attractive. But he said, "Thanks. I don't think I could take Cookie's right now. They've probably gone into the Mazola oil phase of the evening."

Skip shook her head, both at her own delusion and at

59

Steinman's failure to understand New Orleans. "Not a chance," she said. "Nobody as drunk as they're going to be could possibly screw. Can I call you Steve?"

"Sure. And you're Skippy, aren't you?"

"Just Skip."

"The grown-up version."

"More or less."

"Skippy. Cookie. Bitty. What the hell is this—a kindergarten? Isn't anyone named Bill or Sue?"

Skip shook her head and started for the kitchen to get the beer. Steve followed her. "No one," she said. "It's a kind of tradition."

"Preppy."

"Beyond preppy. Southern. But if it helps to orient you, my official name is Margaret." As she turned on the light, roaches scattered over the counter, making the dry, skittery, papery noises that tended to make people who paid any attention slightly sick. The natives, of course, ignored them. Steve turned pale. "How do you stand it? Cookie's got them too."

"They're a way of life in the Crescent City—like the silly names. My folks even have them over on State Street."

"State Street, indeed. That rolled off your tongue awfully easily."

"Cookie must have told you I'm the only cop in town who was a Kappa at Newcomb."

"Kappa—that must be some sort of sorority. We've heard tell of 'em in California."

Skip laughed. "It's refreshing to meet someone who doesn't live and die by this stuff."

Steve held up his Dixie. "It's refreshing to meet you, Officer Post-deb."

Skip winced. "Don't. That's what my brother cops call me when they want to be nasty."

"Sorry. I seem to be a social failure tonight."

"You're wounded. Shall we sit?" They settled in again on

her sofa, Skip sufficiently loaded—not to mention exhausted—to let herself feel almost as if she were having a date. She wanted a good time, dammit—hadn't had one since she returned to this preposterous backwater—and she didn't care if she did entertain Mr. Steve Steinman, murder witness. She didn't care what the lieutenant or the chief or Mr. Steinman himself thought. She, Skip, felt like kicking off her shoes and drinking beer. She proceeded to do so.

"Why exactly," she said, "were you filming the Rex parade?"

"Why? Are you kidding? *Why?* It was going to be part of my chef d'oeuvre, that's why. I'm at AFI and . . ."

"AFI?"

"The American Film Institute. Do you know how many now-famous films started out as AFI student projects?"

"No. A lot?"

"Oh, hell, I don't know. A few, at any rate. Anyway, I wrote this screenplay about a woman who gets involved in a crime and she runs away—to New Orleans—but it's Carnival and what she finds there is worse than anything she left behind, and then she's got two sets of baddies after her. Oh, well, you don't want to know the whole story—I was just trying to get some color shots at the parade today, but everything's changed now."

"What do you mean?"

"How can I do a movie about a fictional crime when I actually saw a real one?"

"You mean now you want to do a documentary?"

He looked embarrassed. "Of course not. Nothing like that. It's just that—I got the idea to come to New Orleans because I knew Cookie and wanted to see Mardi Gras, but now that I'm here, the whole thing seems so much bigger and richer than I thought. I mean, even without the murder. Now I feel like I want to set more of the story here—make it more about New Orleans. I mean—I don't know what I want. All of a sudden my old idea seems jejune, that's all."

"Jejune?" said Skip. "Puerile as well?"

"Callow and infantile."

"Jejune," said Skip again, savoring the silly sound of the syllables. She and Steve laughed like lovers sharing a favorite threadbare joke. "Another beer?"

He crumpled up his can and handed it to her. He said, "Tell me about this guy, will you? I mean, about the St. Amants. Was Chauncey some sort of fancy Creole from a family prominent for generations?"

"By no means. He was from a very middle-class family that lives out by Lake Pontchartrain. I've met his parents—very nice, very ordinary. But Chauncey went to Tulane, where he met Bitty Mayhew, who's a member of one of the oldest Uptown WASP families, and he married her. Her father was then president of the Carrollton Bank—and more or less king of the city, as opposed to being merely Rex—but despite the kid's humble beginnings, he took Chauncey on and they say he was never sorry. Chauncey was smart, and in due time *he* became president of Carrollton. Civic leader too—good works up the kazoo.

"As for Bitty, she drinks too much and always has, ever since I've known her anyway, which is all my life. They have a daughter who drinks too much and lives off her trust fund and a son who's an insufferable brat—and who also drinks too much."

"That would be Marcelle and Henry. I hear there's a best friend too."

"Cookie's been filling you in."

"Not only on the St. Amants. I know the names of every member of your family as well. But the best friend—Tolliver Albert—what's he like?"

"I like him—always have. He's your basic aging bachelor, which in New Orleans usually means a closet queen; but if he's gay, he's discreet. Quite the man-about-town, favorite escort and all that, but never any special lady friends. Who knows about his proclivities?"

"Maybe he was Dolly—maybe he and Bitty were having an affair."

"As a matter of fact, it was Tolliver's balcony she stood on. But he and Bitty aren't an item, believe me. She likes booze, not men."

Steve sighed. "I wish I had more of the hang of New Orleans."

He sounded so wistful Skip wanted to pat him. "It's not easy. The social structure's got more strata than a shale cliff."

"So I gather. You wouldn't want to run a few of them by me?"

"Oh, God, don't get me started. When I lived in San Francisco I never paid for a meal. I just spouted N'awlins lore and I was invited everywhere." She gave him a new beer.

"N'awlins? Is that the correct pronunciation?"

"God, no. I've never actually heard it within the city limits. But outside, it's the folklore favorite. Like, when you land here, the flight attendant says, 'Welcome to N'awlins', and you're supposed to be in the know."

"So what's right?"

"Ah, many, many things. New Awlins if you're very southern. New Orl-ee-uns if you're kind of preppy and affected. New Orlins for most people. (Never New Or-leens, of course.) And New Awyuns, if you also say my-nez."

"Hold it a minute. *My-nez?*"

"For mayonnaise. It's what they say at the very top rung around here. If you hear my-nez or New Awyuns, kowtow. But do not be fooled—if you want to go to Napoleon Avenue and the taxi draver takes you to Na-poe-yun, he probably isn't an aristocrat in reduced circumstances. Even the yats say Na-poe-yun."

"Yats?"

"In good time, in good time. Weren't we talking about strata?" She was beginning to enjoy herself. It was like being in California again.

"Uh-huh. Full speed ahead."

"Well, of course you've got your old Creole families with the fancy French names, and then you've got your uptown WASPs—sort of like me, except my folks are first generation, which is good enough for Rex if you're rich enough and determined enough, but not good enough for the Boston Club, which is upper-*upper* crust, no matter whose ass you kiss."

"You're a WASP? Langdon isn't an Irish name?"

"We don't talk about that. We go to Trinity Episcopal Church, and that qualifies us as WASPs. Then there's your old Jewish families and there's the Petroleum Club crowd—mostly oil execs. And lots of other Johnny-come-latelies with more money than history, like the Langdons. Then there's your slightly less wealthy—or even fairly poor—Ole Miss and LSU grads who work around town and mix in with the Uptown crowd a little. And way, way down the line, you've got your yats."

"Ah, yes."

"It's short for 'whereyat,' which is their greeting. If anyone says, 'whereyat, Steve?', whatever you do, don't say, 'at the corner of Ursulines and Royal' or they'll think you're crazy. Say, 'Hey, cap, how you?'"

"It means hello?"

"Approximately. Yats are working-class whites who originally settled the Irish Channel, on the river side of Magazine Street, and also the Ninth Ward, out beyond the Faubourg Marigny. For reasons no one has yet been able to discern, they speak with Brooklyn accents. A female yat is called a charmer, pronounced 'chawama' by uptown twits such as myself."

"That's how they talk?"

"Yep. They berl up a pot of red beans every Monday and their bathrooms are equipped with terlets and also with zinks, in which they rinch their pantyhose. They also eat s'rimp and ax questions."

"Good thing you're not a snob."

"Just passing on the local color."

"Speaking of which, where do blacks fit into the strata?"

Skip opened a ceramic box on one of the tables beside the sofa. "Now that," she said, "is a subject of much interest. However, the professor cannot go on without sustenance. Would you care to join me?" She held up a joint. Steve looked half eager, half confused. She shrugged, lit the joint, took a toke, and passed it to him. He didn't refuse.

"Blacks are a different caste, just like in other American cities, but they have their own strata. In the days of slavery, the Creole People of Color had their own very well-developed society in the Quarter. They owned businesses and they were rich, lots of them, and well respected. The prettiest girls, meaning the ones with the most obvious Caucasian genes, were sent to the quadroon balls, where they met rich planters, who bought them houses of their own and supported the children of their unsanctioned unions. The children, in turn, were eventually sent to the balls if they were girls, or packed off to school in Paris if they were boys. Anyone who could pass for white did. I expect some of our leading citizens can trace their ancestries back to all that. And look at me." She used both hands to toss her lavish mass of crinkly curls.

"I thought that was just a good perm."

"Absolutely natural. But I don't count because we're 'from away.' However, there was a queen of Comus a few years ago who mortified her whole family by declining to have her hair restyled for the great occasion. People who saw it said that Afro was so high and so thick the crown would hardly sit on it."

Steve laughed. "Her father must not have been in the Boston Club. Surely you have to be racially pure to get in."

"I doubt it. How would anybody know? Anyway, a little thing like ancestry wouldn't stop a true Bostonian from being a rockrib—the point is to pass. However—" she took another toke—"back to strata. The blacks have their own strata, based—are you ready for this?—on skin color."

"I think I might throw up."

"Why? They're just emulating the rest of us bigots. Stories used to be told about black nightclubs where they wouldn't let you in if you were any darker than a paper bag. An 'integrated' club meant one where you could go if you were anywhere from café au lait to licorice. Want another beer?"

"I need one, I think."

Skip gathered up the empty cans and hauled out a brace of fresh Dixies. When she got back, Steve was pulling on his beard, thinking. "I want to use all this stuff," he said. "It's going to be a whole different movie."

"Put me in it, why don't you." Skip put a hand on her hip and started to mug.

"Why not? You're the most amazing thing I've ever seen."

She'd started cutting up because she was high and having fun—she hadn't expected a serious answer. "Thing?" she said. "You think I'm a *thing*?"

"Are you an anthropologist doing fieldwork?"

"I'm a cop. No shit. A cop. I'm just observant, that's all."

"Cookie said you kept flunking out of schools."

"So?"

"I expected a ding-a-ling."

Skip shrugged. "I read a lot." She was getting pissed. She didn't like people telling her what they expected, and for that matter didn't like them expecting things of her. Who cared if Mr. Steve Steinman of AFI expected a dumb cop? Skip was Skip and *not* who he expected, and he was drinking her beer and smoking her dope and he could keep quiet about it.

Steve said, "You have the most beautiful hair I've ever seen. How many cops have gorgeous hair? And almond-y eyes. Maybe you could play the lead."

She didn't speak, wasn't sure she'd heard right. And wouldn't have known what to say anyway. She could have sworn he'd just given her a compliment, maybe two, and done it while she was in the middle of being mad at him.

He said, "You should be at a ball tonight."

Skip was embarrassed. She changed the subject, slipping back into her professorial mode and letting the moment pass. *"You* should be. A Carnival ball is like nothing you've ever seen. Rex and Comus are held in the Municipal Auditorium, which is divided in half for the occasion. They're the most important balls, so they're held on Mardi Gras night."

He slipped back with her, once again teacher's pet. "Do they take the seats out for dancing?"

"Uh-uh. They sink the stage so it's flush with the floor, and that's where they dance. That way no one falls off."

"But what about the rest of the place? People dance in an empty auditorium?"

"Far from it. Spectators spectate."

"Do they sell tickets or what?"

"Perish the thought. You have to be invited. If you're very special, you get a callout, which means you can dance. But only ladies get callouts."

"My head's spinning."

"Okay, it's like this. If you were invited to Comus, say, you'd have to wear white tie and tails. Or at least black tie. You'd get to sit down and watch a bunch of guys in funny costumes dance with ladies in evening dresses. You might recognize the ladies, but of course all the men would be masked. The ladies with callouts would be seated in a special section. They're wives and friends of the families of members. They'd just sit there until a member of the floor committee came to escort them to their partners for their one dance— two at the most."

"And they wouldn't even know who the guy was?"

"If your husband's partner's a member, that's probably who it is. But no one tells you."

"So theoretically you wouldn't even know who you were dancing with."

"Right. It's a little on the weird side."

"How about the queen and her court?"

"That's the part that's a spectacle. For Comus they wear

silver, and gold for Rex—all sequins and spangles. From the seats it looks like something out of a science-fiction movie. The trains alone weigh as much as a Toyota. The big moment comes at midnight, when Rex takes his court over to the other side to pay their respects to Comus and his court—the parvenus bowing to the real power. Quite charming."

"Yick."

"That's the way the sequin sparkles. Just another Fat Tuesday in the City That Care Forgot."

"It's amazing you turned out the way you did."

"I wouldn't say that. It's more or less inevitable, really. Anyway, you poor kids aren't the only ones who had it tough." Suddenly she realized she knew virtually nothing about Steve Steinman. "Or are you poor?"

"Not exactly. My family belongs to a Jewish country club that excludes our brothers of Russian extraction."

Skip threw a sofa pillow at him. "And you've been sneering at *my* friends and fellow townspeople."

"I wasn't sneering. The human condition is just a little disappointing wherever you find it, that's all."

Mollified and suddenly curious, Skip said, "You know everything about me. What's your story?"

"Absolutely untrue, Officer Langdon. I know nothing about you except that you come from what you insist is a social-climbing family and you're a big, gorgeous cop." Skip felt herself flush. "I don't see how you got from one to the other."

"Well, tough luck, I'm tired of talking. Your turn."

"Okay, okay. I'm from Atlanta, went to Duke, where Cookie Lamoreaux was my roommate, and am now in training to be the next George Lucas. I'm thirty years old, unmarried, and want very much to see you again."

"You do?"

"Uh-huh. How about breakfast?"

"I don't think I'm going to feel like it."

"Late, then. Brunch."

"I'll be working."

"Okay, I'll come down and we can talk about whether I need to file that complaint."

"Oh, God, I forgot all about that. Come at three, okay?"

"Not first thing?"

"I'm going to be out of the office."

"No problem. I'll wait for you."

ASH WEDNESDAY

1

Skip had been told to do what Uptown girls would do, and the first thing on the list was exactly what nearly everyone else in town would be doing—going to church. Afterward she'd go to the St. Amants', but first things first—a city that celebrates Fat Tuesday must wake up to Lent. Besides, she was going to need something spiritual in her life after walking through the Quarter.

Despite the efforts of heroic sanitation crews working through the night, Ash Wednesday on Bourbon Street had a sickening morning-after feel to it. True, by now several tons of go-cups, discarded Hurricane glasses (or the shards that were all that remained of them), pointed sticks from corn dogs, beer cans, and worst of all, corncobs would have been hauled away. But the stench would remain—of garbage and vomit, and spilled beer. And anyone who was still on the street probably hadn't been home that night.

Yet Skip craved the walk and the subsequent streetcar ride. If she had time, she often traveled uptown this way instead of driving. She discovered its therapeutic qualities the time someone dropped her at her parents' house and she got into a fight with her father—the last she'd ever had with him, the last time the two had spoken. She'd taken the streetcar home rather than let him drive her. And by the time she hiked to St. Philip Street, she found she'd cooled out.

This morning the benefits were twofold: physical and mental. She had a nagging cobwebby hangover that cried out for fresh air and exercise. And she needed to think about what she'd done last night. Three stupid things. Very dangerous things.

One was having Steve meet her at home. Another was telling Marcelle about it. That one-two combination had already had consequences, and she needed to try to square it with herself.

The third was a different matter—smoking weed with a stranger. With the wrong stranger, it could put her job in jeopardy. It was unsmart, uncoplike, un-Skip-like. So what had made her do it?

Probably a drug worse than a crack and heroin speedball. Testosterone.

The walk should have helped—she should have been able to sort out some of it, at least, but she was wearing heels and her feet hurt too much.

She ended up window-shopping. She'd walked a block over to Royal, which stank almost as much as Bourbon, but at least here there were no sleazy clubs with the smoke still hovering. There were antique shops, filled with lovely things a cop couldn't afford.

71

She was caught up in the journey, in the city, as she had never been before moving away and often was lately. She let herself go with it, enjoying herself, getting the fresh start she wanted. It was wonderful the way, in forty-five short minutes, you could go from the dilapidated beauty of St. Philip to the tawdriness of Bourbon, the commercial elegance of Royal, and finally, once on the streetcar, the magnificence of St. Charles. The farther uptown you went, the more the mansions lining the avenue looked like English stately homes. Skip got off at Jackson Avenue, the line of demarcation between downtown and the Garden District. She wasn't far from Tolliver Albert's, and St. Charles at this point—yesterday's parade route—was nearly back to normal. Skip turned toward the river and Trinity Episcopal Church, as familiar to her as her old bedroom on State Street.

Her parents were at church. She took communion, let the priest smear her forehead with ashes in the shape of a cross, and left with hardly a glance at them. Outside she had an almost uncontrollable urge to walk to the river. She was looking toward it, shivering (she'd worn no coat, only a suit, and the wind had come up) when she heard her mother's voice: "Skippy."

She stopped and turned around, seeing that her mother was wearing black and needed to lose ten pounds. "Hello, Mother." Her mother had wanted her to call her "Mummy," but even the other girls at McGehee's didn't say that.

"Did they give you the day off?" Her mother spoke of "them" as if they were enemies who held her daughter prisoner.

"Not really. They gave me a nice assignment. I'm working on the murder."

"Oh, Skip. It's not as if it were a stranger—it's Chauncey!"

"I think that's why it means more to me than it would to the average cop. It's a good assignment, Mother. Be proud of your little girl."

"Oh, Skip!" said her mother again, as if Skip had told her she'd been arrested.

"I met a nice boy, Mother."

"You did? Someone we know? Is it serious?"

"A friend of Cookie Lamoreaux's." She had dragged out poor Steve Steinman because she wanted to give her mother something—just a little something—to reassure her. But now she could see the pitfalls of what she had said.

"Is he from here?"

"From L.A., but Cookie's known him forever. They were roommates at Duke."

"Skippy, you be careful. We don't know this boy and the world is full of people who can hurt you."

"I'll be careful, Mother. Why didn't Daddy come out?"

"You know how he is, darling. He told me to ask you when you're coming home."

"I live on St. Philip Street, Mother."

"In a hovel."

"I have to go to work now."

"Won't you consider going back to school?"

"I like my job. I'm on my way to the St. Amants'. Are you going?"

"We've already been."

"Good-bye, then."

One day after church she and her brother had walked to the river. It was summer then and the closer they got, the heavier the air became. The last couple of blocks, it was nearly impossible to breathe, the way the air sat on top of your chest and refused to go in. Skip was wearing a fancy dress and ruining it, sweating. Her brother took off his coat and tie and threw them away. There were still mansions on Jackson, some of them half falling down, some still fine, interspersed with roach-ridden apartment houses. It was that way for a block or two, to Magazine Street. And after that it was poor, got poorer as it got hotter and heavier. Her mother had beaten her for it, but it was one of the finest adventures of her childhood.

Doing it now might be dangerous, she thought. Some would say that nowadays a young woman shouldn't even walk through the Quarter to Canal to catch the streetcar. It didn't matter—it was too cold anyway, and she had to get to the St. Amants'. She turned toward the lake and then uptown onto Prytania.

Privately Skip called the Garden District "Rappaccini's District" after the poison garden in the Hawthorne story. She found it as achingly beautiful—in its way—as she found her own neighborhood. But instead of the tumble of structures from three centuries—from Creole cottages to Holiday Inns—the Garden District enjoyed a more leisurely pace. By contrast, its gracious old houses seemed rather like country estates, displaying exuberant front yards right on the streets instead of hiding tiny gemlike courtyards.

There was a nineteenth-century Caribbean feel to the place, more so in recent years, since the fad for old-fashioned gaslights. On a summer evening, with the gaslights on, the improbable scent of mixed magnolia and jasmine in the air, one could almost hear the clack of hooves on cobblestones, see sails in the distance. The gardens were rife with banana trees, crotons, profusions of tropical plants—and each tendril, to Skip, was a viper that would surely strike if you turned your back. She thought it as evil and dangerous a neighborhood as its denizens found Tremé, as stultifying and smothering as she felt the Quarter was liberating.

Yet her feelings had nothing to do with the beauty of the place. They were about her associations with the homes in which she'd visited here, full of air as thick as that near the river, harboring atmospheres that made you gasp for breath.

The St. Amants' house, with its stuffy furniture and its grand piano that no one ever played, was far from one of her favorites. It looked as if someone had gone to as much trouble to make it ordinary as Tolliver Albert had to make his apartment special and personal. Skip thought of the decor as the wing-chair-and-Audubon-print syndrome. Her parents' house suffered from it as well, and that wasn't the only other place she'd seen it.

Today the shiny-finish dining table was covered with a lace cloth and laden with food that probably wouldn't be eaten, though Skip doubted there'd be a problem with leftover drinkables.

In one of the wing chairs flanking the fireplace sat Haygood Mayhew, Bitty's father, white-haired, red-faced and shrunken in height, puffy in body, looking squat and square and rather like a toad. Though retired from the Carrollton Bank, he was still one of the most powerful men in New Orleans, as anyone could see who cared to observe the gaggle of would-be's dancing attendance. The mayor was one of them.

Gossip had it that Haygood had gone along with Chauncey and supported him. Not that he would have had any objection to a black mayor, female mayor, or any other kind so long as he or she was friendly to business in general and to the Carrollton Bank in particular. Haygood wasn't a bigot. Wasn't even a seersucker-suit conservative. Skip had once seen him proclaiming his nonpartisanship on a local TV show. Chauncey's politics—so upsetting to many of Haygood's contemporaries—had probably made the old man chortle with malicious delight.

In the other wing chair sat Bitty, a porcelain statue draped in black. Behind her stood Tolliver, and she was receiving condolences from the only black person in the room besides Mayor Soniat—John Hall Pigott, the musician, club owner, and retired actor. Skip had never seen him in person. She hadn't known he was so tall. His hair was starting to turn white, and he was easily the handsomest man she'd seen since leaving San Francisco. No wonder he'd been in so many movies, though some said he couldn't act a lick. But nobody said he didn't play brilliant clarinet, and he had been Chauncey's staunchest, most influential ally in prying music money out of the city. For years he'd lived in California, but last year he retired from acting, returned to his hometown, and opened his club.

Skip had never seen him in person. She didn't think of herself as the sort who got star-struck, but she noticed she was staring.

2

They thought he was drunk, but then that's what they'd thought yesterday. Despite appearances, he'd never really managed the oblivion he craved. Maybe it was the coke he'd had earlier that day, he didn't know. In the end, he'd had to pretend, slumping all over the furniture and heading upstairs early.

That way he'd be ready in case Bitty needed him, but he could still get away, if not from himself, at least from dingbat Marcelle and a million smarmy relatives.

Today he was doing better. He wasn't exactly drunk—at least not nearly as drunk as he supposed he must look—but he was feeling better anesthetized, less exhausted, more able to play out the unlikely scenario in which they'd all become embroiled. He was an actor and this was his most important role. It was as simple as that. It didn't matter how much he drank—if he kept his mind on the task at hand, he could handle it. The booze would just smooth things out and allow him a little more freedom.

Still, there was one area in which it wasn't working. He couldn't shake an odd feeling he had somewhere in the center of his body—a very uncertain, unsure, mixed-up, confused sensation. It had to do with the ambivalent feelings he'd had for his father. To his surprise, he actually felt grief that Chauncey was dead. Of course, he felt a lot of other things too—relief for one, for another, a kind of dark happiness on his mother's account.

Chauncey was no good for Bitty, never had been, had driven her to drink. She was going to be a lot better off without him, might even kick her addiction. Was she drinking today? he wondered. It was hard to tell with all the pills Langdon was stuffing down her.

How beautiful she looked. The black dress with the blonde hair was about as dramatic a combination as you could find outside a Carnival ball. Henry adored the dress and wondered idly if it would fit him. But of course it wouldn't—there was a reason for Bitty's nickname.

He was continually surprised that she really was a tiny, ethereal creature—like Titania, only more fragile. He had the most delicious memories of sitting in her lap, cuddling at her breast, being picked up and comforted. He couldn't have been more than two or three, but he remembered so vividly that he still sometimes thought of her as big. In a way, in his mind, she was. He'd never said good-bye to the strong happy mother he remembered.

Unlike most of his friends, who seemed to recall only the traumas of their childhood, Henry harbored bittersweet haunting thoughts of the way it was with Bitty and him before Marcelle was born—even after for a while. He was adored and fulfilled. When Bitty started drinking, and when the drinking gradually increased to the point where some days she couldn't take care of him and his sister, the happiest days of his life came to an end.

Yet he never stopped wishing he could have the idyll again. Now that Chauncey was dead, for instance, he wondered what the chances were. For Bitty. For himself. Even, a little, for Marcelle. And for Tolliver—most definitely for Tolliver. For all of them as a family. Yes, he thought of Tolliver as family, and most ardently wished he were.

As he watched the continuing parade of New Orleanians coming to pay their respects, he wondered how many were glad Chauncey was dead. A lot, he suspected, might have reason to be glad. He was sure he had done the right thing yesterday. And had done it very well, in his opinion, though it wasn't the sort of thing you went around crowing to yourself about.

Oh, God, could that abysmally dressed woman over there be the person he thought she was? From the back all he could see was a gray flannel suit, not so much out of style as never there to begin with. Très ordinaire. (And très schlumpy— hips like a retaining wall.) The whole effect was made worse by brown pumps and hair done up in some kind of half-assed French twist, but coming out of the pins in great curly clumps. Oh, shit. There couldn't be two women in New Orleans anywhere near that tacky. Fuck, it had to be.

What in bloody hell did Skip Langdon think she was doing, just coming over and walking among the guests as if she'd been fucking *invited*? Shit and piss. He was going to have another drink and then by God, he was getting rid of her. Bitty didn't need her here, and neither did he.

3

Tolliver stood behind Bitty's wing chair, one hand on her shoulder, like a patriarch in an old tintype. He knew it looked stiff and pretentious, but he couldn't very well sit on the arm of the chair and he wanted Bitty to know he was there, to feel his physical presence—his hand on her shoulder—and draw sustenance from it.

Bitty could draw strength only from him and Henry, and Henry had left, apparently in pursuit of a young woman who was obviously looking for the bathroom. He wondered briefly whether she was an old schoolmate or what.

He smiled, surely as woodenly as George Washington ever had, he thought, as the passing parade paid their respects to the widow. He couldn't keep his mind on the occasion at hand. His life was passing before him.

He was standing there smiling, holding on to Bitty's shoulder, and realizing that he had lived vicariously through the St. Amants. He had done what they had done, gone where they had gone, thought what they had thought, played the perfect doting uncle. He could have lived a "normal" life— could even have gotten married—but he hadn't. Was it too late for him now? Almost certainly. And yet, whether he gained from it or not, he didn't regret Chauncey's death in the least.

"I'm back," said Henry. "Why don't you get yourself a drink?"

"Shall I get one for you?"

"Thanks. Bourbon and water."

Tolliver got the drinks quickly, reluctant to leave Bitty alone with Henry for long. He resumed his spot, and Henry did sit on the arm of Bitty's wing chair, gripping her elbow, looking as if he were using her to prop himself up. Tolliver thought: We must look like some stupid Victorian-era illustration in a book on family life. What a travesty.

Relieved for once of Chauncey's overbearing presence, Tolliver was beginning to realize exactly how much he had hated the man. He thought he had known before, it had been a cancer he'd lived with, but the depth of it hadn't really penetrated till now. Chauncey and his goddamn secrets, his twisted hypocrisy, his vaulting ambition—the things he had done to Henry and Bitty were no less than unspeakable. Surely only good could come from his long-overdue absence. In unguarded moments, though, Tolliver felt a chill of fear, his mind turning crazily to thoughts of Pandora. *If only the demons would stay in the damn box!*

Marcelle approached with a big girl in a gray suit, the girl Henry had followed. "Mother, it's Skippy in mufti—Dr. Langdon's daughter." Tolliver thought Marcelle did well to prompt Bitty, who in turn would be doing well to identify

Marcelle herself, thanks to none other than Skippy's quack of a dad.

"Hello, officer," said Henry. "Going to put us in your report?"

The girl looked confused.

"How about this?" said Henry. "Two of the suspects, Mrs. Bitty St. Amant and her son, Henry, were fried to the gills on the Wednesday following the crime. Oh, and maybe you could make a little note to the side in parentheses: 'as usual,' you could say. Then you could say, 'After prolonged surveillance reporting officer noticed Marcelle Gaudet, the former Mrs. Lionel Gaudet, aka Marcelle St. Amant, flirting with three or four guys old enough to be her father, who was conspicuous by his absence.'

"And maybe then you could mention something about how you searched my father's study without a warrant. Would you mind doing that, officer? Would that little thing be too much trouble?"

Till then, everyone had remained frozen, unable to believe what was happening. Tolliver felt suddenly very dizzy. His body jerked, giving one of those half-asleep lurches, except that this was daylight and he was standing up.

Bitty kept her face a mask—probably was barely able to move a muscle in it anyway—but she dabbed at her eyes, as if that were all she had energy for.

"Time," asked Marcelle, "for Henry's nap?"

Without a word, Tolliver put an arm around Henry's shoulders and marched him gingerly toward the stairs. He didn't trust his legs, hoped he wasn't going to blow it. He'd forgotten again to take a pill. His head was spinning. Henry was worse, and no wonder—he was fried to the marrow, not the gills. His knees were wobbling badly.

Dammit, Henry, walk! I'm going to die on the staircase if I don't get my pills. He thought it, but he didn't say it.

4

Marcelle knelt beside her mother and held both her hands. "It's okay, Mother. I'm here."

Bitty's eyes overflowed. "Skippy," she said, "I do apologize for Henry. We're all so very upset today."

Skip murmured something and started to wander off. "Skippy," said Marcelle. "Please don't leave. I'll just stay with Mother a minute."

She didn't know why. Bitty wasn't going to fall out of her chair, and apparently couldn't care less whether Marcelle stayed with her or not. But Marcelle couldn't be sure. Maybe that detached manner of hers was just the drugs. Still, she hadn't responded to Marcelle when Henry and Tolliver left.

She has a lot on her mind, Marcelle reminded herself. She's doing well just to remain sitting. But she wished she were able to comfort her mother the way Henry and Tolliver did. She couldn't get Bitty's attention—she'd never been able to.

She knew Bitty hadn't yet become a drunk when she was born, hadn't till she was three years old, but she might as well have been one all along—all Marcelle could remember of her early childhood were her mother's "sick days," the way she smelled of sherry and Bloody Marys, and the old sandbox Chauncey and Bitty had built out behind the house for Henry.

Oh, dear God, I hope I can be a better mother to André than she was to me. If I do nothing else on this earth, please let me do that. And the way things are going, it doesn't look as if I'll do another damn thing.

André was upstairs now, watching a movie with some other kids. She'd kept him with her in this house of gloom for two days and she knew it was hard on him, but surely it was better than leaving him with a baby-sitter. Or was it? Why the hell was child rearing, the most important of all tasks, so shockingly unscientific? People knew more about microbes and life in space than they did about how to raise kids, and they wrote more books about that stuff too. Marcelle truly hoped she wasn't making a mess of four-year-old André, dooming him to a resentful adulthood spent on the shrink's couch.

Her own life was rather like that. And if it hadn't been for her dad, she knew she'd be an even worse wreck than she was. Thank God, Chauncey had been there for her—sometimes anyway. At the moment she missed him so much all she could remember were the good times—Chauncey ruffling her hair, swimming with her, teaching her to ride a bike. (Bitty thought bicycles dangerous and didn't want her to have one.)

Marcelle did want her father's murderer punished. But she was worried about something: That in the course of the murderer's arrest and trial, Chauncey's good name would be destroyed. That his human rights work would be not merely forgotten but discredited. Yet how could the murderer be punished if there were no arrest and no trial?

Tolliver was coming back, seeming a little woozy. He didn't look good at all, but what could one expect under the circumstances? Marcelle herself, she imagined, would frighten small children.

Okay. All right. When Tolliver arrived to take care of Bitty, she'd find Skip. She'd asked her to stay; she supposed she'd known she was going to tell her.

Oh, Daddy, why did you have to do what you did?

She found Skip chatting with Jo Jo Lawrence. The sight of him almost made her vomit. Had she really fucked him yesterday? Fucked him while her father was getting murdered?

God, she hoped she wouldn't be questioned too closely about what she was doing at the time of the murder. Should she tell Skippy? Maybe she could keep it quiet. But then she remembered it wasn't important. What was important was to tell Skip the other thing.

"Jo Jo, go away, would you? Skippy and I've got some old times to talk over."

He looked puzzled. "I didn't even know you two were friends."

As he walked away, it occurred to Marcelle that Skip was probably another of his extramarital adventures. She wondered if he'd have been so quick to screw her—Marcelle—if he'd known she and Skip were friends. But he probably would have. Jo Jo wasn't the sort to be bothered by much, and hadn't the brain power to do much fretting even if he had been.

She put a hand on Skip's arm. "Skippy, I've got something to tell you."

Skip nodded.

"First of all, Mother and Daddy didn't have sex. They had separate rooms."

Skip's right eyebrow went up, and her cheeks flushed faintly.

"Now don't be embarrassed. I have to tell you that because it's the only way you can understand. Daddy had other women."

"I see."

"One woman, I mean."

"How do you know?"

"She came to the house once, a few weeks ago. All dolled up with cleavage and high heels. I was here at the time, and Mother was upstairs. I heard Daddy say, 'Don't ever come here again,' in the meanest tone I ever heard him use. Then he slammed the door in her face."

Marcelle paused to sip her drink. "You should have seen her, Skippy. She was young—under twenty-five, for sure—and beautiful. All angles and planes in her face, and copper skin and copper hair. And she looked so *hurt* when he slammed the door. And then furious. She kicked the door. I was here with André, visiting the grandparents. I heard it start, and then I looked out the window and saw it all."

"You think she might have killed your daddy? Is that why you're telling me this?"

Marcelle nodded.

"But I thought you felt it was political."

"Oh, I know I said that. I just wish I believed it. But listen, there might be a chance—maybe this woman didn't kill Daddy and if she didn't, Skippy . . ."

Marcelle thought she might cry. She caught her breath and held it a second. "Oh, Skippy, listen, if it wasn't her, can you please, please keep it secret—about her, I mean?"

"Secret? I don't understand."

"From the newspapers, I mean. Oh, please, please. Because, Skippy, listen, it wasn't just that he was having an affair, it was something else. Something I wish you could be real, real discreet about."

"I'll do the best I can. What is it?"

"She was black."

Chauncey St. Amant, friend of the downtrodden, had sexually exploited a young black woman. Marcelle had been living with it for weeks. She was disappointed in her father, certainly, but ultimately she thought what he did to relieve the terrible despair of living with Bitty was his own business.

However, public knowledge of such a liaison would make a laughingstock of her father's memory. She thought it ironic that in the 1980s, interracial love affairs bore more stigma than they had in the 1800s. And in Chauncey's case, there was much more than snickering at stake. Marcelle had admired her father for his courageous stand on racial matters more than for anything else.

Yet she was glad she'd told Skip. Chauncey's less tangible contributions—the subtle ones having to do with reshaping attitudes—might be in jeopardy. But surely nothing could undo his real work—his affirmative action program, his support of the arts, the things that had helped actual individuals whom one could know and talk to. Nothing could change the election of Furman Soniat.

THE WOMAN

Skip left feeling slightly giddy at having stumbled so easily into Marcelle's confidence. She remembered what Ring Lardner had once said about Ash Wednesday—that he felt like "Rex in a state of Comus"—and smiled. She had never felt more alive. There was something about death that was different from the little deaths of alcohol and drugs—it didn't numb you out, it made you operate on all cylinders.

She was pretty sure she could find Chauncey's mistress. Of course the two stars, O'Rourke and Tarantino, probably could too, but she'd gotten the tip and she could run it down faster because she knew people. She was exhilarated. She wanted to do this by herself, not as third wheel on the team, and she could. She felt it. She'd do it today, but first she needed to go to headquarters to check out a few things—and make sure

85

the stars understood that she was really on this thing. Also, she needed to make friends with them—she didn't know these guys at all except by name.

O'Rourke was fortyish and a heartthrob—sandy hair, cute mustache, nice buns. Married to a sergeant who worked in sex crimes. He seemed a little on the taciturn side.

Tarantino was ten years older, give or take. He was dark, clean-shaven, and overweight in that peculiar pear-shaped New Orleans way—giant shoulders, chest and belly (with emphasis on the belly), but regular-size legs and arms, unfat face. She didn't know if it was in the genes or what, but half the men in town were built like that.

They were there—both of them—when she arrived. Tarantino rose and shook hands. "Skip. Glad to have you. We can use another hand."

Not to be outdone, O'Rourke rose too. "Good to see you, Langdon." He'd been to church—still had a smear of ashes on his forehead.

"I've been at the St. Amants'," Skip said. "I thought we could bring one another up to date."

Tarantino said, "Good idea. Sit down, sit down." He waved at an empty desk. "Use Chuck Bennett's desk, why don't you? He's on sick leave."

Skip sat. "The clothes are a wash," Tarantino continued. "Anyone could have gotten them anywhere. But they probably came from the flea market—or at least the shirt might have. A guy at one of the costume stores remembered the style, but they had it three years ago. The skirt's new, but all the cheap stores have it. Same with the wig and gloves."

"What size are they?"

"Good question." He shrugged his mammoth shoulders. "Medium. The shirt's literally a man's medium, and the skirt's a twelve, which I'm told would probably fit a fairly hefty woman or a medium guy. And it wouldn't have to fit—you could leave it open in the back if it was too small or pin it up if you were."

O'Rourke looked at her through narrowed eyes. She noticed with surprise that they were brown. "What size do *you* wear, Langdon?"

"Huge." She declined to be ruffled. "What about the gloves?"

Tarantino shrugged again. "Men's medium."

O'Rourke said, "How did the outfit fit her? Loose? Tight? Or what?"

He had asked the same question yesterday, but that was before she'd known about the film. If they had that, they could get a better idea; they could blow it up and maybe pick out something useful. She was angry at herself, and she answered sullenly, making a point of using his first name, letting him know she didn't like the way he kept calling her "Langdon" as if he were her supervisor: "I don't know, Frank." Hostility hung in the air.

To cover, it, Tarantino said, "The guns were something else, though. Old Colt 44.40s with the date stamped on the barrels—1912. No serial numbers. Reasonably rare. Like they were in somebody's attic for a long time and then they decided to get 'em out. We're checking gun stores, but I don't think that's gonna get us anywhere. Did you say you were at the St. Amants'?"

"Why do you ask, Joe?" She smiled. At least she could establish rapport with this one.

"Just wonderin' how the other half lives."

"I went to the wake. And I took an unauthorized walk around the first floor." She tried to keep her voice neutral. "And I did find out something interesting. Chauncey had a real nice gun collection in his study."

O'Rourke leaned across his desk. "Anything missing?"

"I couldn't tell. I thought I'd ask Mrs. St. Amant later. She wasn't in very good shape yesterday."

"Shit!" said O'Rourke.

Tarantino said, "Hear she drinks."

"She's a human siphon."

Tarantino gave the requisite appreciative chuckle, O'Rourke let one corner of his mouth go up a quarter of an inch.

"So listen," said O'Rourke, "you think the guy was killed with his own gun or what? Why the hell would you think that?"

"I think he was killed by someone who was at the Boston Club yesterday. Let's face it, Frank—either somebody took Mrs. St. Amant's key or she killed him herself, right?"

"Somebody outside could have had a key. Maybe they took her key some other time—like when she left her purse at some other party."

"It still had to be someone she knew—and someone she knew might have paid her husband a visit and put the guns into his briefcase while Chauncey was getting him a drink."

O'Rourke snorted.

Once again, Tarantino played the peacemaker. "We had a funny call from Tolliver Albert."

Skip felt a twinge. Why hadn't he called her? He *knew* her, dammit. "Oh?" she said.

"We put a police seal on his house, so he spent the night with the St. Amants. But first he went home for some clothes and stuff."

"Uh-huh?"

"Says there was something weird about the deal. You know that Mardi Gras stuff on the balcony? That purple and green and gold stuff?"

"The bunting?"

"Yeah. He says he didn't put it there."

"So Dolly must have. Anybody see her?"

Tarantino leaned back in his chair, hands crossed over his heroic breadbasket. "Nobody's called yet, but we gave it to the *Picayune*. Maybe somebody will when they read about it."

"So, Langdon," said O'Rourke, "what else have you been doing?"

"Hanging out with the swells, like the chief said I should." She hoped she didn't sound too smug, but she didn't much care. O'Rourke was starting to get on her nerves. She stretched. "I even went to church this morning."

"And what are you planning on doing now?"

It was a good question. One possibility was to spend the next few minutes confessing her stupidity about the film. But she didn't feel safe enough, not with O'Rourke's belligerence. She didn't know what it was about—maybe he was that way with everyone—but she wasn't about to make herself vulnerable until she had a better idea.

She looked at her watch. "I've got someone coming at three for an interview, and then I think I'm going to go home and make some phone calls. I'd like to see what kind of gossip I can pick up."

"Shee-it!" said O'Rourke.

She ignored him. "Okay with you guys?"

"It's up to the chief, not us," said O'Rourke. "You're teacher's pet, aren't you?"

Skip's heart pounded. She felt the energy start low in her belly and rise up her spine. She knew that in a minute it was going to turn nasty and come out of her mouth. She took a deep breath and hoped her voice was steady. "I went through the academy just like you. I was first in my class, were you?"

"Second," O'Rourke breathed.

"The chief's my dad's friend, not mine. What I got in this department—which is hired—I got on my own."

Tarantino patted the air with his right hand, keep-it-down style. "Hey, guys, come on—we gotta work together."

Skip said, "I'm not so sure, Joe. If Frank doesn't want to work with me, he doesn't have to."

She left feeling at odds—half deflated, half heartened. Half proud of herself for standing up to O'Rourke, half wondering whether she'd been childish to pull rank. That was really what she'd done. Because even though they outranked her in reality, she outranked them in a weird way. The chief had brought her in as a kind of independent consultant from another division. She may be only a patrol officer, but she didn't have to take orders from them and she didn't have to do the shitwork on the case—the endless calling up of costume stores and gun dealers. She was free to lollygag about with the swells, as O'Rourke apparently saw it.

She could understand his resentment, and she wondered if she should have confronted it directly instead of getting snippy. But that stuff only worked with a reasonable person, and she didn't know whether O'Rourke was one.

Another half was coming up—she was only half convinced. Half convinced that O'Rourke was the enemy. Maybe he was just in a bad mood and she'd gotten in the way. Or worse, much worse—maybe he and Tarantino were Mutt-and-Jeffing her. Maybe they both resented her being assigned to the case and were using this way of keeping her at arm's length, refusing to really cooperate while it seemed Tarantino was trying to. If she were gullible enough, she'd give him what she knew, let them run with it, and gratefully accept whatever crumbs they threw her.

She sighed as she got on the elevator. She was wondering when the famous police code was going to kick in—the us-against-them mentality, the simple belonging she craved. She'd felt it in the academy, but she'd been out a year now and still hadn't carved her niche in the department. Things here weren't so different from on the outside—the smaller, prettier, more submissive women did better with a lot of these guys than she did. It hadn't been all bad, it just wasn't home yet. She'd had two good experiences, working with a woman and with a young man she'd gone through the academy with. But some of the older guys just didn't like big, sassy broads. Or maybe it was her problem—maybe she did something that intimidated them.

Once she confronted a lieutenant who'd nearly made her quit with his constant barking. "I just don't like self-confident people," he said.

What a joke! Self-confident? Skip? But she'd said, "Hadn't a cop better be self-confident?"

He said, "I don't like *you*, Langdon," and she got the transfer she requested.

She didn't give a damn if she did work with Tarantino and O'Rourke. Maybe she was more of a free-lancer anyhow.

Anyway, they don't know about the film and they don't know about Chauncey's mistress.

"Skip, are you two years old or three?"

Hold it, here. Let's think about this. Would it be smart to tell them at this point? Nope. Okay, then. Stop putting yourself down. Do your job and let them do theirs, and don't let them intimidate you. They're not Daddy, okay? You don't have to act as if they are.

She stepped into the sunlight of South Broad Street. The landscaping in front of police headquarters was fairly bleak, consisting only of a desultory fountain and a monument dedicated rather ungrammatically to "police personnel that died in the line of duty." A patrolman had been killed trying to stop a bar holdup a few days ago, and there were six or eight wreaths in front of the memorial. Skip walked over to get a look at them.

It was five of three and as good a place as any to wait for Steve Steinman. She certainly didn't want to get into the film problem with O'Rourke listening in—she didn't want him or anyone else or *anything* screwing her up. She was surprised at the vehemence of the thought and saw that she had plucked a fern from one of the wreaths, and torn it up as it flashed through her head. She released the green wreckage, letting it fall on the ground, letting herself realize how caught up in this thing she was—after only one day and no real action—how deeply she'd been drawn into the thrill of the chase, how much she wanted to work this case, and do it well. She could honestly say she was more excited than she'd ever been in her life and deeply, deeply afraid of blowing it—if she hadn't already. God, what she wouldn't give to see that film!

"Hey, Skip, whereyat!" Steve Steinman was waving from the sidewalk.

"Awright, cher."

"Cher? Like the actress?"

"That's Cajun talk. Didn't you see *The Big Easy?*"

"Yeah. I wondered what language it was in. Hey, you look good in a skirt."

Skip stared down at her plain gray suit and wondered what planet this guy was from. "Thanks."

"You didn't have to meet me out here, though—I'd have found you."

"And where would you have found me?"

"I don't know. Wherever they told me at the door."

"To tell you the truth, they might not have known. Usually I work out of the V.C. District."

"Surely not Viet Cong."

"Vieux Carré. This week I'm detailed here. And thereon hangs a tale." She looked him in the eye, hoping to get a sense of his trustworthiness; she couldn't tell a thing. "Want to hear it?"

"Sure."

"Let's get some coffee, okay? I don't want to talk in there."

Steve looked around, confused. "This looks like the middle of nowhere."

"Uh-huh. Tulane Avenue's right up there. We could walk but—" She hesitated.

"But what?"

She looked down at her scruffy brown two-inch heels. "I'm not used to these." She smiled sheepishly. "I've been to church and a wake. Have you got a car?"

"Uh-huh."

"Forget coffee. Let's go to the Napoleon House."

"Na-poe-yun?"

"Yeah, you right."

"I write?"

She laughed. "How could I have forgotten that one? You gotta say, 'yeah, you right.' It's like in Mexico, you have to know *'una cerveza, por favor'*—it's the one essential phrase that'll get you through anything."

"Hey, Professor Longhair. Who axed for this?" He took her hand as if they were sweethearts.

They sat in the courtyard at the Napoleon House, depriving themselves of its famous peeling paint and ragtag collection of pictures of the little emperor, but gaining the late winter sun. Suddenly ravenous—she'd had only a cracker with cheese at the St. Amants'—she ordered a muffuletta and a Dixie.

Steve had his own Dixie and earned her gratitude by refraining from remarks about cops drinking on duty. They talked a little about Cookie and his coterie of grownup brats while Skip worked on her sandwich. Finally, feeling fortified, she said, "Look, Steve, I feel really bad about what happened to you last night."

He shrugged and touched his lump. "It hardly hurts at all today. I don't even think I got a concussion."

She gasped. "Concussion! You shouldn't have been drinking last night."

"I'm fine. Really."

"But you might not have been, and I didn't think of that. I should have."

"Are you a doctor or a cop?"

She shook her head. "I'm stupid, that's all."

"Hey, what is this? You're not your normal arrogant self."

She laughed. She didn't think she'd been arrogant last night, but she certainly could be, and Steve was smart to pick it up—or perhaps it was just very obvious.

"I had a problem with another policeman. I'm a little shaky, I guess. It's what I want to talk to you about, to tell you the truth. Listen, I really screwed up last night. I put you in danger and—face it—we lost the film."

He put on a benign expression and, behind his glasses, reminded her of her grandfather. "It wasn't your fault. You couldn't know how many people knew I was bringing it to you."

She squirmed inside her wool suit. *I shouldn't have told Marcelle he was coming.*

She said, "Yeah, but none of them would have mugged you on the steps of the cop shop."

He laughed. "I don't blame you. It happened and it's too bad, but maybe something good'll come out of it."

"Like what?"

He looked embarrassed. "Like—we'll get to know each other."

She looked at her plate, now harboring only a crust or two and a trickle of olive oil. Why hadn't she known he meant that? Could it be that this guy really liked her? Or did he want to use her somehow? How, she wasn't sure, but he was a filmmaker and that was a second cousin to a journalist. Maybe he needed a good source in the police department. So? said the other side of her psyche, the part that wanted desperately to connect with someone so intelligent and, apparently, sensitive.

So what if he's interested in cop behavior? Don't animal researchers get close to the dolphins? Make friends with the gorillas?

On impulse she said, "Can I trust you, Steve?" It came out almost a whine, certainly a plea.

He wore that same benign expression. Was it real? "Of course."

"I'm detailed to homicide this week—to the St. Amant case."

Uh-oh. Now his expression was avid. There was no mistaking it. But at least he didn't try to hide it. "God!" he blurted. "I envy you."

"You envy me?"

"Yeah. I was a journalism major—and then a reporter for a while on a paper in Orange County. And now you know what I am. People like me are all frustrated cops—or private eyes, or FBI agents. We want to be where the action is, but we don't have the nerve to really do it. So we get our thrills vicariously."

She felt better. Now *that* had the ring of truth. "Well, listen. I guess you'll understand this. I'm assigned to work with
two older policemen, two really experienced guys who've
worked a million homicide cases and know what they're
doing. Now technically, since I'm assigned to the case, it was
perfectly okay for me to want to get the inside track on the
film—"

The corners of Steve's mouth turned up. "And maybe solve
the murder single-handedly?"

"Now don't make fun. But, yes, there was hotdogging involved, okay? Not, dammit, that those guys wouldn't do it to
me. Either one of them is capable of exactly the same thing,
but, see, they're older and more experienced and supposedly
wiser, so if they did, and the film got stolen, it wouldn't look
so bad. And who'd chew them out about it? Me? Fat chance.
A rookie respects her elders.

"However, it wasn't them that did it, it was me. And one of
these guys is really on my case. I don't know why, and I don't
know if he's really fronting for the other one as well, but he's
giving me a bad time—"

"And you want me to forget about making a complaint so
there'll be no record of what you did."

She did, it was true. But put baldly like that, it scared her.
She wondered if she was turning pale.

"Hey, relax," said Steve. "Listen, no problem. I was just
worried that the cops on the case wouldn't know about the
film and therefore wouldn't know to look for it—it turns out
you're assigned to it, and you can look for it, okay? God!
Don't get so excited. I trust you a lot more than I do those
other jerk-offs."

Skip felt a sudden rare twinge of cop loyalty—the us-
against-them feeling—at his wholesale dismissal of her
brother officers as jerk-offs. But for the moment she ignored
it. She said, "Thanks, Steve. I really appreciate it."

He looked wistful. "If I can help you at all—"

"How long are you going to be in town?"

"Another week or so, I think. Maybe longer if I can borrow some money. Like I said, this whole thing has really turned me around. I've got to rethink this project. I was just here to get Mardi Gras material—the bulk of the film will be shot in L.A.—but now I really want to rewrite the thing while I'm here. I want to do a whole different kind of movie."

"Have you decided how you'll change it?"

"That's the trouble. I really haven't. I just know it has to be more honest, that's all. I think maybe the woman didn't come to New Orleans—maybe she was here all along."

Skip looked at her watch. "I've got to go. Good luck with all that." She offered her hand, but Steve wouldn't shake. He took the hand in both of his.

"Wait a minute. I'd like to see you again."

What for? So I can stand in as a dolphin or gorilla for you? I don't have time for that now.

"I've got a lot of work to do."

"I know. But you have to eat, don't you? Let's have dinner tomorrow."

She shook her head. "I don't think I can make it. Listen, why don't I call you. You'll be at Cookie's, right?"

"Uh-huh."

She left him looking slightly hurt, as if she'd brushed him off. And she might have. She honestly didn't know whether she'd call or not, but she knew he was a complication she couldn't deal with today—and maybe not tomorrow. Romantic attractions—and yes, she admitted, she was attracted to him—took up a lot of psychic energy. She couldn't spare any just now, even for a less complicated relationship than Steve Steinman offered—one in which she wouldn't have to worry about being anyone's dolphin.

She walked to St. Philip, suffering in the unaccustomed shoes, which she kicked off the second she walked through the door.

Quickly, chomping at the bit to get to work, she folded up her unmade sofa bed, changed into jeans, made herself a glass of instant ice tea, and settled down with her Rolodex.

"A" for Albert—was Tolliver a possibility? She didn't think so. If he knew Chauncey had a mistress, he'd announce it when all ten of his fingernails had been pulled off and both knees broken. She needed someone with no discretion and no brains. Cookie Lamoreaux! No—if he knew he'd already have told her.

She dialed Alison Gaillard, one of her long-lost Kappa sisters.

"*Officer* Langdon! I read all about you in the *Picayune* this morning. I was so proud of you! I'm nothing but a little housewife now, and look at *you*. Honey, I wouldn't be surprised if they write a TV series about you."

"You've got a little girl, I hear."

"Looks just like her daddy, thank God. I couldn't have stood it if she'd come out lookin' like pitiful 'ol me."

Skip took a deep breath. Alison could be on the cover of *Vogue*, if *Vogue* got lucky; her husband had the thickset body and dumpling features of the Scotch-Irish (as everyone knew, he was from Georgia).

It was a shame about the baby, but Skip didn't think she should say that. On the other hand, she wasn't sure.

This was one of the many southern styles that left her panicked, searching desperately for the proper response. The practitioner put herself down in what seemed a completely insincere way—indeed an inexplicable way—while extravagantly complimenting someone who didn't deserve it. So was Skip supposed to heap reassurance on her? ("Alison, you're not all that ugly. Really. Just a little eye makeup and you might have gotten a *good-looking* husband.") Or was she supposed to ignore Alison's self-deprecating protests and go to the heart of the matter. ("Oh, that poor little baby. There's just no justice, is there? Well, I hear they're doing wonders with plastic surgery these days.")

She finally said, "I'm sure she's a doll." But that didn't seem to solve the problem completely—she still felt Alison had fished for a compliment. She followed up with, "Nothing wrong with your genes, though. Your Levi's anyhow, when you're in them. That's what all the guys say."

Alison's laugh was a silver flute. "Skippy, you are the *craziest* thing! You're just a nut, you know that? What can I do for you, any-old-how?"

"Well, it's kind of confidential; you won't tell anyone, will you?"

"Of course not, Skippy."

Of course not. And the sun would be setting in the East tonight. "I'm kind of new in the department and, you know, some of the guys don't like me very much."

"Skippy, I'm sure that can't be true. You're just imaginin' that."

"No, really. They think I'm a snob."

Alison laughed the silver laugh. "You! *You* a snob! The same person who used to wear jeans and T-shirts to rush parties? Who wanted to pledge a *black* girl? Skippy, they just don't know you very well."

"Well, they do know I'm a Kappa."

"Oh, I see."

"They think because of that and because my daddy's a doctor and everything—well, you know how it is. I get, like, hazed."

"Oh, yeah. Like they don't really accept you as one of them."

"Mmm-hmm. So they never let me work on any good cases. Anyway, the point is, what I'm going to have to do is prove myself. See, if I can do some, like, free-lance detective work that's really good, and maybe I could get Mimi Jurgenson to put it in the *Picayune*, well, I could prove I'm really cop material and maybe my career would advance like it's supposed to."

"Oh, Skippy. Chief Langdon! I like the sound of it."

"Right now I'd settle for 'sergeant'. And I heard a rumor I thought you might be able to help me with."

"Have *you* come to the right place! Rumors-R-Us." She played her silver flute. "Nothing's changed, has it?"

"I hope not, Alison. Listen, what I heard was Chauncey was cheating on Bitty."

"Well! I wouldn't be surprised, poor man. Has she got a problem, or what?"

Skip let out her breath. She thought she'd set up the whole thing so perfectly. All that effort for nothing? "You mean you don't know about it?"

"Well, there was that little thing a few years back with that girl that does PR for the jazz fest. You know her name— Stephanie something. She went to Sacred Heart. But everybody said it was just a flirtation. He got cold feet and wouldn't really do anything. I never thought it was out of loyalty to Bitty, though. I thought he was scared shitless of old man Mayhew, and why wouldn't he be? Whoever heard of the St. Amants anyway? Chauncey wouldn't have existed in this town if it hadn't been for Haygood Mayhew. His good looks were only going to take him just so far."

"Seems like they took him far enough. He got Bitty, didn't he?"

"Oh, you nut! You're so baaaad! Hey, listen, officer, speaking as a policewoman—what's the inside track? Who did him in? One of those dope-fiend musicians he was always helpin' out?"

"Alison, can you keep a secret?"

"Of course!"

"Well, I think he was having an affair with someone he didn't want around anymore. And she didn't want to be dumped."

"Ooohhh. The plot thickens."

"So who should I call? Who do you think would know?"

"Well, let's see. Remember Annette Alexander? Her husband's been working over at the Carrollton Bank—or there's that little girl from St. Francisville—Bella? Can that be right? Tell you what, Skippy, let me make a couple of calls myself."

"Oh, no. Absolutely not. I don't want you to go to any trouble—uh-huh. I can do it myself. No problem."

"No trouble. Really. I'll enjoy it. Call you right back."

She hung up, Skip knew, to stem further protests, which even Skip, so socially inept she thought of herself as socially diseased, knew she was obliged to keep making. Alison certainly would enjoy it. And Skip had no doubt she'd get right to it. But just to be on the safe side, she applied herself to the Rolodex.

Francie Holloway wasn't home . . . Marigny Pecot's line was busy . . . she got Barbara Lee Lipscomb's machine . . . should she call her brother? He might know. But was it worth the aggravation? She'd almost rather talk to her father.

She dialed Jo Jo Lawrence and got his wife, Baby. (It was said, Jo Jo's IQ being what it was, that he'd married her so he'd never have to trouble his pretty head remembering her name. In intimate moments, he could just holler, "Baby, Baby, Baby," and call it a day.)

"Baby? Skip Langdon."

"Skippy. Jo Jo said he saw you today."

"Yes. At the St. Amants'. I missed you, though."

"I know. I stayed home with the baby." (Oh, God, Jo Jo probably called it Baby too.)

"You and Jo Jo know the St. Amants pretty well, don't you?"

"Jo Jo does, I guess." Her voice sounded slightly sad. "He used to go with Marcelle, you know."

"A long time ago. I remember."

"Not long enough." Skip could swear she was starting to cry. "Did you want Jo Jo? He's still at work."

"What firm is he with now?"

"Haw—" She was blubbering, outright blubbering. "Haw—Hawkins—"

"Hawkins and Sneed?"

"Uh-huh." She hung up.

Skip dialed Jo Jo, wondering if she should say anything about Baby's weird behavior. "Hi, baby," he said, causing her almost to laugh out loud.

"I just talked to Baby."

"How's she doing?" he said. "She was pretty weirded out when I talked to her about an hour ago."

"To tell you the truth, she sounded upset. Is something wrong, Jo Jo?"

"Ah, no, no big deal. Somebody told her some crazy story, that's all."

"Is there anything I can do?"

"No thanks, baby. It'll blow over. No biggie. But, hey, what can I do for you?"

"To tell you the truth, I'm interested in idle gossip."

"Hey! Don't believe a word you hear! Absolutely untrue! Every word."

Not for nothing, Skip mused, was Jo Jo called Dodo Lawrence behind his back. "Not about you, silly. About Chauncey."

"Chauncey? But Chauncey's dead."

"Well, listen, I was thinking about solving the murder."

He laughed. "Oh, I get it. Like Jessica Fletcher. Hey, you've got the right job for it."

"I know. I just *hate* writing traffic tickets."

"Well, go to it, baby. How can I help you?"

"I heard Chauncey was seeing somebody."

"Seeing somebody?" He sounded puzzled. "You mean besides his secretary?"

"I don't know. For all I know he was seeing a cast of thousands. *Was* he seeing his secretary?"

"Sure. At least he was a few years back. Villere girl. Estelle, maybe. Yeah—Estelle Villere. Black girl. You know the old saying."

"Right. Hot, black, and sweet." (The saying, which had

always turned Skip's stomach, compared the preferred New Orleans woman to the local coffee preference.)

"My daddy told me about her and Chauncey—he and Chauncey were asshole buddies, you know. Daddy's pretty broken up about the whole thing—Chauncey getting killed."

"We all are, I guess. Listen, you're a pal, Jo Jo. I'll return the favor sometime."

She looked up Estelle Villere in the phone book and came up blank. She was making another glass of instant ice tea, trying to decide who to try next—Teetsie Delegal or SuSu Sims—when Alison phoned.

"Rumors-R-Us reporting in."

"I knew you'd come through."

"I'd have come through quite awhile ago, but you were on your silly phone."

"I got something too. Estelle Villere, right?"

"Boy, are you behind. She was number three."

"Of how many?"

"Oh, only four. Every one of them his secretary."

"No!" Skip was shocked at the need to control that such a thing implied.

"You better believe it, honey. That was his MO. I don't know whether he fucked them first and then made them his personal serfs, or whether he hired them and then exercised *droit du seigneur*. Listen, I gotta thank you for this. I *never* knew this stuff. I guess sometimes you forget to gossip about people twice your age. Even *experienced* gossips."

Skip laughed in spite of herself. She hadn't had the least idea Alison even knew the word 'serf' much less *droit du seigneur*. "What about number four? And what happened to the other three?"

"Let me look at my notes. Okay, the first one's name was Nancy—I couldn't get the last name on short notice, but if you give me more time—"

"It may not be necessary. What became of her?"

"She got fired. And shortly after, married a nice young

man who had previously been on his way up at the Carrollton Bank. Soon after that, *he* was fired. Now, Officer Langdon, can you see a connection there?

"I can smell one anyway. Number two?"

"You're not gonna believe this."

"Believe what?"

"Her name was Heidi. Honest. Miss Heidi Jones from Lafayette. She only lasted a year. Found herself a better job working for some guy over at Shell."

"And we can only speculate on how she auditioned for it."

"Naughty, naughty, Skippy. You are one of the last living genuine characters—you know that?"

"How about the lovely Estelle?"

"Now, she was around for a while—five years or more. She was practically an institution. And she *was* lovely too. Black—did you hear that part? Real light-skinned, I heard, about six feet tall, and mostly leg. They say guys used to make appointments with Chauncey just to drop by and get a gander. Stelly, they called her. She was famous. And guess what? All of a sudden she wasn't there anymore. No one knows a thing about what happened to her—all Chauncey would say was, 'She's not with the bank anymore.' Even to his closest friends. He had to use Kelly girls till he found a replacement."

Skip felt her scalp prickle. Stelly could have been the woman Marcelle saw—"beautiful" and "light-skinned" wasn't much of a description, but Marcelle's woman fit it too.

"Skippy?" said Alison. "You still there?"

"I'm here. I'm speechless, that's all. When somebody dies, things come out that you can't imagine, don't they?"

"It's a can of worms, all right." Alison didn't sound the least disturbed by it. "Anyway, number four's Sheree Izaguirre."

"Izaguirre? She doesn't sound black."

"Should she be?"

"I don't know." Skip felt confused. She supposed she'd begun thinking of Chauncey as having the prototypical preferences in illicit womanhood of Jo Jo's old saying.

"Well, anyhow, that's the rundown. You want Sheree's address?"

"My God, Alison, I've got to hand it to you."

"See? I'm not the dingbat you think I am."

Skip was glad they weren't speaking face-to-face, because she was dead sure she was blushing. She certainly had underestimated Alison. After getting the address and hanging up—and finally getting the ice tea—she tried to think whom Alison had suddenly reminded her of and realized it was her mother.

Elizabeth Langdon was Liza to her friends, but her own daughter thought of her as Dizzy Lizzie. Lizzie didn't seem to Skip to have a thought in her head except where she wanted to be invited next and how to make it happen. Her conversation—calculated always to please, never to offend—consisted solely of social pleasantries.

There was certainly a low cunning in her mother's machinations, but that wasn't the part that made Skip compare Alison with her. Liza's climbing agenda naturally included charity work, and this was what she did well. Put her in charge of an event and the same woman who couldn't have done her own laundry suddenly assumed the personality of a general.

Skip opened her closet. She wasn't used to being a plainclotheswoman, but the garments there certainly looked perfectly chosen for one. There was the gray suit she'd had on earlier, a beige skirt, blue silk blouse, two more pairs of jeans, some sweaters for winter and blouses for summer, and a pair of black gabardine slacks that her mother had found on sale and bought for her. These she chose now, along with a tan sweater and navy blazer. Plain clothes she had. Very plain.

Sheree Izaguirre lived off Veteran's Highway, in the kind of ticky-tacky apartment house she could have found in any city in the country. Skip supposed the pool was the drawing card—or maybe it was the anonymity, since Sheree was seeing a married man. She wondered if Chauncey had paid for the apartment—had even chosen it himself.

The woman who answered the door was petite, like Bitty, and she had something else of Bitty about her—a childlike vulnerable quality, tiny shoulders that begged for a protecting arm. She was around thirty, Skip guessed, and had dark skin—nicely tanned, most likely, from weekends around the pool—but she wasn't black. Her short curly hair was tousled, as if she'd been lying down. She wore a gray sweatsuit. A simple gold bracelet—one she doubtless always wore, that Chauncey had probably given her—emphasized the fragility of her right wrist. Her face was swollen from crying.

"Yes?"

"Sheree Izaguirre? I'm Skip Langdon from the police department." She showed her badge.

"Yes?" said the woman again.

"I'm here about Chauncey St. Amant. I wonder if we could talk a few minutes."

"Come in." Sheree Izaguirre stepped aside, looking puzzled. Pulling a tissue from a box sitting on an antique foot locker that served as a coffee table, she blew her nose. "I'm a little upset," she said. "Sit down."

Skip sat on a sectional sofa too big for the room and covered with tan plaid Herculon. On the floor was beige carpeting, and at the windows hung dark-blue drapes in a fabric that looked plasticized and probably was—curtains chosen by a landlord. Outside, the lights of the city were beginning to come on. Over Skip's head dangled a spider plant in a macramé plant hanger. A framed jazz-fest poster hung on the wall. Except for the old trunk, the furniture looked as if it had been bought from the floor of a department store—and rather hurriedly, by someone who was bored by shopping. The only discordant item in the room was a toy truck lying on its side in a corner.

Sheree sat down in a pine rocking chair with an orange cushion in the seat. Surveying the room quickly with wide, dark eyes, she twitched restlessly. "It's getting late," she said, and popped up again. She closed the curtains, turned on a table lamp.

Skip said, "I'm sorry for your loss, Ms. Izaguirre. I've known Mr. St. Amant all my life. My father's his doctor— maybe you know him."

"What'd you say your name was?"

"Skip Langdon. My father's Don Langdon. I think he and Chauncey had lunch now and then."

"Doctor Don. Sure."

"We'll all miss Chauncey." Skip smiled, let a beat pass. "There's no easy way to talk about a murder, I guess, so let me just start in the middle. I came to see you because you saw Chauncey every day, you know who else saw him, you know who phoned him. Right now we're all asking ourselves the same question. 'Who'd want to kill Chauncey St. Amant?'"

Sheree Izaguirre smiled through her pain. "I know I am."

"You're in a better position to know than most of us."

"Me?"

"Had he had an argument with someone lately? Received any threatening phone calls? Did he seem frightened about anything? Worried in any way? Those are the sorts of things you might know."

She was already shaking her head. "No. He was always nice to everybody." She dabbed at the tears that were starting to roll out of her eyes.

"Did you ever meet the woman who preceded you at the bank? Estelle Villere?"

She blushed. "No. But I heard about her. Everyone knew

Stelly." She varied the inflection on the name, so that it sounded slightly contemptuous.

"Did you know she and Chauncey were an item?"

She looked at her lap. "Yes."

"Look, Ms. Izaguirre, I know this is painful for you. I'm not trying to make it hard, but I have to ask."

She looked up and smiled again—putting on a brave front. "Sure. I understand."

"Okay, here's a couple of really tough ones—some personal questions I have to ask along with the others. I understand you also were seeing Chauncey romantically. Is that true?"

She nodded miserably.

"How was it going?"

"Going? I don't understand. Fine, I guess."

"Did he want to end the relationship?"

"No. He never said that anyway. Do you think he did?" Her face showed real fear.

"I have no reason to think so. Did you want to change it at all?"

"Change it?"

"Break it off. Or maybe get married."

She looked Skip full in the face. "Officer—uh—Langdon—"

"Skip."

"Skip. I could have been in love with Chauncey, but I held back to protect myself. I don't think he was the kind of man who fell in love, to tell you the truth. Although people say—" She stared into space.

"People say what?"

"That he was in love with Stelly. Our relationship was different—it just wasn't romantic, pure and simple." She shrugged. "I have a little boy in Country Day, and I want to keep him there. Chauncey paid his tuition. That was our arrangement."

"Oh. Where is he now?"

"Jimmy? At his daddy's."

"Did Chauncey talk about Stelly?"

"No. Never."

"Do you know why she left?"

"No."

"Okay. I have a description of a woman I wonder if you know. She's black, young—probably under twenty-five—very beautiful, with an angular face, and light skin that's close to the color of her hair—a copper color, I'm told."

"That's LaBelle Doucette." Sheree Izaguirre was excited. "Omigod, I'd forgotten about her."

"Tell me about her."

"Omigod." Skip noticed that she said "gowad" for "god," the first trace so far of the famous charmer accent. She guessed Sheree Izaguirre had worked hard to lose it. "I can't get over it. She came to Chauncey's office and asked to see him—oh—a couple of months ago. Something like that. But she didn't say her real name. Let me see now—"

She put a hand over her face, thinking. "She only gave one name, but I can't get it back. Oooohh—what was it?" She curled her hand into a tiny fist and beat the arm of the rocking chair. "Lynn! No, that wasn't it. Yes, it was. I'm almost sure. Lynn. Anyway, it doesn't matter, does it?"

"She just came in and said, 'Tell Chauncey Lynn wants to see him'?"

"Oh, no. She said 'Mr. St. Amant.'"

"But something like that?"

"Uh-huh."

"And, considering your relationship with Chauncey, weren't you curious when a beautiful young woman came to see him and gave only her first name?"

"You damn betcha I was!" All traces of tears were gone now. She was caught up in the thrill of the hunt. "And they had a fight too. You asked about fights? They had one—that bitch and Chauncey."

"What did they fight about?"

"I wish I could tell you. I did everything but listen with a glass to the wall, but I couldn't hear any words. Just shouting. And in the middle of it, Chauncey opened his door and pointed toward mine—the door of the reception room—and said, 'Leave this office! Don't you *ever* come here again!'"

"Pretty dramatic."

"But I've got to give her credit. She might have been intimidated, but she opened up her purse and pulled out this little piece of paper she had all ready. She handed it to him and said, 'Here's my phone number if you change your mind.' She went out the door, turned around, smiled, and *waved*—would you believe that? I swear to God, Chauncey turned purple. I'm not kidding, I never saw him look like that or anything close. He took the paper"—

She leaned over, plucked a tissue from the box, and balled it up viciously, making a mean-looking fist.

"—and did this. Then he threw it in the trash can, went back in his office, and slammed the door without saying a word."

Skip gave her a conspiratorial smile. "And you, of course, fished it out."

"Wouldn't you have?"

"Sure."

"Anyway, all it had on it was a name and phone number, and the name sure as hell wasn't the same one she gave me." She put her hand over her face again. "Listen, it wasn't Lynn. I just remembered something. I told Chauncey it was and he said, 'I don't know any Lynn,' and then he came out to see her and she told him her name herself. It was something-Lynn—like Ann Lynn or Faye Lynn, or maybe Ti-Lynn. And when he heard it, he got real serious and asked her to come into his office."

"He didn't know her?"

"He seemed to, once she refreshed his memory. Yeah. She said, 'Remember me?' after she said her name. And then she said, 'From a long time ago?' in this real seductive, sexy kind of way. Anyway, it turned out her name was really LaBelle Doucette—or that's what it said on the paper. That one I can remember perfectly. Because of Patty LaBelle the singer and my next door neighbor when I lived in Arabi. Benny Doucette."

Skip said, "Any theories about what was going on?"

"Sure. What I thought was that all he originally knew was her first name. Maybe it was her professional name—she could be a stripper or even a singer or something. I thought maybe he met her somewhere, had a one-night stand with her, and later, when she found out who he was, she tried to blackmail him." She looked pleased with herself. "What do you think?"

Skip shrugged. "I hate to say it, but I can't do any better than that. That could have been it. But let's see if you can add to the description I've got. Height and weight?"

"Medium tall I guess, but she had on heels. No, on second thought, I think she was pretty average—five five, maybe. But she looked tall because she was so skinny—a hundred pounds, maybe a hundred and five. *Real* skinny."

"Hair and eye color? I'm not sure what 'copper' really means."

"Her hair really did look like copper—metallic. Very metallic. But not so much red as a kind of gold—reddish gold. Copper that's beginning to go a little green. *Real* pretty. Probably expensive to get it that way too. She had it in some crazy Hollywood kind of style—kind of flyaway, like she just woke up. Like Tina Turner, but toned down. And brown eyes."

"Skin color?"

"I remember you said copper hair and skin, and that's how I knew who you meant. Her hair matched her skin. And her skin looked kind of more red—for skin—than her hair did for hair. I mean, you can have hair that's flaming, but skin doesn't get all that red."

"And she was good-looking?"

Sheree nodded resignedly. "She was really something. You couldn't take your eyes off her. Except that her clothes and makeup were awful. Cheap." Her lip curled slightly. "She had nails like those old Chinese guys. Painted K&B purple. Same color lipstick."

"And you're sure she was black?"

Sheree shrugged. "Sure."

"You know, I'm missing something here. How could you tell?"

"How could I tell?" She looked at Skip as if she'd lost her marbles. "I don't know. She just was, that's all. The way she talked, first of all. And her hair texture. Skin color, I guess— not many white people have that kind of reddish skin. I don't know—something about the features, maybe. How do you tell anybody's black?"

"Sometimes it's hard. You could be black, maybe. I mean, you're darker than the woman we're talking about, and you've got Caucasian features, but you *could* be black."

"Well, I'm not. But this LaBelle was. You could see it from a hundred paces."

"I believe you—I was just curious. You didn't look up her phone number, did you?"

Sheree smiled, apparently having accepted Skip as a fellow female, badge or no. "Are you kidding? I looked her up in the phone book to see where she lived, saw she wasn't listed, realized that meant Chauncey couldn't reach her unless he had the scrap, and ate it."

Skip was taken aback. "Ate it?"

Sheree laughed outright. She seemed to be cheering up. "No, I didn't eat it. I flushed it. And no, I don't have the slightest recollection of it."

"I was afraid of that," said Skip, and stood up to leave.

LABELLE

Skip stopped at a K&B with a phone booth to look up LaBelle for herself, nearly laughing aloud at the thought of Sheree's disdain for LaBelle's taste in makeup. The Katz & Besthoff drugstore chain was almost as famous for the purple of its logo as Pepto-Bismol was for its pink, and a bilious hue it was.

True to Sheree's observation, there was no LaBelle Doucette listed, but there were thirty other Doucettes, a circumstance that made Skip wish momentarily that she had a nice job teaching English at Sacred Heart. Had she really been feeling smug about not having to help Tarantino and O'Rourke with the scutwork? She was about to make calls to twenty-nine people who weren't going to want to hear from her—thirty, come to think of it. If LaBelle lived at the home of one of the listed Doucettes, she'd probably rather talk to the Phantom of the Opera.

Skip went home and changed back into jeans. First she called Marcelle for a better description of the black woman.

"Not too tall," said Marcelle. "About my height, maybe—say around five five, five six. But she was a bean pole, like Stelly Villere. Did you ever meet Stelly? Daddy's ex-secretary?"

"No, but I hear she was a real knockout."

"You're not kidding. And a doll too. Sweet as pie and pretty as a picture." She stopped. "Oh, that made me think of Daddy. That's what he used to say about me." Her voice had tears in it. "Anyway—"

"The woman. Did you notice her eyes?"

"No. It was dark out. And I was on the second floor, looking out a window."

Skip went through the hair and skin questions she'd asked Sheree Izaguirre and got similar answers—similar enough, anyway, to convince her LaBelle was the woman Marcelle had seen.

"Marcelle, a question about Stelly—she was with your daddy a long time, wasn't she?"

"Oh, yes. At least five years."

"Do you know why she left?"

"Why? What's Stelly got to do with it?"

"I was just thinking. Could this woman be related to her?"

"Related! How could she be?"

"You just said they had similar body types."

"Oh, but everything else is different. Stelly has black hair and gold skin, for one thing—completely contrasting color scheme. And anyway, she's . . ." Marcelle hesitated. ". . . a lady."

She spoke with defiance, but Skip declined the cue and laughed anyway. "Aren't we nineteenth century?"

"Oh, Skippy, you know what I mean."

"I do. I was just teasing. But seriously, do you know why Stelly left?"

Marcelle's voice had an edge to it. "No, I don't. Why?"

"In police work, you have to check everything. There's no getting around the fact that somebody had a grudge against your daddy—a real bad one. Disgruntled employees have been known to commit murder, you know. And nobody seems to know why Stelly left. We've got a technical term for that in my business."

"What?"

"A mystery."

"Skippy, you're so funny. I'll ask Mother why she left. She might know. Daddy always did seem kind of sad about it. Maybe he caught her embezzling or something."

"Thanks, Marcelle. I'd appreciate that."

There was no putting it off now. Skip settled down with the phone book and started dialing.

"LaBelle? Ain't no LaBelle here!" Slam! as if she'd been a heavy breather.

"Cornell? Cornell's working nights now."

"My mama's not home tonight. She's out playing Bingo, I think. Her name? Her name's Mama. Idn't it?"

Busy.

No one home.

"I'm sorry. I think you must have the wrong number. What number were you calling, please?"

Another busy.

"I don't know no LaBelle, cher, but maybe you'd like to come over and suck my dick."

"Whisper, whisper—heart—not expected—whisper—morning."

"LaBelle doesn't live here anymore."

Skip said, "Thanks. Sorry to bother you," before it sank in that the woman on the line had said something she wanted to hear. Who was she? She'd dialed so many she'd lost count.

"Mrs. Doucette?" she said. "Philomena Doucette? Can you tell me where I can reach LaBelle?"

"I guess she still workin' on Bourbon Street. Never hear from her no more. Don' know, really."

"Bourbon Street? Do you know the name of the place?"

"I b'leeve it's called the Do-It Club. Somethin' nasty anyway. I b'leeve it's the Do-It Club. Do-It's the name I seem to remember—Lord help me." Her voice was draggy and tired and a little scratchy.

Skip knew the Do-It Club as well as she knew any of the hole-in-the-wall clip joints on Bourbon Street. It employed the usual near-nude dancers whose faces said they'd rather be in Philadelphia, and LaBelle, from Sheree Izaguirre's description, sounded perfect for the part.

Skip looked at her watch. Ten o'clock. A little early for the Do-It Club, and she was hungry, the three o'clock muffuletta having finally worn off. In her one food cupboard (the minuscule kitchen had two, but she kept dishes in the other) there was a can of tuna packed in water and another of split pea soup. Since there was no bread for a tuna sandwich, it had to be the soup. She wanted a beer with it but didn't dare smell beery for the meeting to come—a possible meeting with a murderer, she thought with a little thrill. This could really be it. Could she eat with this much adrenaline pumping? Yes, but she couldn't taste.

Did she have to change clothes again? She supposed so. She might have to make an arrest, and it would be tacky to do it in jeans—give the department a bad name. She changed again into the slacks and blazer, tucked her gun into her purse. It was still early, but too bad, she was too nervous to wait any longer.

Seen from the street, the Do-It Club was a black gash in the wall, lit occasionally by the harshness of a spotlight shining on naked, fatigued flesh—merely another money-maker being shaken, business as usual on the tawdriest street in the country. If you looked closer, you saw a runway for the dancers, a bar, a few miserable tables—at some hours, a crowd of party animals as well, barking and pawing the ground and howling at the moon.

Skip elbowed past the surprised-looking young barker. Jesus, the place was the eighth circle of hell. It smelled like spilt, sour beer, weeks-old vomit, urine, sweat, and filthy concoctions from the Tourist Trap School of Bartending. And that was before you even got to the smoke. What was it the EPA talked about? Ambient air? This air was ambulatory. To her horror, Skip started coughing. "What'll it be?" asked the bartender. "You know how many people come in here and start coughing?"

"About fifty percent, I guess."

"About seventy-five. You a cop or what?" Skip stared at him. He was about six inches shorter than she was and a couple of years younger. He was olive-skinned with dark eyes, and he had a very specific accent—not an accent so much as an inflection—kind of a nasal monotone. He wore a blue Oxford cloth shirt.

"I might be," she said. "You went to Holy Name, Jesuit, and now Loyola. Right?"

He gave her five, a gesture she hated. "Hey! Awright! Now I know your rank. Detective, huh?"

"Uh-uh. I'm one of those psychics the cops keep on staff to find bodies and things. Here's how you pegged me—the only women who've ever been in here have either been cops, hookers, or drunken tourists. I'm dressed wrong for a hooker and I'm sober, so I must be a cop."

"The atmosphere in here's interfering with your psychic powers." He leaned over the bar. "Officer, your purse is open."

Skip's hand flew to close it, one finger lightly brushing the exposed gun. "Thanks. Jesus, that could have really been trouble. Let me buy you a drink, okay? By the way, I'm Skip Langdon."

"Eddie Macaluso. You want a drink too?"

"Just a Coke, please."

"I'm going to have to advise you against that."

"Against Coke? Are you a health freak or something?"

"You can have it, but I've still got to charge you seven-fifty for it."

"Good God. Give me a Dixie."

"Seven-fifty for that too." He shrugged and waved at the dancer of the moment. "Hey, you're paying for the show." He gave her the Coke she'd ordered originally; she tasted rum in it, decided she didn't know what to make of Eddie Macaluso, and pushed it away.

For the moment, she watched the overweight redhead in the leopard G-string. The woman had stretch marks on her pendulous breasts and probably track marks on her arms. From the looks of her watery eyes, her brain had taken a quick trip to the outer ring of Saturn, where it was finding no more joy than in the noisome confines of the Do-It Club.

She turned back to the bartender. "Eddie, tell me something."

"UNO."

"What?"

"Not Loyola. UNO. You were right about Jesuit, though."

"That's gratifying. Here's something else I'm not psychic about: Do you have a woman working here named LaBelle? LaBelle Doucette?"

"Never heard of her."

"How about Lynn? Or some name with Lynn in it, like Ann-Lynn or Faye-Lynn?"

"Sherilyn. I like that one."

"Sherilyn? You have a Sherilyn?"

"Uh-uh. I just like the name. Listen, you want to talk to the manager? I've only been here a couple of months."

"I'd love to if it's no trouble." She heard herself speak and didn't like it. She was sounding more like a McGehee's girl than a police officer.

"Hey, Uncle Dutch!" Eddie was shouting, hardly making a

dent in the recorded Country-Western song that the redhead was supposed to boogie to. Or so it seemed to Skip. But a puzzled-looking face peeked out of an aperture somewhere near the back of the club—probably the door to an office. "Lady wants to see you."

"Send her back." The voice was gravelly, as whose wouldn't be, Skip thought, after years in this place. She paid for her drinks (wishing she was paying a lot less for them) and walked to the back, acutely aware of predatory eyes on her. "Hey, big mama!" hollered an admirer. She wondered if she should take a bow.

The man waiting for her was the original Mr. Five by Five, though Skip put his actual height at five seven or eight. She didn't even want to guess at his girth. He moved slowly, dragging one foot a little, and, glancing down discreetly, Skip saw that he wore a corrective shoe, probably for a club foot. A shame, she thought.

The man's hair was oily with some kind of dressing and he smelled strongly of a cologne Skip had noticed a lot of men seemed to be wearing lately—probably some fashionable elixir their daughters gave them for Christmas. It was something dense and exotic that made her think of a *harim*—the scent the sultan would wear when he summoned his favorite of the evening. Except for the bum foot, Uncle Dutch seemed ideal for the part. Put him in a turban with flowing robes and a scimitar and he was the sultan from Central Casting. He had broad, heavy features, hooded, languorous eyes, and the sort of generous, sensuous lips that could make her fall in love with a man.

Despite his size, he would have been handsome in a thuglike, piratical kind of way if his skin hadn't had the sick, gray cast of a life spent indoors puffing on cigarettes. He led her into a room barely bigger than a closet, certainly not meant to contain two people of their respective sizes.

It was furnished only with a desk, chair, and filing cabinets, but the walls were nearly covered with pictures of a handsome family—a dark, pretty woman and two laughing children, a boy and a girl. Beautiful children too. Uncle Dutch himself was in some of the pictures, his arm around the woman, or sometimes one of the kids. Skip's stomach flopped over, thinking that a man who lived like this man obviously did—who was overweight, smoked, stayed up all night—might very well not live to see his grandchildren.

She showed him her badge. "I'm Skip Langdon. With the police department." She wasn't quite sure how to introduce herself—always before, the uniform had done it for her.

"Dutch Macaluso. What can I do for you?"

"You really are Eddie's uncle."

"Who else would hire the bum? Hey, how much did he charge you for your drinks? No, don't tell me. I got a feelin' he's running a little scam up there—overcharging the customers and skimming off the extra—but I don't think I want to know."

Okay, she and Eddie were even now—she had owed him one for telling her about the open purse and now she'd repaid him. She breathed easier—Eddie seemed such a cagey little devil she didn't want to be in his debt. "I thought he was a smart kid."

"Smart! I could tell you stories . . . when that kid was three and a half he figured out a way to wedge a soup can in the terlet so it couldn't be pried out by any plumber in the parish. Whole damn terlet had to be replaced. My poor baby sister, that's all I can say. Sit down, why don't you?" He pointed at the only chair.

"No, thanks. I'll only take a minute. I'm looking for a woman who used to work here, I think. LaBelle Doucette."

"LaBelle. Oh, God, was I sorry to lose her. Prettiest gal I ever had in here—I'm not kiddin'—" He shook his head. "How a gal looked like that could end up shakin' her tail—" The head wagged some more. "Dance! Could she dance! When she could stand up."

"She was a drunk?"

"Junkie." He lit a cigarette and blew smoke in Skip's face.

"I finally had to let her go—really hated to do it—she brought in the customers like I was givin' out free drinks—but there wasn't no choice. Sometimes she didn't come to work two, three nights a week. A shame when people do that to themselves, ain't it?"

Skip turned her head as more smoke came her way. She said, "You wouldn't know where she's working now, would you?"

"I heard she ain't dancin' no more. The rest of what I heard you don't want to know." He was shaking his head again, in sadness and judgment.

"Mr. Macaluso, I'm a police officer."

"Oh, yeah. Well, you're still a woman." He opened his arms, palms up. "I heard she was turning tricks. What would you expect?"

I'd expect her to have been turning tricks since she was thirteen or fourteen—and certainly while she worked here. And I'd expect you, Dutch Macaluso, not to be such a phony bastard. For all I know, you were her pimp.

"I just hope she got her act together," Macaluso said. "I'd hate to see that girl in the gutter."

What would you call this place?

"You want an address for her? I think I still got it."

"I'd appreciate that. A phone number too, if you have it."

He rooted through his Rolodex.

"Did she have any friends who worked here? Or a boy friend?"

"Not that I know of. Here you are." He handed over an address and phone number.

"You don't know anybody else who knew her?"

"Honey, she was only here six weeks. And that was about a year ago."

The address was on Burgundy, a run-down street on the lake side of the Quarter. The building wasn't that different from Skip's, a gorgeous old Creole town house that had fallen on hard times and been divided into apartments. What was left of the green paint looked nearly as old as the structure itself. The windows were barred.

Skip rang all four doorbells and got no answer. Surveillance was clearly called for. She walked home, got her car, went back to try the bells again, and again got no answer.

It was about twelve-thirty, barely an hour later, when someone stopped in the doorway across the street. It was a plump black woman in a miniskirt and a young white man, a laborer of some kind by the looks of him, the sort you saw in working-class bars making racist pronouncements. His right hand was clutching her buttocks. The woman searched her purse. "Now don't you worry, that ol' key's got to be someplace."

Silently, Skip joined them. "Excuse me."

Both turned around to find themselves staring at her upheld badge. "I'm looking for a woman named LaBelle Doucette."

"Don't know her," said the man. "'Scuse me, I've got to be going now. That okay, officer?"

He was probably as sexist as he was racist, Skip thought, and momentarily relished his submission. Quickly, she smashed the feeling, knowing all too well that too much of it turned good cops into sadists. "Sure," she said.

The man walked away briskly.

"Look what you done, Miss Cop-Ass! Maybe you don' care I got a baby to feed. I ain't had a trick all night—you got any idea what you jus' cost me?"

"Maybe you haven't heard, Miss Ass-for-Sale, but prostitution's still illegal. Now calm down and cooperate, okay? And maybe I won't follow you when you go back out and bust you for soliciting. What's your name?"

"Jeweldean Sanders."

"I'm Skip Langdon, Jeweldean. I'm looking for—"

"Yeah, I heard you the first time. You lookin' for LaBelle Doucette." She was short and had to look up at Skip. The face, though currently hostile, had a round, bovine prettiness marred by a scar near the right corner of the mouth.

Skip nodded and watched the hostility melt.

"Well—every cloud got a silver linin'. Come on in. This my chance to get back at that bitch. What's she done now?"

"I just want to talk to her."

"Yeah, I know you gotta be discreet. I hope she in baaad trouble, that's all. You want me to testify against her, you got me. I wouldn't even have to perjure myself. If it's bad enough, she done it—you can count on that one."

She led Skip up a flight of scruffy stairs and into what looked like a one-bedroom apartment trying to pass as a bordello. A door to the right was closed.

"Sshhh," said Sanders. "The baby's asleep."

"You leave your baby alone at night?"

"Well, he four now. Anyway, I come back every hour or so. Check on him after my trick."

Part of the living room had been partitioned with makeshift curtains that looked like sheets dyed black and then spruced up with silver and gold glitter. A few plants, an old red-velvet sofa, and a scratched coffee table made up the visible furniture. Over the mantel hung a very bad painting of a naked black woman.

"Tha's my office," said Sanders, pointing to the curtains. "When LaBelle was here she use the bedroom. Billy Paul, he was stayin' by his grandmama then, but I got him back now that bitch outta here."

"You and LaBelle used to share this place?"

"Tha's right. Till she ran off with two hundred dollars I had saved up. I was gon' get Billy Paul a color TV—he just got a ol' black and white, and you *know* how kids love their TVs. That LaBelle, jus' one day she was gone and all her stuff and all my money. Jus' like that." She snapped her red-tipped fingers. "So now I can't buy no TV and I gotta turn twice as many tricks to pay the rent, and tha's why I'm about to tell you where the bitch is stayin' at."

Skip followed her into the kitchen, where a wall telephone hung above a counter strewn with telephone messages and a

faux leather address book. Sanders waved at the counter—
"Tools of my trade." She picked up the address book.

"How long ago did LaBelle leave?"

"Oh, 'bout six months."

"Had you had a fight or something?"

"Nothin'! No reason in hell for that kind of behavior! Come right out of thin air." She fingered a line in the book. "Okay, you ready?"

"Hold it. It seems pretty weird she took all your money and left a forwarding address."

"She ain' leave no forwardin' address. I do business with a ol' dude named Calvin manages a big ugly place over in Tremé. He tol' me she stayin' there now."

"Why don't you just go over there and get your money?"

Sanders stared at the backward child that had found its way into her kitchen. "What I'm gon' do? Shoot her?" Skip forebore to ask why she hadn't reported the robbery. She knew what would have happened—LaBelle would have said the money was hers and no one would have been able to prove otherwise.

As Sanders handed over the address book, Skip had a thought. "I noticed you had a white client tonight."

"Something wrong with that? You prejudiced?"

"I was wondering about LaBelle. Does she see white clients?"

"Oh, law, don't get me started! Thought she was Queen of Comus or somethin'. She had this notion of her sorry self seein' only a Very Exclusive Clientele by out-call only, dawalin'. Miss La-de-da! I tol' her, tha's a good idea, and you got the looks and all, but how you gon' meet 'em? Send 'em a brochure? You jus' cain' do that if you a free-lancer. And—I might as well say it—if you got a jones like that girl does. She could make jus' enough money to pay the man, and then she was noddin' out and cudn't work for hours and hours. How she gon' set herself up in business that kind o' way?"

PAIN PERDU

Marcelle woke up crying, but not for Chauncey, the way she'd done yesterday. The first wave of missing him was starting to pass, and now she was remembering what life was like before Mardi Gras. She was crying for herself.

She could hear André in his room singing to himself, probably playing quietly with his ships and trucks—boy things. Soon it would be guns—so far she'd held off on that, but it couldn't last. People would give them to him, all the other kids would have them, it was inevitable—she couldn't do anything about it, but no surprises there. She couldn't do anything about anything.

He needed his breakfast; she needed to get up and give it to him. Oh, hell, André didn't need her. André was the most self-sufficient child in Orleans Parish, perfectly capable of pouring cereal and milk into a bowl. She turned over, feeling the sun streaming in on her satin comforter.

Glancing at the clock she saw that it was eight-thirty. She couldn't put it off forever. She really would have to get up pretty soon. Okay. She would get up and make André his breakfast. Pain perdu. She had loved it when Bitty made it for her. No, not Bitty; Bitty never had, that she could remember. It was Louise, maybe, who had made the pain perdu, or Tonetta, one of the ever-changing stream of black women who worked for the St. Amants. They were always leaving for better jobs, Bitty said, and nothing could have been more true, Marcelle was sure. They always left partially crippled or maimed, with Henry grinning evilly in the background. When Louise bent down for her dustpan, Henry had jabbed a hatpin half an inch into her ample behind. Marcelle was next door at the time, with a playmate, Betsy Labadie. When the screams went up, she was so sure her mother was being murdered she had wet her pants. Instead of calling the police, Mrs. Labadie picked up an iron frying pan, just in case, and flew next door herself, probably more out of curiosity than anything else.

She certainly wasn't worried about Bitty, as she had stopped long enough to reassure Marcelle that there was no possibility her mother's life was in danger, since Bitty would never have hollered, "Oooohhhhh, sweet-Jesus-gracious-Lord-Holy-Father, my black ass! Oh, Lordy, my black ass hurts!"

Bitty, as it happened, had been "lying down" at the time, having had a long lunch that apparently had indisposed her. Hearing the screams she had gotten up, of course, but had been put back to bed and fussed over by a reassuring Henry, who explained that old lazy Louise had sat down when she ought to have been working and impaled herself on an upholstery tack she had dislodged with her huge bulk.

It was left to Mrs. Labadie to nurse Louise's posterior with ice wrapped in a towel. Marcelle herself had first found a pair of dry panties, then phoned Chauncey, panicked and crying, to race home and rush Louise to Touro for a tetanus shot. Louise came back just one more time, to learn that Henry's story and not hers had become St. Amant Family Truth. She left once again remarking upon her lower anatomy, but in a different context. Her exact words had been, "Upholstery tack, my ass!"

Later Marcelle had sneaked into Henry's room and searched it, finding the hatpin in an envelope marked "Louise" in a leather stud box his grandfather had grown tired of and given him. She could have shown it to her parents, but if she had, one of two things would have happened. Henry would have denied ever seeing it before and claimed Marcelle must be really sick and crazy—you could tell by the way she was always trying to get attention. Or, if that hadn't worked and Henry got nailed—say his handwriting was recognized—he might have gotten revenge, and Marcelle had some theories about the dangers of being the object of Henry's wrath, especially after what happened to Tonetta. So Marcelle had kept quiet about it—tattling wasn't going to bring Louise back anyway.

As for Tonetta, she fell down the stairs one day. Fortunately it was only the fifth step from the bottom that she tripped on, and she ended up with nothing worse than a broken ankle. She said she stepped on a toy truck and lost her balance when it flew out from under her. No toy truck was found in the vicinity (though there had been plenty of time for retrieval in the ensuing confusion) and, under questioning, Henry was shocked and hurt that anyone could imagine he would be so careless as to leave his toys on the stairs.

He said simply that he had been taught the dangers of carelessness from early babyhood, had learned his lesson well, and had never been known to leave toys on the stairs—had he? The argument was completely convincing, of course, to a pair of parents to whom the idea of a planned accident simply didn't occur.

It had certainly occurred to Marcelle, though. She knew she wasn't the one who'd killed her own goldfish by putting purple ink into the water, though she'd been punished for it. If you put that together with certain other incidents, like the time one of her tricycle wheels unaccountably fell off, or the broken glass she'd found on the floor of her room one night when she came out of her bath, pink-cheeked and barefoot as usual, you'd conclude it was best to be very wary of Henry.

Oh, hell! Why couldn't she shake this mood? Probably because it was so unfair, so unexpected about her father—he had been the only normal one in the whole family.

Daddy's funeral is today. How in hell could I have forgotten? She knew how she could have. The shrinks called it denial. Okay, fine. So she was doing that again. She sat up and pulled aside the curtain, the one that was already letting in the sun that had awakened her.

A little girl was sitting on the front porch of the double shotgun across Burdette Street. She had on a navy-blue dress and black patent-leather shoes with little white socks, as if she were going somewhere. Her hands had fallen down between her knees, so that she was leaning into her skirt, and the sun glinted on her brown hair. Something about her looked touchingly forlorn, as if someone had forgotten her. The house, badly in need of a paint job, seemed to echo her mood. The scene was so beautiful, so moving, someone should paint it. Marcelle knew that Degas, exactly the right person for the job, had lived in New Orleans once, on Esplanade. She thought of his beautiful pictures of children and of the shimmering visions of Paris she'd recently seen in a traveling exhibit of Impressionist works. New Orleans was surely as beautiful as Paris, and she wished it could be painted by resurrected Impressionists. This moment should be preserved forever.

Maybe, she thought, she should take some more art history courses. Nothing gave her greater pleasure than exceptional beauty—not just in paintings but in other things too.

If she were an archaeologist, she might unearth an Etruscan vase, and touching it would be the thrill of a lifetime. If she were a veterinarian, she might palpate a tiger one day, or a giraffe, and she could lie down and die; life could surely hold no more delights. It would be like looking at André asleep. And yet she could do that every night and life was still empty.

She adored André—surely no parent could be more adoring—but she wasn't a career mother. That she knew now. André was a person, not a piece of clay for her to shape and mold and tear up and mold again if she didn't like the first way he came out. She recognized her hardest maternal task as that of letting him be the person he was rather than trying to turn him into the shape-shifting windup toy, sometimes a wooden soldier, sometimes a teddy bear, that she wanted for herself in her darker moments. When she was with him for very long the tension of letting him play out his own life, encouraging him in his own path rather than trying to control, nearly tore her apart. Thank God for day care, or she'd have a four-year-old basket case on her hands, and she wouldn't be much better herself.

Oh, God! Who said she was? Certainly no one who had seen her lately. The truth was, she needed that lump of clay to shape. Not André, but something of her own. Something to fill that empty hole, to relieve that deep longing that booze and sex had never eased. Even Henry had his acting. She had nothing. Maybe she should take the metaphor literally—the one about the lump—and try ceramics.

Oh, come on! You've got about as much talent as that ceiling fan up there.

Even as a child she'd brought home lopsided clay bowls while the other children's were smooth and symmetrical; crayon drawings of stick figures when everyone else had graduated to first-grade realism.

She was no more an artist than she was a career mother. But her love for art—for the beautiful—rivaled her love for her child. She sucked in her breath and let it out slowly, trying on the thought. She hadn't put the two thoughts together before. Art history, then. Definitely.

But what could she do with art history? Teach? No. She wanted to be around the artworks, to have them actually in her life. Maybe—oh, God, here was an idea! Here was an idea that gave her a weird tingling in the pit of her stomach, that was how powerful it was. She knew that tingling and what it meant. It was fear. When she thought of something good, something she wanted, something she really wanted a whole lot, that tingling started. It meant she was afraid she couldn't have it and she'd better just stop thinking about it.

The idea was this—maybe she could apply for a job at Uncle Tolliver's antique store.

He would teach her about antiques and she could take some courses as well. And every day she'd be there with them, able to look at them, touch and caress them whenever she wanted. She wondered if she would cry when she sold a particular favorite.

Quickly, she squashed the thought. She was already sold, already committed, already in love, and that wasn't going to work. If she felt that way, she knew she'd never apply for the job. That's what always happened when she wanted something. She wanted it for only about ten minutes. Then she let it recede to the back of her mind and stay there till she forgot about it. Zoning out, she'd come to call it. Whatever seemed important, necessary for quality of life, she just zoned out.

She was going to have to get some distance on this thing if she was going to make it happen. But of course she probably wasn't going to make it happen. She never made anything happen. She wished she could be like Skippy Langdon. Skip knew what she wanted and went after it and got it. She was Marcelle's idea of a true woman of the '90s—strong, competent, sure of herself, and bold enough to do a job usually considered blue-collar, male, and dangerous. If only Marcelle could be like that. If only there were something she wanted to do the way Skip wanted to do police work. She was somewhat in awe of Skip, even intimidated by her, and always had been, throughout their childhood. As a small child, she was afraid to try to be friends—she knew somebody like Skippy Langdon could have only contempt for a wimp like her. As she got older, she'd become more secure in the friendship—after all, they really had known each other all their lives, and Skippy had been in her wedding. Surely she wasn't going to just go away now.

Though of course she would be filled with justifiable contempt if she had any idea how many men Marcelle had been to bed with in the past two years—how much a part of her life, how compulsive random seduction had become for her. The beautiful things she had lately been appreciating were men's bodies.

That was her favorite part of sex—looking at the bodies, touching them as reverently as she *would* touch a tiger or an Etruscan vase if she had the chance. That was all that was really left now—that and the momentary pleasure. *The cheap thrill*, she thought contemptuously.

Before, sleeping with everybody she'd grown up with, everybody who'd married everybody she'd grown up with, everybody who was new in town, and everybody who was just visiting, had given her little bursts of self-esteem. For a while she felt like some twentieth-century Scarlett O'Hara, some magnolia-smelling version of *la belle dame sans merci*, tiptoeing heedlessly through a field of male tulips and stomping when she chose. There was a lot of strength in having absolutely nothing invested in sex, nothing emotional except aesthetic pleasure and erotic gratification. She felt beautiful and powerful—not lonely, empty, not the way that, deep in her heart, she really was.

She would gladly have gone on with it forever if she hadn't started feeling more like Blanche DuBois than Scarlett O'Hara—some pathetic, broken thing dependent on the kindness of strangers to satisfy her needs. Lately she'd been feeling not powerful but impotent; not beautiful but tattered, slutty. Desperate.

She sank down under the comforter, restraining herself from actually pulling it over her head. It's okay, she said to herself.

You're allowed to be this depressed two days after your father dies— your father, your only living relative (formerly living relative; try to grasp that, please)—your only relative who gave a damn about you and, let's face it, whom you could stand.

The sobs rose in her throat.

I never had a mother at all, and now I have no father.

Bitty was always dressing her up, putting her into little black-velvet dresses and little red-felt jumpers, and little black patent-leather shoes, like the ones the little girl across the street had on. Bitty's little girl had to be perfect—a perfect little extension of Bitty's beauty and Bitty's breeding. Everything was about public appearances, nothing was about her and Bitty. And she had to be what Bitty wasn't too—competent, alert. Shit, *awake.* If Bitty'd been half awake herself, maybe she would have seen that Marcelle needed someone to hug her once in a while, someone to kiss her knee when she skinned it, not someone who wouldn't let her ride a bicycle for fear she'd skin the goddamn knee.

That was the other thing about Bitty. She was afraid of her shadow and wouldn't let Marcelle do anything more adventurous than take a walk around the block holding tight to Louise's hand, or Tonetta's, or whatever hand was attached to the current all-too-temporary surrogate mother. Mostly, Bitty just wasn't there. She was in her own amber-colored haze, emerging only long enough to set new restrictions or demand some new perfection. The perfections were easy. They all had to do with being quiet and unobtrusive—fading into the woodwork until called upon to step out of the corner and curtsy—to pass the hors d'oeuvres at a party, say, perfectly dressed, perfectly mannered, quiet as a kitten.

The restrictions were something else again. Once, about

3:00 in the afternoon when she knew Bitty hadn't eaten lunch, she'd made her a sandwich—cream cheese and pineapple, cut it into ladylike, bite-size fourths. She could hear her mother now: "Marcelle, baby, you didn't cut this yourself, did you?"

"Tonetta's gone home . . ."

"You know you're not supposed to play with knives! Now take this and throw it out! Go on. And I mean throw it out, Marcelle—don't eat it. You're already Little Miss Chubs and you've got your daddy's fat genes."

In those early years—God, it hurt to remember!—Marcelle understood perfectly well that she'd been placed on earth for the sole purpose of pleasing her mother. That was okay. That was fine. She would have been thrilled to please her mother, if only she could ever really have achieved it. But no matter how much she worked at it, no matter how hard she tried, she couldn't make it pay off. She couldn't get Bitty to notice her, couldn't get close to her.

She didn't know how old she was—maybe six or seven—when the pain stopped, when she stopped beating her head against the wall. But she knew that at some point she had made a decision—had quit trying to get Bitty's attention, had become resigned to not having it, and had replaced the struggle with nothing at all.

She no longer did anything, felt anything, or thought anything—that is, no longer held opinions. She made no more decisions, she stopped wanting what she couldn't have.

The funny thing was, it was perfectly obvious what she didn't want. She hadn't for a moment wanted her husband, Lionel Gaudet.

I didn't even want André! I just couldn't make up my mind whether to have a baby or an abortion.

She married Lionel for a very distinct and specific reason— so she could go on doing nothing, feeling nothing, holding no opinions, making no decisions.

Lionel experienced her as a juggernaut in his path—an

analogy she rather liked but found utterly laughable. "Don't you understand," he had raged, "that you have all the power in this marriage? *All* of it."

She had simply stared at him in disbelief. How was it possible to be so completely off the mark? She had about as much power as a junior clerk at Lionel's company.

"As long as you aren't participating, you aren't giving me any slack at all. How can we change anything if you won't negotiate?"

"What is there to negotiate?"

"We're not living, Marcelle. We're only existing. We're not having a marriage. Don't you want one?"

No!

So Lionel hadn't worked out. And all those years of strategic withdrawal hadn't either. Because she could no longer not feel anymore. She didn't know why, but she'd come to the end of her resources on that. Now she felt far, far too much—and all of it bad.

Oh, Chauncey, why did you have to die? And why couldn't you have left me something better than a trust fund and your fat genes? You could always do things—why didn't I inherit that?

The phone beside the bed rang. "Marcelle? Jo Jo. I just wanted to see how you're doing."

"Okay, I guess. Daddy's funeral's today."

"Listen, baby, I'm sorry I fell asleep on you the other day. God, I was so hot for you I could have come in my pants; I woke up thinking about you, wanting you so bad just like in the old days, but I reached for you and you weren't there. I don't blame you, I don't blame you a bit—"

She hung up, she had to, she was getting sicker with every word. Was she going to throw up? She swallowed. Maybe not. She lay back on the pillows, feeling glad to have escaped. He'd been about to ask to see her again, and for once she wasn't even slightly tempted. Tempted! It didn't even enter the picture. Temptation rarely went hand in hand with nausea.

"Mommy?" called André. "Are you awake yet?"

"Good morning, baby. Come on in and give Mommy a kiss."

As the small feet failed to patter on the bare floor, instead clomped like a pachyderm, delivered like a cyclone, she wondered what Jo Jo meant about falling asleep.

THE FUNERAL

1

This new eye shadow had to be applied with a tiny wet brush and then smoothed out with a slightly bigger dry one. It went on as a bruised shade of aubergine, but—ah—now it was smoothing out. Sort of a raspberry. Nice.

Now a lipstick to match, blusher, eyeliner, and lots of thick sable mascara. Henry was particularly fond of applying mascara. He opened his eyes as wide as he could and stroked—his eyelashes with one hand, his penis with the other, through the black dress he'd put on in honor of his father's funeral, a little taffeta number he'd bought at the flea market. It wasn't really meant for daytime, and certainly not for a funeral, but, oh, please, dahling, details! It wasn't meant to be worn by a man either.

Under it he wore a black garter belt to hold up his black silk stockings, but no panties, as that would defeat the purpose of the exercise. He also had on a bra stuffed with baggies full of cornstarch, which did for the dress what Henry's chest couldn't, but that wasn't its main purpose. The bra was what got him hard. Something about that confined feeling, that uncomfortable wrapped-up-ness, did it every time.

He had tried to analyze it. He quite enjoyed bondage as well, and thought the two things were connected. A bra was a kind of harness that made you want to twitch your shoulders to get comfortable, but if you did, it not only ruined the effect, it didn't help. So you didn't. You endured the confined feeling so you would be more beautiful for your lover, or possibly in the quiet knowledge that your lover would soon be taking it off—he wasn't sure where the excitement came from. In his case, only rarely would a lover be taking it off, as he didn't go in much for two-person sex anymore, and anyway had developed his whole drag routine as an amusing method of autoeroticism in the first place. Amusing and effective. A ritual that built, becoming more and more exciting like a great play, until it reached the same delicious point, the satisfying climax. A catharsis—after a morning in this getup, he'd be so balanced he could go through half a dozen relatives' funerals.

He crossed his index fingers and held the hex sign up to the mirror, warding off his own reflection, as if it were the one thinking appalling thoughts. Hmmm—a beauty spot would look good. And a short black wig—he'd be Liza Minnelli. He'd need pearls, of course, with the basic black. He rooted through a drawer, found an opera-length rope, and draped them around his neck. Stepping into the specially made spike-heeled shoes that had to be mail-ordered in men's sizes, he stood in front of his full-length mirror. Good. The dress had a full enough skirt that his now nearly bursting penis didn't ruin its lines.

Now for the finale. He was about to get the wig when the metallic buzzing of the doorbell sounded. Jesus, loud! Like the hornet that ate Cleveland, he thought, feeling the lovely hard-on starting to disappear.

Shit! What if it were Tolliver? He lived in fear that Tolliver was going to find out about his penchant for drag. But seeing Tolliver would be almost as good as concluding the ritual. He could say he was just out of the shower and then take a minute to change and get the makeup off. If it were anyone else, he could simply say he was busy.

He spoke into the intercom. "Yes?"

"Henry? It's Skip Langdon. Can I talk to you for a minute."

Fuck! For this he'd lost his hard-on? "I'm busy now."

"It'll only take a minute."

Actually, he could see having some fun with this situation. Tubs Langdon, post-deb cop, probably wouldn't be the least bit amused at his outfit. Her idea of mean streets was probably those with frozen-yogurt stands instead of ice-cream stores. He could play it very Noel Coward—perhaps a cigarette holder . . . on the other hand, she *was* interrupting his ritual.

"It's about LaBelle."

Oh, shit. That settled it. He remembered to say, "Who?" while pushing the buzz-in button.

Should he replace the dress with a robe for a gender-fuck effect? (A smoking jacket would be ideal, but he didn't have one.) No. This way would be more fun. He flung open the door. "Good morning, officer."

She was wearing the hopeless gray suit again, though she'd added a blue silk blouse. "Nice blouse," he said, and fingered the collar like a housewife in a fabric store.

Her expression changed as she took in his outfit—from neutral to amused. Oh, hell, this wasn't going according to plan.

"I bet I know where you got those shoes," she said. "I have to order mine too."

"Shall we sit down?" This goddamn blasé attitude of hers put a whole new light on the scene. He wasn't sure how to play it.

He minced to one of his two director's chairs. He also had a rattan sofa, but he left that for Tubs. Settling her bulk, she said, "So. You doing *Cabaret*—old chum?"

Jeez, she was brittle. Well, hell, at least the Liza look was working. "I'm going to a funeral."

"Are you?" She looked utterly charmed. "*Tout* Nouvelles Orleans will be whispering with delight." As she spoke she clasped her hands, turned her head slightly sideways, chin down, and frankly mugged.

Who the fuck was the actor here? Had she no respect? His father was being buried today, for Christ's sake. Okay, one more shot. "I thought I'd take a date. Black, for mourning, of course. Do you know Jackson Robichaux?"

"Bartender at Lafitte in Exile, or bellman at the Richelieu? Both well known around the department. Personally, I think the bellman's more your type. He's short."

"Bitch! What the hell do you want, anyway?"

"For openers, how about an apology. For our little encounter yesterday?" Lots of Southern girls had that weird interrogatory way of speaking. There was usually something submissive about it, but when Tubs did it there was an edge of sarcasm instead. He lapsed into Tallulah Bankhead. "So sorry, dahling, but ectually, I have no recollection of it. I was a bit under the weather, they tell me." He'd gone British. Glenda Jackson, say, doing Tallulah. "It was my father who died, you understand."

The corners of Tubs's mouth turned up in a goddamn superior way. "Apology accepted," she said. "I really came about something else. Do you know a woman named LaBelle Doucette?"

"Why do you want to know?"

"She may have killed your father."

Jesus, she certainly went for the jugular. He wished like hell he had a drink. He said, "I see. And what's that to you?"

"God, you're a heartless brat. Don't you care who killed your father?" She mimicked him. "'It was my father who died, you understand.'" She swished a limp wrist around as she spoke, which he took as an insult, knowing perfectly well that a man doing Tallulah in makeup, heels, and taffeta cocktail dress in broad daylight had a hell of a nerve.

Furious, he nonetheless contained himself, staying in character. "Since you ask, no, dahling, I most assuredly do not care who killed my father, as I myself had the best of motives for doing so. Perhaps you are unaware that I am a homotheckthual." He spat the last word like a viper.

Ah . . . what was this? A laugh out of old Tubs. Well, he *had* done the lisp rather well. "I wath, acthually."

Oh, shit, she wanted to play games. He dumped Tallulah, stood up, and went big-voiced, Orson Welles. "Are you also aware that I am an actor?"

"Henry, I'm not even going to touch that one." Laughing again.

Bitch! "To say that my father did not support me in either endeavor would be understatement in the extreme." Damn! The role really called for pacing, but he couldn't see it in three-inch heels. "He promised to 'disinherit' me, whatever *that* may mean, if I did not abandon my sinful and, far worse—embarrassing—ways. Chauncey St. Amant, as you know, was a famous patron of the arts. But did he support his son in his own artistic endeavor? He did not! He was a famous advocate of civil rights, but did he respect the right of his only son to the sexual preference of his—ah—choosing? He did not!"

Dear God, he had slipped into what's-his-name, the actor who died of lung cancer, doing Hamilton Burger, district attorney. Oh, hell, who cared? He liked it. "Instead, he insisted upon a made-to-order son, a son of his own invention, a banker, family man, and civic leader, exactly like himself. A clone of Chauncey St. Amant—a shorter, blonder and *swishier* clone, perhaps, but a clone nonetheless"—he almost said "ladies and gentlemen of the jury"—"was the son Chauncey St. Amant demanded. Nothing less did Chauncey St. Amant demand than a thoroughgoing personality transplant, to be accomplished by that most drastic of all means, the taking of a master's of business administration." (Appropriate laughter from the audience.) "To be followed by psychotherapy toward one end and one end only—the reversal of the son's theckthual preferenthe." He did the spitting viper again, turning on Tubs and actually spewing saliva at her.

"Bravo, Sir Larry—"

"Lord Larry."

"Lord Larry. Or whoever you are. Joanne Woodward, maybe, in the *Three Faces of Eve.* So I take it you murdered your father to get him off your back."

"Of course not. It would have been to save my portion of the St. Amant fortune before he could make good on his terrifying threat."

"To disinherit you."

Henry nodded.

"Tell me, how long had he been making the threat?"

"Oh, ten or twelve years, I guess." He kept his voice nonchalant, not wanting her catching on to when he was serious and when he wasn't.

"So. *Did* you kill him?"

"How could I? I was at the Boston Club."

"I thought you took a walk. No one saw you for a while. About half an hour, as a matter of fact. Plenty of time."

"How would I get through the crowds?"

"Tell me something, Henry—how did you get to the Boston Club in the first place?"

"Drove. You wouldn't expect the small but regal Bitty St. Amant to walk, would you?"

"But you live here in the Quarter—you could easily have walked."

"I picked up my mother so we could all go together."

"Picked her up?"

He sighed impatiently. "I walked there and drove her car back. Passengers were my mother, sister, and Tolliver Albert."

"And where'd you park?"

"The bank parking lot—Dad's space."

"The bank is about two blocks away from the Boston Club. And well off the parade route. Right?"

"Right."

"So all you'd have to do was lift your mother's keys—you had to get the key to Tolliver's apartment anyway—shoulder your way through two blocks of crowds, and drive down any street but St. Charles. Is that right?"

"Are you saying I did?"

"Asking, Henry. I'm asking if you did."

"Well, what gives you the fucking right to ask?"

She fumbled in her purse for her badge, held it up, and grinned that superior grin of hers. "You've forgotten I'm a civil servant?"

"You're not on this case. I've talked to the guys who are— O'Rourke and Tarantino."

"Oh, but I am on the case. O'Rourke, Tarantino, and Langdon. We're a team. Call them up if you don't believe me."

Why the hell had he let her in? The idea of shocking her with his outfit suddenly seemed incredibly childish. At least now his question was answered—he knew why she was asking about LaBelle, which, goddamnit, she was doing again.

"O'Rourke, Tarantino, and I were wondering if you know a LaBelle Doucette."

"Never heard of her—"

"Yes?"

God! He'd almost said, "Never heard of her black ass." *Watch your* honky *ass, Henry.*

"Maybe you've seen her, then." Skip described her.

"Uh-uh. Who is she?"

"Someone who visited your father both at home and at work. I can't tell you anything more than that."

"Because you don't know or because you don't want to?"

She shrugged. God, he hated cops.

She said: "Do you know what a Colt 44.40 is?"

"A gun, I presume."

"An old one. And your father had a gun collection. I'm wondering if he owned a couple."

"You're asking *me*? The homo—".

"—theckthual?" she spat, along with him. "Stupid idea. Right. I'll bet you don't know anything about baseball either."

"Will that be all, officer?"

She stood up. "I think so. And I'd like to thank you for your cooperation. See you in church."

She strode to the door and left without throwing him so much as a glance.

See you in church? Shit!

He looked at his watch. Double shit. He hiked up his skirt and started unfastening his garters, fumbling in his haste. Fuck Tubs Langdon and the cellulite she walked in on. He had a run in his goddamn silk stockings.

Was there time for a drink before the funeral? There would have to be. They couldn't start without him anyway. His hands were still shaking as he got out the ice and other stuff for a vodka martini. He tossed half of it down in a swallow and shook his head to clear it.

There. Better. He had twenty minutes to get into a suit and up to Bitty's house. Carefully now, he began to unfasten his other stocking and apply himself to the new problem as well. LaBelle. How the hell did Tubs know about LaBelle? Could Marcelle have told her? But how could *she* know? He didn't think his sister even knew LaBelle existed.

2

Bitty had a deal with herself—all she had to do was make it through the service (including the grueling trip to the cemetery), and then she could drink her miserable heart out. The house would be full of people, but Bitty, as its chatelaine, could withdraw to her private chambers and comport herself as disgracefully as she chose.

She couldn't allow herself either alcohol or drugs until afterward because of all the damn getting up and down. It was hard enough if you were sober.

As the priest mumbled on (it didn't occur to Bitty to listen), she saw her father's mouth draw tight in an effort not to show feeling. He might have been remembering the talk they had all had before the wedding about whether the children would be raised Catholic or not. The Mayhews were adamant that they would not be. If they expected opposition, they didn't get it. Chauncey was happy to be married to a Protestant, to raise his children as Protestants, probably would have been happy to convert if anyone, including himself, had given a damn. He'd never bothered much with religion at all, and so had remained formally if not very devotedly a Catholic. Which meant they were all having to contend now with the unfamiliar ritual, the strange prayers.

André stirred next to her. She wondered if Marcelle had been wise to bring him, but he was such a grown-up boy for his age. Would André hold her hand, she wondered? What a little man, with his hair combed back like that. She started to inch her hand toward his but felt intimidated. He didn't need her. Marcelle never had, and André was just like her.

Marcelle had come into the world fully armored, like Athena, it seemed to Bitty. She was a beauty from the first and, by three, had mastered all the social graces. Perfection itself was Marcelle. Never a moment's trouble. Cleverer, more practical than most of the adults around her almost from the start.

When Henry cried that he was afraid of the dark, Bitty would lie down with him. Marcelle went out and bought him a night-light with her own allowance. Bitty hadn't even thought of it.

When she thought of the golden pleasure of those few, early years, once the children started coming, she forgot where she was, what had happened to Chauncey, that it had all been over for nearly a quarter of a century.

At first being with Chauncey was enough for her. But during the years she couldn't get pregnant, their lives became incomplete, marred with worry and failure. Then Henry came and he and Bitty fell in love.

Three years later, when she tucked Marcelle into Chauncey's arms, his eyes lit up in a way they hadn't when he first saw Henry: "*This* one's pretty."

"She looks like you," said Bitty.

He was shocked. "She does. She looks exactly like me."

Bitty said, "Of course she does. Did you think I was cheating on you?"

He kissed her forehead. "Don't say that."

She loved him so absurdly, so ridiculously—beyond human imagining, that was all. And beyond human endurance, which was where her good friend booze came in.

As she sat now, defeated, shoulders bent in her black suit, the memory washed over her like morning sun. It was a forgotten time, another life, someone else's.

The one she had lived before that seemed more real to her now, was easier to call back, to feel. Remembering, she felt tears start to destroy her careful makeup, and thought it ironic that she was crying at her husband's funeral over the shards of her childhood. When do we grow up? she wondered, sobbing into one hand, fumbling for a tissue with the other. Is it ever over? Any of it? For any of us?

Her father put his arm around her. She shivered, thinking she'd prefer the embrace of a boa constrictor. The touch of her bourbon-smelling, blunt, ruthless father was loathsome, and she was usually extremely good at avoiding it. But at the moment she could hardly get up and move. She sank down, unable to bear it.

And now he put both arms around her, trying to hold her up. She was going to scream. She couldn't stand this. She could feel the scream rising in her throat. Oh, thank God. The congregation were getting to their feet.

"Are you all right?" he whispered.

"Yes. Let me go, please."

The Christmas Henry was two, he had a wonderful time and got tired out. But he didn't want to give up his wonderful time. He raced screeching through the house, trying to make it last, trying not to get caught by a grown-up and sent to bed. Bitty laughed. She didn't mind if he raced and screeched for a minute. It was her house and he wasn't hurting anything. Chauncey had sighed and rubbed his head, as if fatherhood wasn't what he had in mind after all.

Her father had picked Henry up and sat down with the baby imprisoned, Henry's legs between his own, holding both of Henry's hands in one of his, the other clamped over Henry's mouth so that Henry couldn't move at all, even his head. Bitty was sitting on the sofa. For a moment she stared unbelieving, frozen. And then she melted, woke up almost, as if she'd blacked out for a second, and found herself standing, clawing at her child, screaming, "Let that baby go! Let go of that poor child!" as if her father was a Nazi officer about to turn her baby into soap.

"Bitty, what is it? What's the matter?" her father inquired, concerned, looking puzzled, never letting go of Henry. Not even thinking about it.

Chauncey stroked her hair. "Bitty, darlin', it's all right. Henry's coming to Daddy, aren't you, sport?"

"Take the little monster," said her father. Henry leaped into Chauncey's arms as if from the clutches of a kidnapper.

Later Chauncey said, "Don't you think you overreacted

when your father picked Henry up? Are you tired out after all the excitement?" He kissed the top of her head.

She didn't answer because she didn't know if she'd over-reacted or not. She'd been seized by some primeval, elemental force, which might have been the Mother Bear instinct, or it might have been a memory come back to haunt her. Bitty thought it was probably a combination of the two. She was almost sure, when she thought about it, that her father had done that to her at Henry's age, whenever he wanted, picked her up like a toy and pinned her and gagged her. Her reaction was too visceral, too desperate to leave much doubt.

Her father didn't let anything get in his way, certainly not another human being, and most assuredly not one smaller than he was. He wanted what he wanted right now, and if it happened to be peace and quiet, he silenced the noisemaker.

She was pregnant that Christmas. She didn't know it yet, but she was pretty sure, and the thought of having another baby made her strengthen her resolve, the vow she made when she learned she was pregnant with Henry. Sometimes she thought it took her so long to get pregnant because she was afraid of what would happen to her children, that her body simply rebelled at giving her children until she knew she could handle it, that she wouldn't hurt them. Her vow had been to protect her children from violence.

Her mother, christened Marianna MacDuff Scarborough, earned the nickname Merrie Mac in the first two years of her life—ostensibly for her sunny disposition, but Bitty thought it appropriate that it derived from a battle.

If Merrie Mac had ever been merry, it had been well before Bitty's first memory of her, of Merrie Mac buttoning her dress and then smacking her bottom in dismissal, performing a distasteful chore and sending away the small irritation that kept getting in her way. Bitty couldn't once remember her mother hugging her. She did all the necessary mother things but always in the same grudging way she performed the dress-buttoning. Bitty knew she was a nuisance and tried to stay out of the way, especially when her parents were fighting, which was most of the time.

Her mother would speak just as the soup was served, at the optimum time to make Bitty and her father lose their appetites. "Haygood, did you forget the milk again?"

"What milk?"

"I told you this morning we were out of milk."

"No, you didn't, Marianna."

"I most certainly did."

"You did not tell me we were out of milk. I would have remembered, just like I always do, if you had told me we were out of milk."

"I opened the refrigerator and I *said*, 'Oh, Haygood, there's only enough milk for Bitty's cereal,' and *you* said, 'I'll pick some up on the way home from work.'"

"Marianna, I didn't even have breakfast here this morning. I had breakfast with Hugh Del Monte at the Roosevelt."

"You did too. You sat right there in that chair and drank your coffee."

"I did not, Marianna."

"You did. Are you telling me I'm a liar?"

He would shake his head in disbelief. "I don't know what you're talking about. If you'd talk to me about a subject I could understand, I'd be glad to talk to you."

"You sat right there in that chair, Haygood."

"I did not sit right there in that chair."

And so it would go.

They would fight about a quart of milk, but Merrie Mac would never ask to move—to get out of that drafty, dark, old house on Louisiana Avenue, that house that she complained of all day long to Bitty and then at night to Haygood as well. She'd say she got so depressed in there she felt like slitting her wrists; and she'd say it was so drafty she guessed that's why she was sick again. But she'd never say, "Haygood, let's move."

She was afraid of him, and so was Bitty. Before she was nine, Bitty figured out that bickering and complaining was her mother's way of getting back at him because she didn't dare ask for what she wanted. Bitty didn't question why Merrie Mac never asked. She knew. Her father would give something only if it suited him. He didn't give a damn what anyone else wanted unless it meshed with his own plans.

Bitty got the bicycle she wanted for Christmas, but little Gilford Del Monte also got a bicycle that year and Haygood didn't want to be outdone, so he got her a better one than his friend Hugh got for his son. It wasn't the color she wanted, and it was too big for her. She was afraid to ride it, and the first time she did she fell off.

When she asked for a puppy, Haygood said, "You wouldn't take care of it, Bitty; you know that. Look at that bicycle just rusting out in the garage."

He hadn't wanted her anyway. He wanted a boy. She had to learn to hunt and fish instead of taking ballet lessons, even though she hated worms and, frankly, anything outdoors at all. For a while she even had to take riding lessons, but she was so terrified of the horses that eventually the teachers wouldn't allow the screaming, clinging little creature in her specially made miniature jodhpurs anywhere near their stable. ("Another reason you couldn't take care of an animal. You're scared to death of 'em.")

Merrie Mac was sick nearly all the time. She didn't have any one thing, but she had the flu a lot, and stomach complaints, and inner-ear trouble, and sometimes headaches. She had two favorite topics of conversation—her husband's failings and her health. In the afternoons, after school, she would tell Bitty what was wrong with her this time and what the doctor had done about it and how it hadn't worked and what he had done next and how that hadn't worked either, and what he was finally trying now.

When Bitty met Chauncey he had seemed a miracle—vigorous, full of life, not sick like her mother, not a drunk like her father. She wanted him to save her from their darkness. And she wanted to have children with him—strong, healthy children that she couldn't have with just anybody, given her background. Perfect children she'd never neglect, and neither would Chauncey.

Hurt, Tolliver had said, "Somehow I always thought you and I—I guess I just assumed . . ."

"Oh, Tolliver!"

Thin, pale Tolliver? So quiet, almost effete. But she could see why he'd thought that. He had plenty of reason to think that. Their families were close. They'd grown up together, almost—gone out with groups of kids, paired off and dated. She loved him and felt more comfortable, safer with Tolliver than she ever had with anyone. He was like a first cousin who was almost a brother. And, when she thought about it, she'd never dated anyone else before Chauncey—never had the least inclination or interest. She supposed, in some corner of her mind, that she had "always assumed" as well, or would have if she'd thought about it.

But she hadn't. The idea of marriage hadn't come up yet. If Tolliver had proposed, she'd probably have married him, but only after taking time to think about it and wondering why it hadn't occurred to her before.

Chauncey was like one of those horses she'd been so frightened of—a force you couldn't argue with. She'd always known—with the horses—that riding would be the most exhilarating thing she'd ever done if she weren't so afraid. She knew it would be that way with Chauncey—and she wasn't afraid for a second.

The priest was doing something odd now. He was starting to talk as if there were just a few people gathered in the cavernous church instead of hundreds, from the mayor to some of the street musicians Chauncey had befriended. He was talking about Chauncey, telling Chauncey anecdotes, and then his tone changed. He talked about the fact that after a death the living tend to feel guilty for being alive, and how they must learn to accept themselves as they are, without guilt for another's death. And then he said they had to accept the dead too. He said, "We must all accept Chauncey now, as he is now—which is dead." Bitty's sobbing stopped for a moment. He did not say that Chauncey had gone to his maker or been claimed by Jesus or any such nonsense. He said dead.

Chauncey had been dead to her for years.

3

They buried him at Metairie Cemetery or, more properly, entombed him, as New Orleanians, because of the high water table, have historically preferred this method. The Mayhews apparently had claimed him as their own—to the Mayhew plot he went.

Skip, shivering in her silk blouse and suit jacket, thought the obelisk-centered plot, with its imposing tombs and monuments, its careful carving, and most of all, its vast size, might more properly have been called the Mayhew acre. With the Mayhew estate on it.

She saw Chauncey's parents, the St. Amants, standing together, huddled against the wind, like a couple of out-of-place old retainers, except that now Mrs. St. Amant claimed intimacy by taking the tiny hand of André Gaudet. Mrs. St. Amant wore a plain black-and-white tweed coat. Mr. St. Amant wore a brown suit. He was an accountant, Skip thought.

The morning sun hadn't lasted. On a day like today, overcast and windy, the place was properly eerie. New Orleans cemeteries were called cities of the dead, and Metairie was the biggest city of all, and probably the most beautifully landscaped. The tombs were like small houses—in some cases large ones—set on carefully manicured streets. The Mayhew plot, with its own obelisk, which in turn had its own moat, and with so many tiny buildings to contain the bones of so many bygone Mayhews, was like a self-contained little necropolis within the larger one. The "estate" was as crowded as if an outdoor concert was about to be presented.

Skip had caught a glimpse of her parents in the church, and she saw them again here, her mother leaning against her father in the cold, both of them looking slightly ill in black. She made no attempt to say hello.

Even her brother was here. He wasn't with her parents, but with a woman, she saw—probably some Mayhew relative he was going out with. Conrad had inherited the family hobby of social climbing. The woman turned and she saw who it was—Sara Ann Gaillard, one of Alison's sisters. Alison and her husband were standing with them.

God! Everyone she'd ever gone to Miggy's or McGehee's or Newcomb or Trinity with was here, and everybody from her old neighborhood on State Street, and all the next-door neighbors of all the little girls at whose homes she'd played as a child.

There was Judith Harmeyer, Tolliver Albert's redoubtable gray-haired sister, and her husband, Arthur. Tolliver and Henry stood near Bitty, whose father had an arm around her, holding her up perhaps. Bitty looked defeated, as if she'd crumple to the ground if someone didn't hold her, but Skip had glimpsed her in church and her color was good. She was ethereally beautiful in her widow's black. Tolliver, though— God! He was paler than usual, and his eyes were sunken and deep-circled, as if he hadn't slept. And that was the least of it. Skip didn't know when she'd seen such a look of misery on a human being's face. He was staring at Bitty as if she was drowning and he couldn't swim.

The musicians seemed at home, seemed to feel Chauncey had been public property and it was fine for them to be there. John Hall Pigott, the black star who'd returned to his roots, was standing with some of them. At the edge of the crowd were a fat guy in a dumpy-looking suit and a tall guy in a nicely fitting blazer who were hanging back, hands behind them, shifting awkwardly from one foot to the other, looking as out of place as Chauncey's parents. Watching them did Skip's vengeful heart good—she was pretty sure it was O'Rourke and Tarantino. They looked like parasites who couldn't quite get a grip on their hosts.

Near them, but closer in, was Marcelle, like Bitty stunning in black, except that it made her look vibrant rather than fragile. Now that André had gone to his grandmother, she looked as if she hadn't a friend in the world.

Skip started toward her and ran into a man holding a go-cup. She couldn't believe it—a go-cup at a funeral. Something foul-smelling—scotch, probably—splashed all over her suit. When the shock wore off, she stopped staring at the Rorschach on her breast and raised angry eyes to the mischievous blue ones of Cookie Lamoreaux.

"Sorry, officer."

"Cookie, you're incorrigible," she whispered.

"Hi," said a whispered voice behind her. She turned around to see Steve Steinman, looking supremely uncomfortable in a pair of summer khakis—probably just right for L.A.—tweed jacket, and knit tie. Could the tie be choking him? He certainly looked as if it was. He leaned into her ear and said, "Good to see you. Did you see who's here? John Hall Pigott. The movie star."

She nodded and continued toward Marcelle. Steve followed, catching her arm, nodding to whomever Skip nodded, finally saying, "Where do you want to go?" She pointed toward Marcelle. Steve took her hand and led the way as if he was her date.

The service ended and they had to go against the tide of people trying to leave. Without being prompted, Steve was acting as a buffer between her and the members of the dread uptown crowd who were bearing down, wanting to talk small talk, maybe even pump her about the case. He was politely sending them away, drawing Skip toward her goal. This, she thought, must be what it's like to have a boyfriend—a presentable, socially adept guy you could take out in public, not some married semiliterate. She liked the sensation quite well, and thought, Well, fine. If he wants to use me, just fine. Right now I'm using him, and I like it a lot.

"Oh, God," she said, "faster. There's my yuppie brother."

He pulled her into a sort of clearing. "Marcelle," she called.

Marcelle was no longer alone. She was surrounded. But at Skip's call, she broke away and threw her arms around her. "Oh, Skippy! It's hard."

"I'm so sorry. I know it is."

A loud yowl went up—André. Marcelle disappeared, leaving Skip feeling peculiarly touched. She wasn't sure why she felt so compelled to comfort this woman she hardly knew—and had never really liked—or why Marcelle had responded as if Skip was a close relative.

Relishing the thought, she relaxed and chatted with old acquaintances now, introducing Steve, feeling oddly proud of having him with her and much more comfortable than usual with these people. The social amenities seemed so much easier to get through when there were two people to do the work. She hoped Tarantino and O'Rourke were getting an eyeful of her in her Uptown element, eating their hearts out, watching her receive earfuls of helpful gossip and red-hot tips. She had a meeting with them that afternoon, and she had no idea what she'd report.

Steve said, "Are we still on for dinner tonight?"

"I was supposed to call you!"

"Forgot, didn't you? No problem. The Bon Ton, eight o'clock." He left before she could refuse, using his huge body as a battering ram to get through the crowd.

She watched her parents, in a knot of their own acquaintances, stare curiously after him. Her father, as usual, glanced away when she looked at him. Her mother's eyes held big, reproachful tears. Neither of them tried to speak to her.

4

If it hadn't been for LaBelle . . . For once the simple nurturing act of watering his orchids wasn't working. Tolliver had started raising them because even mild fiddling with his few houseplants had opened up a new way of feeling to him. It wasn't like the buying and selling and stroking and worship of antiques, which was stimulating. This was restful. It was like going into a trance, some satisfied place where you could forget what had gone before and just be *here*, watering these plants, playing in this earth. It wasn't the sort of thing a sophisticated person talked about in public, but people didn't mind discussing the blossoms he produced and they frequently used the word "magic" in reference to them, which couldn't have been further from the truth. Which was, of course, that nothing could have been more basic, more natural, more predictable, and less "magical." He might have bought "mystical," but he knew the word wouldn't come up if he lived to lunch at Antoine's on his hundredth birthday.

Today the magical-mystical process refused to swallow him up. His hands shook and he kept spilling water. He went through the normally loving acts mechanically—even wiping up the spills mechanically, just getting the job done, unable to silence the tape that was running over and over in his head.

If I could just goddamn have left well enough alone. Goddamn LaBelle! And goddamn me.

To his amazement, Chauncey, whom he'd hated for so many years, kept gnawing at the edge of his consciousness. But not the Chauncey who was dead—the Chauncey who had been his friend at Tulane, that confident, vital, compelling young man with the bright future. Even then he was driven; Tolliver knew that, but big deal. He was ambitious. And why not? He wasn't an Albert or a Mayhew, he was from out by the lake. Ambition was appropriate for someone like Chauncey. The kind of energy it produced invigorated Tolliver. Chauncey reminded him of a line from a poem: "healthy, free, the world before me." The whole world. But that was before Chauncey became a prisoner of his own desire.

Tolliver laughed, spilling water on his coffee table. Jesus, he should be writing cover copy for women's beach books. But it wasn't only the melodrama that amused him—it was the unwitting pun. LaBelle had brought the whole house of cards down and she was product, prisoner, and victim of Desire with a capital "D"—the Desire Project, an eerily apt name for the worst slum in the state. Chauncey himself didn't need any project—he was just a victim of small "d" desire, with the consequent damage not only to himself but to his wife and son.

Worry about Bitty was just a numb ache today. Maybe it really was too late for her. Or maybe he was just in a worse funk than he thought. At the moment, he felt worse about Henry. The boy had always been so close to Bitty, never able to break free, to become his own person.

I'm no different. He shook his head to clear it. The thought remained and expanded. *What makes me any different? Except that, with me, it isn't only Bitty. It's all of them. The whole St. Amant family.*

He set his watering can on the rug and collapsed on the blue sofa. He was no different from Henry. And now the inevitable had happened—he tried to save them and he ended up destroying them. Indisputably destroying Chauncey. But the rest of them? Was it over for them too? Could they pull out of it? They might, if people would leave them alone.

Dammit, it was a family affair. The cops had no business in the middle of it. Skip Langdon, whatever you said about her father, was sharp. There was no question in his mind she'd get to the bottom of it. Most cops wouldn't know where to start, but Skip had more things going for her than her quick wits. It wasn't that complicated, after all. All you had to do was know whom to ask which questions.

Oh, God, what had he done? But here was the real question—could it be undone? If he hadn't had such a terrible headache the day of the wake . . . but no matter, she could still be stopped and he thought he knew exactly how. There wasn't much time, though; he'd have to be fast.

SWEET CHARITY

"Officer." Lieutenant Duby nodded to her, ever the gentleman. Skip was late—the other two had already arrived.

As she slipped into the vacant chair, Tarantino said, "How's it going, Skip?"

O'Rourke said nothing. Skip didn't get it. How could a guy who was married to a cop take this kind of attitude? She couldn't believe she ever thought he'd be an ally.

Duby said, "I had a call from the mayor this morning before the funeral. Guess who he'd had a call from?"

Skip was pretty sure she knew, but she hung back, giving the other two a chance to speak. When neither did, she said, "Haygood Mayhew."

"You got it."

"I bet he mentioned poor Furman would never have been

elected if it hadn't been for his son-in-law, Chauncey St. Amant, and he thought it was a damn shame Furman's goddamn whole police force hadn't even been able to solve a murder committed in full view of half the city."

Tarantino and Duby laughed. Duby said, "Sounds like you know the old gentleman pretty well."

"Gentleman, my ass. Old turkey buzzard's more like it."

"Well, the old turkey buzzard more or less runs the city in case you three aren't aware of it. So I thought we'd better compare a few notes here."

"Hey!" Tarantino looked hurt. "We're going as fast as our chubby little legs'll carry us."

"No need to get your feelings hurt, Joe. I just want to know where we are, that's all. Who wants to report first?"

"We've been talking to some of the people at the Boston Club that day," said O'Rourke. He spoke matter-of-factly, but Skip thought she caught a hint of triumph in his voice, as if he thought he was stealing her thunder. Tarantino was staring at her—trying to gauge her reaction?

"The logistics of the thing are pretty damn simple," O'Rourke continued. "You could walk to Albert's and back in forty minutes to an hour, going on back streets. You'd have to get through some crowds first, but you could probably do that in about ten or fifteen minutes. If you had transportation nearby, like a bicycle or scooter, you could do the whole damn job in half an hour."

Duby said, "You're going on the theory the murderer was someone at the Boston Club?"

Tarantino shrugged, "That's where the key was."

O'Rourke kept talking as if the interruption hadn't occurred. "Tolliver Albert was seen leaving the club approximately half an hour before the murder. By his own admission, Henry St. Amant went out 'for some air.' No one can remember seeing either of them return. The club has a reception committee on Mardi Gras, so there's usually someone at the door. But I'm told they get talking to someone or have to piss or whatever, so people *could* come and go without being noticed. Also, there's a gate that opens onto Canal St. from the patio."

He consulted his notes. "A Mrs. Del Monte remembers talking with Mrs. Chauncey St. Amant some forty minutes before the murder was reported. Or possibly thirty or twenty minutes before the murder. Mrs. St. Amant excused herself to go to the ladies' room. No one else remembers seeing her until a few minutes before Officer Langdon found her in the ladies' room. A Mrs. Anne-Marie Delamore also reports seeing her there—"

Duby said, "She was in there for forty minutes?"

O'Rourke shrugged. "Don't know, sir. But she was there at the beginning of the forty minutes, and the end of it. Or maybe it was thirty minutes, or twenty—Mrs. Del Monte says she can't be sure. Maybe Langdon wouldn't mind asking her."

Skip nodded.

"Then there's Mrs. Gaudet. She was seen leaving shortly before the murder with a Mr. Jo Jo—uh—"

"Lawrence?" said Skip.

O'Rourke glared at her. "Yeah. Lawrence. How'd you know that, Langdon?"

"They used to go out. And anyway, Jo Jo's got a reputation."

"Well, no offense, but so does your friend Marcelle Gaudet."

Duby leaned forward. "Oh?"

"You've heard of the Whore of Babylon? The lovely Mrs. G. makes her look like an amateur."

Tarantino looked sympathetically at Skip. She wished she could trust him. She had this weird idea he felt bad because her friend was getting creamed. Duby gave her an uncomfortable glance as well.

Skip shrugged. "What's everybody looking at me for? Just because I've known her forever doesn't mean we're best buddies. Hey, Frank, say what you like about her. I don't give a shit."

"You were hugging her like a sister at the funeral."

"That's called sympathy, asshole. Her father got killed, remember?"

"Officer!" Duby spoke sharply, angry eyes on Skip. "What's going on here?"

"Sorry," said Skip. "Nothing's going on."

He turned to O'Rourke. "Frank?"

O'Rourke turned his palms up and shook his head.

"All right, we'll deal with it later. Go on with your report."

"Somebody saw Lawrence and Mrs. G. sneaking upstairs." He stared at Skip. "That's where the lying-down room is."

Duby said, "What does Lawrence say?"

"He says he was drunk and she had to help him upstairs. That she helped him lie down and he doesn't remember anything else till someone shook him awake after we showed up down there."

"And Mrs. Gaudet?"

"We haven't been able to get to her."

Skip said, "I'll be glad to talk to her."

Duby nodded and turned back to O'Rourke. "All right. Go on."

"That's about it, sir. We're concentrating on these four right now. But it's worth noting that Albert lied about leaving the party—he says he didn't."

Skip said, "I think I have something to add. Did you know about the car?"

Tarantino shook his head; O'Rourke glared.

"They all came together, and parked at the Carrollton Bank, about two blocks away. Mrs. St. Amant's car key was with her key to Tolliver Albert's apartment. The killer could have taken them both at the same time."

Skip liked the way this was going. Apparently these guys hadn't stumbled onto LaBelle. For a while, she wanted to keep that whole aspect of the case to herself. She wanted to keep it from these two. In her head she could hear Duby saying, "Good work, Skip," then turning to O'Rourke and Tarantino: "You guys check it out."

Duby said now, "Is that all, guys?" When O'Rourke nodded, he turned to Skip. "You ready?"

"I guess so. I've been trying to gather personal information about Chauncey that could point to some kind of motive. I'm wondering about the four people you're concentrating on—"

O'Rourke said, "Shee-it! You're wondering! Lieutenant, could you please tell Officer Langdon the statistics on domestic violence?"

"Pipe down, Frank!" Duby was angry. "Whether you like it or not, Langdon's on this case. Work with her."

Skip continued as if nothing had happened. "I guess wives have plenty of reasons to kill husbands, and sons and daughters inherit, of course. But I don't see a motive for Tolliver Albert."

"You know, you could really help us on that," said Tarantino.

"I could?"

"Yeah—get us some scuttlebutt. We figure he was getting it on with the wife, but—"

"Uh-uh," said Skip. "That definitely isn't the scuttlebutt. You do know about Bitty's drinking problem?"

O'Rourke snorted. "Yeah, and we heard of the Super Dome too. We talked about it before—remember, Langdon?"

She glared. "For years the scuttlebutt's been the same. Tolliver turns up at parties with a lady now and then, often not. People think he's probably gay but discreet. As for Bitty, romance would cut into her boozing time. What I could do, though—I could see if I can find any other motive for Tolliver."

"We'd sure appreciate it," said Tarantino, seeming almost childlike in his gratitude. Skip wanted very much to like him, but she didn't dare.

"Do you know about Henry's relationship with his father?"

They didn't answer, so she continued. "Apparently they hated each other. Chauncey was ashamed of Henry's homosexuality—"

"The kid's a faggot?"

She stared at O'Rourke. "He's a drag queen. Worse than that, he's an actor. Anyway, he and Chauncey have been at each other's throats for years. I don't know about Marcelle, though—she was crazy about Chauncey."

Tarantino shrugged. "All we know is she's got no alibi."

Duby stroked his mustache. "What else have you got, Skip?"

"Chauncey was having an affair with his secretary, but I guess you two know that."

O'Rourke said, "Sheree Izaguirre. She was at the parade in Algiers at the time of the murder. With her mother and her kid. And some people the mother works with."

"What people?" asked Duby.

O'Rourke looked uncomfortable. Tarantino said, "The mother works as a housemother at a home for retarded women. She took some of 'em to the parade."

"So Izaguirre's alibis are a kid, a bunch of retards, and her own mother. Right?"

The two men nodded.

Duby said, "Keep checking her out. What else you got, Skip?"

"Well, it seems as if Chauncey was big on secretaries. He had an affair with one a few years back who left under mysterious circumstances."

O'Rourke said, "What circumstances?"

"If I knew they wouldn't be mysterious, would they?" To Duby, "I'd like to work on that."

"Sounds pretty thin, to tell you the truth. You gotta remember, whoever did it had a key to Albert's. What else you got?"

"That's about it."

"That's all?"

Skip nodded.

"Well, frankly, it's not much. I'm not blaming you, Skip— or not just you. I mean all of you. This is the most important murder case in the history of the city and between the three of you, you haven't got diddley. My hottest homicide team, and the bright young rookie with all the great connections. What the hell's the matter with you guys anyway?" He addressed himself to O'Rourke and Tarantino. "Especially you two. Now get out of here."

When they'd left, he said to Skip, "I don't know about you. The chief wants you on the case, but you're throwing O'Rourke off his stride and you're not coming up with enough to justify it."

"Throwing O'Rourke off his stride!"

"He doesn't like you, Langdon."

"That's my fault?"

"I don't know. Is it?"

"I walked in yesterday and he got abusive. That's it. I haven't done a damn thing to antagonize him."

"You called him an asshole."

"Jesus! That was a reaction."

"Well, don't react to him, okay? He's one of my best men, and I can't afford to have him upset."

"I guess I'll have to steer clear of him."

"Stay on this another day anyway. Get that stuff the guys asked for."

He lowered his head to his paperwork, not bothering to dismiss her.

She liked Duby. He had an easy manner and a diplomatic way about him—it was no wonder he'd come as far in a difficult department as he had. In the dark suits he always wore, he looked more like a lawyer or a banker than a cop. He was a graduate of UNO. Skip was at ease with him because he seemed familiar to her. And because it was his job to put people at ease—difficult people, egos at odds with each other. But what had just happened was blatantly unfair.

O'Rourke was going to get away with treating her any god-damn way he wanted to just because—face it—he was the more valuable officer. By doing nothing, she was "throwing him off his stride." Putting herself in Duby's shoes, she could see his point. In his eyes, O'Rourke was half the team that would eventually break the case. Skip was a harmless fluff of lagniappe the chief had asked for. He didn't expect anything one way or another from her; but if she got in O'Rourke's way, however innocently, she was a liability to him. So what she had to do was start looking valuable. She was starting to think she'd made a mistake by keeping LaBelle to herself. And yet, he'd pissed all over her idea about Stelly—it was proba-bly too early to mention LaBelle. All she knew at this point was that Chauncey had some reason to be angry with the woman, certainly not that she'd killed him.

She sat down at a computer and asked it for LaBelle's rap sheet. For good measure, she also asked for sheets on Henry, Marcelle, Bitty, Tolliver, and Chauncey. She was looking over the printouts when she felt a hand on her shoulder.

"Hey, Skip." It was Tarantino.

"Hey, Joe." He smiled and sat down.

"Listen, don't pay any attention to Frank. He's got a bug up his ass."

"So I noticed."

"It's not about you. It's personal problems. Even I can't stand him right now. Usually he's a great guy, really."

"Frank O'Rourke and Vlad the Impaler."

"Who?"

"Another really great guy. He doesn't like me, Joe. It's that simple."

"I know, but it's nothing to do with you." He looked em-barrassed. "It'll blow over. Give it time."

She smiled again. The guy was adorable. "Okay. I'll try to be nice." She applied herself to the rap sheets.

"Whatcha got?" Tarantino looked over her shoulder. Bitty's

sheet was on top, showing several arrests for drunk driving. "You know what? We forgot to get sheets on our four guys."

Was he a bit too innocent? She felt wary again. "I can save you the trouble. Chauncey, Marcelle, and Tolliver are completely clean. Bitty's got this"—she tossed it over—"and Henry got busted for drugs once. Marijuana."

She slipped his sheet and LaBelle's into her purse and stood up. Tarantino said, "Can I see Henry's sheet?"

"Sure." She pulled it out. "Keep it, why don't you?"

She didn't look at LaBelle's sheet until she was safely outside in her car. Tarantino looked like a doll, but Charles Manson had fooled people too. Anyone that close to Frank O'Rourke couldn't be all good.

There were no surprises—just routine busts for prostitution, drugs, and shoplifting.

Glad it was still daytime, Skip drove to Tremé, to the address Jeweldean Sanders had given her. Except for police officers, not that many white people ventured into Tremé—except to go to the Municipal Auditorium, where the fanciest Mardi Gras balls were held, or to Louis Armstrong Park, but ever since a tourist had been murdered there, there had been fewer carefree park-goers.

Nothing in the neighborhood seemed to have seen new paint in the current century. When a window broke, which seemed to be often, boarding it up was frequently the best the residents could manage. Except for a few new brick ones, the buildings were as lovely as any others in New Orleans—or would have been if they hadn't been falling apart.

There were a lot of people on the street, unemployed people, probably. Skip felt the stench of poverty in the air, its strangling oppressiveness, as dense as smoke over a forest fire.

LaBelle lived in one of the very few newish brick buildings in the neighborhood. This one looked nearly as much like a jail as it did an apartment house. It was a no-frills box with windows so tiny they were hardly worth bothering with. The space that could have been a yard had been paved over for parking. The building next door was burned out.

Aware of how conspicuous she looked, a white woman in a suit, she rang LaBelle's doorbell. Getting no answer, she rang the bell belonging to the building manager, the man named Calvin with whom Jeweldean Sanders "did business." Once again, she got no answer. She wondered whether she could be seen from inside.

Well, she'd recognize LaBelle if she saw her. She parked her car on North Villere and settled down to wait. Within fifteen minutes she'd been propositioned by two men, warned away by a worried old woman, and panhandled by several children. She was there nearly an hour before the robbery attempt. Three young men surrounded the car and asked for her money. Hell. It was nearly impossible to keep a low profile on the damn street. Reluctant to identify herself as a policewoman—and get known in the neighborhood—she simply started the car and took off, narrowly missing one of the would-be highwaymen but wishing in some dark corner of herself that she hadn't, that she'd hit the son of a bitch.

Shit. You practically had to be black to do surveillance in the goddamn place. And even that might not help—a lone woman would probably be noticed and approached no matter what she looked like. A couple of guys might work out if they were black and looked as if they were doing something you'd do in a car, like drinking. But much more than an hour, and even they'd be noticed. There were just too many people out and about. Maybe she could talk Calvin into letting her use his apartment. She'd taken his name from his mailbox— Calvin Hogue. She'd see if he had an arrest record. Maybe he could be bargained with.

For now, though, she couldn't think of anything else to do. She could hardly go back to North Villere—and anyway, Steve Steinman was expecting her at the Bon Ton. Thinking about it now, she realized she'd never really intended to go;

hadn't thought she could take time out. It looked as if she had no choice, though. And anyway, maybe he'd drive her back to Tremé after dinner. They could see if there was a light in LaBelle's window.

Skip doubted she entertained clients there, though. Not if she catered to whites. More likely, she took calls and met them in hotels. Probably even had a beeper so she didn't have to sit by the phone and wait.

Back in her apartment, she looked at her watch. Nearly two hours till her date. Plenty of time to primp. Kicking off her shoes, she fell in a heap on the unmade bed. Jesus, a date! Officer Skip Langdon didn't date. Occasionally she spent a couple of hours drinking with someone with whom she later had sex, but she hadn't been out to dinner with a nice young man since college. Had she? Well, there had been once in San Francisco. . . .

It occurred to her to wonder why she lived this way. Was it because of her size? Too tall and too big, not a really great combo for attracting men. But that wasn't all—she didn't like the men she knew in New Orleans, the ones she'd known all her life from subscription dances, and there wasn't anyone else in the whole damn town, except policemen who were wary of her, and married Cajun bartenders. Was that it? Thinking about tonight, the lack of enthusiasm she felt for it, she thought that wasn't it at all. She just wasn't in the mood.

"Yoo-hoo! Officer Darlin'!" It was her landlord and neighbor, Jimmy Dee Scoggin, standing outside her door doing his come-hither falsetto.

Smiling, she opened up. "Dee-Dee Doll, it's been forever."

He swept past her, handing her a joint as he walked. He was about five feet nine, spare, and already gray. The way he lived, he'd come by his hair color honestly. "Well, look at us, just *do*! God, that's an awful outfit. You look like you're going to a funeral."

Closing the door, Skip stared at the joint in her hand, trying to make up her mind. "I *have* been to a funeral, Do-

Do." Oh, hell, why not? Shrugging, she took a toke and passed the joint back to Jimmy Dee.

He lay down on her bed. "Oh. Chauncey St. Amant's, I guess. Well, la-di-da. Aren't you . . . too much . . . too soon . . . to know."

"Guess what, Dee-Dee? I've got a date tonight. Eat your heart out, darlin'."

He sat up. "With a man?"

"A big one."

"Ooooohhhh. Be still, my heart. And what are we going to wear, my dainty darling?"

Handing the joint back to Skip, he leaped up and opened the closet. She took another little toke while Jimmy Dee surveyed her wardrobe. He came out looking bemused.

"Not spending that giant salary on clothes, I see."

"I guess I haven't got anything, huh?"

He gave her a wicked look. "No, but I have."

"Dee-Dee! Since when have you been into drag? Anyway, we wouldn't wear the same size, you runt."

"Don't I know it, Your Bigness." He took the joint and left like a small sirocco. By day, Dee-Dee worked for one of the city's stuffier law firms, causing secretaries to swoon and partners' wives to introduce him to eligibles. Skip knew the swish act was strictly to amuse her, whom he considered a project. He felt she was deeply depressed and probably wouldn't survive without his antics; he told her so roughly three times a week. She wondered if he wasn't the one who was depressed, or at least one of the ones, but deep down, she knew he was probably right. She needed him.

She folded up the sofa bed, getting more and more stoned as she waited for him. He was like Tolliver, she thought. He kept his private life private, indeed. Hardly anyone knew for sure he was gay.

He burst back into the room, throwing her an oversize black sweater with some sort of abstract metallic design on it.

"I found it in the bathroom after Carnival. Don't ask," he said.

She held it up and stared in the mirror. "It's not really my style."

He held his hand to his forehead. "Thank Gawd!"

"What do I wear it with? The gabardine pants?"

"Oh, Skip, Skip, Skip, what would you do without me? With jeans, darlin', with jeans! And sweetheart, a favor, okay? Don't wear your jogging shoes." He turned to go.

"Dee-Dee, wait a minute."

"What, do I have to do your hair too?"

"Do you know Tolliver Albert?"

He looked puzzled. "Doesn't ring a bell."

"Good-looking. Runs an antique store on Royal."

"Mmmmm. Maybe we should meet. That is, if he's under twenty-three."

"I want to know if he's gay. Can you ask around?"

"Is that who you've got a date with, little one? You fruit fly!" The door closed behind him, and Skip, as usual after one of his performances, doubled over laughing.

It wasn't only from the clowning either. Dee-Dee's controlled substances were always of the highest quality. She felt floaty and fine. Normally she took showers, but tonight a bubble bath seemed in order. That way she could play with the bubbles.

It was seven-forty when she stepped in front of the mirror in the black sweater, which really was quite chic, a pair of tight jeans (due to certain circumstances, she didn't own any other kind), and her one pair of all-wrong brown heels. Well, hell, at least they were unobtrusive, and she didn't have a choice—she'd promised Dee-Dee she wouldn't wear her jogging shoes.

There was time to walk—should she? Yes, definitely. She was still a little stoned. She'd trip lightly over the pavement like a dancing hippo from *Fantasia*.

She stepped out the door and locked it. She heard a step,

just one, behind her, but it was too close. She started to whirl around, light as a hippo, but never got past the intention stage. The thought of whirling flitted in and out like lightning before the back of her head exploded. She sank to her knees, holding on to the doorknob.

The light was hellish. No way she could sleep anymore. She could remember voices, when some people had found her, and being lifted into a vehicle and brought to the hospital. She knew she was at a hospital, she even knew which one. It would be Charity (because nearly all the city's accident cases went there), and she would be in a tiny room marked "Trauma 7," where they took the closed-head injuries and where she had once spent a grisly hour or so with a victim who wouldn't let go of her hand. (That is, she'd be there unless she had an open-head injury, but she couldn't remember any blood being mopped up.) Okay. She wasn't unconscious (though she wanted very much to sleep some more); she wasn't even disoriented. She knew exactly where she should be—only she wasn't.

This wasn't Trauma 7, with its almost cheerful clutter. This place was too white, too stark, and she was moving; her whole body was on some kind of track, moving through a white arch. And it was so terribly cold here.

"Skip? Skip, can you hear me?" It was a woman in a white coat—doctor, nurse, or technician.

"This isn't Charity."

"Yes, it is. You're fine. You're okay. We're just doing a CT scan to make sure there's no bleeding and no fracture."

Fracture! There probably was one, the way it hurt. She realized the pain was what was making her so sleepy—or not the pain itself, but the need to get away from it. Okay, enough of that. She knew that phrase "extreme drowsiness," and what it meant with head injuries. It meant "serious," maybe even "life-threatening." This wasn't that kind of injury. She concentrated on waking up.

The white-coated woman said, "It looks fine. We're going to do a couple of other evaluations—neurology and ophthalmology—and then I think we can send you home."

They sent her back to Trauma 7 first and left her there for a long time. At least she was warmer there.

A man popped his head in. "Skip? I'm Dr. Saul. How're you feeling?"

"What's your first name?"

He looked confused. "Uh—Gilbert. Why?"

"I'm feeling fine, Gilbert."

He looked even more mixed-up. God! She thought, I wonder if you have to have an IQ in three figures to get through medical school. "There's—um—someone here to see you. Do you feel—?"

The man couldn't seem to recover from having his title stripped off—or maybe he was always a wimp. Being the daughter of a doctor—to her mind, the consummate phony—she hadn't a moment's patience with anyone in the profession. Damn! Her head hurt. Maybe the visitor was her father. Would they have notified next of kin? Oh, God, of all people she didn't want to see. "Who is it?" she said.

But too late. A face appeared over Gilbert's shoulders. A handsome Irish face, the face of a pushy cop who didn't mind shouldering his way through sacred medical bastions and into trauma rooms where he had no business.

She said, "Oh, shit. Not you."

O'Rourke said, "We were worried about you, Langdon. Silly of us, wasn't it? You got a hard head."

Gilbert fled.

"I think it was real sweet. Where's Joe?" She could have bitten back the last two words the moment she said them—maybe she was just falling into their little Mutt-and-Jeff trap. *Oh, face it, you're already in too deep to get out.* The reality was, she'd love to see Joe right now.

"On his way."

"Would you mind leaving me alone for a little while?"

"I just wanted to be sure you're your usual bitchy self." He turned and left. She heard his quick angry steps retreating and thought, What's wrong with him? But she knew what it was. She had hurt his feelings.

Goddamn! Why was she supposed to nursemaid some asshole who was nothing but nasty to her while her head hurt like this? She wanted to drift off again, but out of stubbornness—O'Rourke would have said bitchiness—she stayed awake.

Several centuries later, after sessions with the neurologist and the ophthalmologist, she was given a final evaluation and sent home, with instructions: Come back if she suffered vomiting, noticed the famous extreme drowsiness, or had trouble moving her extremities. And have someone wake her every hour to make sure she was properly oriented. Oh, great. Who? she thought. O'Rourke?

He was waiting with Tarantino to take her home. Tarantino hugged her, giving her a sustaining whiff of that comforting male smell they all had. She had wondered sometimes if it was a pheromone but thought it couldn't be; it relaxed instead of aroused. "You okay?"

"Pretty much. It still hurts, but you can't do anything for it. Can't drink. Can't take codeine or anything. Only aspirin."

"Concussion?"

"Yeah, but that's all. No fracture."

"We'll take you home, okay? I'll get the car."

She was left with O'Rourke for a few minutes. Did that mean anything? If they were really Mutt-and-Jeffing her, surely they would have had enough sense to have Joe stay with her. In her weakened condition, there was no telling what she might say. She wanted to lean on someone large and strong, but certainly not on Frank O'Rourke. He said, "Langdon, you better sit down." But where they were standing, in the waiting room part of the emergency setup, every seat was already taken. O'Rourke made no move to find her a vacant one, no move to help her stand.

"I'm fine," said Skip, and forced herself not to sink against a wall.

In the car, he said, "What happened, Langdon?"

"Hey," said Joe. "Come on. Lay off."

"I just asked what happened."

"Leave her alone. Can't you see the poor kid feels like a dog's breakfast?"

What *had* happened? She was trying to make up her mind whether to drive or walk to the Bon Ton . . . "Oh, no!"

Joe said, "What is it, Skip? You feel sick?"

"I had a date!"

"Your date clobbered you?"

"No! I stood him up. Oh, no!"

"Yeah, well, don't tell anybody," said O'Rourke. "They might take you out of the Social Register."

"I'm not in the goddamn Social Register!"

Joe said, "Leave her alone, okay?" To Skip, "Here we are. Frank'll walk you up while I park."

"No!" She flung herself out of the car and raced to her doorway, but it was no good. O'Rourke was behind her. She'd run only a few steps, but she was dizzy from the effort.

O'Rourke said, "Easy," and put an arm around her.

Without a word, even to protest the offending arm around her waist, she unlocked the door and started up the stairs. O'Rourke dropped the arm.

In her own apartment she hesitated, unwilling to turn on the light. Jimmy Dee could see it from the slave quarters where he lived in relative splendor. He might pop over smoking a joint as usual. But surely he wouldn't—he'd assume she'd brought her date home. While she was still debating, O'Rourke flipped the switch himself. Skip had hung up her suit but left her pantyhose on the floor, where she'd thrown them in disgust. Thank God, she thought, she had made up the damn bed. She swooped down to get the pantyhose, dislodging something, it felt like. Something cranial.

"Ow." She got up slowly and checked her message machine. Three messages. Two more than usual, considering Jimmy Dee checked in now and then, but he wouldn't have tonight. So three more than usual. They'd all be from Steve, and they'd be increasingly angry. She certainly wasn't going to play them for O'Rourke's amusement. Instead, she merely ignored him. He could sit down or not, she didn't give a damn. As for her, she did, on the sofa, and dialed Cookie Lamoreaux's number. Steve answered.

"Steve. Skip. Listen, I'm really—"

The click was loud, so loud O'Rourke had to have heard it. As she hung up, he said, "So who whacked you, Langdon?"

"I didn't see anyone. I was locking my door."

He shook his head in disgust. "You sure you went to the academy? Or did they just sneak you in the back door?"

"Could I ask you something, O'Rourke? Why do you hate me?" She thought he could not have looked more surprised if he'd been the one who got clobbered.

"I don't—" He stopped, and she knew he'd started to say he didn't hate her, but he couldn't because he did.

Maybe it was the head injury, or rather, the lost inhibitions caused by the injury, but she knew she'd hit it. He and Tarantino weren't pulling something on her, and it wasn't a case of simple dislike, as Duby suggested. Frank O'Rourke really hated her, she thought he hadn't even caught on to it himself till right now.

The doorbell rang, and he let Joe in, not out of consideration, she was sure, but to avoid having to face her and her stark accusation. She didn't let up. As Joe's heavy steps pounded up the stairs, she said, "What have I ever done to you?"

She thought his ruddy complexion lightened up, but she couldn't be sure.

Joe stood at the threshold. He said again, "You okay?" She nodded. "We gotta talk a few minutes."

She realized he was waiting for her to ask him in. It was an effort, but she smiled. "Come in, Joe." The moment with O'Rourke was lost.

Though her head throbbed and she wanted nothing more than to lie down, she let the two men have the sofa, while she sat in her director's chair.

O'Rourke said, "This has got something to do with the case, doesn't it?"

"My getting hit? I don't know. I told you—I didn't see who did it."

"Langdon, the people who found you were pretty shocked to find a gun in your purse. Your wallet was there too. Did you count your money?"

"No."

"Do it now."

"No."

"Goddamnit, you're impeding a murder investigation." As if she wasn't a cop.

"Leave my house, please."

"What are you talking about?"

"I'm talking about your rudeness and disrespect."

For once O'Rourke looked confused; for a split second he wasn't his usual arrogant self. He said, "Joe?"

"Skip's upset. Why don't I stay with her awhile?"

"We came in your car. How am I gonna get back to the damn hospital?"

Tarantino stared him full in the face. "Walk, maybe. It might cool you off."

O'Rourke stomped out of the apartment and down the un-carpeted stairs like a herd of buffalo.

Tarantino turned to Skip. "Like I said. Sometimes the bastard even gets me upset."

"He hates me."

"Yeah, he really does. But don't take it personally."

Even through the pain, that struck Skip as funny. She started to laugh but found that made the ache worse and stopped, rubbing her head. Catching Joe's eye, she saw he looked hurt.

He said, "You know, this is pretty hard for me—with you guys hating each other like this."

"Do I provoke it, Joe? Do I even react to it nine-tenths of the time? All I fucking well do is refuse to take any more abuse every third day or so." Her voice rose with every word, and as it did, the throbbing increased. She ended with a moan.

"Oh, poor baby," said Joe, in a voice that bespoke years of tending children. "Let me get you something." He went into the kitchen, gasped when the skitter of roaches began, and opened the refrigerator.

While he poked around, Skip tried Steve again. This time no answer.

Tarantino came back popping the top from a Diet Coke, which he thrust into her hand. "Drink this."

"Do you have kids, Joe?"

"Two."

"I thought so. Does Frank?"

"One. A little girl."

"I pity the poor child."

Tarantino hunched his shoulders in frustration. "He's got problems, Skip. I can't tell you any more. I'm sorry."

She leaned over and covered his hand with hers. "Listen, thanks for being on my side just now."

"Ahhh—he pissed me off."

Skip picked up her purse and counted her money. "Yeah, it's all here. I didn't mind counting, I just didn't want to be ordered to count—you know what I mean?"

"Sure."

"So if I wasn't robbed, I must have been hit because of something to do with the case—is that your theory?"

Tarantino nodded. "We think you know more than you're telling."

"I do. I just wanted to hang on to it awhile—I didn't want you guys to waltz away with it."

"Skip, I swear to you, I'll see you get the credit you deserve."

For a moment she felt the distrust she'd decided to abandon. He kept talking. "You've got to come clean for your own safety. It looks simple to me. You know something, somebody knows it, they think you're the only person who knows it, and they tried to take you out. Have you thought about that? Somebody really tried to kill you."

She said nothing, wondering whether it was true.

"Tell me what you know, kid, okay? Let Uncle Joe get you out of this."

"I tried to talk about it, and everybody pissed all over it."

"You did?"

"Remember what I said about the secretary?"

"That's all it is?"

"No, there's a little bit more, but let me sleep on it. Can we talk tomorrow?"

"Sure."

She followed him to the door, and as she was about to close it, she found herself saying, "Joe? Take me somewhere, will you?"

She was consumed with guilt for having stood Steve Steinman up. Normally she wasn't even given to guilt, an emotion she considered wimpy at best and self-destructive at worst. But now she felt it, felt the need to be free of it, like a compulsion.

On the way to Cookie Lamoreaux's, Tarantino left her alone with her thoughts. The image of herself popped into her mind, pacing her tiny apartment, holding cold cloths to her head, crying, unable to sleep. I'll go to Jimmy Dee's, she thought, knowing she needn't go through that. But the picture of herself sleeping happily in the vast antique bed in Jimmy Dee's spare bedroom wouldn't come. Even here she paced and cried. The image told her what the guilt was—a cover for her loneliness and fear.

Even through the throbbing, there was satisfaction in that. *I always knew guilt was phony.* And then: *God, what an arrogant bitch!*

The lights were out at Cookie's rambling old house—an

inheritance he couldn't really afford to maintain. Tarantino said, "You sure you'll be all right? I'll wait for you."

When Steve Steinman appeared at the door, tugging on a bathrobe so small it was obviously Cookie's, Skip planted her foot in the doorway. She waved the car away quickly, delivering herself into his near-stranger's hands.

"Skip." He stepped aside to let her in, not looking angry, only puzzled.

Suddenly she was furious. "You hung up on me!"

He winced. "I didn't—"

"You wouldn't even let me explain!" To her horror she was suddenly blubbering, crying her eyes out, her chest heaving so hard she felt she would vomit up her lungs, her liver, whatever was in there, by a kind of bellows action of the diaphragm. The physical part was agony, but almost nothing compared with the embarrassment. The more embarrassed she felt, the harder she cried.

Steve stopped struggling with the robe and put his arms around her. She felt bare skin—he wore only briefs under the robe.

"It's okay," he said. "Let it all out." He didn't know that if she did, she'd have no internal organs left.

She held on to the robe, a blue terry-cloth one, grabbing bits of the fabric in her fists, steadying herself so she wouldn't fall, and he began to stroke her hair. She tried to move in time, to avoid the inevitable, but she wasn't quick enough. As he touched the injured spot, she cried out and flung her head, connecting with his chin. She heard his teeth snap together.

He said, "What is it? What is it, Skip?" and then he caught on. "You got hit."

She nodded, unable to speak yet. Finally the heaving stopped and she rested her head on his shoulder. He maneuvered her to a sofa. "I'll get you some brandy."

"No. And I was right before—I should never have given you any. Oh, God, it hurts. Did it hurt you this much?"

"I don't think so. I'm so tall I'm kind of hard to hit."

"I'm sorry I couldn't call. Someone found me and sent me to Charity. I've been there all night. To tell you the truth, I forgot for a while—that I was on my way to meet you."

"I should have known. I thought it was the damn job—"

"You couldn't have known I got hit."

"I mean—that it was something you couldn't help."

"But if it had been the 'damn job,' that would have been something I couldn't help."

"Look, it's not really that. I was just upset. I guess I was afraid you wouldn't come and I had more invested in seeing you than I thought."

She stared at him, looked for signs of lying or insincerity. He said, "What's wrong?"

"Did you really mean that?"

"Of course. Why not?"

She started to cry again. "It's so sweet." But she wasn't crying out of sentimentality. She was crying for herself, because she wouldn't dare to say a thing like that. He held her again.

"How's your head?" she said finally.

Automatically his hand went to his own injury. He grinned. "Still hurts."

"That's what I was afraid of."

"Listen, Skip, stay with me tonight. Let me take care of you."

"Stay with you?" She wasn't sure what he was asking, and sex seemed out of the question to her.

"Just let me be sure you're all right. Cookie has a million bedrooms—and he's not using any of them tonight."

"Well, there's one thing. I do need to be waked up every hour."

"That's why you came, you bitch. You're just using me."

He sounded furious, and she wasn't thinking fast, but in a moment it came to her that he was joking. She said simply, "Yes."

"Okay, it worked. Do you know Cookie's cousin Camilla?"

"Oh, sure. Little blonde from St. Francisville."

"You can have her room. Cookie left it made up since she was his only Carnival guest who didn't fuck a stranger every night—or at least an old friend. Except for me, I mean—I was at your house with a headache."

"One night anyway," said Skip, and allowed herself to be led up the stairs.

Steve brought her a T-shirt and left her. She heard him brush his teeth, and then heard a tap on her door. He entered without being asked. "You okay?"

"Uh-huh."

In the darkness he crossed over to the bed. "You can use my toothbrush if you like."

"Thanks."

"Good night." He bent to give her a good-night kiss.

As he moved away, kiss accomplished, she seized his face and held it. Without making a decision, she pulled it back toward hers. As they kissed, she let his face go, moved her hands to his shoulders, embracing him in earnest.

He whispered, "Your head. We'll hurt your head."

She didn't answer. She didn't feel the pain as they made love, didn't feel anything except searing need, not so much for him, Steve Steinman, as not to be alone, to be reassured, to do something to prove to herself she was still alive, she was going to be all right. Afterward she hated herself for her neediness and moved to the other side of the bed.

He woke her up in an hour, as promised, and made love to her again, this time his idea. She was sleepy and hurt. He took time to arouse her, to make her want him, to get back what she had taken from him, and she was grateful. He had evened the score. And this time she felt close to him, was glad to be with him rather than just someone.

SIBLINGS

1

Once again staring at the ceiling fan, still for the winter, Marcelle felt the tears sliding down her face. André had pointed to the tomb and said, "Mommy, are they really going to put Poppy in there?" and she wished she hadn't taken him to the funeral. He was too young to know about death, to have to experience it the way grown-ups did. But she didn't want him to be left out. She wanted him to be an active, participating, wanted member of the family, not someone on the fringes. She'd miscalculated this time, though. She'd done it wrong. He had clung to her, and later he had nightmares.

Yesterday, in the end, they hadn't had time for pain perdu, and she had to give him cereal. Today she'd make the pain perdu. Then she'd take him to day care and then she'd go to Uncle Tolliver's to apply for a job.

She sat up, smiling. The tears were gone. She actually felt . . . happy. Wasn't that what this feeling was? It felt light, strange, too good to be true. What was it? Relief that her father's funeral was over? Or could it really be the first tiny green shoots of happiness?

"Mommy! Mommy!" First the terrible clatter of feet, then the squirmy torpedo on her lap.

"André-Pandré! Good morning!"

"Can we do something fun today?"

"Of course. You were such a good boy yesterday. So brave, like a great *big* boy. We can do anything you want."

"Mommy, I'm glad Ma-Mère was there. She held my hand—you know—when they *did* that to Poppy. But she was so sad."

She stroked the small wriggly back. "I know, honey. We were all sad." The tears came back with the word.

"I didn't know you could die before your mother and father."

She held him close and rocked him, crying again, but hoping he wasn't. "Oh, honey, you can't, usually. We just got very very unlucky in our family. It won't happen to you, sweetheart. I promise."

"I wish it would, Mommy. I don't want you to die first."

"Honey, look at me." *Oh, no, don't, I'm crying.* He couldn't, the way she was holding him.

"Mommy, I can't. Let me go."

"Okay, but first pull my hair."

"Pull your hair?"

"Uh-huh. Pull as hard as you can."

He pulled. "Ouch," she said, and released him. "You know why I wanted you to do that?"

"No."

"So you could know I'm really here. And I'm not going

anywhere. Okay? I'm not going to die, and you're not going to die. Do you believe that?"

"I guess so." He wasn't convinced. She could kick herself for taking him to the damned funeral.

You had to use stale bread for pain perdu, and it was never a problem finding any in Marcelle's house. She soaked some slices in milk and eggs, with a little sugar and vanilla, then fried them to a gorgeous gold. Sweeping them triumphantly onto a plate, she called, "André!"

As the small feet pounded, she dusted her creation with cinnamon and powdered sugar. She poured milk as André sat down. Without even looking at his plate, he picked up the glass and drank half the milk. Then, big eyes staring up at her, milk mustache still in place, he said, "Could I have some Freakies?"

"Sweetie, we're having pain perdu this morning."

"But I don't like this stuff."

"You liked it last time I made it."

"Did not."

"André, you like it. Don't you remember?"

"It's yucky."

"Just try a little, okay?"

"No!"

"Come on, just a little." She speared some with a fork and held it to his mouth. He pushed the fork away, dislodging the small piece of French toast, dropping it into his lap.

"My pajamas! You got my pajamas dirty!" He got up and ran from the table, feet pounding back to his room.

I've got to get a carpet for that fucking hallway. She sat down and started to eat the pain perdu herself, but the powdered sugar stuck like sawdust in her throat.

André came back with no pants, wearing only a forest green long-sleeved T-shirt, looking like a cherub. "You can't have Freakies," she said. "You've had them three times this week. How about some shredded wheat?"

"I hate shredded wheat."

"André, won't you just try a little bit of the pain perdu?"

"No!" He took off again.

Should she give him the Freakies? She had to admit that she would have if he hadn't refused the damned pain perdu. But now she'd said no. Could she go back on her no? Wouldn't that give him all the power?

She went into her bedroom and picked out a deep blue sweater to go with tight, tapered black pants. It was hard to know what to wear the week your father died. All black seemed melodramatic, but she didn't feel up to bright colors yet.

By the time she had her makeup on, she had the answer to the breakfast question. She went to find André's jeans. "Let's try these, sport." She helped him step into a pair of under-pants, then the jeans. "You hungry?"

"I want Freakies!"

"How about an Egg McMuffin?"

"Oh, boy! Can we really?"

"Uh-huh."

"And then what? Can we go to the zoo?"

"Sweetie, I have to be somewhere this morning." *I wish.*

"You said we could do something fun!"

Oh, God, she had said that. She'd completely forgotten she had other plans—it was so goddamn rare. "I know I did, sweetie. I just forgot I had to do this other thing. Tomorrow we'll go to the zoo. I promise."

Without warning, the little face twisted and collapsed. He threw his arms around her legs, screaming. "You promised! You promised!"

"André, for heaven's sake, we'll do it tomorrow." She tried to pry the curled fingers away, but André held tight.

"Mommy, you promised!"

Fury rose up in her. Why couldn't he let her be, today of all days? Why did he have to pick this one to be clingy? The only day in his short life that she'd actually had something to do other than screw?

She pulled him off her, tugging hard, all the gentleness used up. She practically dragged him to the car, drove him to the nearest McDonald's, and left him screaming while she got his Egg McMuffin. She thrust the McDonald's bag into the hands of the day-care attendant. "When he stops crying, give him this, will you? He hasn't had breakfast."

She left André with his hands outstretched, screaming, "Mommy! Mommy!" as if he was panicked within an inch of his life.

She hadn't gone two blocks before she thought, I wonder if they have a microwave? His breakfast'll be cold. Should she stop somewhere and get him a doughnut? No. She couldn't go back there—he'd never let her get away. Why did he have to behave this way? Why? Today, of all days? It was as if he knew she was about to get a job—to do something that would take her away from him. He could be so devious sometimes. But it wouldn't work—she was going to do what she had to anyway. He couldn't stop her.

The tight feeling in her throat that had been constricting a little more by the second had developed into a hard knot of pain. Suddenly she knew what was about to happen and she pulled over just in time. Sobs poured out of her—great, wracking sobs that convulsed her body.

When she could drive again, she went home, repaired her makeup, and drove purposefully toward the Quarter, amazed at her own resolve.

Uncle Tolliver looked haggard and rumpled, not quite his dapper self. *But none of us are ourselves this week.* She wondered if the makeup had really disguised the swelling around her eyes.

She tried her best, widest (and today, phoniest) smile. "Hello, Uncle Tolliver."

"What are you doing here?" His face was gray and his

shoulders slumped forward, making his chest hollow in a way Marcelle had never noticed before.

"I—uh—gosh, you don't seem glad to see me."

"I'm a little busy, that's all."

Marcelle glanced quickly around, confused. There was only one other person in the shop, a man with his back to them, fingering some china. "Maybe I should come back another time."

"No, honey. What is it?" He looked suddenly alert. "Your mama's all right?"

"Fine." She didn't know that. She hadn't called Bitty.

"Does Henry need something?" He rubbed his head, preoccupied, intimidating.

"No. It's nothing. I'll come back." Horribly embarrassed, she started to leave, knowing she wouldn't come back; she'd never have the nerve. She had thought he'd receive her warmly, take her in the back, give her tea, sit her down for a chat.

He called her back. "Marcelle, what is it, honey?" His voice was irritated, the voice parents use with tiresome children.

She had her back to him now, and the male shopper had come into focus—he was Dulles Moorehead, with whom she'd spent a hideous night of frustrated passion about three months ago. She could see Dulles's pathetic penis now, pink and shriveled on his blubbery belly. Marcelle prided herself on arousal techniques—a person who slept with as many drunks as she did had had to learn quite a few—but Dulles proved impervious to her best efforts, and only his snoring had persuaded her to give up.

The night with Dulles may have been the worst in her career as a wild creature of the night—in the top ten anyway. There was the time Conley Butterfield had called her tarantula cunt, and the encounter with the two guys from Houma who thought she was going to take them both on. And of course Hilly Jordan throwing up in her bed. But the memory of Dulles's worthless anatomy had more than once passed unhappily into her consciousness, sometimes with titles: "Moby's Dick," "Watermelon With Worm," "Tadpole on a Field of White." She had actually thought of trying to paint it, so vivid was it, and so poignant, it seemed to her. But she could not paint, and remembering that, she recalled, to her surprise, how much she wanted the thing she had come for. It was like her at this point to blur it out, lose track of what she wanted, go into that beloved numbed-out state she lived in.

That wasn't happening now, she didn't know why. She felt alert, alive, much more so than was comfortable. She felt a sudden tension in her lower belly and a quickening in her genitals, a concrete, sexual excitement that she knew was desire, need. She felt her resolve return, go coursing through her like a vitamin.

She could walk forward, to Dulles Moorehead, metaphor for impotence, and for her life. Or she could turn back to Uncle Tolliver and ask for what she wanted and needed more than anything she could think of. In that instant, it all seemed clear as an alpine lake.

"Uncle Tolliver, I want to ask you a favor." She heard her voice, fresh, crisp, optimistic. "I mean, not a favor. I really think I could be an asset to you."

He looked as if he was in pain, as if he wished he were anywhere but here. But Marcelle wasn't about to stop now. She heard her own voice start to sell herself, and the sound was so novel she felt detached from it. But not from the desire. She was firmly, single-mindedly, fixed on that right now. She was *wanting* in a naked, abandoned way that felt like destiny. "I'd like to help you in the shop, Uncle Tolliver. You know, I was a docent at the museum for a few months and I've had some art appreciation courses. I thought I could take some more . . . I'll do anything to learn the business. I just . . . want a chance." She was speaking in little bursts, running out of breath, because now fear had started to replace desire. Her heart fluttered, her throat had started to close.

"Are you asking me for a *job?*" He practically yelled. He sounded furious.

Too intimidated to answer, she managed only a nod.

"Marcelle, I can't deal with this now." He turned and disappeared into the bowels of the shop.

"Marcelle? Marcelle, is that you?" Dulles Moorehead was headed toward her, about to kiss her on the cheek.

She winced only slightly as he did so, pulling herself together, becoming once more the perfectly oiled little manners machine she had been all her years with Bitty and Chauncey. "Hey, Dulles. How're you doing?"

He held both her hands in an utterly fake gesture of sympathy. "I'm so sorry about your daddy."

"Thanks, Dulles. It was a shock to all of us." Hating the well-bred android mouthing the expected clichés.

"What are you doing with yourself, Marcelle?"

"Oh, same old thing, you know how it is, Dulles. How's Amy?" Amy was his wife.

"She's fine. Just fine." His chins wobbled as he widened his phony smile. His little pig eyes fixed hers. He whispered, "I'd like to see you again. Sometime when I'm not so drunk."

"We'll just have to see about that." This line delivered with a spirited toss of the head; now she was a fragrant magnolia machine. "Bye now."

She undulated out, as the role required, and once on the sidewalk made a face. "Ichhhh!" she said aloud, causing a tourist couple in matching canvas hats to give her a wide berth.

Dulles had flipped her back into neutral, into the automatic mode she'd run on during the wake and funeral—during most of her life—but it didn't last. By the time she reached her car, she was deep in depression.

Instinctively, she knew what she needed to soothe it—

water. She drove to the West End, out onto the pier, and watched the wind churn the lake. It was overcast again, and very windy, so that waves were regularly smacking the retaining wall, each time sending up an exuberant surge of spray. Every time a wave hit, Marcelle jumped a little, excited; it was something else getting hit, not she.

She was horribly embarrassed at having asked for something so obviously out of the question that it had actually made Tolliver angry. She honestly hadn't known she was quite as hopeless as his reaction indicated, and the knowledge was paralyzing. What was the point of taking courses? Of hoping for anything of her own? Clearly she wasn't going to get it, and she might as well live off her trust fund and call it a day.

That was probably the long and short of it, but she felt an overwhelming bewilderment too. Uncle Tolliver had never treated her so perfunctorily. Never. But of course she'd never asked him for anything. Had she been invisible to him too?

"Marcelle, could you get Tom Sawyer for us? It's time for Henry's chapter."

Bitty read to Henry every night, though he was the older one, while Marcelle would play on the floor with her dolls, listening, pretending she didn't care. She was mixed up about the painkiller Tom gave the cat. Surely he didn't do it out of meanness and yet, that was what the story made it sound like.

"Was the kitty sick?" she asked.

Henry said, "This is my book. *You* don't get to listen to it."

Bitty had gone on reading, as if she hadn't asked the question.

She didn't know what she was doing. She didn't have any idea. But I do. And my child is never going to feel like that. Never!

She would rather die today than go to her grave knowing she had ignored her child the way Bitty had, hadn't been any better a mother than her own mother, hadn't learned a damn thing by a bad example. Rather die? She'd rather André die.

He was the most important thing in her life and she wasn't going to forget it, ever again, even for a moment. The hell with Tolliver, and the hell with her stupid idea. As she backed up and turned around, she mentally thanked the lake for its restorative powers.

She felt wonderful, liberated, by the time she got back to the day-care center. Her step was light, she was smiling. André and another boy were building a giant fort with Leggos.

"André? Mommy's back."

"Hi, Mom. I'm building a fort." He looked up at her, then at his fort, showing off.

"I see, sweetheart. Guess what? Mommy's got the rest of the day free. We can go to the zoo now."

André stared at the floor, looking heartbroken. Was he still angry with her?

"André, I'm sorry we couldn't go this morning. But we can go now. We'll have just as much fun, I promise. Guess what, honey, we can take a boat. There's a real boat that sails down the river right to the zoo."

It would mean driving downtown again, all the way to Riverwalk, but she owed that to André after walking out on him.

André still stared at the floor. "Don't want to go now."

"Of course you do, honey. They have white alligators, darlin'—baby ones that somebody found in a bayou. Hardly any kids in the world have ever seen a white alligator, and you can see a whole bunch of them."

André didn't answer. She took his wrist as a signal he should come with her. He didn't rise. He shouted, "No!"

"André, come on!"

"No!"

She pulled him up now, and saw that he was crying. "Honey, please don't yell at Mommy." She didn't deserve to be yelled at. She was being a good mother now. This morning she'd been a bad mother, but how much did André have to punish her for that?

He stood there sobbing, looking as if he'd just been told his daddy was going off to war. She picked him up and carried him out to the car.

2

"Hollandaise *and* creamed spinach?"

"Yes ma'am."

The woman wrinkled her face up.

Her husband said, "Oh, try it, Marilyn. Be adventurous for once."

They had New York accents that sounded like a fingernail on a blackboard in the sweet southern morning.

"The soft-shelled crab wasn't enough?" She turned to Henry. "The thing looked like a giant spider. Right on the plate. You wouldn't believe how disgusting . . ."

He forced a smile. "Perhaps Madame would prefer an omelet?" He said "Modomme" instead of "Maddum"—the tips were bigger that way. Sometimes he even did a phony French accent.

"Well, *I'll* have the Eggs Sardou," said the husband, smug in his solitary adventurousness.

"You'll have a triple bypass too." To Henry, "Could I just get some fresh fruit?"

You don't come to Brennan's for fresh fruit, idiot. You come to clog your arteries and die.

He had dreamed of death last night. He was in the cemetery again, and they were going to open the family vault. Chauncey was already in there, it wasn't for Chauncey. It was for Bitty. Even this morning, in the bustle of the restaurant, he felt the shroud of sadness from the dream drop over him again. The casket was there, like Chauncey's, ready to be entombed. He couldn't stand it. He wasn't going to let them bury Bitty. He was going to save her, take her away. He

190

opened the casket to get her out and saw that it was all right. It wasn't Bitty in there but himself.

He'd been afraid he was going to continue missing Chauncey, be sorry he was dead after all. But the feeling was gone now. The dream showed it. Chauncey was dead in the dream, and yet it didn't matter. It didn't matter at all, had nothing to do with the plot, and Chauncey had nothing to do with their lives anymore.

"Watch it, son!" Another waiter, carrying a tray full of Ramos fizzes, sidestepped him skillfully.

At the funeral he felt he needed to be with Bitty and had stuck to her like an old retainer. To his regret, he'd only briefly been able to see the only relatives he could stand besides his mother—his paternal grandparents, Poppoo and Mommoo. Or Pa-Père and Ma-Mère, as stupid Marcelle, eternal Doris Do-Right, still called them. As soon as he was old enough to think of it, Henry had Anglicized the nicknames, which seemed too fancy and not at all to fit his down-to-earth grandparents. The names had been Chauncey's idea, a salute to the St. Amant heritage, for once.

Before Henry and Marcelle were born, Bitty's mother, Merrie Mac Mayhew, had inherited a friendly old house in Covington, on the Bogue Falaya River, large enough to accommodate the rambunctious and numerous MacDuff clan in the sticky summer months. Bitty had spent summers there as a child, and after Merrie Mac died, her father gave it to her. Bitty and Henry and Marcelle spent most of every summer there, leaving Chauncey to work at the bank. He joined them on weekends, and every now and then Geegaw, Henry's Grandfather Mayhew, did as well. Mommoo and Poppoo were there most of the time.

Henry had loved those summers. In those days, as soon as you got off the causeway you were in the woods. Covington was a place of pines and sycamores and magnolias bigger than you could imagine, so that standing outside was like being in a high-ceilinged, earth-smelling room. Merrie Mac's house creaked with character and old age. It had a pointed roof, front porch with swing, side yard, and sleeping porch with screens.

One day Henry had said: "Want to go down to the river, Poppoo?"

His grandfather answered without missing a beat: "Sure, Kiddoo." From that time on, neither of them called the other anything else.

Remembering Poppoo and Mommoo, Henry slammed an empty tray down, drawing stares from his colleagues. What made him angry was that Chauncey had no excuse for being the kind of father he was. Poppoo and Mommoo were the salt of the earth, polar opposites of anyone else he knew. Simple folk. Poppoo was an accountant, Mommoo just a grandma. Poppoo spent every day with Henry while Mommoo cooked and Bitty mooned about. Mommoo would make a big pot of gumbo, or boil up some shrimp and they would all eat outside. Every night was a picnic; every day was peaceful as the river itself.

Poppoo was a big, dark, gentle man who would fish all day and bring his prizes back to Bitty as if they were piscine keys to heaven. Both of them adored her, Mommoo and Poppoo, and adored Chauncey too.

Poppoo would say, "How are things at the bank, Chauncey? Shaping them up over there?"

"Things are fine, Dad," Chauncey would answer, and Poppoo would address someone else, "Chauncey's a golden boy, the boy with everything. He's a leader, always was. Always had the best grades, always the best in sports."

Chauncey would smile. "I knew I'd better be."

Poppoo would cuff him on the arm and they'd both laugh. Poppoo treated Chauncey like a prince, made him feel like a king who could conquer the world. All summer Poppoo would tell stories about his golden son, the apple of his eye.

"We had this ol' worthless Irish setter named Murphy, used to do nothin' but come in the house and scratch fleas all day.

Chauncey wadn't but a little fella, hardly in the first grade, when he brings home this picture he drew of ol' Murphy. I swear, I couldn't believe a six-year-old had done it—looked like a professional piece of work it was so good. But I didn't let on 'cause I had me a plan. I said, 'Chauncey, you know, that dudn't quite look like ol' Murf to me. You gotta show him scratchin'. That dog's always got a flea.' Little fella looks up at me and says, just as serious as you please, 'Daddy, where do you think I should put the flea?'

"I say, 'Right there. Right there behind the left ear.' Little fella goes away. When he comes back he's got a whole new picture and, I swear that dog's come *alive*. Chauncey's got his hind leg up behind his ear, looks like it's goin' about a mile a minute. So I say, 'Chauncey, that's so good I want to borrow it, take it down to my office, can I do that?' Chauncey says, 'Of course, Daddy.'

"He didn't know it, but I been readin' in the paper about a contest for a scholarship at this art school a lady was startin' in the Quarter. So I just entered the picture and guess what, it came in second!'"

Bitty, to whom Poppoo was telling the story, made appropriate noises, and then Poppoo said, "I told him, Chauncey, you'll just have to do better next time. He said, 'But, Daddy, I don't want to go to art school.' I said, 'Sure you do,' and you know what? Next year I did it again. I entered the contest without tellin', and that year he won." He stopped and chuckled. "That Chauncey. Always had to be number one. Nothin' else was gonna do for my boy."

He let a moment go by and then he said, "Turned out he loved that art school. Didn't you, boy?"

Chauncey said, "I don't remember, Dad."

Henry flew into a fury every time he thought of the story. He too had brought home a drawing of a dog and Chauncey had said, "Looks like a cat, son. Why don't you make its ears longer?" Henry was too humiliated ever to show him another picture.

He picked up the Eggs Sardou and the fruit for the New York couple. The fruit wasn't the fresh stuff the woman had asked for. He had talked Modomme into Bananas Foster, which she was going to love, and which would put at least two pounds on her and which would get him twice the tip he could expect for an unignited breakfast. He hoped he could pull himself together enough to do the flambé.

As he lit the rum, Modomme's eyes lingered lovingly on him, approving, as if he were her own grandson; she was about Mommoo's age, and she had gray hair as well (though it was sleekly cut instead of frizzed with a home perm).

Henry made a resolution to call Mommoo and Poppoo, to see them this week. Chauncey had snubbed them. He never invited them anywhere, instead spending his time courting Bitty's horrible parents. Henry wished they hadn't had to suffer for Chauncey's ambition. And that went double for someone else he wished he could call. For LaBelle, the woman Chauncey had treated more ruthlessly even than himself or Bitty or his parents.

He poured the rum on the bananas. *"Bon appétit,"* he told the New Yorkers.

REBELLIONS

1

Cross, head throbbing, feeling in no shape to work, Skip put on work clothes—a sweater and the beige skirt. At least the ugly shoes went with the damned outfit.

Her romantic mood had faded in the harsh light of the morning (which wasn't overcast for once), as Steve set pancakes before her and tried to make her eat them. She had asked him to take her home, but he wouldn't until he had fed her. Pushy, pushy, pushy.

Staring at the doughy discs, she thought nostalgically of Claude at the Abbey. Perhaps she simply wasn't cut out for domesticity. She took a bite and forced herself to swallow. Or perhaps this wasn't the guy for her.

She didn't trust him in daylight. He had waked up, rolled over and said, "Stay with me today."

"I have to work."

"Take me with you."

Take him with her! She was a police officer. "You know I can't do that."

"Why not?"

"Would you want me with you while you were filming?"

"Sure. I'd film you." He smoothed her eyebrow with a forefinger.

"I'm a cop, Steve. I can't do it."

"Can't do what?"

"Can't endanger a civilian. Can't let myself get distracted. Can't treat this case trivially. It isn't a movie, it's real life." She hated the way she sounded.

He did too, if the Bronx cheer he emitted was any indication.

"Sorry, I just can't do it, that's all."

"I understand."

She wasn't sure he did, though, or he wouldn't have been so insistent. He wasn't treating her seriously as a professional. She wondered again if it was just her job—the information she could give him, the color—he was interested in and not really her at all.

Come on, Skip. You started this, not him.

Maybe she was just in a bad mood because of what she had to do this morning. Putting it off as long as possible, she stopped first and got Calvin Hogue's rap sheet. Good—the guy looked like a small-time dealer. That might give her some leverage.

She dragged herself onto the elevator and went up to see Duby.

"Skip. Sit down. Are you okay?"

She shrugged. "Just a concussion. Nothing time won't take care of."

"The guys think the St. Amant killer whacked you—they think you know who it is."

"I didn't know they gave me that much credit."

He waved a hand. "Ahhh, they're just paranoid."

"I think I do know something. There's a woman involved in this, and I can't find her."

She told him everything she knew about LaBelle. When she was done, his expression didn't change. He didn't venture an opinion, he didn't give Skip a back pat. He said, "Are you well enough to work?"

"Of course." Though she wasn't so sure.

"Find her."

"I'm doing my best."

"Look, she has to go home sometime. Go back to her apartment and stake it out. Just stay there till you see her go in. It's that simple."

Not so simple for a white woman, she wanted to say, but thought that would sound whiny and unprofessional.

She said, "Alone?"

He nodded.

"Are you going to staff this around the clock?"

"How many officers do you think I've got, goddamnit?"

A one-person stakeout was very unusual. But Duby's irritation at her second question had told her what was behind it—it wasn't a matter of being short-staffed. It was a matter of pleasing the chief and doing something with her, even something Duby thought unimportant. She didn't care. Except for the fact that she found stakeouts a form of hell, there was nothing she'd rather be doing if it meant finding LaBelle.

She went into homicide to look for Tarantino—to have the promised talk with him. Neither he nor O'Rourke was there, which was fine with her. Her head hurt too much to talk. She left Joe a note.

She wanted to get to Tremé as soon as possible, on the off chance that LaBelle was still there, sleeping after a hard night plying her trade. But the way Skip's luck had been running, she didn't think she would be. So she went home first and changed into jeans, dark sweater and a blue bandanna. She'd still look white and alien, but less like an easy target for rape or robbery.

Neither LaBelle nor Calvin Hogue answered her ring. La-Belle's apartment was on the first floor, the center right one, it looked like. She slipped to the right side of the building. Curtains, shades, blinds, or pinned-up sheets covered every window of the first floor—apparently privacy was much prized in this neighborhood. The center apartment had rice-paper curtains, one with a tiny tear near the bottom, about the size of a nickel. Skip found two bricks to stand on and hoisted herself up. If this was LaBelle's apartment, at least she hadn't flown the coop. Skip looked into a neat bedroom furnished with a platform bed, made up; '30s-style dresser; and the usual lamps and tables. A sweater lay on the bed, as if LaBelle had been dressing, changed her mind at the last minute, and rushed out still pulling on whatever garment she'd chosen instead.

Skip went back to North Villere. The burned-out house was going to have to be her surveillance post. But it was boarded up and removing the boards was bound to draw attention. She circled it, hoping to find a window that couldn't be seen from the street. When she found it, it was obvious someone had been there before her. Looking in, she saw they were still there—three teenage kids dividing up a haul of ones and fives. Shit! They'd probably just knocked over the corner bar. She could call for backup, but that would draw attention she didn't need.

Through the window she said, "Hey, Frito banditos—where'd you get the green stuff?"

They looked up slowly, cool and aloof as cats. One of them had on an orange T-shirt. He said, "We run a stud service, mama. You want a poke?"

She held up her badge, "Try again, stud."

"Uh—lemonade stand?"

His two buddies collapsed in giggles.

"Shut up!"

Silence.

"What are your names?"

"James Guyton."

"Albert Tree."

Orange-shirt said, "Ralph Leonard."

"James. How much money is that?"

James wore a baseball hat turned backwards. He looked at the floor like the baby he still was. "Eighty-fi' dollar."

"Where'd you get it?"

"We sold somethin'."

"What?"

"Somethin'."

She yelled, "What, goddamnit?"

Ralph said, "Keep quiet, James." He started to walk toward Skip, who was leaning in the window. She pointed her gun. "Freeze."

Ralph stopped and very slowly put his hands up. "Hey. I wadn't gon' do nothin'."

"Stand back.

"Okay, who's got some ID?"

James Guyton threw her a driver's license. "Good. You still live at this address?" He nodded. She put the license in her pocket. "Okay, guys, here's the deal. You're not going to jail, and you're keeping the money. If you stole it, mail it back. You've got three days. If I hear about any $85 robbery in this neighborhood and the money doesn't get returned, I'm coming after you. Understand?"

They nodded, mystified but smart enough to humor an oversized woman with a gun. "If I don't hear anything, I mail the license back. That's what I'm doing for you. Now here's what you're doing for me. Kick out that window over there, leave through it, and don't come back."

"Then what?" said Albert Tree.

"Behave yourselves and don't get in any more trouble."

Ralph asked, "That's it?"

"That's it."

Without stopping for further conversation, they followed instructions. The window she made them kick out had been boarded up and now provided a pretty fair view of LaBelle's building. Sitting on the floor across the room, chin tilted up, she could just see the door. The scorched smell of the place was god-awful.

She tried sitting with legs folded, legs jack-knifed, in the lotus position, and hugging her knees. She stretched, paced and did toe touches. She watched a near-violent domestic argument and what could only have been a drug deal. She saw three fairly young children go into the building and one older man. She would have killed for a Coke. After a while, the rumblings of her stomach were louder than the street noise.

The need to urinate was what finally made her leave. She knew a million stories about stakeouts that had gone awry when the cop looked away long enough to tie his shoe or something; she also knew what her orders were. But she was damned if she was going to drop her jeans and pee in a corner of a burned-out house.

While she was out she had a hamburger and came back ready for another few hours of hell. First she looked in La-Belle's window, just to make sure she hadn't returned. The sweater was still on the bed. She rang the bell, got no answer, and rang Calvin Hogue's. A male voice came over the intercom. "Yeah?"

"Police," she said.

The man who met her at the door was forty-ish, wearing an undershirt and khaki pants. He had a scar on his right cheek and eyes with yellow whites.

"Jeweldean Sanders tells me you know LaBelle Doucette."

"Know her to see her, tha's all. She pay the rent on time."

"Has she lived here long?"

"Six months, maybe. She travel a lot, though. She be gone a lot anyway. I think she works conventions, tell you the truth."

"She must be doing well."

He shrugged. "She still live in this dump."

"Does she ever have any visitors?"

"Nooo-ho, indeed. Not Miss LaBelle Doucette. She no sooner bring a john here than ax the guv'nor to tea. Miss LaBelle—she got a *Uptown* clientele."

"I wasn't thinking of johns. I was thinking of women—a sister or friend maybe."

"Uh-uh. Nobody but the one person she want to see. He sell her what she need."

"Junk?"

Hogue nodded. "Guess tha's why she still live here. Cain't seem to get out of that hole she in."

"You friends with her?"

He thought about it, finally shrugged. "Not specially."

"Good. Then you won't tell her I'm looking for her."

"Don't even know when she gettin' back. Hadn't been around for two–three weeks."

"Two or three weeks!"

"At least. She do that sometime. Goes for weeks at a time."

"You know where she goes?"

"I tol' you. I think she works conventions. Maybe goes to Atlanta, Dallas—stays there awhile." He shrugged. "Maybe jus' Baton Rouge."

Skip was thinking. No way was she going to wait around for LaBelle to get back from a trip. "Listen, I took a look at your rap sheet today. You could use a friend like me."

"Oh, yeah? What you gon' do for me?"

"I don't know. Depends on what you need. Like if you got arrested again, maybe I could say you're a good guy, helped me out on a case. Maybe I could come up with some money if you'd rather have that."

He turned down the corners of his mouth like a pouting child. "I ain't no snitch."

"You don't have to snitch on anybody. Just let me know when LaBelle gets home, that's all. She's no friend of yours, right? And you probably know what she did to Jeweldean. She's not a nice woman, Calvin."

"Hey, now you got somethin', speakin' of Jeweldean. You get me a freebie?"

"Consider it done." If Jeweldean wouldn't donate it, she could always pay for it herself.

She gave Hogue her number, took his, and left feeling as if she'd pulled off a fabulous scam. She could get used to this working alone. There was nobody to find out how you operated.

2

"Mr. Albert, could you spare us a few moments?" It was the dark one who spoke, the friendly one.

I couldn't spare you a nickel if you were starving. Go away and leave us all in peace.

"Hello, Inspector—Officer—"

"Call us Joe and Frank. Joe Tarantino and Frank O'Rourke." He remembered them from the Boston Club, but hazily. He had known they'd be around, but he hadn't expected Marcelle. She'd unsettled him and he wasn't ready for these two.

"How're you doing with the case? Any leads?" He'd heard the words on television.

"We think we're getting close, but we need you to answer a few questions for us."

"I'll be glad to do whatever I can." He hoped he could pull this off. He'd blown it with Marcelle.

"About that bunting on your balcony—you said you didn't put it there."

"I never saw it before."

"Can you think of any reason the killer wanted it there?"

He let a moment or two go by, as if he were thinking. "None," he said. He hoped his eye wasn't twitching; it felt as if it was.

"Mr. Albert," said the other one, the good-looking blond. "You said you didn't leave the party on Tuesday."

Tuesday. Mardi Gras, they meant. The party at the Boston Club. "That's right," he said.

"Well, Mr. Albert, we were wondering if you went out after all and maybe you just forgot about it."

"With all due respect, officer, it was only two days ago."

"You were seen leaving the club, sir."

Tolliver covered his face with a hand. What to do with this one? "Seen leaving the club?"

"Yessir."

"May I ask by whom?"

The fat man pulled out a notebook and consulted it. "A Mrs.—uh—Kerlin. Teata Kerlin."

"Tea-Ta."

"Sir?"

"Tea. Ta. Not Teata. Her older sister gave her the name, but I'm surprised anyone remembers that part; Deeanna's been dead ten or twelve years. Tea-Ta must be, oh, seventy-five by now." And still a beauty too. White hair done up in what used to be called a chignon—surely it was called something else now, but maybe not, considering Tea-Ta wore the hairdo exactly as it had been worn thirty years ago. She'd married an Irishman, but Tea-Ta was very much the Creole aristocrat, with a lot of Spanish in her. She'd have mooned the crowds from the Boston Club balcony before she'd have had a nose job, and her beak was the size of a modest penis. It was magnificent on her, with her hair like that, and those cheekbones. That day, Mardi Gras, she'd been wearing mauve lace . . . "Yes. I did see Tea-Ta. It's coming back to me now."

"What time was that, sir?"

203

"Time? I don't know, really. Before the parade. Forgive me; before the murder." He straightened his shoulders, conscious of putting up a brave front. Tea-Ta had said, "Leaving, Tolliver?" But he couldn't speak right then.

"She was just coming in. I remember it now."

"You were on your way out?"

"Yes."

"Where did you go, sir?"

"I had a headache. I went to get my pills."

"And did you get them?"

The pills were at the apartment. "No. The crowds were murder."

"Where were your pills?"

"In my car."

"We understood you drove down with Mrs. St. Amant."

He was sweating; his head was starting to hurt. "In her car, I mean. I left them in the glove compartment. But I never found the car."

"You never found it, sir? You mean it wasn't where she parked it?"

He opened his palms. "I never got there, you see. The crowds were so thick I couldn't get through them."

"The murderer got through them."

What was he supposed to say to that? "I wasn't feeling well that day."

The blond spoke again. "One last thing, Mr. Albert. Do you have a key to Mrs. St. Amant's car?"

"Why, no. Why do you ask?"

"How did you plan to get your pills?"

He leaned his chin in his hand. "Well, I couldn't have gotten them, could I? I see what you're saying." He paused a moment and then shrugged mightily, hoping he seemed convincing. "I wasn't thinking clearly." He tapped his head. "The headache."

"Were you drinking a lot, Mr. Albert?"

"No, of course not."

The blond said, "You know, this story's pretty damn thin.

First you say you didn't leave the place, then you say you did, but you didn't do what you left to do, and then you say you couldn't have done it anyway."

The dark fat one plucked at his sleeve. "Frank. Take it easy."

"I wonder if you could leave now?" said Tolliver. "I think I've answered all the questions I can."

He turned and went to the back of his shop—why, he wasn't sure. Just to get away. He jumped, hearing a noise behind him. But it was only someone coming in. Every little thing startled him lately.

Skip Langdon, of all unwelcome people, was standing in the middle of the place, next to a display of porcelains, looking exactly like the proverbial bull in a china shop. What an unfeminine woman she was! Particularly in those awful jeans that made her hips and thighs look like the foothills of a small mountain range. Pretty face, though. If she'd lose thirty pounds and cut that hair . . .

What the hell was she doing here anyway? This was a girl who'd known the St. Amants from the day she was born—they'd probably gone to her christening. Her father had taken care of the whole family all her young life, and before that even. Why, he'd been Merrie Mac's doctor after his partner died—old Dr. Eustace. Why couldn't this woman, of all people, leave them alone?

"Hey, Mr. Albert."

"Skip." He hoped he sounded unwelcoming.

She came closer. "Is something wrong? You okay?"

"Not really. Two of your colleagues just left."

"Oh. Tarantino and O'Rourke. Tell me, was the blond surly and the other one kind of friendly?"

"You've met the gentlemen."

"That O'Rourke hates me. I just wondered how he is with other people."

"Like he took police lessons from TV." That got a smile out

of her. "Darlin', you're not here for the same thing, are you? Ol' Tolliver's 'bout been through it."

"Well, I was just wondering . . ."

"You people have got to stop this." He was shaking his head like an old man, couldn't stop. "This is too hard . . . on me, on Henry, and specially on Bitty. You know how fragile she is, darlin'. You people just can't go on with this.

"We can't take much more, especially from you. You ought to be ashamed of yourself. A girl from a good family, father who's taken care of everyone in the city for the last quarter-century, mother who's done such good work for so long. You could have done anything you wanted. What on earth do you get out of being a policewoman? Snooping around, dogging people . . . really, Skip, it just doesn't make sense. . . ."

He had a dim feeling, though, a funny feeling he shouldn't be doing this, that he was somehow out of line. But out of line in what way? Everything he said was perfectly true. The *girl* was out of line. And he was just telling her; somebody had to. That social-climbing quack of a father she had obviously couldn't do a thing with her.

"Look, I can take this. I've taken a lot in my life and I can probably take a lot more. But Bitty! Poor little Bitty! You know what she's like, how she's been ever since she lost the baby. It's just not right."

"Baby? Bitty had a miscarriage?"

"No, no, no. The *baby*. You remember."

"I don't really think I do."

"But everyone knows about it." Didn't they? Or was his life so intertwined with those of the St. Amants that he thought everyone was privy to every moment of their existence, like characters on "Dynasty"? "The third child," he said, "that came after Marcelle and that died soon after she was born. That's when Bitty started drinking."

"I see. You're really close to them, aren't you?"

"About as close as you can get and not be a blood relative."

A lot closer than Chauncey's parents; he hated them, and Bitty had told Tolliver why.

"Did you know Chauncey's former secretary, Stelly Villere?"

He felt calmer now. The pill must be working. But he didn't like the turn this was taking. "Yes. Everyone did." There he went with the "everyone" stuff again. He sounded like a small-town gossip.

"I understand Chauncey was involved with her."

"I wouldn't know about that."

"Do you know why she left?"

Because Chauncey was such a bastard to her.

"I assumed she left to take a better job." *Motherhood's a better job, isn't it?*

"Oh? Do you know where?"

"No idea."

"I hear Chauncey made a practice of getting involved with all his secretaries."

"You've certainly had your pretty ears open." There. That sounded more like him, the charming Tolliver all the ladies liked.

"What about prostitutes?"

"I beg your pardon?"

"Did he get involved with prostitutes?"

"Where on earth did you hear that one?"

"Tolliver, I really don't understand you. You talk about what 'everyone' knows so long as it isn't damaging to your precious Chauncey. You know as well as I do that 'everyone' knows about the secretaries. But I'll tell you something you may not know—Chauncey *was* involved with a prostitute. She came once to his house and once to his office. On both occasions she seemed extremely angry with him. I think it's a fair assumption he was killed by someone who was extremely angry with him, don't you?"

Oh, God, she knows about LaBelle!

She put a hand on his, suddenly the girl he'd known all her life. She spoke softly. "You can't protect him now, Tolliver. Help me find the killer."

He tempered his next speech to suit her new mood. "Skip, don't you think I want to? Don't you think I'd do anything to help you? Honey, I'm really sorry I was so defensive with you. It's true what you said. Of course he was involved with Stelly and Sheree and every secretary he ever had. 'Everybody' does know that. But prostitutes! That's a whole other thing."

"Not streetwalkers. Maybe I didn't make myself clear. This girl is more like a call girl. Gorgeous, I'm told. Probably caters to a pretty good clientele."

He shrugged. "I don't know a thing about it, honey. You know, frankly, I think the murder was politically motivated—always have. He had enemies on both sides of the fence, and he was powerful enough—"

"Tolliver, I've got to find out who this woman was. Could she have been someone he knew outside her professional life?"

"Honey, how should I know? I don't know a thing about her."

"She'd be black, for openers. Her name's LaBelle Doucette. Does that ring a bell?" He shook his head.

She described the woman. "Ever seen her?"

"Never."

"Think way, way back. Could she be somebody you might have seen with Stelly?"

"I don't *think* so. Stelly's been gone a long time." He shook his head and flailed his hands, aware that he was dithering.

REACTIONS

1

One step at a time. Bitty held tightly to the banister and moved slowly. Wasn't that what they said in AA? No, but it was close. It was days they talked about. Lately Bitty had had many days without alcohol, and she hoped to God she'd never have to have another one. This morning she'd had a Mimosa for breakfast, and then another, and another still. She would have liked a Ramos fizz, but she wasn't up to fixing it, and she wasn't about to ask Yvonne, who worked for her now and who was the only reason Tolliver and Henry could be induced to go home. They hadn't wanted to leave her, and she loved them for that, but she needed to be alone for a while. To drink herself to sleep and then to sleep. And to get up and cry and drink and sleep again.

After her morning Mimosas, she'd slept. It was getting on toward midafternoon now and she knew she ought to have lunch, but that was the last thing on her mind. She wanted wine. Lovely chilled white wine. And she wanted it fast. The pain engulfed her, imprisoned her, made her a thrashing fish in a net. She stumbled, caught herself, and saw a tear fall on her hand, white as it pressed against the banister.

"Miz St. Amant?"

"Yes, Yvonne."

"That you? You up?" Yvonne came into the foyer, wiping her hands on a tea towel.

Bitty stopped, unwilling to let her see how unsteady she was. "I was just coming down for some lunch."

"Lemme h'ep you." Yvonne must have weighed two-fifty. Having her help you was like walking with a pillow for support. "Those l'il shoes you got on slippery on these stairs."

"Yes," said Bitty, perfectly aware of the farce they were playing out.

Yvonne leaned into Bitty's ear as Bitty transferred her weight. "Young lady from the po-lice here to see you. I tol' her you were sleepin', but she say she wait. I could take you back upstairs real quick, say you felt faint or somethin'."

But it was too late. Skip Langdon stood in the foyer, apparently having followed Yvonne to the stairs.

"Hey, Mrs. St. Amant. I won't stay but a minute."

A black plume of despair spiraled through Bitty's body, entering at the top of the head, settling in the stomach as numbness. It wasn't so bad; she could handle it. It was even rather like the oblivion she had been about to get in another way. It freed her from the feelings and made it possible to cope. Only briefly did she regret the sweatsuit in which she'd been sleeping. At least she had combed her hair.

"Hello, Skip. I was just coming down for lunch."

"Really, a minute's all I need."

"Thank you, Yvonne," said Bitty as they reached the ground floor. She led Skip into the living room.

Skip said, "I won't even sit down. I just had a little question for you. I'm working on a timetable for the day of the murder." She laughed nervously. "You know how it is—low man on the totem pole."

Bitty nodded, wishing she'd get on with it.

"When I found you in the bathroom, how long had you been in there?"

"Two or three minutes, I guess."

"Someone saw you go in there about half an hour before that . . ."

Bitty nodded.

"You went twice?"

She nodded again.

"I was wondering . . . do you recall what you did in between?"

"I beg your pardon?"

Skip was looking increasingly uncomfortable. "I mean, who you talked to . . . what room you were in—that sort of thing."

Bitty paused and thought. Nothing came to her. At last she said, "To tell you the truth, I don't have the faintest recollection."

Skip smiled. She really was a very pretty girl when she wasn't wearing that awful uniform. "Stupid question, I guess. Only one other thing—do you know if Chauncey has a pair of 44.40s in his collection?"

"Collection?"

"His gun collection."

"Oh. Those are guns. I don't know what he had, or even if he kept a record of it. Why do you ask?"

"That's what the murder weapon was. The 44.40's an old gun—kind of a cowboy weapon—the sort a collector might have."

"But . . . how could it have come from here?" Fear clutched at her.

"We just need to check everything out, that's all. Listen, I'm really sorry I had to bother you."

Bitty saw her out, nibbled at a tuna sandwich and actually got down some tomato soup before the burst of coping strength left her. She was on her second glass of wine by then, but it wasn't enough. The feelings started again. So that Yvonne couldn't see her crying, she went back upstairs, carrying the half-empty wine bottle. She was thinking of her second daughter.

After the years of infertility, she'd never dreamed of using birth control, never in a million years expected the bountiful blessing of a third child. And certainly never expected the pregnancy to go full-term. Nearly everything had gone wrong that could go wrong, and Bitty had spent the last two months in bed. But it was supposed to be longer than that. The baby was early, a wrinkled and pruny thing, even more so than Henry, but to Bitty's mind the most gorgeous child ever born, more beautiful than Helen of Troy, after whom she had named her.

The loss of her, that sudden, disastrous wrench, had been far worse even than this net of despair that enshrouded her now, the cumulative pain of a lifetime. This was a dull, dismal, hopeless misery. Losing her daughter was a sharp stab in the vitals.

It was worse than anything that had happened in her childhood. And sometimes, as a child, Bitty would think, *Nothing* could be worse than this, nothing unless I am taken prisoner by alien forces who rip my eyeballs out and tie me up and let wild animals gnaw on me whenever they're hungry, biting off little bits of me until I have no fingers or toes or ears.

When things were that bad she would lie in the dusty dark under her bed. She did not know why she went there, just that it was a good place to think about whether she would like to die or not.

2

The sheets were torn from Skip's unfolded sofa, every drawer of her dresser dumped on the floor. The back window was broken. In the kitchen it was the same, only worse—all the drawers dumped and a few glasses smashed for good measure. Skip's feet crunched on their shards.

"Shit!" she yelled, loud enough for Jimmy Dee to hear her in his outbuilding. But he wouldn't be there, he'd still be at work. Frantically, she picked up her lamp, set it back on its table, just to be doing something, to stave off the panic that was rising in her. Whoever had hit her had done this, had gotten into her apartment. She could see how too—by putting up Jimmy Dee's ladder in the back, maybe wearing workmen's clothes, and busting out the window with something wrapped in cloth to muffle the noise. The back courtyard was kept locked, but you could climb over the gate if you were bold, and Jimmy Dee kept a ladder in his storeroom, the same one that was still sitting under the window.

Somebody was trying to show her she wasn't safe, even in her own apartment. Who? LaBelle or friends of hers? Had Calvin Hogue ratted? But she didn't even meet him till today and she'd been slugged last night.

She was starting to lose it, freaking out—she needed to call a friend. But who? Not Jimmy Dee—she'd phoned him once at work and knew he hated it. Steve? No. She wasn't going to make a habit of being dependent on him.

She couldn't file a police report—she wasn't supposed to be home, she was supposed to be staking out LaBelle's place. *Shitfire!*

She sat down and began to take deep breaths. As she breathed, became calmer, Marcelle came into her mind. "Oh, Skippy, poor baby," she would say, and make her warm milk or something. There was something sweet about Marcelle that she'd never noticed before this case. But Marcelle not only wasn't a real friend, she was a suspect in a murder investigation.

How about Conrad? Her yuppie brother? Uh-uh. He'd say this was what came of becoming a cop. He hated her being one not because it was dangerous but because it was blue-collar. Conrad was a snob and a twit.

The oxygen rush—or whatever you got from deep breaths—was good for only about thirty seconds. The terror was returning, and Skip's hand was snaking toward the phone. She dialed a number that was becoming increasingly familiar.

"Get out of there," said Steve. "Wait for me at the Blacksmith Shop."

"But he's gone." She was confused. "There's no one here."

"That's not the point. You'll get more and more depressed." He rang off, apparently sure she'd follow orders, and she was more than glad to.

She went into the dark, damp bar—a genuine one-time blacksmith shop—and ordered a beer despite her concussion, thinking, May as well, the whole place smells like beer; why fight it? The beer helped, but it was true what they said—having your house broken into really did feel like a rape. She'd heard it before and thought, 'Patooey! Tell that to a real rape victim,' and now she knew what it meant.

Steve came and held her and took her back upstairs. "Okay," he said, "do you want to help or do you want to watch?"

"Watch what?"

"Watch me clean up."

She didn't feel like moving, was still numb, but she couldn't let him do it alone. "I'll help."

"You take the bedroom." (The kitchen, of course, was the real work.)

As Steve swept up the glass in both kitchen and studio she began desultorily to pick at the piles of her meager possessions. "Good thing I'm poor," she said, "or we'd have really had a mess."

"Now there," said Steve, "is a cockeyed optimist." He whistled as he wrestled her cheap flatware back into drawers, her canned soup back onto shelves.

It was true what she had said—because of the paucity of things to ransack, they finished the job in a little more than an hour.

"And now," said Steve, "for the purification ritual. Put your hands up." He pulled her sweater over her head.

"Oh, Steve, I don't think—" She didn't want to make love, but didn't want to say so.

"Shhh. You have to do this part in utter silence." He unsnapped her bra and took it off. "Sit down," he said, and then produced a box of incense, removed a stick, and lit it. "Now stand up."

He unzipped her jeans and pulled them to the floor, along with her underpants. At a sign from him, she stepped out of them. He picked up the incense stick and dusted her body with smoke, chanting, "Oh-wa, ee-wa, ooo-wa—"

"I thought you had to be quiet."

"Shhh. Except for the chant. Oh-wa, oo-oooh—waaaah—" It sounded as if he was making it up as he went along.

When she was well dusted, he gave her the stick and placed her hands at her waist. Feeling like a caryatid Skip looked far into the distance, letting expression fade from her eyes, getting into the ritual spirit. And getting very turned-on, standing there naked while Steve undressed, an action she could see from the corner of her unfocused eyes.

He took the stick away from her and held her hand, not pulling her toward him as she expected. Instead he took her into the bathroom, turned on the water and stepped into the shower, bringing her in after him. Solemnly, still not saying a word, he washed her, even her hair, and so carefully that he didn't hurt her head wound. Then he dried her and wrapped two towels around her, one like a sarong, the other around her head. "Now," he said, "it will look different."

He led her back into her apartment, which was just now

dark, and turned on the lamp. Skip gasped. It looked wonderful, cleaner than before.

"Better?" said Steve.

She threw her arms around him, but still he didn't respond sexually. He said softly, "Hungry?"

"Uh-huh. Shall we order something?"

"No. There's another step in the healing process. Let me dry your hair."

"That's it?"

"No, dummy, but you can't go out with your hair wet."

He made her remain naked, but tucked her in a quilt for warmth, while he ran the hair dryer.

God knows what my hair will look like, but I don't care if it comes out in dreadlocks. This is probably as close to paradise as I'm ever going to get.

And then, of course, she thought of lighting a joint.

Which was Jimmy Dee's cue to bang on the door. "Margaret? Mar-griiit!"

Steve turned off the hair dryer. "Another suitor?"

"Just my neighbor. Let him in, will you?"

"This," said Jimmy Dee, "is a first." He handed Steve a joint before introducing himself. "A straight man holding a hair dryer. You are straight, I presume?"

"He is," said Skip. "Steve Steinman, Jimmy Dee Scoggin."

"Officer Darlin', you're naked! I turn my back for one minute—"

"Dee-Dee, shut up, there's a lot to tell."

"So I *see.*" He minced over (the hair dryer having set the tone) and got the joint back from Steve. "Don't let me interrupt anything."

"Okay," said Steve, and went back to working on Skip's mop.

Jimmy Dee sat down at the opposite end of the couch and stared. "I think I've died and gone to heaven." He found Skip's foot under the quilt. "How about if I suck your toes while he's doing that?"

She kicked. "Shut up, Dee-Dee, and listen. I spent last evening in Charity."

"Oh, Gawd, you had a date last night. The One-Minute Pregnancy? Oprah for sure, Donahue maybe . . ."

"I got slugged."

"Slugged?" His voice was a hiss.

Almost yelling over the sound of the hair dryer, Skip told her story, with Dee-Dee wailing at appropriate moments, "Oh, my dainty darling! Why didn't you call me?"

Because I called Steve instead—God help me.

They were all deliciously stoned by the time Skip's hair was dry, but Steve apparently wasn't overcome by feelings of bonhomie. Skip would have asked Jimmy Dee to join them. He said, "Skip and I were just going out—"

"Good God, yes, young love; don't let l'il ol' me stand in the way—nice to meet you, Steve." Skip got the feeling he didn't think so at all. He turned at the door. "Oh, Margaret, about Tolliver Albert. Queer as a three-dollar bill." He paused for effect. "But straight as a dick. I mean stick."

"Beg pardon?"

"He's weird, darlin', weirder than shit. But probably not gay. He doesn't belong to any of the gay krewes or hang out at Lafitte, or hang out period. You didn't tell me how good-looking he is, by the way. Plenty of guys have tried cruising his shop—to no avail."

"So what makes him weird?"

But the door shut on the last word. "Toodle-oo." Skip thought he had heard her question.

Steve stared at her. "What's wrong with him?"

"I guess he was pissed that you didn't ask him to join us."

"Are you?"

She paused to consider. A moment ago she had been, but the feeling had passed, probably because Steve was now caressing her left breast. "No. I'd rather be alone with you."

She wished she could take back the words. They weren't her style.

The rest of Steve's elaborate purification ritual also involved water, in the form of the mighty Mississippi. They went to the

Jax Brewery, where they could eat fairly good (if not great) food and stare at a scene out of the nineteenth century. The old-fashioned stern-wheelers and paddle-wheelers plied the river once again, this time carrying tourists instead of gamblers, runaways, and stolid folk off to visit their kin.

Steve said, "I don't know about this Jimmy Dee character. Are you sure you can trust him?"

Trust Jimmy Dee! The real question is, can I trust you?

"Trust him for what?"

"I don't know. It sounds as if you had him doing legwork for you."

She shrugged. "I just asked him to pick up some gossip. In his way, Jimmy Dee's as respectable as Chauncey was, by the way. He owns my building and lives out in back in a slave quarters got up like the Gallier House; works in a big law firm—never, never gets swishy in public."

"If he owns the building he should fix it up a little."

"Hey." She took his hand. "You don't have to be jealous of Dee-Dee." *Just because he'll still be around after you're long gone.*

"I'm not jealous of Dee-Dee. I mean, *Mr.* Scoggin. I just think you have to be careful who you confide in right now."

"I know."

"Who knew you were going to meet me last night?"

Skip thought a minute. "Just Dee-Dee." *And you, of course.*

"I don't like this."

"Dee-Dee can't even kill a cockroach. I'm serious, I have to do it for him. He once raised a baby bird that fell out of its nest. He took it to the office so it wouldn't miss its feedings."

"Look, I'm not accusing Jimmy Dee. I just don't think you should be working alone on this."

"You don't? Mr. Steve Steinman of Los Angeles who's never been a policeman a day in his life doesn't think I should be working alone. My boss thinks otherwise, big fellow, and he's a thirty-year veteran of NOPD."

He held up a traffic cop's hand. "Okay, okay. I'm sure you can take care of your tiny self—"

218

"Oh, stop it, you sound like Jimmy Dee."

"—I meant you can take care of your Amazonian magnificence. I just wanted to offer my help if you need it, that's all."

She didn't answer right away, afraid to ask. "Thank you—there is something."

"What?"

"I'm not too keen on spending the night there alone. I mean I'm—" She groped for the right word.

"Spooked?"

"Spooked."

"Anybody would be. Do you want to come back to Cookie's?"

"No. I want to sleep there. Will you stay with me?"

"Of course." And then he explained to her there would be two other steps in the purification ritual—a movie for continuity with the real world and a brandy for soporific purposes. As it happened, she added a step of her own—a postmovie stroll on the Moonwalk, taking further advantage of the healing waters of the river.

Skip truly did feel purified as they returned, a bottle of cognac tucked under Steve's arm, or she would have if she'd thought about it. She was chatting happily about the movie, her troubles forgotten, as they turned onto St. Philip. She fumbled in her purse for her key, her eyes down, and so it *was* Steve who first saw her door.

"Oh, shit," he said, and her stomach turned over.

"What?" But now she saw it. Blood had been splashed against the door at knee level, and a chicken foot left on her threshold. Above the main splash someone, using the blood for ink, had made a number of x's. "Gris-gris."

"Excuse me?"

"A gris-gris's something in voodoo—like a spell or a charm. I guess that's what this is. I've never seen anything like it."

"The chicken foot! It does smack of voodoo."

"And those must be hex marks or something. They're all over the tomb of Marie Laveau." She pointed to the x's.

"Well, hell. Let's scrub it down." He picked up the chicken foot.

She was grateful for his matter-of-factness; without it she was pretty sure she'd have fallen apart at this point, run screaming down Bourbon Street, and probably ended up being taken to DePaul's by a couple of brother officers. A tidal wave of hysteria was starting to overwhelm her; she didn't seem to be able to make a move without being persecuted. Steve's voice, his touch as he put an arm around her, were keeping the wave at bay.

She threw herself into the homely business of washing off the chicken blood (surely it *was* chicken blood). "Could this be the work of the same person?" She was thinking out loud.

"The person who slugged you and broke in? We don't even know if the same person did those two things. But I think he did—or she did. I don't know about this weird stuff, though. Do you know anybody in a cult or anything?"

"No. I don't know a thing about this stuff. But I think mostly black people practice voodoo."

"There aren't any black people involved, are there?"

"There may be." She snapped her fingers. "You know what I need to do? Check something out. Would you mind taking a ride with me?"

They went to LaBelle's, where Skip pounded on the door, to no avail. She tried Calvin Hogue; he said LaBelle hadn't been home.

Later, in bed with Steve, the cognac coursing cozily through her veins, she felt safe. She wondered idly if LaBelle was really out of town at all; maybe she had taken refuge with her mother.

DAUGHTERS

1

How could you run an antique shop feeling so anxious and tired and out of control? You couldn't, Tolliver thought, and yet, why not? You've done it before.

This was worse, though. This was far and away the worst it had ever been. His hands were jerky, his shoulders twitchy; it was like having St. Vitus's Dance.

"How much is this?"

How much was what? What in hell was the customer pointing to? "That—uh—little table? Three-fifty, I think."

Was the damn thing three-fifty or not? And where was his sales spiel? At this point he was supposed to explain what a fine table it was, and why. But he couldn't remember. It was on the tip of his tongue, he just somehow couldn't seem to wrap his brains around the relevant facts.

"Is it American or European?"

"American. Federal."

It wasn't Federal, didn't even resemble Federal; it probably wasn't even American. He hoped this joker didn't know antiques. The customer gave him a puzzled look and left. Tolliver couldn't find it in himself to care. He wasn't himself, and he knew it . . . he really must call that doctor on Monday.

He had a lot on his mind today, including the fact that that organ wasn't functioning very well. It was Marcelle who had done this to him. Her crazy, pathetic visit had brought on the attack and now she was haunting him, like a tiny saucer-eyed ghost.

She may have been the most beautiful child he had ever seen—more beautiful than Henry, and Tolliver adored Henry like his own son. Marcelle had those amazing eyes, and she tried so hard to please. She did please—she succeeded in her little-girl ambition; she did something sweet or cute and you appreciated it, and that was that.

He had heard Chauncey say to her, "Dollin', you know why I wanted a daughter? Because I knew she'd always be there for me. No matter what happens, you'll be Daddy's girl, won't you? You'll never leave Daddy, will you?"

Marcelle, sitting on his lap, had said, "'Course I'll be Daddy's girl. I wouldn't leave you, Daddy." She spoke seriously, obviously wanting very much to be believed.

"You'll take care of me in my old age?"

"'Course!"

"Will you give me some sugar? Right now."

Marcelle threw her arms around him and covered him with kisses.

She was always that way, wanting to do whatever you wanted, doing it, then quietly fading into the background. There was something sad about her, though, something that had come upon her, a heaviness, after Bitty lost the baby and fell apart. Tolliver was amazed at himself, only seeing it now for the first time. The simple fact was that he just didn't think much about Marcelle.

So much attention was focused on Henry, with his father always trying to make him into a carbon copy of himself. The kid acted out a lot, and he screwed up, though now that Tolliver thought about it, the order was probably reversed. He'd lose a chess game to Chauncey, say, and then pitch a fit, throwing the board across the room, scattering pawns and bishops. Chauncey thought it was because he was spoiled rotten. Something told Tolliver it wasn't that. It was frustration and a feeling of impotence because he hadn't performed brilliantly and pleased his father. Poor kid, in those days he idolized his father; he was probably scared to death. He beat Tolliver sometimes, and Tolliver could beat Chauncey. But Henry never could.

Marcelle was already perfect and didn't have to be made into something else. Except for occasionally eliciting from her those silly, extravagant protestations of eternal love, Chauncey more or less ignored her. *We all did.*

He realized he didn't have a single memory of Bitty with Marcelle. Not one. She and Henry were so tightly bound to one other he thought of them as a unit. He didn't realize how hard it would have been for another child to penetrate it. When the baby had come, the second girl, Henry was at a rebellious stage; she might have had a chance, that girl, with Bitty's pride and joy slightly distant from her. But Marcelle didn't. It was simply a club they didn't let her join. *Why didn't I see it? I really had no idea.*

As for Tolliver, he had put his own energy into helping Henry. He wanted to try to build his self-esteem . . . *face it, Tolliver, you tried to be the kid's father. Well, Chauncey wasn't doing it, somebody had to.*

He thought that someday, when Bitty left Chauncey, or Chauncey died, or Tolliver killed him, he would be Henry's father. But it wasn't just that—he loved Henry almost as much as Bitty did, in a way that a family friend or favorite uncle didn't usually love a child. Or wasn't supposed to anyway. He loved him with a kind of dark passion born out of despair. His own and Bitty's and Henry's own.

Marcelle had remained outside that black circle—such a self-contained, happy little thing. Or so it had seemed at the time. But her visit had brought vividly into focus the fact that he didn't even really know her. Marcelle interested in antiques? Asking for a job? *Working?* How preposterous all that seemed. She was a beautiful creature without a thought in her head and not a shred of ambition. Tolliver winced at his own stupidity.

And now he'd killed her father, the one person who noticed her now and then. He never ever, for one second thought he'd be sorry. He'd planned the murder so many times, in so many different ways, over the course of so many years.

How many times had he imagined the pleasure of watching Chauncey die as he stood over him with one of his own guns? The look of surprise on his face as his best friend, the dear friend who had straightened out so much of the repeated shit in his life, relieved him at last of his worries. Bitty had told him Chauncey said he liked helping—that he, Tolliver, did—because his own life was so boring.

For that, Chauncey, pain before you die. Maybe the kneecaps first, a little writhing before the coup de grace.

There were quieter ways as well. Chauncey had a penicillin allergy, something only a very close family friend would know. (Tolliver liked the irony of that.) Such a friend would also know when Chauncey was taking medication for some minor ill or other and could switch a pill—just one that Chauncey would come to in time. Maybe not the first day, maybe not the second—Tolliver would actually enjoy the suspense, be thrilled by the knowledge that Chauncey would die soon and Tolliver would be responsible.

A fantasy he really loved—his favorite, probably—was the

one of the cat burglar. While Bitty and the children were in Covington, Tolliver would turn off the St. Amant alarm (which he knew very well how to do, having many times taken care of the house when the family was away), break into the house, and stab Chauncey as he slept. Stab him in the heart. Always in this one Tolliver saw the hilt of an antique dagger protruding from Chauncey's bloody chest. This one had so much power over him that twice he had done it—or almost done it. Once he had broken into the house when no one was home, groped his way into the bedroom, and pantomimed the murder. Another time—recently, very recently—he had gone in when Chauncey was there alone. He had actually walked over to the bed and listened to Chauncey breathe, longing to make him stop. But he hadn't brought his dagger, had deliberately not brought it. He wasn't ready yet.

Even through the pain in his head, there was satisfaction in these thoughts, as always. He could not remember which weapon he had finally used until her wraith floated insouciantly, when he was thinking of something else, into his mind's eye. It was LaBelle. LaBelle herself was the weapon. She had come to his house, LaBelle, with her red, fiery, fierce beauty and her awful accent and that smell about her—he didn't know much about women's perfumes, but this was new, he was fairly sure of that, and reminded him of stories he had read, of Chinese concubines and Egyptian ladies of fashion who rubbed themselves with love unguents before bewitching their unsuspecting targets.

Her violet fingernails clashed with her skin—or perhaps clash wasn't the word, perhaps the effect she wanted was one of discord and danger. She was like a succubus with her siren scent and her deep red, angry energy rechanneled in the most ambitiously imaginative ways. He felt he was too old, too depressed, to fully appreciate her, though he could certainly marvel in admiration. In the end she had enthralled him after all, but she had done it with the tools of Scheherazade rather than with those of Lilith or Circe. In her gutter English she had told him the story that cost Chauncey his life. He hadn't intended it to work this way. It was so far from the ways he'd imagined. It was so sad this way.

He was too sad now to continue the charade of trying to work. He closed up his shop and went home.

2

Yvonne had Saturdays off, and Bitty saw no reason she shouldn't have this one as usual. She was delighted, in fact, to know no one would come to her house today, no human being for whom she had to pretend. She had a lovely bottle of scotch in her bedroom and so there was no need to make a show of getting up. Henry and Tolliver were working and wouldn't be around. She could lie here all day and anesthetize herself to her heart's content. Or she could have if Marcelle hadn't shown up. Bitty had forgotten about her.

Using her own key, Marcelle simply came in, made Bitty coffee and eggs and toast, and brought it up to her. "Mother? Good morning, Mother." Bitty blinked as Marcelle opened the curtains.

She sniffed the air and Bitty knew she was taking in the aroma from the scotch glass at her bedside, but knew also that she was far too polite to say anything.

Bitty said only her name, unable to think of anything with which to follow it up. She had been thinking of her other daughter again. Marcelle was an intrusion.

"Yes, of course, it's me. And André's downstairs, being a perfect little lamb, waiting to see his Mo."

"Oh, dear. I don't feel well today."

"Eat something, Mother. Please."

She had sat down and stared at Bitty, who really didn't think she could manage more than a bite or two. She tried a sip of coffee and found it strangely comforting. It seemed a long time that they stayed this way, a tableau almost, except that from time to time Bitty would do something with her fork, pretending to eat. She knew that Marcelle would not go away until she felt she had done her duty as a daughter. She must try to eat the toast at least.

Bitty could defy her, of course. She could pull out her scotch bottle and know that Marcelle wouldn't take it away. But she was too proud.

"Mommy?" called André. "Can I see Mo now?"

Marcelle smiled at her mother. "The cartoons must be over. Shall I have him come up?"

"Oh, Marcelle. Please try to understand—I'm really not myself yet. I need to spend the morning in bed. Dr. Langdon said it'll take me awhile to get my strength back. After the stress of everything."

"We'll come back later. Shall we?"

"Of course." She managed a maternal smile. Later would be fine. Just so long as it wasn't now.

When Marcelle was gone she poured herself a couple of inches, neat. Relief washed over her as she sipped, leaning against the pillows.

Sometimes Bitty thought she was the only one in the world who had given a damn about that little girl, the second one she had known so briefly. And yet, insult on top of injury, when she lost the baby, it was as if she lost her parents as well—not her real parents, but her adopted parents, the parents she hadn't had till she was grown-up. Chauncey's parents, Ma-Mère and Pa-Père. Chauncey suggested the names when Henry was born, and Bitty had used them from that moment on; they sounded like parent names, and she liked that.

But they blamed her for the baby's death. They shunned her afterward. They would have nothing to do with her, except out of politeness, though they spent every summer with her and the children, all of them in the Covington house together. But it was all form and no content.

They even tried to get Henry and Marcelle away from her,

as if they thought it wasn't safe for her to be around children. They had come to visit about a month after she lost the baby; Bitty was barely able to get up at all then, in the state she was in now more or less. Too many feelings that wouldn't leave her alone, wouldn't stay buried. Dr. Langdon's prescriptions helped some, wine helped more. She was so depressed she could barely get her clothes on. But that was no reason to take her children away. She had plenty of household help— she could manage; her children were fine.

She had been resting that night, hadn't known Chauncey's parents were there. Ma-Mère had wandered into her bedroom. "Bitty? How are you, dawalin'?" Bitty smiled, remembering how charmed she had been by the accent—Ma-Mère grew up in Chalmette.

"Fine, Ma-Mère. I still get tired very quickly."

"Dawalin', you're so pale! You need some help, baby doll. We've been talking to Chauncey, and we want to do something for you."

Bitty's stomach turned over; some instinct told her.

"We thought we could take Marcelle and Henry for the summer while you recover."

"Marcelle? Henry?" Bitty's lips were so dry she could barely speak. She knew what Ma-Mère was saying, but she couldn't bear to let herself believe it. She had just lost a child. Not her others. No!

"Over in Covington, dawalin'."

"But we'll all go to Covington. Like always."

"Baby doll, you need your rest. You'll come over with Chauncey on weekends, and we'll all be together. And during the week you can work on getting your strength back."

Bitty fell back on the pillow and closed her eyes, knowing not to argue, that there was no arguing when Chauncey had made up his mind—that nothing she could do would stop him. That she was helpless.

She had to visit her own children that summer, as if she were the grandmother, not Ma-Mère. They treated her like an outsider, Chauncey and his parents, like someone who didn't belong in her own house with her own family.

Once she was there without Chauncey and she asked to borrow Ma-Mère's car to get some wine. "I'd rather you wouldn't, baby doll," Ma-Mère said. "I don't let anyone drive it anymore." As if she were some stranger off the street.

Ma-Mère took over—simply overwhelmed Bitty, outvoted her, outmaneuvered her. Bitty would say, "Time for your bath, children," and Ma-Mère would say, "I was just about to draw their water. Come on, dollies, come with Ma-Mère."

She would say to Bitty. "I know you're not really up to coping; I want to make it as easy on you as possible."

Bitty went in to hear their prayers and Ma-Mère was there. She said, "Dawalin', your breath—you don't want them to know." Bitty was not permitted to kiss her own children.

The St. Amants thought the baby had died because of her, because of her body, because she was small, her genes weren't good. They were strong, vigorous, earthy people. Bitty must have looked anemic at best to them. Her family, with its aristocratic inbreeding, must have seemed weak and pallid. That was why they decided to hate and ostracize her, because they thought she had killed their grandchild with her sheer inadequacy.

Now she ached for them, the loving parents she had had so briefly before they deserted her. But she hated them that fall when they tried—*really* tried—to take the children. When summer ended they tried to keep them, tried to talk Chauncey into it. (Only Chauncey wasn't about to be talked into it—how would it look to Haygood, after all? There would have been a rift and Haygood would have destroyed his whole world was what would have happened.) And so Bitty got to keep her children.

But they said—Ma-Mère and Pa-Père—the argument they used was that she had harmed Marcelle. Bitty's chest ached when she remembered, as if Ma-Mère were even now turning the knife in it. She couldn't even imagine how such a story got started—or more accurately she couldn't remember. She knew there was something. *Something* had happened. She knew because she had some vague memories of it, and one very sharp one. The sharp one—she couldn't get it out of her head—was of Marcelle's terrified eyes.

Bitty had been drunk and upset about the baby, the little girl whose growing up she would never see. She could remember that, and she could remember Marcelle on the floor, staring up at her with those eyes, and then herself sitting on the floor and Ma-Mère picking up a screaming Marcelle. The memories seemed damning, but the one of missing the baby made her certain that, whatever had happened, she could not have hurt Marcelle. She of all people would never blame one child for not being another one. Certainly not Bitty, whose father had so much wanted a boy, had tried to make her behave like a boy, had given her boy toys, had made her kill a rabbit.

She poured scotch and drank quickly. That she could remember. She had not hurt a child, but she had most assuredly killed a rabbit. Her gorge rose. She couldn't even get down another swallow of scotch. It was the only thing either of them had shot that day, and it had been tiny. Tiny! You couldn't eat a bony little thing like that, but her father was so proud of her, he made her bring it back to show Merrie Mac. Disgusted, Merrie Mac made them leave it on the back porch.

Bitty went back that night, to say good-bye to it, and touched its brown body, meaning to stroke it, to console it or perhaps console herself. She'd expected a familiar animal softness, but it was stiff and alien. Not like a puppy or a kitten, not like a rabbit. Dead. This was what dead meant. She hadn't known. When she had first shot it, it was still warm and supple, not like this, with its poor little legs sticking out. In shock she drew her hand away and screamed. Screamed and screamed. Couldn't stop. Merrie Mac came out to find her.

"Oh, Mother, it's dead," she screamed. "It's so horrible. I killed it. I *killed* it." She kept repeating the confession, begging for absolution. She wanted her mother to hold her, but she was afraid to ask her to.

"Serves you right, Bitty! I *told* you to leave that revolting thing alone and you disobeyed me again! Serves you *right!* I hope it *haunts* you!" She yelled the last part, about the haunting, having to yell to be heard, because Bitty was screaming so loud. As she delivered the curse, the back of her hand connected with Bitty's cheek. "Shut up and act your age. You're nearly twelve years old." She went back into the house, leaving Bitty alone with the rabbit, afraid to follow her. (When Merrie Mac told the story later, she said that poor Bitty had been hysterical, that she had to slap her to stop her screaming.)

After the rabbit's death, Bitty had cried for weeks lying under her bed. Even now she could remember the vast, yawning despair of touching the animal, knowing in that moment the difference between life and death, understanding the lonely inevitability of it.

Her father had bought her stuffed rabbits and books about rabbits. He had made her sit on his lap, breathing fiery fumes at her, caressing her and holding her tight. "Who's my dollin' baby girl that's just too soft-hearted to go huntin'?" And he would give her a big wet kiss on the ear. Jesus! When he wasn't making her a boy, he was treating her like a girlfriend.

One day he had come in smelling of booze and looking like the Cheshire cat, so smug and pleased with himself. "Look what I brought for my angel. You're going to love Daddy for this, baby dollin'."

"What, Daddy?"

"First, give Daddy a big ol' kiss."

She kissed him. And he drew from a cardboard box a shivering baby bunny, a white one that looked like the ghost of the one she had killed. It wriggled in his big, rough hands, its pink eyes desperate. Before she could catch herself, Bitty

231

screamed. But then she remembered herself, clapped a hand over her mouth and ran, knowing that if she screamed again, her mother would come and slap her.

3

"Is Mo finished with her nap now?" André managed to get the words out between sobs. Marcelle had taken him to see a reissue of *Bambi* and now, for the second time in a week, could kick herself for exposing him to so much pain. She should have remembered how sad and brutal it was, should have had better sense than to take him to a movie that would make both of them cry. They had held on to each other, blubbering and miserable, but immobilized, unable to walk out of the theater.

Afterward she had bought him frozen yogurt, which had momentarily cheered him—if not her—but now he seemed to be having a relapse. She was touched that he wanted to see his grandmother and hoped to hell Bitty was up to it. "We'll go see her," she said. "If she's still lying down, maybe we could—I know! We'll go for a surprise."

She knew what she wanted to do with André—how she wanted to surprise him—but she couldn't bring herself to say it yet, couldn't quite make the commitment either to herself or to him. She wanted to get him a kitten, something alive to give him hope now that he'd lost his Poppy; something soft and positive to remind him that love was still possible even in his grief, and to remind them both that each was not the only living being in the other's life. But some hesitancy nagged at her—a dim fear that she would lose her nerve or that there would be no kittens at the pound, that somehow he'd be disappointed.

To her relief they found Bitty sitting at the kitchen table eating chicken soup. "Oh, Mother. I would have made you some lunch."

"Yvonne left this for me. All I had to do was turn on the heat."

What, Marcelle wondered, had made her mother get up? She had expected to find her dead to the world and reeking.

Bitty called André, who was shrinking back, waiting to be noticed. "There's my big boy! André, come to Mo, darlin'."

André didn't move, except for his hand, which wandered self-consciously to his mouth, but he smiled the shy smile that told Marcelle he had reached the pinnacle of happiness. If he'd been a puppy he'd have been wriggling, but he was André and not given to vulgar displays of delight.

All of a sudden, apparently without having the least idea he was going to, he threw himself into Bitty's arms and began sobbing as if Bambi were losing his mother again. "André? What is it, baby?" Bitty raised alarmed eyes to Marcelle, who realized intuitively what it must be.

"He hasn't been alone with you since Daddy died," she said.

Bitty nodded. "Shhh, child. I know you miss Poppy—"

"It isn't that," said Marcelle, wondering how she knew. "He knows that you're sad. He's crying for you."

"We both miss Poppy," said Bitty, not missing a beat. "We miss him together, don't we?" In a little while, he hushed and let Marcelle find him a place for his nap.

Marcelle marveled at what had happened—she had experienced nothing like it as a mother or as a daughter; it had been a rare, almost psychic moment among three generations, the tiny silver lining you get when it's cloudy out, she thought.

She returned to find her mother still sitting, not drinking, waiting for her. "Marcelle, I want to know if you remember something."

Her voice was uncharacteristically steely, making Marcelle wish for a drink herself.

"Do you remember spending a summer with Ma-Mère and Pa-Père? Over in Covington?"

"You mean without you?" The memory was vague, and gave her a funny, fluttery feeling, but Marcelle knew very well that was what she meant. She didn't want to talk about it.

"It was the summer you were three and a half—Henry must have been about eight."

Marcelle nodded. Why was she getting that funny, uncomfortable feeling?

"You do remember?"

Marcelle nodded again.

"Marcelle, listen, this is hard for me. But I need to know something."

Marcelle knew what the feeling was now. It was fear.

"Did something happen to you?"

Yes.

"Did I hurt you, Marcelle? Was there some kind of accident—something that frightened you? I've been trying so hard to remember. Could I have hurt my own child?"

Yes. Yes again. Marcelle was amazed. That wasn't what the fear feeling at the base of her spine was about—that had to do with Ma-Mère. But there was something else, something about Bitty that was creeping into her consciousness.

She said, "Oh, Mother, of course not. Why on earth would you think that?"

Her mother's eyes brimmed. "It was a terrible summer—terrible things happened that summer."

You're not kidding.

She made Bitty a vanilla milk shake, thinking she needed something more substantial than the chicken soup, and watched her let it melt as she pretended to drink it. She seemed to fade after the odd interrogation, and to have trouble sitting. Marcelle knew what she really wanted, that she was too proud to say so, and she felt guilty keeping her mother from her only pleasure. When André whimpered in his sleep she made an excuse to wake him up and leave.

Dear God, what *had* Bitty done? It was hard to imagine

drunk, incompetent, uncaring Bitty even noticing Marcelle long enough to abuse her. But something violent had most certainly happened that summer. Marcelle had seen a not-so-instant replay—or bits of it—in Bitty's kitchen. She had seen her mother lunging at her—holding an object, something large, terribly frightening—and hitting her. Marcelle had fallen, she could remember the blow, could almost feel it again, feel the wind knocked out of her. You couldn't make that up, that feeling, Marcelle was sure of it. It must really have happened. But if her mother had hit her, then why? What had Marcelle done to provoke it? The hell of it was, she thought she knew, she just couldn't bring it into focus.

That night she woke up screaming, or thought she did. She checked André—he was still asleep. If she had actually made noise, she hadn't waked him. He would probably be all right, he would probably escape. He was four now and hadn't had night terrors—age three was when kids tended to get them.

She had learned that when she was reading child-care books, preparing to be a mother, and had realized that she had had them that summer in Covington. Every night she woke up screaming and wailing, terrified, inconsolable.

"What is it?" Ma-Mère would say, her eyes blazing, furious.

Marcelle was too frightened to answer, probably didn't know anyway, she thought now.

"What *is* it, Marcelle? You'll wake up Pa-Père and Henry." Ma-Mère would shake her, perhaps trying to jar loose the answer.

"What is it, chère?" Marcelle would flail about, probably, if she had done what the books said children did, and would cry all the harder.

"Shut up! Shut up or I'll give you something to cry *about!*" And she would. She would pull down Marcelle's pajamas and spank her with a hairbrush.

The books said children forgot abuses, and perhaps Marcelle had forgotten her share—what had happened with Bitty, for instance—but those memories of the hairbrush stung even now, like Bakelite on bare flesh.

Pa-Père took Henry fishing every day and paid practically no attention to her. But she heard him telling Henry how to fish, she supposed—she didn't know what they talked about—she heard him and he frightened her, just by the way he talked. Even now his voice frightened her. As an adult she had been able to put a few things together, and she could see that her grandparents were indeed very stern—much more so than her own parents—but then they had seemed frankly terrifying. The best thing about Pa-Père was that he turned his attention to Henry instead of to her.

But being in Covington with them had seemed a prison sentence. Marcelle knew—she had always known—that she was sent there for a reason. It was because she had been bad, and had somehow hurt her mother. Henry had told her that. Now, trying to sleep after the nightmare, after learning Bitty had been angry enough to hit her and knock her down, she tried to dredge it out of the muck of nearly a quarter of a century.

An image from the nightmare came back—a doll thrown against a wall, but splattering blood, not a doll at all, a real baby. Her mind ran the dream backward—it was the splattering that had awakened her. Now the mental camera panned back toward the person who had thrown the doll—Marcelle, laughing.

That was it. It was the summer her sister was born. The dream was so vivid now. In it she hated the doll—loathed it. (Loathed her sister, surely.) And she was afraid of her. How could you hate and fear a baby so much? *Wait, you were only a baby yourself. You were jealous.*

Marcelle hadn't a single memory of the baby, had only those waves of hatred she could feel even now.

4

"What's up?"

Skip had hoped to slip out before Steve woke up, to avoid what was beginning to seem an eternal argument between them—the one in which he tried yet again to be her partner and she explained to him one more time that the fantasies of a lifetime of TV and movies didn't make him a law-enforcement officer.

She said: "I have to go out for a while."

"This isn't Saturday? I thought it was Saturday."

"I have to do something I should have done yesterday. Or Thursday maybe. Several things, to tell you the truth."

"And I can't go with you, right?"

The long and short of it was, she was so bowled over that he was finally getting the idea, she'd gone out to breakfast with him and made a date for that night. So it was midmorning by the time she got to the Desire Project, a nightmare of a neighborhood that most assuredly evoked desire—the desire to stay away from it, or to get away, she supposed, if you were someone like LaBelle Doucette.

It was built of red brick, and that was a good thing, Skip thought, or it would have fallen down from neglect. The place was a mess. Garbage was strewn everywhere, windows were out, steps broken, glass from newly smashed light bulbs crunched underfoot. Here and there someone nodded out or slept, and young men gathered in tight knots around dealers, probably. Or maybe, she thought, I've just acquired the famous cop's cynicism. At any rate, the project made Tremé look upscale—which, from here, it was.

The reputation of the place was so rancid she'd been tempted to wear her uniform, but, not wanting to frighten Mrs. Doucette, she contented herself with keeping her badge displayed and a bored look on her face as she ran the usual gamut of "Hey-Big-Mamas."

"Yes, ma'am?" Philomena Doucette looked about a hundred, but she was probably closer to eighty. She was so thin and small, brown skin taut over tiny bones, that every wrinkle looked deep as a ditch. She was slightly hunched and wore a blue cotton dress with a large white collar that was not only unmistakably homemade but made from a pattern that seemed to have been bought twenty or thirty years ago. It hadn't ever been in style, really—it was simply generic dress. Like my skirts and blazers, Skip thought. I'll look like this someday—a giant version of her, though.

She introduced herself and said she'd come about LaBelle.

"Oh, LaBelle. She ain' been roun' in three—fo' year."

"She might be in trouble," Skip said.

Mrs. Doucette's hair had been straightened and pinned back in a kind of bun. Her face jumped out at you, every emotion naked to the casual viewer. There was fear on it now, fear and some kind of deep, cosmic pain—something that had to do with more than LaBelle, Skip thought, something about the human condition as Mrs. Doucette knew it.

A male voice said, "Lookin' good," and Skip jumped as its owner grabbed a chunk of her behind. She wanted to turn and yell at the man, maybe arrest him, but this wasn't the time for it. Her own face must have been fairly transparent as well. Mrs. Doucette said, "Come in, child."

Skip was touched by that and felt silly about her internal debate regarding her uniform. She knew that with or without it, Mrs. Doucette would see her as a child to be protected.

The apartment she entered was like an inn in the Himalayas—a warm spot in a vast and inhospitable wilderness. If Mrs. Doucette could make dresses, she could also make slipcovers. The light-green flowered ones on the sofa and two chairs were worn, clean, and covered with crocheted antimacassars. Antimacassars had also been pinned to both arms and the back of an old blue overstuffed rocking chair that was probably horsehair. Tables stood by each of the chairs and a coffee table sat in the middle, the surface of each covered with dime-store vases and china knickknacks, some so old they were probably now kitsch collectors' items. The tables were cheap and twice as old as Skip, probably, but gleamed and smelled of lemon polish. A stripe of sun streamed through ruffled curtains, coming to rest on the coffee table, revealing not a speck of dust. Skip was sure one couldn't be found in the place.

"Ice tea?"

"Thank you." If you accepted a beverage, people didn't really expect you to leave until you'd finished it. (Or so Skip's theory went.)

Mrs. Doucette brought the tea on a tray, in glasses that looked as if they had once held jelly and were at least as old as some of the china gewgaws. Lemon slices were rakishly attached to them. Skip's hostess handed her her tea with a coaster that had a cat's face on it.

When Mrs. Doucette was comfortably seated in the rocker, tea held ladylike in her lap, she said, "LaBelle in jail again?"

"No. Nothing like that. We need her for questioning in a case we're working on. But I can't find her. Frankly, I'm getting a little worried."

"She ain' been home?"

"No."

Mrs. Doucette's lips set in a tight, straight line. "Tha's La-Belle. The good Lord forgive me, sometime I be sorry I ever took her."

"Took her? She's not your daughter?"

"Oh, law, chile, LaBelle's not but twenty-one. Do I look like I got a daughter that age? LaBelle's my great-grand-daughter. My daughter Verna Ruth passed away so long ago I cain' even hardly remember it; she didn't have no husband, so I raise *her* daughter. Tha's two generations of daughters and that was enough, I'm tellin' you. By time LaBelle come along, I done be too old. The worl' changed too much, I couldn't do nothin' for that chile by then."

"Did something happen to your granddaughter?"

"Somethin' good happen to her. She got a chance to go to college." From the table nearest her, she picked up a framed photo of a moon-faced young woman. "See here? That's my Jaree. She teach school now."

"You must be very proud of her."

"Sho' am, honey. She's my pride and joy. I feel real bad about LaBelle sometime." Her face crumpled as the comparison came to mind, and she reached into a hidden pocket for a tissue. "That chile didn't have no chance, with her looks and this kinda worl' we got. Too pretty for her own good, that was LaBelle. Always boys, boys, boys, wasn't nothin' nobody could do about it. Men too. And they always had dope, boys and men either one. Only good thing 'bout these kinda' days is they got birth control now. Shoo, honey! I had LaBelle takin' them pills before she was leben. Just in time too. With all her misbehavin', she never did get pregnant. Not so I knew about nohow."

"Mrs. Doucette, this may sound like a strange question, but what sort of person is LaBelle?"

"Wild, honey! She a wil' chile, pure and simple."

"I mean, her personality. Outgoing? Sullen? Sweet? Sour?"

"I hear what you sayin', I jus' don't quite know how to answer." She thought a minute. "I don' know if I'd call her mean, exactly—she grabby, though. She wants somepum, she takes." She shook her head. "Honey, LaBelle ain' got no conscience."

"Do you have any relatives named Villere? Or did LaBelle have a friend named Estelle Villere?"

Mrs. Doucette rocked back in her chair, thinking. "No relatives. And I don't think no friend girl either. Don't b'leeve I know."

Skip set down her ice-tea glass, feeling the interview was drawing to a close. "How long has LaBelle been gone, Mrs. Doucette?"

"Fo' years, I b'leeve. Uh-huh, fo'. She lef' when she was

seventeen. Went to live with her mama was what she said. Didn't, though. Just came 'roun now and then for money."

"Is she in contact with her mother now?"

"Not that I know of." Mrs. Doucette's eyes looked into the distance. Skip thought perhaps she was tiring but was too polite to say so.

She said, "I'd like to ask her if I could. Could you give me her name and address?"

"Sho', honey. Go see Jaree. She married now. Got a family of her own."

Which, thought Skip, doesn't include Big Sis, product of a youthful indiscretion in a world Jaree had probably left far behind. She felt a momentary pang of sympathy for LaBelle.

Jaree (aka Mrs. Purcell Campeau) lived in a neat house in Mid City and was just leaving as Skip arrived. Or at any rate, someone was leaving, backing out of the driveway in a late-model Toyota. Waving, so as to look friendly, Skip did the unforgivable and blocked the driveway.

"Mrs. Campeau? Your grandmother sent me." The woman in the car didn't get out.

Skip walked over and offered her hand, which the other woman disdained. "I'm Skip Langdon from the police department."

"Police! Oh, Jesus, not LaBelle again." She was much lighter than her grandmother, slightly reddish, and she had thinned down. The former moon face, nicely made-up, peeked out from under a sleek hairdo.

"I'm afraid so."

Her eyes flashed fury. "What, then?" She glanced ostentatiously at her watch. "I have to pick up my daughter in ten minutes and then I have exactly an hour to make groceries before I have to get my son from the gym, drop him off, get to the beauty parlor, and get ready for out-of-town guests at three-thirty."

"I'll get out of your hair in thirty seconds." The other

woman visibly relaxed. "I just want to know if you're in touch with LaBelle."

"We haven't spoken in two years. Would you mind moving your car now?"

Flustered, Skip said, "Of course. Sorry to bother you," and trotted quickly to her car, caught up in Campeau's urgency.

Feeling snubbed (and also ravenous), Skip went home, changed to jeans, picked up an oyster po' boy to go and strolled to the Moonwalk, impressed at how peaceful the river had been the night before, wanting to watch it as she mulled her case and munched her sandwich.

Who in the hell was LaBelle Doucette (besides the daughter of Jaree and the great-granddaughter of Philomena), and why wouldn't she turn up? She was almost certainly still a prostitute and probably something of a loner. If Jeweldean Sanders's experience was any indication, she wasn't the sort who had a lot of friends.

It wasn't fair! Skip thought childishly. She knew she had been put on the case because of her Uptown sources, but the answer obviously wasn't Uptown. She didn't see how her famous sources could possibly cover this material. Irritated, she threw a bit of her sandwich to a hovering gull. And as the gull caught the crust, her mind came free of its rut and she realized her best source was a member of her own family. Her egregious brother, Conrad, to her disgust, had once been terribly fond of mentioning self-importantly the visits his fraternity brothers paid to ladies of the night.

Swallowing her pride, she phoned. He said, "Hello, Black Sheep."

"Hi, Pride of the Langdons. I need some help."

"On Saturday?"

"I'm trying to find a woman—an upscale prostitute, black, probably specializing in white tricks."

"Well, you've certainly come to the right place. I happen to be in bed with her, but she can't talk right now, her mouth being otherwise engaged."

"You are *so* disgusting!" She hated the sound of her voice, twelve years old and whiny; they had played out this scene dozens of times.

"Hey. Did you call or what? Who asked the question?"

"Not me, big brother. In case you didn't notice, I did *not* say, 'do you, in your great world wisdom, happen to know her?' I was *going* to say, have you heard anything?"

"Uh-uh. Who was that guy you were with at Chauncey's funeral?"

"None of your business." Jesus. She had almost said "beeswax." "I'm sorry. I didn't mean that. It was a filmmaker from California named Steve Steinman. Extremely nice man."

"But Jewish."

"Conrad, you fucking bastard—"

But he was laughing. "You fall for it every time, stupido."

He was right. Skip was famous for stomping out of rooms when their father made racist or anti-Semitic remarks. Conrad was also heartless, but too sophisticated to admit to similar views. However, now and then he'd pretend to be a bigot just to make her mad.

"Damn it, Conrad, why don't you grow up?"

"Why don't *you*?"

Hell. It was a standoff, as usual. "Conrad, I really need help. It could mean my whole career, no kidding."

"No shit. Gosh, your whole career. Now there's a valuable commodity."

"I guess I shouldn't have called." She was feeling humiliated and hooked into all the old games that he always won.

"Wait a minute. Maybe we can make a deal. I've gotten quite a few tickets lately."

"Parking tickets?"

"Uh-huh."

"How many?"

"About a dozen."

"God!"

"If you can't help, say so."

"Well, maybe I could help the least little bit—"

It ended up with her agreeing to fix five of the tickets and Conrad signing on to call around about LaBelle. She'd fix the tickets all right—by paying them herself; if he kept getting tickets, Conrad might even turn into a nice little source. She wondered if she could get snitch money to cover the fines.

Truth to tell, she didn't have much hope for the deal, but Conrad called back in two hours with a name. One thing she'd say for His Otherwise Worthlessness—to Mr. Young Making-It-In-The-Big-World, a deal was a deal. He'd simply stayed on the phone until he could deliver. What he delivered was this—an aging Deke named Hinky Hebert knew a call girl named LaBelle Doucette; he'd be at Tipitina's that night.

If there was a single person in New Orleans Skip thought more worthless than her brother, it was Hinky Hebert; and if she had to choose the single worst location in town to conduct an interview, it would have to be Tipitina's.

5

Shit! It was his sister. Christ, and André too. Henry was feeling about as avuncular as a lamppost. And about as fraternal. He was feeling pretty awful, pretty much wrung out just keeping it together. He didn't feel like coping with family right now. Earlier, Bitty had nearly done him in.

The stair clomping stopped, and he opened the door. "Hi, Sis." She kissed him on the cheek.

"Hi. Can André go in the bedroom and watch TV? I need to talk to you."

She needed to talk to him. He was taken aback. He couldn't remember ever having a heart-to-heart with Marcelle.

"Sure. Come on, Sport." He took André's hand and led him to the television.

When he got back, Marcelle was drinking a glass of wine. Having sworn off alcohol, Henry hated her for it. "Help yourself," he said.

"Thanks." She didn't even notice the sarcasm. "Henry, I've remembered something. Remember the summer we spent at Covington without Mother? When she only came on weekends?" She was in worse shape than he was; he saw it now. Her voice was coming in little whispered bursts, and she was gulping the wine.

He nodded, signifying that he remembered. (He was not likely to forget.)

"Mother attacked me."

"Marcelle, have you lost your tiny mind?"

"She did. She even asked me about it yesterday. And then I remembered it."

"What did you remember, pray tell?"

"She came at me with a weapon of some sort."

"A weapon? Bitty?" He was going extra-heavy on the sarcasm. "Our little ninety-nine pound bundle of utter helplessness?"

"Something big."

"An M-1 carbine, maybe?"

She chewed her lip. "Not a gun. She was only going to hit me, I think."

"Only going to hit you. As opposed to what? Murder you?"

"I don't . . . know." There was a lot of time between the last two words, as if Marcelle really had to think it out.

"You don't know? Do you hear yourself, Marcelle? Excuse me, but did you just accuse your own mother of trying to kill you?"

"I did not! You're the one who brought up murder!" To his horror, she started to cry. She turned away from him, ashamed, he supposed. "Anyway, she had a good reason." She wheeled back abruptly, going in for the dramatic, he thought. She said in a low, level voice, "I killed the baby, didn't I?"

"You what? You killed the baby? What baby, for Christ's sake?"

"Oh, Henry, please. Do you know how absurd you sound?" Brattily, she imitated him: "What baby?" Then she paused and spoke in an understated way he'd never heard before—quietly but with echoing undertones. "Look, I'll be okay. I swear to you I'll be okay. Just *please* quit trying to protect me, like everyone has all my fucking life." He hadn't thought she had so much passion in her.

"I'm not trying to protect you. I just don't know what you're talking about, that's all. What baby did you personally dispatch at age three and a half?"

"Our sister, goddamnit! And stop condescending to me!"

"Our sister? You remember killing her?"

"See! I did, didn't I?"

"You might have wanted to—"

"Oh, God, I did. I did. That part I can remember perfectly. And I probably dumped her out of her crib or conveniently dropped her when it was my turn to hold her. Didn't I? Please don't protect me, Henry. I need to know what happened. Please?"

"Marcelle, she never came home from the hospital. The baby never fucking made it home, okay? There's no way you could have killed her."

"She didn't?"

He shook his head slowly, hoping the deliberateness of it would have a sobering effect on her. "Furthermore," he said, "Bitty never attacked you."

"I remember it."

"You remember wrong."

"The baby never came home from the hospital?"

"Definitely not."

"Then what did she die of?"

Henry shrugged. "I don't know. Do adults tell little kids?"

"When they're big kids."

"Well, they never told me, okay? I don't know what she

246

died of—she just . . . *died*, all right? God, Marcelle you're unbelievable. In case you haven't noticed, there actually has been a murder in our family. Like this week, cookie."

Her saucer eyes blazed at him. "You've got a hell of a nerve to bring up Chauncey. *You* never gave a shit about him. You hated him!"

"So goddamn what, Marcelle? He was my father. Don't you think I feel anything? But listen, who am I anyway? Just the worthless faggot-actor brother—forget about me." He wheeled on her, trying her own tactic. "But what about *Bitty*? What about your mother? How do you think she feels right now? And you've got to invent your own little imaginary drama in the midst of a real tragedy. That's right, Marcelle— this is real. Your daddy's dead and your mother's suffering, all right? Would it be okay if just this once you didn't grab all the attention for yourself?"

"You self-righteous asshole." Marcelle spoke con- temptuously but in a normal tone of voice, not yelling. She let a beat go by, and he saw an unmistakable glint of cunning in her eyes. "I arrived at our suffering mother's house early this morning and made her breakfast, which I practically had to spoon-feed her. At her request I left so she could take what she called 'a nap,' and I returned after taking André to the movies. When I arrived, she began asking me about that summer. She brought it up, I didn't." She paused again, mad- deningly. "Where were you all day, brother dear?" She said it with a bitch smile.

Maybe she was the one who should go into acting. He said, "I was working."

"And after that?" Still the smile—it was unbelievable what a bitch she could be.

After that, he *had* dropped by; Bitty had been stinking drunk and incoherent. Too depressed to stay, he had left and found a trick to spend the day with. And now he hated him- self. For leaving his mother, for being unable to help her, for having meaningless sex, for betraying Tolliver—he shook his head in midthought, surprised to see that he felt quite that way about Tolliver.

But what was he to do now that he had given up drugs and alcohol? Sex was all he had.

He said, "I saw Bitty. While you were at the movies, I guess. She was asleep."

"That's easy enough to say, isn't it?" *Still that goddamn superior smile.*

"Marcelle, get out of here. Just get out. And take your brat with you."

"Believe me, I wouldn't leave André with you for two minutes."

He swung at her. She stumbled out of the way and fell backwards, landing on the floor.

He didn't help her up. He stood there shaking while she scrambled to her feet, watching warily to see if he would try again, and scuttled off to find André. He was unable to move or speak, his mind and body occupied with the almost impossible task of taking in the fact that he would have hit her if she hadn't got out of the way.

His door slammed and he heard her running, obviously carrying André, not willing to risk staying on the premises even as long as it would take to walk a toddler down the stairs. As he realized the implications of her fear, his heart beat faster and faster.

He understood that something large and uncontrollable, something that took odd, hair-raising twists, had been set in motion by their father's death. Very glad he wasn't drunk or stoned, he let himself see that it was something much more terrible than he had first thought, with wider-reaching consequences. He wished to God Marcelle hadn't started this pyrotechnical remembering of hers.

PARTNERS

"So what shall we do tonight?"

Steve had on jeans and a sweatshirt, a signal, Skip imagined, that he didn't want to do much of anything. She had on jeans herself, and the sweater Jimmy Dee had supplied for their first-almost-date two days ago. Slipping into the recycled outfit, she had felt her head with surprise, realizing it hardly hurt now, and something else had occurred to her, something that never had before. She had got it into her mind to try to please Steve, to be as nice to him as he had been to her for the last few days—to trust him enough to allow herself to do that.

"Everything," she answered. "That is, if you wouldn't mind accompanying me on a little police business."

"Not at all." She thought he was only pretending not to be surprised.

"But let's eat first."

They went to Liuzza's, with Steve preinstructed to call it Lye-oosa's, not Leeootza's, like some Yankee from California. Still, he shook his head over the menu, grumbling that a place with such a name, however mispronounced, ought to have more pride than to list "wop salad" for your dining pleasure. They ordered it anyway, along with garlic bread, fried dill pickles, overstuffed eggplant, pasta full of shrimp and oysters, and giant schooners of beer. When she picked up the tab, she thought he was going to fall on the floor. "Skip, you can't afford this."

He didn't know the whole works had come to only eighteen dollars. "Of course I can, once in a blue moon. Anyway, I wanted to thank you for the last few days. For your kindness." It was hard to say the word.

"You'd have done the same for me." He shrugged.

But she wouldn't have; she would never have gone so far out of her way for someone she hardly knew, would never have had the patience or imagination to dream up the elaborate "purification"—in a word, would never have been that kind.

"Let's check something, okay?"

They checked LaBelle's apartment, finding it dark as always, but Steve's appetite was only whetted. "Let's go look in the windows."

"I've already done that."

"But I haven't. What harm can it do?"

None. And I dedicated this evening to Steve, didn't I? Even if he doesn't know it.

"Okay," she said.

Steve parked on Governor Nicholls Street around the corner from the building. Skip led him to the side of LaBelle's building, where she had peeked through the hole in the rice paper. She turned her flashlight on the hole so Steve could see, but took a peek herself first, to make sure the sweater was still lying on the bed as it had been before. The place had been trashed.

"Oh, shit!"

Obviously unable to be polite a second longer, Steve snatched the flashlight. He took one quick look, tried the window and moved on to the bathroom window, still holding the light. "Was this window open before?"

He stood aside, letting her see that it was now. "No. Jesus."

"I'm going in."

"You can't do that."

But he had hoisted himself up to the sill. Too late to call Calvin Hogue, to call police headquarters, to do anything except arrest him—or follow. Without wasting a second she followed, finding footing on the toilet, from which Steve was just stepping. They came out of the bathroom into a hall, Steve first, the light in his hand. A sudden, surprised movement caught Skip's eye. Quickly, Steve turned the light toward it and a figure dressed in dark clothing turned, ran a few steps, paused to unlock the front door, and fled. Steve ran after it, getting in her way.

"Halt!" she said firmly. "Police." As she ran through the door, she paused to close it—ever the good citizen—and cost herself seconds.

The running figure—man or woman, Skip couldn't tell— was nearly a block away, Steve's bearlike form trailing by a good half block. She made a poor third.

"Halt!" she shouted again. The figure didn't even consider halting. It rounded the corner of Governor Nicholls and turned right. Good. She would let Steve pursue on foot while she got the car and closed in. That way the figure couldn't duck into the shadows while she was busy starting the car. She was getting comfortable with the idea when an unpleasant thought came to her.

It won't work. It's Steve's car.

But Steve, apparently of the same mind, stopped and began fumbling for his keys. As Skip passed, he said, "You continue on foot. I'll catch up." It was a good plan and she knew she ought to applaud his quick thinking and the fact that he hadn't given her some crap about looking out, but she was furious. A civilian had just given her orders on what was undeniably police business, and it didn't matter what civilian; she was furious. But she pounded after the intruder, beginning to reach for her gun. He rounded the corner of Tremé Street and by the time she had caught up, he had disappeared. Looking right and left, now holding her gun, she felt like a fool. *Where the hell could he be?*

She heard a car behind her now, Steve's almost certainly. Her eyes still swept the street as Steve's car rounded the corner, and now she felt an almost unbearable embarrassment. She, the policewoman, had let the burglar get away in front of an amateur Dirty Harry.

"Skip, get in."

She waved Steve away, not taking her eyes off the street, determined somehow to psyche out the person's presence.

"Get in!" His voice was urgent. "There he is!"

A car was pulling out of a place no more than a few yards ahead, burning rubber. She knew in an instant what had probably happened. He had rolled under his car to the street side and crouched to open the door, which he'd fixed not to trigger an inside light. She had simply been looking away when he slid carefully into the driver's seat.

Skip jumped into Steve's car, now so furious (at herself more than Steve), so full of adrenaline, and so caught up in her mission that the consequences of a high-speed chase in a private car didn't even occur to her.

Shitfire, he was fast. He led them around absurd twists and turns that got him only as far as North Rampart before he was stopped by a light. He turned left and then right onto Elysian Fields. Here in the Marigny was a good place to force him off the road. Steve tried, but the guy was nervy and fast enough, he apparently thought, to lose them in the labyrinth of small twisty streets here. He turned right onto Burgundy and then the wrong way on Frenchmen Street. They nearly hit a car at Washington Park.

Skip held her breath until they were on Esplanade again, going toward City Park, a straight shot. She knew their quarry wouldn't keep going straight for long, but she hoped he would until they could catch him at a light. She had a feeling lights were going to be his Waterloo. He was stopped at one now.

Undaunted, he went back across Rampart into Tremé and turned right onto North Claiborne, obviously meaning to get on the expressway. And if he made it they were dead. Damn! He did make it, with a U-turn on Touro. The ramp here went on forever, and tilted; the way Steve was driving Skip felt as if she was on a carnival ride, sweaty palms and all.

"What the hell," said Steve, "are we going to do if we catch him?"

"Radio for help?" She let a beat pass. "Oops, forgot— wrong car."

Steve's face was set, and he didn't answer. She was glad she had been flip. There was something about this long ramp that was helping her recover her equilibrium, both within herself and in her relationship with Steve. In this situation he had to know who was boss—it could save both their lives.

She said in a softer voice, "We may be able to force him off the road—it was good that you tried that on Elysian Fields. Frankly, it's probably our best shot."

"I'm glad you know what you're doing." She saw that perspiration was running down his nose. His adrenaline rush was wearing off.

"Are you okay?" she said.

"Fine."

But she wasn't sure he was. To calm him, she continued to talk. "What kind of car do you think that is?"

"Top-of-the-line Toyota—I forget what they call it. About

an '85, I think." His voice was coming back stronger now that they were in an area where he felt competent.

She said, "You didn't get a glimpse of the license plate, did you?"

He shook his head, apparently reluctant to continue, wanting only to concentrate on his driving. He was beginning to feel like a weight to Skip—she supposed this was some version of "smelling fear." But she knew it would do no good to try to persuade him to abandon the chase, and he wasn't yet so frightened he would make bad decisions.

They flew past the LSU Medical Center, past the Superdome, and onto South Claiborne. Suddenly the Toyota turned onto Washington and they were going through the projects. It seemed so quiet here, so desolate somehow. Skip shivered, suspecting she had a touch of white man's paranoia, something that hadn't even touched her in Tremé. She wondered if the driver ahead was experiencing it too—or if he were even white. Steve floored the accelerator, but still the Toyota kept well ahead. They were on Washington for miles, it seemed, and then the Toyota hit a light. In keeping with his strategy, the driver turned left, onto St. Charles.

Skip couldn't stand it. "This is absurd!" she screamed.

"What's absurd?" Steve spoke softly, as if trying to calm a hysteric.

Oh, great. Now he seemed back in control, and the way he'd gotten there was to imagine he had to be masculine and take care of a woman who was losing it. "Don't be so condescending," she said. "I'm not losing it. I'm just frustrated. Don't you see what we're doing? We're going back Downtown."

"So?"

"We just went Uptown!" She guessed only a New Orleanian could understand the stupid circle they were making and on second thought, she guessed stupid didn't enter into it—the guy was just trying to lose them whatever way he could. Clearly he had no plan—he was just driving aimlessly. Now that she thought about it, she realized this was in their favor. If only the damn Toyota wasn't so fast.

Calming down, she rubbed Steve's thigh and turned to him. "How're you doing?"

Briefly, he too turned and smiled at her, "I'm having the time of my life, to tell you the truth."

Oh great, again. He wasn't taking seriously the fact that they were in hot pursuit of a criminal. Or maybe he was just trying to reassure her. She wished she knew, and wished desperately that she hadn't gotten involved in this. *On the other hand, if it turns out right I might be arresting Chauncey's murderer sometime in the next few minutes.*

At Lee Circle the driver of the Toyota took the little jog at Howard that gets you onto Camp. From Camp he turned onto Canal, which curves as it gets close to the river, and the curve fetches up at—too late, Skip realized the driver did have a plan—the curve ends at the Canal Street Ferry. As they arrived, the Toyota was driving aboard.

Skip glanced quickly at the traffic light. Green. There was still time. She said, "I don't believe this," and Steve, instantly grasping the situation, drove triumphantly down the ramp.

They stared at each other, grinning, unable to contain their mutual delight.

"Trapped!" said Skip, banging her leg with her hand.

Steve said, "Like the rat he is."

"Or she is."

Skip was out of the car, gun stuck in her waistband, almost before Steve had turned off the ignition. This time she didn't want him in front of her, messing her up. As she slammed the door, she said firmly, "You stay here. I mean it," knowing it would do no good.

The driver had parked forward on the ferry and had hunkered down, probably aware now that he had been almost unbelievably stupid to have panicked and driven onto the boat. But the rat metaphor held—trapped animals were violent, and he might have a gun.

Skip held up her badge and bellowed, "Police. Get back, please. Get back."

A few lollygaggers got back, Steve along with them, she was happy to see.

Standing behind the Toyota, she spoke to it. "Let me see your hands. Sit up and put your hands on your head. Now."

Nothing happened. What to do? She could give the driver a count of five, hoping he'd lose his nerve, or she could rush the car. She needed another officer; she wished she could ask Steve to open the door so she could be quicker with her gun, but she couldn't endanger his life any further.

Forget the count of five. I'm too nervous.

She pulled the door open on the passenger side. No one was in the front seat. Roughly she pulled the seat back forward, but by now she knew what she would find—nothing.

She kicked the car, hollered loudly, "Shit!" and made for the stairs up to the passenger deck, steps pounding behind her—Steve's, she was sure. Behind her someone said, "Language!" and the group of men laughed.

As she reached the upper deck, the ferry started to pull away. "Shit!" she said again, sure now what had happened. She had been outsmarted by a rat. The Toyota driver had simply climbed upstairs and walked off the ferry. "Double shit!"

Steve put a hand on her shoulder, but she shook it off. She wasn't in any mood to be comforted.

Only one person was riding on this deck, a black man, snoozing. Sticking the gun back in her waistband, she touched his shoulder. "Excuse me, sir." He came awake with a jolt. "Did you see someone walk off the ferry a minute or two ago?"

He shook his head and closed his eyes again. Briefly, she wondered if this was the man who had been driving the Toyota, but she thought he was the wrong build—too stocky by far. And his shirt was yellow, whereas the burglar had worn something dark.

Steve said, "What do we do now?"

"We go to Algiers," she said. "Look, there's a chance he's still on the boat. I'm going to look around. Can I trust you to stay here?"

"He's not on the boat."

Her belly, getting one of its twinges, told her it was true. "I've got to look anyhow."

She walked away, not glancing at him again, pretending to herself that she was confident he'd follow orders.

There was only one other woman on the boat and she was too old, too heavy, and too short to have been the person they were chasing. Among the men there were one or two candidates, but none looked exactly right—either their clothing or body types seemed slightly off.

Skip went back to the Toyota, thinking to search it, and found Steve there standing guard (for which she was grateful). No point, she thought, worrying about prints on the door handle since she had probably spoiled any such opportunity. She opened the car and saw, as she hadn't before, that there was a woman's stocking lying in the front—or rather half of a pair of panty hose that she surmised had been used as a mask—and a pair of plastic gloves. There was nothing in the glove compartment but maps, and nothing else in the car, not even keys.

At Algiers, everyone got off except Steve and Skip. No one claimed the car. Skip hunted up the captain for help on a thorough search of the boat. But there were no stowaways.

On the ride back they went up to the passenger deck, able to relax for the first time in an hour or more. Even now, in winter, Skip could feel the heaviness of the river. It was cold, and Steve tried to draw her to him, but she pulled away.

On land she made a quick call to get the Toyota towed and handled with care, and to have its license number run through the computer. It was registered to a Horton Charbonnet, a name she didn't know. But her mind wasn't on the car—it was on getting back to LaBelle's, where she'd be met by people from the crime lab and homicide. She and Steve said almost nothing on the drive over. Skip was worried about what she had to tell him.

But he had guessed. As he parked he asked, "Do I have to wait outside?"

"I'm sorry. It's a crime scene."

"Should I just leave?"

"Not if you want to go to Tipitina's."

"You've got to be kidding. You want to go dancing? After this?"

"Not exactly. I have to interview someone there. Want to come with me?"

He shrugged. "Sure."

"When the others get here, I'll come get you. You were a witness, and we'll have to interview you. Just do me a favor—make it clear I couldn't stop you from going through the damned window."

She gave him a kiss on the cheek and went back into the apartment. The place was a mess. There was dust and a dead plant, indicating the owner hadn't been around lately, and there were the signs of a systematic search—things not destroyed, but moved fast and thrown to the floor. Surveying the house, she saw that the searcher had not quickly found what he was looking for; every room had been torn apart, every picture pulled from the wall as if to find a safe—a preposterous idea, thought Skip, in such a building. Having no gloves, she plucked one of LaBelle's tissues to use as a handkerchief.

There were few papers—only records of bills LaBelle had paid, but no tax records, and no books. In the living room, though, there was a good collection of records, mostly jazz and other music by black artists, each record pulled from its jacket, some of the jackets torn apart. On the coffee table, open facedown as if it had been shaken, was a dime-store scrapbook, ivory-colored and held picturesquely together with cord rather than bound. Using her tissue, she turned it over.

It was a scrapbook of newspaper clips, stories about the St. Amants, particularly about Chauncey. But each time Bitty or Marcelle went to a luncheon and got a mention in the society column, the entire column had been clipped and the relevant item underlined in plain blue ink, the lines sometimes shakily drawn. Every time Chauncey moved, practically, he got his name in the papers—for political contributions, for serving on boards, for being president of a bank that did a lot of business in the city. There were only two clips on Henry— one saying a play was about to open in which he was one of the actors, and then a review of the play.

It was a meticulously kept record of more than a year in the life of the St. Amants—fourteen months, to be exact. It went back no further than that.

One other item caught Skip's attention—a framed painting of a New Orleans street scene, a picture inexpertly but lovingly painted by an obvious amateur—Philomena Doucette, was Skip's guess, in some senior-center art class. It had been tossed facedown on the floor and she thought she saw tape marks on the back, as if something had been torn from it. She was staring at it, wondering what it meant, when her homicide contact arrived—Sylvia Cappello, young, bright, and all business.

A man from the crime lab came and busied himself while she filled Cappello in on the case and the burglary, then showed her the scrapbook and the painting with the tape marks. Cappello seemed dubious about the painting, but at least she was polite about it. She was a little brusque—maybe insecure—but definitely someone Skip could work with. She'd gladly have traded O'Rourke for her.

Cappello interviewed Steve politely and efficiently, except for a little impatience when he got to the part about breaking into LaBelle's. He claimed now that he'd heard a noise— though Skip hadn't heard it and he hadn't mentioned it before.

Cappello pointed a pencil at him. "You were with a police officer. Why didn't you report the noise to her?"

"I didn't think. I was excited."

"When one civilian enters another's home, it's called breaking and entering."

Steve didn't answer.

Cappello said, "I think Officer Langdon would have already put you under arrest if she felt that was in order, but I'm sure she gave you a stern warning; I'm going to give you one too." She had very black eyebrows, and the way she bunched them was its own warning.

"I understand. I'm sorry," Steve spoke very quietly, barely above a whisper, and Skip almost believed he meant it.

It was shortly after eleven-thirty when they left for Tipitina's—early yet. Her original thought had been to go there alone—Hinky Hebert wouldn't even turn up till most decent people were already home from their Saturday night dates, snuggling down for a long winter's night. She could easily have begged off spending the night with Steve and gone out again after a full evening, with Steve none the wiser. She had decided to take him in that moment, pulling on her sweater, when she made up her mind to give him the evening.

"This is your Uptown joint?" asked Steve as they approached what anyone could have seen was a joint, and a crowded one at that, a frat rat type of clientele spilling onto the sidewalk.

"Uptown is a state of mind but also a place," Skip said. "And we are most undeniably Uptown, aren't we? Besides, look at that crowd."

"How the hell can you tell one kid in a Hard Rock Café T-shirt from another?"

"You have to look at their tennies," she said. "Reeboks mean the same thing here as anywhere."

The inside was a dark barn with corrugated metal walls, bar, stage, and a bunch of kids drinking Dixies. Skip clenched her teeth as they elbowed their way to the bar, thinking Hinky Hebert was a little old for this scene.

Yet, looking around her, she remembered her own days here. Then, as now, the students felt it was their own special purview, but nonetheless, even then the crowd had been sprinkled with kids of all ages. There had always been a few just-over-the-hills, like Steve and herself, in casual clothes; bohemian-looking types of any age at all wearing God knows what; and much older people, the forty-to-sixty crew, dressed for a gala evening—sometimes, especially during Carnival, in evening clothes. Tipitina's was a very "in" joint and therefore often scorned by the jaded, older (meaning mid-twenties) natives such as herself, who would just as soon leave it to the kids and the Hinky Heberts. But every time she was dragged there, kicking and screaming all the way, she remembered what its charm was—the music was absolutely unbeatable.

Tonight the headliner was Charmaine Neville, and now the stage was dominated by a big mama named Marvella Brown. She had the usual girth, the Mae West kind of moves and jokes, the cynical songs that put her men in a bad light. And she had the usual three female backup singers, two in the usual seductive outfits, the other in a black skirt and plain jacket, prompting Skip to wonder if she'd rushed straight from the airport without even a moment to change. Steve said no, she probably belonged to some Christian sect or other, a notion hard to reconcile with some of Marvella's material.

Hinky Hebert's skinny shoulders were nowhere in sight. Skip kept scanning the crowd, every now and then recognizing younger brothers or sisters of her peers, none of whom recognized her. Too stoned, too drunk or, in more than one case, too stupid, she surmised.

Marvella was throwing her several hundred pounds into her finale when Skip spotted the white shirt and khaki pants of Hinky Hebert's best friend since grade school, Bobby Alexander. Aha, where Bobby was, Hinky couldn't be far behind. Bobby had his arm around a female who looked to Skip too small to be his wife, but couldn't be anyone else—Tipitina's on a Saturday night wasn't a sneaking-around kind of place. Sure enough, Hinky was approaching now, carrying three Dixies. Bobby let the woman go and took one; as the woman leaned forward for hers, Skip broke out in a sudden apprehensive sweat. Oh, God, the woman had seen her. She was waving. The others turned round and waved. The woman was Mary Earle O'Rourke, wife of Frank the Oppressor.

By the time the break had begun, and she and Steve had purchased fresh Dixies, her heart had stopped pounding. She was saved from having to search through the crowd by her quarry himself—or by the rest of his crowd at any rate, which amounted only to Bobby and Mary Earle. (Like Tolliver, Hinky never had a date, although no one seriously imagined him a homosexual. They assumed he was usually far too drunk to be interested in anything other than music.)

When Skip had introduced Steve, Mary Earle said, "I hear you and Bobby know each other."

"Have since kindergarten. But I didn't know you two did."
She let her eyes travel from Mary Earle's face to Bobby's.

"Meet my new fiancée," said Bobby.

Skip stared back at Mary Earle, bewildered. "He's not kiddin', honey," she said. "I left Frank six months ago—or hadn't you heard?"

"I hadn't."

"We're living together," said Bobby. "It's been kind of hard on JoAnn—"

"I think it's been hard on Frank too. And believe me, I'm in a position to know. I've been working with him."

Mary Earle said, "I hear he's a bear lately. Somebody told me even Joe can't stand him anymore."

"You wouldn't consider going back to him, would you?"

Bobby grimaced. "Do we have to talk about Frank?"

"Can I get you a beer, Bob?" asked Steve, perfectly able to see Bobby already had one, and Skip loved him for it. She used the interruption, as she knew he meant her to, to get away.

Hinky Hebert was leaning against the stage, both arms around the waist of an Italian-looking beauty of eighteen or so. "Hi, Romeo."

"Hello, Skippy darlin'." His speech was only a little slurred. He released the girl and threw his arms around Skip. "How's that brother of yours?"

"You should know. You talked to him today, didn't you?" Over his shoulder, Skip watched the young beauty slink away. Hinky released her.

"Talked to him?"

"He didn't phone to tell you I'd meet you here?"

"Is this a fix-up?" Hinky roared, apparently finding the idea the funniest he'd heard lately.

"Sort of. Police business, baby. You sure Conrad didn't talk to you?"

"Positive."

"So how'd he know you'd be here?"

He roared again. "Darlin', I'm here every night of the week. Everybody knows that. And if I'm not here, I'm at Jimmy's and if I'm not at Jimmy's I'm at the Maple Leaf and if I'm not at the Maple Leaf—"

"I get the idea, Hinky."

Skip didn't like it when she caught herself thinking in stereotypes, but Hinky made her think of white bread. Despite his French surname (and possibly Catholic faith, Skip didn't know about that) he seemed to her as bland and pallid as any WASP who ever sprang from the imagination of Woody Allen. Not the gorgeous rich kid of regattas and ski resorts, but the cousin from out of town who drank so much and acted so weird he quickly became the fraternity mascot.

No wonder he never had a date, Skip thought—he was a joke, with his narrow shoulders, pasty skin, spectacles, thinning brownish hair, khaki trousers just like Bobby's, and utterly blank expression. You looked, you thought, "nobody home," and you were about to move on when he said something either stupid, offensive, downright mean, or simply eccentric, depending on how drunk he was. And sometimes you stayed to talk, fascinated by his smallness.

"Listen," she said, "What's with Bobby and Mary Earle?"

"Haven't you heard? Alison Gaillard must not have been living up to her reputation."

"Alison and I aren't close," she said, uncomfortable that this was true and that, in spite of it, she'd used Alison for information.

"Darlin', this is prime." The glasses were very thick, but Skip thought that she could see a malicious glint behind them. "Somebody broke into Bobby and JoAnn's and attacked JoAnn. Mary Earle—" his voice went up on the name—"was the officer assigned to the case."

"Oh, my God."

Hinky held up his right hand, as if being sworn in as a witness. "It's true."

Skip wondered if she was turning green. "How do you mean 'attacked?' Raped?"

"*Mary Earle* says not. *Mary Earle* says the medical evidence showed nothing of the sort. And guess what? The so-called rapist stole JoAnn's engagement ring. Remember it? The one Bobby had made out of three rings of his grandmother's—about fifty carats, all told? Tackiest thing you ever saw?"

Skip nodded. No one who'd ever seen the ring was likely to forget it.

"Well, Bobby found it about a week later when he just *happened* to be rooting through JoAnn's lingerie drawer. And once he found it, it suddenly occurred to him that the case needed further discussion with Sergeant O'Rourke. And furthermore, it occurred to him not to mention to JoAnn that he'd found it—after all, a stolen item couldn't be stolen, could it?"

Skip was awed. "So she couldn't report it again."

"Brilliant, wasn't he?"

"But what was JoAnn up to?"

"*Well . . .*" he pronounced the word campily, wringing every bit of drama out of it. ". . . according to Alison Gaillard, JoAnn has been seeing Jo Jo Lawrence—"

"Hasn't everybody?"

Hinky gave her an evil look. "You too, darlin'? I wouldn't have thought—"

"Of course not, you idiot. I meant everybody else." Damn! She'd gotten sucked into his game.

"Well, anyway, JoAnn thought she was pregnant and Bobby's tight as a tick, you know, which meant she couldn't even get an abortion without him finding out about it. So she pawned the ring to pay the doctor and staged the so-called rape. But the next day she got her period, and redeemed the little bauble. Ingenious, don't you think?"

"Oh, Hinky, for heaven's sake—why didn't she just borrow the money? Or get it from Jo Jo?"

"You're missing the beauty of it, darlin'. This way she never had to wear that fuckin' ugly thing again."

Skip laughed. "All that from Alison?"

"Well, actually"—Hinky came as close to blushing as she'd ever seen him—"one night early on in the romance, when Bobby was out with Mary Earle, JoAnn and I—"

"Don't tell me, I can't stand it." Skip put her hands over her ears, but she needn't have bothered; Charmaine Neville had begun her set, tossing her wonderful wild hair to a salsa beat. Hinky had turned back toward the stage. Holding his beer in one hand, he was beating the other against his thigh.

Skip leaned over and yelled in his ear. "Hinky! I need to talk to you."

He looked at her in surprise. "Weren't we talking?"

She felt an arm snake around her waist. Without turning around, she snuggled against the barrel-shaped chest she knew must be Steve's. She raised one hand to touch his cheek. It was a show for Hinky, to distract him with the promise of fresh gossip, but it didn't work. Seeing she was occupied, he went back to the music. Quickly she whispered to Steve that this was the man she had come to see and once again she yelled in Hinky's ear. "Come outside for a second. Please?"

He stared at Steve. "Darlin', there's not a thing I could do for you that guy couldn't do a lot better."

"Oh, Hinky, can it. This is about a murder case." She was shouting so loud she was getting hoarse.

The bland eyes flickered behind the glasses. "Chauncey?" She nodded.

"Later," he shouted. "Charmaine's my favorite."

"Skip," yelled Steve. "I really need to get home."

"Go ahead. I'll get a ride with somebody."

"I'm not leaving you."

"Go. I'll be okay."

They were yelling so loud people were starting to stare.

"No. I'm not leaving without you."

"For heaven's sake, leave. I'm fine."

Hinky turned back toward her with a disgusted look. "Okay!" he shouted. "We'll go now. That way at least I can catch the second half of the set."

Skip turned to Steve, who gave her a quick wink. She winked back and mouthed "thanks." Aloud she said (or rather shouted), "I'll just be a minute."

But Hinky pulled at her sleeve. "Uh-uh, I want to meet this guy. I've been hearing about him."

They filed out behind him, Skip marveling once again at the small-town quality of the place. She had been dating Steve for less than a week and already everyone knew about it. But she reminded herself that it was her own fault—they had been rather obviously together at Chauncey's funeral.

The night air was slightly chilly. She shivered, taking a long pull at her Dixie (now in a go-cup) to repair her scratchy vocal cords. While she drank, the men introduced themselves. Hinky said, "I *heard* our Skippy finally met a guy big enough for her."

Steve laughed. "I'm not big enough to call her Skippy, though. She's made that pretty clear."

"Tell me," said Hinky, "is it true you screwed Simi *and* Susie Barclay over at Cookie Lamoreaux's house the Monday before Mardi Gras?"

Skip gulped.

"Not true at all," said Steve. "That was a fellow named Joe Paul Carter. Ol' boy down from Winona, Mississippi. Looks a lot like me."

Skip had to work to keep her jaw from flapping open. *"Ol' boy"? Can this be Steve Steinman speaking?*

Hinky said, "Shee-it. I thought it was you."

"Hinky," said Skip, wanting finally to get down to it, "I hear you can tell me about a woman named LaBelle Doucette."

"Well, that's kind of a personal question, officer."

"Excuse me, but did you just ask my friend here what he did with whom on a particular day? And what he did with whom else?"

Hinky emitted his roar. "I guess I have to answer, huh?"

"I guess you do."

"Well, LaBelle's a black call girl. Best lookin' little piece o' ass in Orleans Parish. Whooo!"

"Go on."

"Want to know what positions she likes?"

"She doesn't like any of them, honey. Prostitutes lie about that sort of thing."

"Now don't go feminist on me, officer."

"Oh, for heaven's sake, call me Skippy." She turned to Steve. "You didn't hear that."

"Did you say this has something to do with Chauncey's murder?"

"It might." She felt a funny twinge in her belly, the beginnings of regret that she'd mentioned Chauncey.

Hinky was chewing on a nail. "Something sounds right about that. I wonder if he was the 'important New Orleanian.'"

"Maybe you should start from the beginning."

"Well, LaBelle's been getting around quite a bit lately. She's cut quite a swath through the old crowd; I forget who discovered her—Jack Kincaid, maybe—but everybody knows her now."

Skip was shocked—not at the notion of call girls. You lived with that in a place where the Madonna-whore separation was so much the recognized norm that plenty of Uptown women—lots of them not even Catholics—claimed they'd made love with their husbands only when their children were conceived.

What shocked her was that the "old crowd" had apparently managed to blot the AIDS danger out of their consciousness. In a mood to make trouble, she said, "I heard she's a junkie."

Hinky shrugged. "Could be, darlin', but she carries her own rubbers. Likes to say, 'no glo-o-o-ove, no l-o-o-ove,' in this real sultry voice. And if you happen to bring your own (the supersensitive kind) she'll make you leave 'em in your pocket. It's latex or nothin' with that young lady. So everybody feels safe with her. I mean, it's not like anybody wants to *kiss* her."

"What about the 'important New Orleanian'?"

"Miss LaBelle has some very high-falutin' fantasies about herself—or else pretending she does is part of her routine. *Moi,* I think she's nuts. The gist of it is that she claims she's the illegitimate daughter of some bigwig."

"White or black?"

"Who asks? No, wait—white. I know because that *is* part of the routine. She tries to make you think it's your own dad—says things like, 'I could be your sister,' and asks you what you've always really deep down wanted to do with your sister and like that. Didn't go over too well with me—I've always wanted to strangle the little bitch. So I made LaBelle quit doing it and she switched to some pirate and slave girl number. She probably has a million of them."

"Did she ever say anything to make you think there might be a grain of truth in the story?"

Hinky kept quiet for a minute, as if he was thinking, an exercise with which Skip wasn't sure he was familiar. Finally he said, "No. I can't honestly say she did."

"Okay, one more thing, on another subject. Did you ever know a woman named Estelle Villere? Worked for Chauncey St. Amant?"

"I've heard of her, but I never actually saw the lady."

"When you want to see LaBelle, how do you get in touch with her?"

"First of all, you have to book weeks in advance—she goes out of town a lot. And it has to be at your place or a hotel—she only does out-calls. If I give you her number, can I go back and catch the end of Charmaine?"

Steve was all for going back with him, but Skip pleaded exhaustion. When they were in the car he said, "I really appreciate your letting me hear that. I feel like maybe you trust me."

She liked his California style of saying so if you were pleased with your lover. But at the moment she wasn't particularly pleased with herself. She said, "I didn't have any choice, remember? Hinky had an important question for you."

He ignored her. "What do you think? Is Chauncey 'the important New Orleanian'?"

The truth was that Skip was as eager to talk about the case as he was, and after what he had heard, discretion seemed absurd. She told him about the scrapbook. "But that doesn't mean she really is his daughter. Maybe she has a relative who is or met someone who is, and that's where she got the idea—"

"Could you be a little clearer on that one?"

"Sorry. I was just thinking aloud. Chauncey had a long affair with a black woman named Estelle Villere. She was his secretary, and she quit very suddenly. If she had a baby, I think it would have been younger than LaBelle. But LaBelle could have met the child somehow and picked up the idea for that story she told. Baby-sitting, maybe."

Steve laughed. "Before she figured out an easier way to make a living. Anyway, suppose she is Chauncey's kid. Does that give her a murder motive?"

"Yeah, I'd say she had a motive. You should see where she grew up. If that place turned her as mean as it would have turned me, she could have killed him just for dumping her there. But somehow I can't see it—she was probably making a pretty good living as a call girl . . ."

"Good living my ass. Haven't you noticed that hellhole she lives in?"

Skip didn't answer.

Steve said, "Okay, how about this scenario. Whoever Mom is—"

"She's a woman named Jaree Campeau. I've spoken to her."

"Okay." said Steve, "Jaree gets drunk or angry or something and tells LaBelle who her dad is—I presume there would have been hush money . . ."

"Yes. LaBelle's great-grandmother said something good happened to Jaree—that she got to go to college. Maybe Chauncey paid for it and Jaree sacrificed the kid by letting her grow up in the project.

"But say LaBelle came back. Come to think of it, Jaree and Mrs. Doucette said she did. And suppose she asked for money. And Jaree didn't have any or got tired of buying drugs or maybe still had a lot of hidden anger toward Chauncey—anyway, in a moment of pique or something, she says, 'get it from your father if you can,' and spills the beans."

"Exactly what I was thinking," said Steve. "So LaBelle gets up this whole fantasy about herself and how she ought to be taken care of by her dad and she invites him to support her. But he won't, so she kills him."

"Of course that doesn't explain where she is, or who tore her place up." Skip yawned.

"Tired?" He started the car.

"Really beat." And tomorrow she had to try to track down Horton Charbonnet, Toyota owner, if Cappello hadn't found him; and she still hadn't found Estelle Villere. Suddenly she felt panicked. Overwhelmed. She had vowed to give Steve the evening and she had. That was as far as she could go. "Would you mind if we didn't spend the night together? I've got a full day tomorrow."

"Of course not." A muscle in his cheek twitched, and she knew he did mind. She minded herself. They had met at the wrong time.

Her apartment felt strange to her and there was a draft—Jimmy Dee hadn't yet had her window fixed, and she had had to tape paper over the hole. She hadn't slept here alone since the burglary. She felt oddly forlorn.

Reluctantly, she admitted to herself that she was afraid. *Not really afraid—I'm a cop, for Christ's sake. But spooked. Definitely spooked.* She had some brandy left from the other night. A couple of quick belts and she was out.

She wasn't sure what woke her—some sort of bump, she thought later, but when her eyes flew open she saw the figure in the half-light; LaBelle's burglar, the Toyota driver. It was still dark and the person was still only a shape wearing a stocking mask.

The shape was standing over her, holding something, as if he planned to hit her with it. She rolled quickly to the other side of the bed, feeling for her gun, but unable, in her fog, to remember where she had put it. The figure ran out the front door.

Skip felt groggy and her head hurt, probably from the brandy. It took every ounce of her strength to get out of bed, locate the gun, and run down the stairs, but this asshole had broken into her home twice, this time obviously meaning to harm her; it was not something she could let go.

She turned onto Bourbon heading Uptown, not sure what else to do; a block ahead she saw a running figure. "Halt!" she yelled, knowing he couldn't possibly hear her. The last of the Saturday night carousers were beginning to stagger their way home. He would blend easily into the crowd. But what about her? A six-foot wild-haired, barefoot woman in a nightgown and brandishing a gun? Common sense told her to go back home immediately, but she could not. The feeling of violation was too great. Her head was clear now; she was furious.

"Halt, Goddamnit!" she yelled as she passed a knot of revelers in their early twenties.

"Help! Herbie, help!" squeaked one of the girls.

Someone answered, "Careful! She's got a gun!"

What if they call the police?

The notion of being handcuffed by officers who didn't know her and were under the impression she was a madwoman was too much. The burglar would get away—there was no question of that—and Skip would end up in a nightmare if she didn't go home now. She stopped running and crossed the street so as not to pass Herbie and his friends again. She looked straight ahead, trying to look sane, but knew in her heart it was hopeless. Herbie's group, shrinking against the buildings, was going quietly into one of the still-open bars, to call the police, she knew. Well, then, the hell with looking sane—the thing to do was to get off the street before they got there. She jogged home, rather enjoying the sensation of running barefoot in the cold.

The burglar had come through the already-broken window—damn Jimmy Dee for not having it fixed before he left for the weekend. On closer inspection she could see that not only had he used the same window, he had once again used Jimmy Dee's ladder, which Jimmy Dee had simply returned to his still-unlocked storeroom. Damn him again!

Pulling on a sweatshirt and jeans, and pinning up her hair, to look as different as possible from the lunatic the cops would be stalking, Skip went around to the back and dragged the ladder into her own building, leaving it downstairs in the entryway. As she worked, she heard a siren and was shocked to find herself frightened by it. If she had been spooked before, that was nothing.

The break in the window was small—just large enough for someone to ram a hand through and unlock the window. She had taped the paper on it at Jimmy Dee's request rather than board it up and leave nasty nail holes. Should she board it up now?

No. She couldn't handle spending that much time here. She would call a glazier as soon as it was late enough and send the bill to Dee-Dee, damn him again.

For now, she had to get out. Even as she locked her door and headed to her car, she wasn't sure where she would go.

GENEALOGY

1

"André, can you play in your room, darlin'? Mustn't wake Skip, baby."

"Will you come with me, Mommy?"

Marcelle definitely didn't want to play four-year-old games before she had had her coffee, but it wasn't fair to André to shut him up alone while Skip was sleeping on the sofa. And she couldn't wake Skip after what she'd been through. What to do?

Make a deal, as usual: "Honey, Mommy needs her coffee right now. Could you play alone for a while? And we'll go to the park later."

"Okay."

He padded off like the little gentleman he was, and Marcelle marveled at her good luck. It had to be that—dumb luck—because much better mothers than she had perfectly awful children.

She made coffee for herself and Skip, not knowing if Skip would even wake up before it cooled but wanting compulsively to do something for her. After the initial fear attached to having her doorbell rung by a policewoman at dawn, she was childishly grateful to Skip for coming to her. This must truly mean they were friends—and surely no friend would destroy her and what was left of her family. Surely as long as Skip slept on her couch the St. Amants were safe.

She wondered if there were any eggs.

"Marcelle? What time is it? Is it afternoon or anything?"

Skip padded in, barefoot as André, wearing the T-shirt Marcelle had given her to sleep in.

What fabulous thighs she has. If I had that much weight on me, I'd ripple like Jell-O in a hurricane.

"It's only about ten. Would you like some coffee?"

"I'd love it." She sat down at the kitchen table. "Marcelle, I've been trying really hard to find the woman you told me about."

"Oh, Skip. You don't think she's the one who broke in, do you?"

"No, because that person also broke into her house."

"You know where she lives."

"Uh-huh, and her name and everything. I just can't find her, that's all. She's LaBelle Doucette—does that mean anything?"

Marcelle chewed a cuticle. "I don't think so."

Skip looked up at her, compassion in her green eyes, and sadness, Marcelle thought. "You know that old saying about omelets and eggs?" Skip said. "I hate to mention it, but I think you and I need to have a serious talk."

Marcelle pulled warm, lovely French bread from the toaster and gave it to Skip. Her own throat was closing. Skip buttered her toast lustily, apparently oblivious to the fact that Marcelle was shaking as she sat down to join her.

"Is it going to be awful, Skippy?"

"Only a little. Can you stand finding out some things about your father that you never wanted to know?"

Marcelle couldn't find her voice. She shook her head, wanting the whole conversation to disappear.

Skip spoke reasonably, calming a child: "It's important, Marcelle. I think we need to do this to find out who killed him."

It was not bad enough her father was dead. Now he couldn't even be her father anymore, the Chauncey who had held her and made her feel as if not having a mother wasn't really the worst thing in the world.

Skip didn't wait for an answer, but kept talking. "Let's talk about the day of the murder first." Quickly, she corrected the faux pas. "I mean, about Mardi Gras."

Marcelle managed a small smile. "It's okay. You can say the 'm' word."

"Can you remember more or less what happened that morning—who came and went when?"

"Oh, Skippy!" Before she could turn away, giant tears were running down her face. "Oh, Skippy, it's so humiliating."

"You can tell me."

"I wasn't even there, hardly. I mean, I was, but not so's you'd notice."

Skip waited.

"Promise you won't tell this."

"I'll do my best."

"I know you will. I'm so ashamed." She composed herself, biting a hunk out of her lower lip to keep it from trembling. "I was upstairs screwin' Jo Jo Lawrence."

"In the *Boston Club*?"

Skip sounded so shocked Marcelle felt a chuckle rise in the back of her throat. Something about the italics seemed so innocent she felt suddenly like a sorority girl exchanging confidences. "They have this 'sleeping room' upstairs, I guess in case somebody gets too drunk to go home."

"Oh, *sure.*"

"No, really—I mean, it's definitely not for screwing. There's not even a lock on the door."

Skip's eyes twinkled. "Anyone peek in?"

"I don't know. I was facing the wrong way."

They both collapsed in giggles. But Skip was not distracted. When she had wiped the tears from her eyes, she said, "I need to ask you something about Stelly Villere."

"You already asked why she left. I don't know."

"Did you know your father had a pretty well-known affair with her?"

No. It can't be true. Stelly taught me how to French-braid my hair. She didn't answer.

"I'm really sorry, Marcelle, but she could be involved in all this."

"Stelly could? She wasn't the woman I saw."

"I'm still wondering if that woman could be a relative of Stelly's, though. Or a friend."

Marcelle couldn't make sense of this. "I don't see how Stelly fits into it."

"I don't know that she does. But she left her job very suddenly, and no one seems to know why."

"But that was years ago."

"You must have been no more than a teenager."

"I was nineteen, and Stelly must have been in her early thirties. I couldn't bear the thought of never seeing her again." She shrugged. "But I guess I must have fallen in love or something—or maybe I lost my nerve because she was black. I don't remember what happened. Anyway, I never called her."

"You had her phone number?"

Marcelle nodded. "I remember getting it out of Daddy's Rolodex." She shrugged. "I probably still have it."

"No kidding! Could you give it to me?"

"Sure." She searched in her own file. "Oh, look here—two numbers. One in New Orleans and one in Harvey. The one in Harvey's marked, 'after Nov. 1.' I copied it down."

Skip hugged her. "I don't believe it. You're a wonder."

"It may be outdated."

"It's the best I've gotten so far." Writing down the number must have reminded her of something. She grinned and said, apropos of nothing, "Did you know Bobby Alexander moved out on JoAnn?"

"Oh, sure. Moved in with that policewoman—there was a rumor it was you for a while. But I told Alison Gaillard no *way* would you look at that wimp. Which reminds me—how about that filmmaker guy you brought to the funeral?"

Her heroine, the female new centurion, blushed like a seventh grader. "He's nice." She shrugged, looking entirely uncomfortable. "I like him."

"Seeing him every day?"

Skip didn't answer. "Listen, I hate to say it, but the hard part isn't over yet. I want you to think very carefully about this. I've had a tip about LaBelle, the black woman. It might not be true, but I have to check it out."

Frightened again and once more unable to speak, Marcelle only nodded.

"Have you ever heard of a woman named Jaree Campeau? Or, wait—her maiden name was probably Jaree Doucette."

"No."

"Your father never spoke of her?"

"Who is she?" Marcelle croaked.

"LaBelle's mother. I think there's a chance Chauncey was her father."

"He couldn't have been." Her throat was opening, her voice getting strong again. "My father wasn't like that."

Skip was silent, looking into her cup.

"I mean, maybe he fucked around a little. Do you know about alcoholics? I do, there's no way I couldn't know, is there? I've read quite a bit of stuff on it. What happens is that the 'chemical-free partner,' as they call it, stops respecting the alcoholic and loses interest in sex. Can you blame him?"

"It's an awful situation."

Damn! Why did she have to be so coolly diplomatic and noncommittal?

"How would you like to go to bed with someone who smelled like booze was coming out of his pores like sweat? Well, my mother smells that way. Of *course* Daddy had to have sex with someone else. I can't blame him for that, can you?"

"I guess nobody could," Skip said carefully.

"Okay, so maybe he screwed around, but he would never, never in a million years have abandoned a child. He just didn't have it in him."

"What would he have done? Brought her home to live with you and Henry and Bitty?"

Marcelle was taken aback. *What would he have done?* "He would have taken care of her—"

"I think he tried to. I think he gave Jaree some money."

"He wouldn't have treated any daughter of his like he treated that woman. I saw it! No way in hell he would have ordered her away and slammed the door on her—he just wouldn't have."

Again, Skip didn't speak.

"You think I'm idealizing him, don't you? Okay, look, I guess that's only normal under the circumstances. But listen to this—Chauncey heard Henry say 'bastard' once, when he was about twelve, I think—I must have been seven or eight. He forbade him ever to say it again. He said the word was not acceptable in our house, that no one should ever be judged by the accident of birth but by their achievements, that we were all created equal and what was important about a person was not who their parents were but what they did with their lives."

"I see why you loved him."

Marcelle felt the all too familiar tears starting up again. "Of course neither Henry nor I did a damn thing with our lives."

"How can you say that? You have a darling son and Henry's an actor."

"Daddy didn't really consider anything an achievement unless it paid off. He didn't look at Henry's acting in aesthetic terms."

"Which is odd, since he was such a supporter of the arts."

"I guess it's different when it's your own family. You want them to be like you." She shrugged. "Anyway, he did consider André a magnificent achievement. I guess you could safely say he operated on the double standard."

"It's a funny town. If I did nothing, my dad would be happier than he is with what I am doing."

"Oh, but you've really done something."

"Not to hear Don Langdon tell it. He wouldn't be happy till he heard I was picking up some man's dirty underwear—some rich, socially prominent man's."

"Of course then you'd have a maid and wouldn't have to." They laughed. Marcelle would inherit money now, and she could have a maid herself. It wasn't what she wanted.

She said, "Daddy was a wonderful man, Skip. Really he was. He *did* believe in the arts; he tried like hell to help all those poor musicians and never held it against them even if they *were* junkies. He said it was a crime the way this country treats its artists. And he felt that way about poor people too, which is why he worked so hard in politics. He really *cared*, Skippy. And he tried to give Henry and me a sense of—I don't know, social responsibility or something. As well as ambition. He wanted us to work as hard as he had to, not just to be little rich kids who didn't know how to do anything." She made a face. "Like me."

"You know how to be a mama."

"It isn't enough." As she spoke, she put it all together for the first time—her need to do something, to have something of her own—with Chauncey's values. She felt momentarily strengthened, as if her father were still with her, as he had been at her first piano recital, whispering, "You can do it, baby."

Skip said, "I'd better go. Could you think real hard about one last thing?"

"Okay." Why not? She felt strong now, with Chauncey's ghost whispering.

"Was LaBelle in the house the night you saw her? Or might she have been at some other time?"

Marcelle closed her eyes. Could Chauncey have let her in and then made her leave when things turned nasty? Not very likely, but—

"Maybe," she said. "Why do you ask?"

"I think there's a chance your father was shot with a gun from his own collection."

"No!"

"I'm not sure. Do you know if he had a pair of Colt 44.40s?"

"No. Are those guns?"

"They're the ones we found at Tolliver's."

"They didn't look familiar," she said doubtfully, "but I've never paid the least attention to the damned collection. If you like, I could look and see if anything's missing—I mean, if there's a piece of shelf that isn't dusty or something. Would that help?"

"A written record of what he had would be better."

"Okay, I'll go through his desk."

"I'd appreciate it."

When she was gone Marcelle fell in a heap on her bed, unable even to make André's breakfast. Staring at the ceiling fan, she wondered if she had known her father at all. Speaking to Skip, she had felt perfectly confident that her father couldn't have had an illegitimate child, couldn't have kept such a thing from his family. But he had had a secret love affair with his secretary, who had treated Marcelle like a younger sister.

She thought of the scene she had seen Chauncey enact with LaBelle. Bad enough if she were his mistress, but intol-

erable if she were his daughter. And if Marcelle found it intolerable, how about the larger community? She had worried
that her father's affirmative action work would be endan-
gered. What if he had had a daughter with a black woman—
this Jaree—and then shunned her? He would end up not
merely a laughingstock but an object of hatred.

2

In the bright light of midmorning, Skip's postmidnight panic
returned. The day was getting away from her. She called
homicide. Cappello had gone as far as it was possible to go on
the Toyota owner for the moment, but the news was frustrating.
It seemed Horton Charbonnet worked for an oil company and
lived near Carrollton. One Jeanette Nelms, a UNO student
whom he had hired to take care of his dog and three cats, told
Cappello that to the best of her knowledge Charbonnet was
where he said he was—visiting friends in Houston—and would
be there until Wednesday. He hadn't left a phone number and
hadn't said a word about a car. She had gotten the house-sitting
job through an ad, didn't know him, and didn't have the
slightest idea whom he might have lent his car to.

Damn! Charbonnet could be the key to the whole thing—
unless he'd simply parked his car on the street for a few days
and somebody'd stolen it.

She called Steve, just to touch base, soothe any hurt feelings he might have from the night before.

He said, "I missed you last night. I wish I'd been with you."

"I missed you too."

"You did?"

"I certainly did. Especially when LaBelle's burglar came in
my back window."

"You're kidding."

"I wish I were. I can't talk about it now, though—I've got
to get on the road."

"Can you come over tonight? Cookie's cooking. He says he's going to get a date and everything."

"I think so. I'll call you later."

She tried the second number she had for Stelly Villere, the one in Harvey, figuring the first had long since been disconnected. A teenage boy answered "Hello?".

"I'm calling Estelle Villere."

"Who?" He sounded outraged, as if she'd invaded his home and asked for Jabba the Hut.

"Estelle—"

"Oh, *Stelly.*" Very superior. "Stelly back in New Orlean. Huh husband work there now."

"Do you have her phone number?"

"No."

"Does your mother?"

"She ain' here."

He hung up, leaving Skip to curse everyone under twenty, an age she hadn't left so long ago herself. She called back again. "Listen, what's Stelly's husband's name?"

"Peeler."

"What's his first name?"

"Peeler."

"Okay, what's his last name?"

"Johnson."

"Thanks for your kindness and cooperation on this beautiful Sunday morning."

There were half a dozen P. Johnsons in the phone book, all of whom Skip called while a man repaired her window, and four of whom knew no Estelle Villere, the other two not being reachable.

She went over to LaBelle's, told Calvin Hogue about the burglar, and asked him again to phone her if LaBelle turned up. Then she grabbed a sandwich and drove out to see Jaree Campeau.

Jaree was napping, but her husband, a light-skinned man with kind crinkly eyes, said it was about time she got up anyway. Skip sat uncomfortably in the living room, where a girl of twelve was watching TV, while Jaree got dressed. Jaree entered wearing jeans and crewneck sweater, still patting her hair into place. Not greeting Skip, she snapped, "Turn that thing off, Shirley Ann. It's a beautiful day outside. Go get some exercise."

Skip stood and told Jaree her name, sure she would have forgotten.

"I remember you, officer," said her hostess. "I was hoping you wouldn't be back. Hoping I'd heard the last of Miss La-Belle Doucette."

Skip hated her coldness. LaBelle might be a disappointment, but she was the woman's daughter. Unable to control herself, she said, "A child is a lifetime commitment."

"Tell me about it. I can honestly say I wish I'd never seen or heard of that girl."

I can honestly say people like you don't deserve children. May Shirley Ann marry a white man and decide she's too good for you.

Skip's feelings must have shown in her eyes. Jaree said more mildly, "Sit down, officer. I know I sound hard, but if you knew that girl and what she's put me through and my grandmama through and my husband and chirren through. . . ."

"I'm sorry to tell you this, but I'm afraid she may be involved in a serious crime."

"Whoo! Serious crime. She's already been involved in every kind of crime you can name."

"This is murder, Mrs. Campeau."

Jaree didn't move a muscle, didn't flick an eyelash. "I'm not surprised. Nothing that girl does would surprise me."

"I'm still trying to find her."

"Well, I still haven't heard from her. Believe me, if I did, you'd be the first to know."

"I was wondering if she might be with her father."

"No chance of that, honey. She doesn't have the least idea who her father is."

"I heard she tells stories about him—she says he's a white man, a prominent New Orleanian."

Jaree smiled a cold, smug smile, the kind, Skip thought, an executioner who really loved his work might permit himself as he delivered the coup de grace. "He probably is, officer. But LaBelle doesn't know who he is, and neither do I."

Skip tried not to let her jaw drop as she tried to imagine the prim Jaree in the role of LaBelle's predecessor as sweetheart of the regiment.

"Like mother like daughter you're thinking," Jaree said. "But you're thinking wrong. It is a pure delight to tell you that LaBelle is not my natural child. I adopted her when I was seventeen, and I wish to God I'd stayed working as a maid instead."

Skip waited, sure there was more. Jaree sounded as if she was starting to enjoy herself. "That's what I was doing at the time," she said. "Trying to earn enough money to get myself through college. And suddenly this offer came, out of the blue. The family I was working for offered me $25,000 to raise a child that needed a home. Lord, if I'd known what I know now! My grandmama really wanted that baby—I thought they'd make each other happy and I'd get a college education out of it. Well, I should have got a job as a waitress—like you say, being a mother's a lifetime commitment and I wasn't ready for it, and I *sure* wasn't ready for a daughter like LaBelle."

"Tell me, was it a legal adoption?"

"Are you kidding?"

"No, I guess it wasn't. Do you mind telling me the name of that family? The people you worked for?" Skip spoke carefully, trying to conceal how much she needed the answer.

"Not at all. It was Harmeyer. Arthur and Judith Harmeyer."

She knew the Harmeyers well, had last seen them at Chauncey's funeral. Judith Harmeyer was Tolliver Albert's sister.

SUNDAY KINDS OF LOVE

1

Bitty looked at the mirror, at her petite self in her black suit, her blond hair as shiny as ever, unable to believe it was really she. They had all fussed over her at church, said how good she looked. She thought it was true and she was looking at herself soberly, not having had a drink yet today. She couldn't understand it—she was dying inside.

Yet she looked like a young widow who was coming beautifully through tragedy. She must have one of those pickled livers that keep working against all odds. Her father had one—why not she?

She tore at her clothes; they oppressed her. Pearl buttons flew off her cream silk blouse.

286

Where was Henry? Working, of course. They would go out to dinner that night, if she lived so long. At the moment she wondered, seriously wondered for the first time, what it would be like to kill herself quickly, as opposed to the slow way she had been working on for two decades.

She was so lonely. She didn't understand why Tolliver hadn't called, either last night or this morning. She had thought he loved her.

Perhaps that was what had her so upset—not hearing from Tolliver. Still in her slip and bare feet, she phoned him.

Not home. And not in church. Her father had taken her to church, had called late last night and offered to do it, and Bitty had been so surprised she had said yes and then had been too proud not to be ready when he arrived. Her father did not do things for other people; it was not his style. It was Tolliver's.

She changed into a peacock-colored running suit and looked in the mirror again. She could be in her early thirties. She looked wonderful. She could probably find a new man if Tolliver didn't want her. But surely he did if the rumors weren't true, and how could they be? She knew him better than anyone.

She lay down on her bed for a moment, knowing that she would go down and make herself a mimosa in a moment or two, but prolonging the pleasure, the anticipation.

Ah! I'm not dying. I do want a mimosa.

Was it possible to live? She tried to imagine a life without Chauncey, a real life, not the waking sleep the last twenty years had been. A life in which she was married to Tolliver.

He would probably make love to me.

The thought came with a jolt. It must have been seven years or more since she and Chauncey had made love, and probably another year or two since the time before that.

Tolliver would make love to her, and he would love her. Chauncey did not love her, had never loved her, had married her for what her father could do for him, and she had adored him. Or at least she had at first. For years she had hated the bastard. She smiled to herself, remembering how much he hated that word, and went downstairs to get her drink.

Could she have married Tolliver? She had come halfway to accept over the years the general wisdom that he was a homosexual, and so maybe he wouldn't have married her after all. But he had made love to her once. It was rushed and painful, and he had kept saying her name. When she thought of it now, she flushed, not with pleasure but embarrassment. She had hated his saying her name, hadn't known how to answer. She knew that something was happening to him that she wasn't able to share.

It was her first experience with sex, and it was no experience at all. She had closed her eyes and watched Tolliver and herself from someplace in the air above their two bodies, merely an observer. She was pouring orange juice when the odd spectacle came back to her—the picture she had seen with her eyes closed so long ago. She had not thought of it in thirty years.

She had not wanted to do it again and had put Tolliver off by saying she was too afraid, and it was only two weeks later that she met Chauncey, whose first touch, as they shook hands, stimulated nerve endings all over her body.

She never thought of Tolliver in a sexual context again. By the time she was settled with Chauncey, the first flush having faded, she noticed that Tolliver was there, that he had always been there. She must have assumed he always would be. She had wondered about his personal life hardly at all, had considered him an adjunct of herself and Chauncey, had not needed to know anything else. He was just there, that was all. And now that she needed him, he wasn't at home.

2

Henry found her snoring on the living-room sofa, the carpet beside her reeking from a spilled drink. He had arrived several hours early for their dinner date, thinking to coax her out of the house and to distract her from becoming stinko, for once.

He cleaned up the mess, embarrassed for her, and let her sleep another hour before he shook her gently. "Bitty. Bitty, darling, it's your baby."

His heart turned to jelly as she touched his face and smiled. She must have made this gesture a thousand times. He literally didn't think he could get along without her, would probably die without her in his life.

He was a fool not to have moved back in for the week, at least, maybe a few weeks until she was on her feet a little better. He was shocked that it hadn't occurred to him that he could do that, had still thought of this house as his father's house, a house in which he wasn't welcome.

"Henry? Baby, is that you?"

"Rise and shine, Mother."

"Did I oversleep?"

"No. I came a little early. I thought we might take a drive or something."

"What a nice idea, baby. Help me up the stairs, will you?"

By the time they had reached the top of the stairs, it was obvious she wasn't going anywhere but back to bed. He tucked her under a satin comforter and went downstairs to watch television.

He couldn't watch; he was too worried. What would happen to her now? He had asked her to dinner tonight to give her something to look forward to and it hadn't worked. Since he had had to work that day, and Tolliver hadn't returned his call, he had arranged with Geegaw, of whom he was half terrified, to take her to church, thinking he'd come over soon after. But he saw that he hadn't been quick enough, that she must simply wait every day until she was alone and then head straight for oblivion.

He needed to move in; that was obvious. He would do it tomorrow.

He heard her stirring, running a bath, at about five-thirty. She was wonderful—never missed an engagement, apparently possessing an inner clock capable of rousing her even from a stupor.

When she came down she was beautiful in midnight-blue silk. In response to his compliment, she said, "I must get some more black clothes. I only have the suit."

"I'll take you. Tomorrow if you like."

She answered vaguely, and he knew she would end up pleading a headache.

At the restaurant she pushed her salad around her plate, not eating and trying to hide it. But as she drank her wine, a pink glow colored her cheeks and she chatted quite cheerfully.

"Do you remember when you and Marcelle were little, when the three of us went out together every afternoon?"

Every afternoon it had taken hours to get Marcelle ready, and then they could only go to places where babies could go and Bitty had to watch Marcelle every second. Henry had to play by himself most of the time, but when he could get Marcelle alone, he threw dirt in her face.

"Remember how much fun we had together?"

"I always thought Marcelle was kind of a drag."

"Oh, darling, you know you love your sister. You were so cute with her at that age, so worried something might happen to her."

"Was I?"

"Oh, heavens, especially that time she had strep throat. Remember that? She was in the hospital overnight, and you came to my room the next morning to ask if she'd died."

He hadn't the least recollection of it.

290

"I was thinking of those days last night. This week is so hard, Henry."

"I know, Mother. You need someone with you. I'd like to come stay with you awhile."

"I'm fine alone. Really. I was thinking last night that everything's all right, that I can make peace with myself."

The waiter took away her barely touched salad and brought their entrées.

"I was thinking about those days—just the three of us together—and realizing that I was genuinely happy then. How many people can say that?" He smiled, saying nothing, inviting her to continue. "Your life has meant something—it hasn't been wasted—if you've had something so perfect, just once."

"Mother, of course your life hasn't been wasted. What would I do without you?"

"You don't really need me. But it doesn't matter, you see? That's what I'm trying to tell you—I've had a happy and satisfying life already. I don't need anything else."

Fear wrenched at his gut. Surely she wasn't suicidal. Not after all that had happened this past week. He couldn't take it. He said, "You aren't depressed, are you, Mother?"

"Of course not, dear. That's what I've been trying to tell you. You're not to worry about me, and you're not to consider moving in. You have your own life to lead, and I don't want to be a drag on you."

"Come over tomorrow night. I'll cook for you."

"Don't be silly. You can't spend every night with your mother."

"I would if I could." He gave her a flirtatious smile.

She leaned over her plate to take his hand, a fold of her dress flowing into the sauce meunière. Her hand felt as cold and bony as a chicken's claw. "I know you would, darlin'." She smiled bravely and squeezed.

The smile stopped, but the squeeze continued. A tear ran

down her cheek, but she made no effort to brush it away. She simply kept staring at him, squeezing his hand.

He should do something to help her now. He tried to think what to do. She said, "You're not a bit like Chauncey, are you?"

He didn't know what the answer was, whether she wanted him to assure her that he was indeed exactly like Chauncey, that she still had that to hang on to, or whether he was supposed to agree with her. Paralyzed, he missed his cue.

She began to sniffle and had to let go of his hand to pull out a tissue. "You wouldn't do what Chauncey did."

"Mother, you can depend on me for anything you need. You know that."

"Oh, Henry, what am I going to do? Tolliver didn't call me today."

Tolliver?

"We'll get through this," he said.

"I'm so miserable. I have no one in the world anymore."

"No one? What about me?" How could she say this to her only son, who would happily devote his whole life to her? "How about Geegaw and Marcelle and André and—I don't know—Yvonne and Mommoo and Poppoo—"

"You don't understand. I'm completely alone now." She was sobbing.

"Mother, I think we should go." He realized now that the sudden somersault into despond was simply another manifestation of drunkenness, just as her earlier mood had been. All of New Orleans would understand that too, and would know about it by morning. It was too late to avoid that, but he felt an overwhelming need to get her someplace safe, where people couldn't stare, as quickly as possible. He signaled for the check.

"I'll be all right. I'll be good." She poured herself another glass of wine and sipped, her tears wiped away, a strange childishness, a pathetic need to please, overcoming her melancholy.

He hated this. "Oh, Mother."

"I'm sorry, Henry. I didn't mean to disgrace you." She said "dishgrashe."

"Mother, please, you don't disgrace me. I just want to help you and I feel so helpless." He took a deep breath and a big chance. "Let me take you to the Betty Ford Center. Please. You need a boost. You know you do."

"You don't think there's any hope for me, do you?"

"Of course I do. That's what I'm saying."

She dipped her napkin in water and dabbed at the dress, having now seen the stain she'd acquired. "I feel so awful."

"I'll help you. I'll take care of you."

"I could never go that far from home."

"Someplace here, then. Or no place—just AA."

"I couldn't go to AA. Chotsie Carruth goes. She says everybody smokes."

"Mother, you're killing yourself."

"I want to die."

She looked suddenly seventy years old. Beautiful Bitty, an ancient tragedy mask. He couldn't stand it. He had to do something to get her out of this.

"I need you, Mother."

"No, you don't. Not really."

"No, really, Mother. Really, really, really." He threw his napkin on the table for emphasis. "I need to know you're there. I need you to be strong for me."

She dabbed at her eyes again, trying to force a smile and ending up with a grimace. "No, you don't, son." Her voice came out in a whisper.

"Mother, pay attention to me. I need you. You know what I'm talking about."

"No, Henry."

"I'm talking about Skip Langdon."

"What do you mean?"

"I mean, I'm probably going to be arrested."

She screamed. Not a particularly loud scream, a muffled

one, but unquestionably a scream. Three waiters hovered instantly, shielding their table from the other diners. "Is there a problem, monsieur?"

"My mother is ill. Help me, will you?"

The waiters moved with startling efficiency, two attending to coat-getting and door-opening, one helping him support Bitty, the other acting as escort, trying to hide them and not succeeding while Bitty blubbered and tried to walk on rubbery legs, though really they had to half-drag, half-carry her.

3

Could Skip get *Cookie* a date? She simply did not believe the message on her machine. Was Steve Steinman out of his mind? No woman in New Orleans would go out with Cookie Lamoreaux, and with good reason. Everyone had already done it once, and no one was dumb enough to do it again. Though nearly thirty, Cookie was the original teenage gross-out king—arriving drunk, puking in the daisies, groping women, insulting elder statespersons, having to be driven home and poured out of his car—these were a few of his endearing little trademarks.

The message not only asked her to get him a date, but specifically mentioned Marcelle. Marcelle! Aphrodite reborn as a mortal. Not bloody likely, Steinman. The alternative, however, was spending an evening with Steve and Cookie alone. Cookie would tell endless tales of drunken ribaldry, and she and Steve would end up playing audience to him. Skip thought hard. Maybe there was a policewoman who hadn't met him yet.

In the middle of her reverie Marcelle called to see how she was and if she wanted to go out for a bite, and Skip was desperate enough to pop the question. Amazingly, she was willing to do it—seemed eager, even, but couldn't because of

André. Even more amazingly, Cookie, confronted with the situation, invited André.

Due to sartorial indecision ending in a promise to herself to go shopping soon, Skip arrived to find the others well into the cocktail hour. As advertised, Cookie was cooking, leaving Marcelle and Steve to huddle together on the living-room sofa. Skip had finally broken out an almost-new red sweater with which to top her jeans; Marcelle's outfit could technically have been called sweats, but the pants were tight and tapered, the shirt long and sexy, the fabric magenta with leopard spots. Skip felt an urgent need to go and stake out LaBelle's and realized with horror that this was serious jealousy. She was hooked on Steve Steinman.

He got up to give her a hug worthy of Mighty Joe Young. Guilt, she thought. "Ouch," she said, and rather testily.

"Sorry. You looked so pretty, that's all. I just want to—" He bit her ear.

"Not here, King Kong."

Marcelle got up to deliver her own hug. "About time you got here. Can you imagine how hard on the ego it is to try to talk to a guy who keeps checking his watch and glancing toward the doorway?"

Could she be serious? Skip decided not to think about it, to be grateful they were both polite at least. Steve followed her when she went to say hello to Cookie. "Marcelle's nice. I like her."

"What guy wouldn't?"

"Weird taste in clothes, though."

From his post over a hot stove Cookie hollered, "Kojak! Who loves ya, baby?"

Skip gave him the requisite sisterly kiss, noting that he looked unusually spruced-up. "What's the occasion?"

He shrugged. "I thought we should all be friends." Skip thought he probably had a long-term crush on Marcelle. She'd never seen him quite so civilized.

"So, Kojak, tell us about the big case." Deftly, he turned the fluffy-looking shrimp he was frying.

"No shop talk, okay?"

"Not okay. Why do you think I invited you?"

Marcelle drifted in. "Cookie, please." She looked as if she were about to cry.

"Oh. Gosh, sorry, Marcelle. I must be crazy." His face glowed like a tequila sunrise, and Skip didn't think it was just from the heat. "Women out of the kitchen. You're making me nervous. Steve, you can help me."

The women took their drinks into the living room. Except for the exercise bike by the front window, it looked not only presentable but actually nice. Cookie had swept, dusted, vacuumed the furniture, and stuck some daffodils into a green pitcher.

"Cookie's . . ." Both spoke at once.

"Go first," said Skip.

". . . different. Changed."

"You're not kidding. In the last few hours apparently."

"Really? You mean it hasn't happened over the years?"

"You haven't seen him lately?"

"I guess not." The saucer eyes were wistful. "We used to go out. A long time ago."

"You've gone out with everybody in town."

She lowered her head and when she raised it, she was blinking away tears. "Skippy, I never thought you, of all people . . ."

"What is it? What did I say?" But, too late, she knew. She remembered O'Rourke's "whore of Babylon" remark.

"You know what you said."

Weirdly, she felt almost as much of a pang as when Steve got angry with her. She had hurt Marcelle, and Marcelle was someone she was coming to care about. The thought astounded her. *Marcelle St. Amant, girl airhead, my best friend.* Well, she might really be an airhead, Skip wasn't sure yet, but she was a warm and generous soul. If she wasn't a murderer.

"I'm sorry. I just meant you're so pretty and popular . . . I didn't know you and Cookie were an item."

She smiled, apparently mollified. "Well, we were fourteen at the time."

"You're kidding."

"He dumped me. My first broken heart."

"Cookie dumped *you?*"

"I've never gotten over him. We didn't speak for years. In fact—till now."

The plot certainly thickened. Who would imagine the gross-out king and the bruised magnolia as star-crossed lovers?

The men arrived with the shrimp, heralded as Cookie's Famous Cajun Tempura, which their host was serving as an hors d'oeuvre and which proved to be, logically enough, shrimp tempura spiced Cajun style. Cookie had even made some without the spices for André, who withdrew temporarily from a TV somewhere upstairs to stuff his tiny face.

There was a salad course after the tempura, and then the best paella Skip had ever tasted. Cookie said, "Shucks, honey, it's nothin' but jambalaya with a funny spelling." But Marcelle's stream of compliments continued to flow.

"You should open a restaurant, Cookie, really you should. This is the best stuff I ever put in my mouth."

"What this town needs—another restaurant."

Skip shrugged. "There were a million restaurants when K-Paul's opened."

"Which reminds me," said Cookie. "Did anyone ever hear of blackened *anything* before it did?"

No one had.

"You see. Even Prudhomme had a gimmick." His voice had an edge to it.

"Wait a minute," said Skip. "I think I just detected something."

"I'll drink to that." Cookie raised his glass. "Kojak has detected something."

They all drank, and all accepted refills.

"What have you detected, Kojak?"

"You've thought it out about restaurants. You really do want to open one."

"Ah—not really."

But she could tell he did.

Marcelle said, "If you could do anything you wanted with your life, what would it be?"

He stared at her. Skip expected one of his cracks, but he looked down at his lap. Finally, he said, "Cook, I guess." She thought it probably cost him to say something serious, even three words.

Marcelle said, "You're so lucky."

He stared as if she were the Pythian Sibyl, about to dispense wisdom such as he had never heard before. "You have something you love." She let a beat pass. "To do."

No one spoke.

"You all have it," she said. "You don't know what a gift that is."

"You have André," said Cookie, whose disdain for children was famous among the women he'd dated.

Skip had to stop herself from slapping at her ear to make sure it was really working right. Next these two would climb up on the table and sing a duet.

"I love him to distraction," said Marcelle. "But it's not the same as having something to *do*." Her voice rose to something that was almost a whine.

Thank God. Back to normal.

"Steve, you're the luckiest of all."

"Me?"

"Because you're an artist. What it must feel like to make something! To start with nothing and *make* something that's really yours."

"Cooking is like that." Cookie spoke a little huffily, but Steve was still preening.

"You know, not many people understand that. They don't

think about it. They only think, 'film, wow, glamorous' or 'dance; gee, talented.' They don't think about the *process*, about what's it's like to live with the thing inside you trying to get out."

Cookie said, "Maybe we can get you a cheap abortion," but no one so much as glanced at him.

Skip was thinking guiltily that indeed she hadn't stopped to think about it, about what Steve really did, and what it meant to him.

Marcelle was rapt. "I've thought about it a lot. I think about it every time I look at a picture I love or a statue or even a beautiful piece of furniture. I think of the wood-worker, planing his wood, and touching it and rubbing it and applying oil to it. When I see Henry act, I can't believe it's my brother who can do that. I'd give anything if it were me. It makes me want to cry." She teared up.

Cookie said, "What? What makes you want to cry?"

Skip thought she would talk some more about how de-prived she was, poor little Southern girl who couldn't do *any-thing*, she was jus' so helpless, but Marcelle flushed and spoke in a whisper. "Beauty," she said. "Art."

An embarrassed silence fell. Skip thought, no one says things like that. They think them, but they don't say them. And she realized how very much she felt like that herself. Or used to. She had let that part of herself die in recent years. But now she remembered a one-woman show she had seen in college, how she couldn't stop staring, how she had felt a lump in the back of her throat. She was stoned at the time and thought it was that. But the feeling had been back, it came up at least once every time she set foot in a museum; sometimes she felt it looking at certain blocks in the Quarter. She ignored it; she pretended it wasn't there.

The name of the artist from the college show flashed into her mind and she knew she had seen it in the paper recently. She wanted one of the paintings on her wall—something by that artist, something that gave her that feeling. She saw her dump of an apartment suddenly covered with beautiful paintings, not heavy-metal posters at all, and she smiled, picking up her glass to invite a toast.

"To art," she said.

"Hear, hear."

"To artists," said Marcelle, so obviously including Cookie that he stopped pouting and served dessert.

Among many half-drunken assurances that it was a work of art, a masterpiece, a chef d'oeuvre and competition for the Mona Lisa, they washed down a multilayered chocolate cake with champagne, and Skip felt an unaccustomed mellowness that had nothing to do with drink spread through her body.

She wondered if they were all actually growing up, putting away old resentments, old prejudices, and becoming different people—people, she thought with a jolt, who would actually like to know one another—be friends, as Cookie had suggested. Was she ready for that?

TOLLIVER

1

She woke up early and kissed Steve awake. They had spent the night at Cookie's. "I gotta go, D. W. Griffith."

He pulled the pillow over his head. "Oh, my aching head. I can't believe we really had that conversation."

"*In vino veritas,* Roger Corman. I'm taking you a lot more seriously from now on."

"How about just taking me?" He pulled the sheet off to show her his erection.

God, it was beautiful; she could almost taste it already. She started to slide down his body, hormones suddenly activated to full throttle.

But there isn't time; it's Monday morning and you're a cop. Remember?

She sat up. "Oh, shit. I can't. I've got to go home before I go to work."

"Damn." He rolled over.

"Yeah."

She was probably scheduled for the stakeout at LaBelle's today, as she had been for days, but she needed to check her machine.

Jimmy Dee's voice trilled at her first: "Good morning, my tiny true love. I suppose there'll be nothing left of you but a bone and a hank of hair if you're out rutting with that elephantine friend of yours. Give scrawny old Dee-Dee a call if you've still got a mouth left."

And then Duby's flat, emotionless voice: "Skip, I hope you haven't left for your stakeout. We've closed out the St. Amant case. Report to your usual district this morning."

Closed out the St. Amant case?

Her finger shook as she dialed. "Lieutenant. I must have been in the shower. What's going on?"

"Have you heard about Tolliver Albert? It's all over the radio."

She was silent, trying to take it in.

"I'm sorry if he was a friend of yours. He's dead. Took pills, probably Saturday."

"No!"

"You knew him well?"

"It isn't that—"

"His neighbor found him. He was supposed to have dinner last night with her and her husband. He'd asked if he could bring Mrs. St. Amant, so she wouldn't be alone, but Mrs. S. says he never even phoned her about it. When he didn't show, the neighbor investigated. Found the door unlocked, the body lying on the bed, fully clothed, hands folded on chest."

Skip's heart was pounding. She sat on the floor, trying to

ground herself, to keep her mind from racing. Hoping she sounded normal, she said, "Did he leave a note?"

"Oh, yes, he left a note. In which he confessed to the murder of his best friend, Chauncey St. Amant."

"But why? Did the note say why?"

"He was in love with Chauncey's wife."

"Bitty? But—"

"But what?"

She had been about to say, "but she drinks," and then realized how stupid that sounded, how blind she had been to the obvious. She said, "Go on."

"It seems that Mrs. St. Amant rejected him for his trouble and, overcome with remorse and heartbreak, he decided to do himself."

"I don't believe it."

The lieutenant spoke very gently. "I know it's a shock, Skip. But believe me. He's dead."

"It sounds so fishy."

"The note's definitely in his handwriting. And there was something else—a holographic will."

"My God. Leaving everything to Bitty?"

"No. We don't know yet if this will supersedes another. It didn't mention everything, only his business, the antique store. He left it to Marcelle Gaudet."

"I didn't even know they were close."

"Who knows? Anyhow, we're mopping up the case— thanks for helping out on it."

"Oh, God, I feel awful."

"I know you do, Skip. I'm really sorry."

"I mean physically sick. This has never happened before—"

"You've had a shock. Why don't you lie down for a while? Come in an hour or so late."

In an hour, Skip called her sergeant at V.C., her old district, and pleaded serious female trouble, probably an ovarian cyst, she'd had them before and they could—

Eager to avoid the grisly details, he cut her off with a gruff,

"Okay." Not even, see you tomorrow, just get off the phone, lady. She'd thought he'd feel that way.

She couldn't stop now. Too many cans of worms had been opened, the biggest one named LaBelle. If Tolliver had killed Chauncey for love of Bitty, why had he burglarized LaBelle's apartment? Why had he killed himself after less than a week? Surely he hadn't fallen for Bitty, whom he'd known all his life, any time recently. It must have been years ago. So maybe it took him some time to get up his nerve to kill Chauncey—or to go nuts enough to do it—but after waiting years for her, why give up after less than a week? Logically, he would have expected her to go through a period of mourning and then he would have begun a formal courtship. It was too early for any of that to have happened.

Skip knew that the theory about going nuts would technically cover those objections, but nothing she knew or could imagine covered LaBelle.

She put on her gray suit—she had a sympathy call to make—and then she looked up the two P. Johnsons she hadn't yet reached. If she was going to talk to Stelly, it had to be this morning, before Stelly heard about Tolliver—the body had been discovered too late to make the morning paper, but already she could have heard it on the radio. The first address was out in New Orleans East, and a woman answered. "Mrs. Johnson?"

"Yes?"

"Is this the Peeler Johnson residence?"

"Yes, it is."

"I'm with the gas company. Our meter reader's having trouble finding your meter. I was wondering—are you going to be home for a while?"

"Another hour probably."

She thought at first she had the wrong house. The kid sitting on the steps was unmistakably white. But the address was right. "Do the Johnsons live here?"

"Uh-huh. My mom's inside." He sounded like he had a cold.

The house was a small redbrick one, an Ozzie and Harriet-style dwelling with a nice lawn and a bicycle on the front walk. She heard the kid's mother before she saw her.

"Mark? Mark Anthony, who told you you could go outside?" She opened the door and stepped out, in jeans and an old black sweatshirt, faded more or less to charcoal. Her hair was caught up with combs into a sort of fluffed-out ponytail. "You get back in this house this minute, you hear me?" She sounded like a common scold and even in the faded sweatshirt looked as if she belonged on the cover of *Vogue*. Skip figured her waist measured about the same as one of her own upper thighs.

"Mrs. Johnson?" she called.

But the woman was occupied with opening the screen door for the boy. She cuffed him as he went in. "You feel good enough to sit on the porch, you're not sick enough to stay home. Tomorrow, you're going to school, I don't care if you got pneumonia."

"Mrs. Johnson?"

"Can I help you?"

Skip identified herself. "I'd like to talk to you about Chauncey St. Amant."

"Chauncey! I haven't thought about Chauncey in years. Until he got murdered, I mean."

"I wanted to ask about an acquaintance of his."

"Would you like to come in?" Good. She probably hadn't heard about Tolliver.

"I think we should talk out here. You may not want your son overhearing—"

"My son!" Her eyes flashed anger as she caught on that her privacy was going to be invaded. "What are we going to talk about, officer? What is this anyway? I haven't even seen the man in ten years or more. What are you doing coming into my home talking about Chauncey St. Amant?"

"Mrs. Johnson, I—"

"I'll tell you anything you want to know about Chauncey St. Amant if you've got a strong enough stomach." She had transferred her fury, but she hadn't tempered it. Skip half expected lightning bolts to sizzle out of her eyes, which had turned as dark and threatening as the river.

"Aren't you afraid your son—"

"My son's got nothing to do with Chauncey St. Amant."

Skip realized she'd been assuming, because of the boy's Caucasian hair and features, that he was Chauncey's son, that in just these few moments she'd made up a whole story about Stelly's leaving her job because she was pregnant. But now that she thought of it, Mark Anthony had blue eyes, not Chauncey's brown ones.

"Why'd you come here asking me questions?"

"I want to know if you know a woman named LaBelle Doucette."

Johnson stepped down and began to walk Skip away from the house, having apparently decided on prudence where the boy was concerned.

"Never heard of her. Who is she? Chauncey's latest 'secretary'?"

"I think she might be involved in his murder."

"Mmmph." It was a strangled sound, as if she had had to swallow a lot and was ready to cough it back up. "I imagine she might be if he treated her anything like he treated me. I've thought a woman must have killed him. I've thought it many times. And I've cheered her on, too. Somebody should have killed that bastard a long time ago." She spoke loud and angrily, apparently not caring about the neighbors now that Mark Anthony's ears were out of the picture.

"He must have done something terrible to you."

"Terrible? *Terrible?* You know what that bastard did to me? Shouldn't happen to a dog, shouldn't happen to an *animal!*" Tears of rage flowed down her cheeks. "We were lovers, you know about that?"

306

Skip nodded.

"Everybody in town knew. But I was dating Peeler—my husband—at the same time. He knew about Chauncey, but Chauncey didn't know about him. Peeler wanted me to marry him, but I couldn't make up my mind to do it. I was so high and mighty, having this fancy white dude sugar daddy I just couldn't settle down. My mother'd say, 'Stelly, you ridin' for a fall' and she wasn't kidding either.

"Well, I got pregnant. Didn't know who the daddy was, didn't care. All I cared about was that baby. The minute the doctor told me, I was so happy I wondered what I'd been waiting for. So I told Peeler I'd marry him and told Chauncey I was getting married and Chauncey said, 'You pregnant?' Just like that. Just 'cause I'd gained five or six pounds and got sick every time I smelled coffee or cigarette smoke, I guess he figured it out. I said, 'Yes, are you happy for me?' He said, 'Stelly, what if it's mine?' I said, 'I'm not gon' bother you about it. Not gon' ask you for a penny. I'm leaving here and getting married.'

"Well, he said I couldn't do that. Can you imagine?"

"I guess he didn't want to lose you."

"It wasn't that. Wasn't even close. He didn't want me having that baby. Said what if it looked like him—what if Peeler left me and I couldn't support it, what if I decided to sue him, what if I asked for money. I said, 'Don't worry about it. Nothing's going to happen.' So you know what he did then? He offered me money to have an abortion. Cash money—$10,000—to abort my child. You ever hear of anything like that?"

Skip shook her head.

"Well, I said no, of course. He said he'd like to give me some money anyway—for a wedding present, and he asked if he could come over for a drink—to say good-bye. He made me have one with him. I just had fruit juice, because I was looking out for the baby, but next thing I knew I was waking up in some doctor's office. I tried to find out where I was and somebody gave me a shot. When I woke up again I was home, stuffed up to my chin with bloody gauze. And I wasn't pregnant anymore." She turned the incipient thunderbolts on Skip. "Now what do you think of your Mr. Chauncey St. Amant, civic leader, friend of the downtrodden and of black people most particularly, *and* king of Carnival?"

The question, thought Skip, is what do I think of this story. She said, "Are you telling me he drugged you and somehow got you a forced abortion?"

"That's exactly what I'm telling you."

"But no doctor would do that." She wished she believed it.

"Oh, no? Not for Mr. Chauncey St. Amant, civic leader? You don't think so? Honey, wadn't no lawyer or Indian chief put that gauze in my twat." For the first time she lapsed into black dialect. "You realize what he did? It was illegal what he did. What would you call it, officer? Assault? Hah! Murder's more like it. You can't *do* that to people."

Skip made herself ask the question. "Do you know who the doctor was?"

"I didn't care about that. I just wanted my baby back." When Skip didn't reply, Johnson turned to her, and mischief had replaced the storm in her eyes. "Funny thing was, I got pregnant right away again, and ended up with a whiter-looking baby than I probably ever would have had with Chauncey. Peeler's my color except with blue eyes. I guess Mark's the color of one of his great-granddaddies—but I knew I couldn't sue Chauncey, claim it was his baby after all, when I saw those eyes."

Skip wished she had never heard of Estelle Johnson, wished she could take back the whole damn morning and her stupid lie about her ovary, wished she were walking her beat, chatting up old ladies and giving teenage punks threatening looks. She turned her brain inside out but couldn't think of a reason on earth for Johnson to lie about such a thing. Her gut told her she hadn't. The tears and the thunderbolts were entirely too real.

The hell of it was, she knew Chauncey could do it. Maybe plenty of cops wouldn't think he could get away with it, would really believe what she had said—that no doctor would do such a thing—but Skip knew the St. Amant family doctor and, maybe more to the point, the Mayhew family doctor, all too well. She could see just how it could happen. Chauncey would mention that he needed to get out of a possible jam with his father-in-law. Or maybe he'd taken the problem to old Haygood Mayhew first, said he was afraid of getting into trouble with Bitty, thereby defusing him, making him a coconspirator against the scourge of the Southern male, the Southern female. And then Haygood had taken it to the family doctor, who referred him, at least, may even have done it himself.

She wondered what her father had gotten out of it. Even Haygood Mayhew couldn't get an upstart like him into the Boston Club. Maybe the Louisiana Club, something like that. Something. Skip was sure of it. Her father would happily sell his soul, but he wouldn't be stupid enough to give it away.

Angrily, she drove to police headquarters, wondering why she was so mad. She should be sad—for Stelly, for her aborted child, for her own aborted child. For being born into such a poison garden of corruption. And maybe she was, underneath. On top she was mad, probably at Skip Langdon, investigator extraordinaire, for unearthing this garbage, exposing her own nostrils to the stink of it.

Thanking her stars that Tarantino and O'Rourke weren't in the office, she went up to homicide and typed the written request she would need on her next errand. Then she headed for the state office building, which housed the Bureau of Vital Records.

There she had a clerk check for birth certificates under four names—LaBelle Albert, LaBelle St. Amant, LaBelle Doucette, and LaBelle Campeau. For mother's maiden name, she tried Caroline Mayhew (AKA "Bitty"), Jaree Campeau, and Estelle Villere. Date of birth was a problem, but the computer program could make checks within five years of an approximate date. None of the combinations yielded a birth record. That made two dead ends in one morning.

She was still so shaky from talking to Stelly that she did something she rarely did—had a beer with lunch. Then she bought some breath mints and drove to the Harmeyers' house in the Garden District.

A graceful old iron fence enclosed the yard, as if for children, but Judith and Arthur hadn't had any. And no wonder, in Skip's opinion, as she couldn't imagine either of them mating with anyone. Arthur was a small, stoop-shouldered man with wispy hair and a great number of broken veins on his face. Tolliver's sister was the personification of "battle ax."

She had iron-gray hair, permed into quiescent waves away from her face and sprayed so stiff a hurricane couldn't dislodge them. Her makeup was peachy-pink and inches thick, as if exposing the skin on one's face was tantamount to public nudity. Her bosom was deep as quicksand (and probably similarly textured once you removed the armor), her hips a mighty fortress—the whole, neck to knee, was corseted so tightly that bumping into her would bruise. She couldn't have been more than sixty, and probably not that, but she seemed frozen in time, an old trout from the Eisenhower era. Probably, Skip thought, Judith had simply turned into her own mother.

A uniformed maid assigned to door duty led Skip into "the front parlor," where the clan was gathered, along with various friends. To her horror, Skip saw that her parents were there. Well, it would be only half awkward. Since her father wouldn't talk to her, there was only her mother to fend off, and fend her off she must—if mixing boyfriends with police work was difficult, how much worse was having your entire family around to supervise?

Bitty and Henry were here, but not Marcelle. And not Bitty's father—he had probably been over earlier. Not John Hall Pigott either; he probably hadn't known Tolliver, but with a twinge of disappointment, Skip realized she'd been hoping to see him. Bitty was seated in a wing chair, just as she'd been at her own house a few days ago, and this time Henry stood behind her instead of Tolliver. It seemed odd to have Tolliver missing.

Skip felt a surge of sympathy for Bitty, for her having lost two men she loved in less than a week. And yet if you read between the lines of the note, you could make an argument that she had been the cause of both deaths. If Tolliver's death was what it seemed, she must have given him cause to believe she was in love with him.

Skip's mother had made her way over. They hugged mechanically—Skip found it hard to feel warm toward someone who nearly always greeted her with disapproval. Today's hello was, "Oh, Skippy! Not that old suit again."

It was on the tip of her tongue to say, "It's all I have," but she knew what that would start. She said, "Hello, Mother. How's Daddy?"

"He's sitting right over there."

"He looks fine."

"Why don't you go over and speak to him?"

"I don't think so." In a different mood she might have. But after what she'd learned this morning, she was glad to have an excuse for avoiding him. She stared for a moment, though, trying to decide if he looked like a criminal. What he had done—if it had been he—was something like rape. She thought you could also make the case, as Stelly had said, that it was something like murder as well, but as a pro-choice woman, Skip figured she wasn't the one to try. It certainly was an invasion of a woman's body it made her sick to think about. It implied a heartlessness, a being out of touch with others, with their feelings, and with your own, that was almost unfathomable. Did her father look heartless?

No. Not to her. Old Haygood Mayhew looked as if he had long since made the Faustian bargain, and probably hid cloven hooves under his custom-made shoes. Her father looked so completely like what he was that her heart went out to him—he looked like a man trying to keep up appearances. But not merely the superficial sort of appearances that obsessed him. He looked as if he was trying to hide from himself the central fact of his life—that he had thrown it away, that he knew nothing more of himself than he did the day he was born. He had somehow failed to notice when he reached his limit, to realize that, even though he was a poor boy from Winona, Mississippi, who could become an intimate of the rich and well-born, he could not control the universe. But she knew—his face showed his struggle—that he could control his own feelings in a halfway sort of way simply by refusing to acknowledge their petty existence. And by God, he would do that if it took all the bluster bred into him by a family that traced itself back to the Confederate army and had been perfecting macho posturing for at least the last hundred and fifty years. When blustering didn't work, he simply withdrew. If a piece of the universe—say, the piece named Skip—refused to be commanded, it didn't exist.

For Skip he was the perfect paradigm of the Southern male—a wimp of the first water thinly coated with what she thought of as Naugahyde machismo, so phony it wouldn't fool a five-year-old.

Wait a minute here! I thought I was going to put all that behind me— be friends with Cookie Lamoreaux and everything.

But Cookie hadn't performed any abortions on unconscious women that she knew of. Her father's wimp factor had turned nasty.

You don't know that.

She didn't, but she couldn't figure a way to find out as long as her dad wasn't speaking to her. And working that one out wasn't going to happen today.

Her mother whispered, "Did you know you have a run in your stocking?"

"Damn! Do I?" Her attention drifted below her knee just long enough to make sure it was true. "How are the Harmeyers?"

"Doing very well. It must be hard—"

"I have to speak to them. Excuse me." She extricated herself abruptly, perhaps rudely, she thought, but she mustn't get involved in more than small talk with her mother or the afternoon was shot. If Skip's father wouldn't speak to her, her mother made up for it. She could hold forth for hours on the one subject in which she had any interest—how thoroughly embarrassed she was by her daughter's very existence. Skip suspected she wasn't the only one who had to listen either. Her father was probably becoming so deeply sick of the subject he'd no doubt joined two or three new civic clubs or committees, filling his nights with meetings, blessedly away from home.

Bitty was alone now, looking inexpressibly sad and too small for the black dress that billowed around her. Arthur Harmeyer was approaching, taking her hand. . . .

Skip said, "I'm so terribly sorry about Tolliver; I know how much he meant to both of you."

Bitty gave her a strange, hurt look, as if she wanted to cry but couldn't because her face was sprayed on. Neither one answered. Skip felt herself flush as she realized what they must be thinking—that she, alone of all the guests, could know what was in the note. Because of course the content wouldn't be publicly released.

She turned away, confused, with the odd sensation of having her cover blown. Across the room, Henry was huddled with Judith. Both of them turned and looked at her. Then Judith walked toward her. "Hello, Skip. How are you, dear?" She gave Skip her hand.

"Mrs. Harmeyer, I'm so sorry—"

"I know you are, dear. Let's walk out to the foyer, shall we?"

Skip allowed herself to be propelled, not sure what was going on. As they reached the door, Judith said, "Thank you for dropping by, dear. I know it must have been hard under the circumstances."

She means I shouldn't have come.

She said, "Not at all. I was 'raised to—"

"Of course, dear. And we do appreciate it." Pointedly elbowing the maid aside, Judith opened the door herself.

"Mrs. Harmeyer, I feel as if I'm being given the bum's rush."

"Of course not, dear. Your mother and father are very welcome here. But it *is* rather inappropriate—really, I know they'd feel more comfortable—"

Skip felt rage rise up her spine like the Kundalini fire they talked about in San Francisco. She stood her ground, noticing that someone else was coming up the walk. "Do you remember Jaree Doucette?"

Judith didn't react at all, simply smiled more broadly, showing a perfect set of upper teeth and rather crooked bottom ones. "So nice of you to come, Skippy." She turned to the new arrivals, an elderly couple, and before Skip's eyes, let tears slide down her cheeks as if she had turned on a faucet. She buried her face in the man's shoulder and sobbed, "Oh, Jonathan, I jus' don't know how I'm gon' make it through this."

You could make it through the Hundred Years' War without even getting wrinkled, you bitch.

She clattered down the front steps in the horrid brown shoes, walked fast till she was out of sight, then ran to her car and kicked it. She felt like pounding it as well, but someone might see. Instead, she got in and took deep breaths.

Well, it had to happen sometime. New Orleans was simply not going to put up with a police spy in its midst. But it wouldn't have happened today without the intervention of asshole Henry St. Amant.

Damn the little twit!

She kicked out again and bruised her instep on the brake.

2

Marcelle was folding laundry in her bedroom. André had a case of the stomach flu—poor baby, it wasn't surprising, considering the stress he'd been under lately—and he was watching TV in the living room. She had had two hours of TV already and couldn't hack it any longer. Besides, she needed some time to mourn Tolliver.

Since she couldn't get out today, she couldn't do that with her mother and Henry; she certainly couldn't do it with André. She didn't even want him to know yet about Tolliver's death. One death was almost too much to bear at his age; she didn't know how he could handle another. She would have to think of a way to tell him, would have to choose the time and place carefully. One of the other day-care mothers was a child psychologist—maybe she'd get some advice from her.

Here, alone in her room, she could cry as long as she did it silently. And so, as she balled up socks and smoothed T-shirts, she was letting the tears go, snuffling into a tissue, using it to gag herself when the sobs came. What a mysterious, strange, dear man was Tolliver. The revelation of his being in love with Bitty didn't surprise her in the least. She'd never considered it before, but now that she thought of it, it explained everything.

It was so obvious now why he'd never married, why he stayed so close to the St. Amants, why he never seemed interested in women. Had Bitty had a years-long affair with him, she wondered? *Her mother?* God, it seemed unlikely, and not because Marcelle thought Bitty was any saint either. She just didn't seem to have a lot of sexual energy.

Something must have happened to Tolliver, though, to flip him over into violence—into killing her father. Marcelle knew she was still crying for her father, partly, and she hoped some of her tears were those of forgiveness for Tolliver, but she also felt a genuine grief and compassion for him. For her father's murderer. It was *so* peculiar how things turned out sometimes.

Now she could track perfectly their odd transaction on Saturday. When she had come in and asked for a job, he must already have been planning his own death—must have known he wouldn't live out the day. And then, seeing her, he had remembered, or maybe realized for the first time, how much she loved her father, and he had been overcome with guilt on her behalf. And so at the last minute he had left her the store.

Marcelle didn't know how to respond to that, and thought she better not try to sort it out. It was a dream fulfilled, pure and simple. But at what a cost! And with emotional strings that could work themselves handily into a noose if she weren't careful.

The other thing was, it had come so suddenly. She didn't know if she was really ready for it—not for the details of running a shop; she didn't know a thing about that, but she could learn. But for getting what she wanted. It felt so odd and unfamiliar. She didn't feel she deserved it.

She couldn't think about that now. It was too much, just as two deaths were too much for André. For right now she was just going to feel crummy and cry as much as she wanted, and the hell with trying to make sense out of anything.

"Mommy, someone's at the door."

"Okay, say I'll be just a second."

She looked in the mirror to see what repairs were needed but was instantly distracted by the sound of the front door opening. Damn! She'd meant him to speak through it.

"Hi, Skippy. She said just a minute."

"Hi, André. How's my boy, huh? How's my big, gorgeous André?"

She heard the sounds of a small boy being scooped into the arms of a doting auntie. She called, "Watch out, Skip. He's got the flu." As she rubbed a little cover cream under her eyes, she felt some of the gloom lift. Of all people she could think of (except maybe her mother), Skip was the one she most wanted to see right now. Her anger from yesterday morning had faded as the day wore on—that was why she'd phoned her about dinner the night before. To make peace, cement the friendship she felt they could have.

She'd wanted it but had doubts it was really possible while Skip was still probing her family and friends. But now all that was over. Surely Skip had come here out of friendship.

From the look on Skip's face she knew the makeup hadn't worked, that it was obvious she'd been crying. She said, "André, darlin', aren't you glad it was Skippy? What if you'd opened that door and it was somebody who wasn't invited?"

He looked at her gravely. "Was Skippy invited, Mommy?"

"That's not the point, young man. The point is, you know you're not supposed to open that door without knowing who it is. Skippy, I hope you didn't get too close. Did you hear me call? He's got the stomach flu."

Skip held her stomach and bent over. "Waaak!" she squawked and staggered over to the sofa, where she pretended to die, ending with eyes crossed and tongue hanging out. For the first time that day—in days, when Marcelle thought of it—André laughed. Fell down and laughed and rolled, wrapping his blanket around him, rolling and unrolling, like some kind of small contented animal.

I don't play with him enough. I mother him too much.

To Skip she said, "I think you've cured him."

She turned off the TV and sent him off to his room to play. Skip said, "It's amazing he'll do that."

"People tell me I'm very fortunate. They tell me how awful their kids are, and I just thank my stars."

"There are no bad kids—only bad parents."

Did Skip really believe that or was she just being flattering? "You'd be a good one," she said. "André loves you."

"It's because I never grew up. Listen, I'm really sorry—"

Marcelle waved her into a chair. "It's awful, isn't it? I'm still trying to assimilate it. My daddy's best friend killed him because he was in love with my mother. And then on top of that, my favorite almost-uncle killed himself. And they're the same person. Is that what happened?"

Skip spread her palms-up hands. "That's what my lieutenant says."

"It doesn't seem possible."

"*I* didn't think so. It doesn't to you either?"

"My mother and Tolliver—they just didn't seem . . . I don't know, maybe the daughter's the last to notice something like that."

"Didn't seem what? In love?"

Marcelle whispered, "No."

"She did have a key to his apartment."

"The flowers . . . but of course she'd have to have an excuse. She was always going over to Tolliver's; I guess it made a perfect cover. It just seems like—"

Skip waited, not saying anything.

"I mean, don't you think you'd notice if your father's best friend was in love with your mother?"

"Have you asked Bitty about it?"

"Are you kidding? She's been in a coma, just about, for the last week, and today she's even worse, with those damn pills the doctor gives her . . . oh!" She remembered who the doctor was.

"It's okay. Listen, your mother's not perfect, neither's my dad." Her smile of dismissal looked genuine.

"Sorry. Well, anyway, that's Bitty. You know what it's like living with an alcoholic? Have you read much about it? The whole family participates in a conspiracy not to talk about it—only in our case, we didn't do that. We could talk about it with each other, just not with Mother." She stopped to ponder. "I just thought of something."

"Um-hmm?"

"Tolliver. We didn't talk about it with him. The taboo extended to him too."

"Why?"

"That's what I'm wondering. If you read about this stuff, you'll see it follows a pattern. Nobody knows how the taboo gets there. It just is. It's almost like ESP. You just know—psychically or somehow—what the rules are. I think you know"—she was formulating it for the first time as she went along—"you have an exaggerated sensitivity to other people's feelings. So you know what will hurt and what won't. Daddy could talk about Mother"—she spoke wonderingly, putting it together—"But Uncle Tolliver couldn't. I guess that should have been a clue. But you know what doesn't make sense? Daddy fell out of love with her—why didn't Tolliver? He saw her at her worst, just like we all did. Look, she's gorgeous, all right?"

Skip nodded.

"And no amount of boozing it up ever seems to change that. And she can be sweet—so sweet—you should see her with Henry sometimes. She must have been a real knockout as a young woman—I mean, she still is, but when she had her faculties, it had to be a boost, don't you think?"

They laughed, the tension of the tragedy starting to dissipate a little.

"Then when she started drinking . . . after Hélène died—"

"Hélène?"

"My baby sister. The one I told you about. You know the story, I know you do. 'After she died, Bitty was never the same.' Meaning she never drew another sober breath."

"The baby's name was Hélène?"

"Yes, after Helen of Troy, because she was so beautiful,

Mother always said." Marcelle had always been wildly jealous of that description.

"What did she look like?"

"Look like?"

"You don't remember?"

"I never saw her." *But I did. I must have.*

"You're sure?"

"Sure? Skip, I was only three years old. How can I be sure of anything? I don't remember her, okay? Anyway, I couldn't. She never came home from the hospital."

"Oh?"

"What do you mean 'oh'? Do you believe me or not? Listen, I was just *three*. I know she didn't come home because Henry told me. Recently."

"What did she die of?"

"I don't know. We didn't talk about her. I guess that was another of the family taboos." *But why was it taboo?* She wondered if she could talk to Skip about it.

"What year was she born in?"

"What?"

"When was she born?"

It wasn't that Marcelle hadn't heard the question, it was that it seemed so off-the-wall she doubted her ears. "I don't know," she said. "I'm twenty-four, and I was three when she was born—she'd be twenty-one, I guess."

"Maybe 1968?"

"I guess."

Skip made a show of looking at her watch and stood up quickly. "Oh my God, I've got to go report in before I can go home today." She leaned forward awkwardly to kiss Marcelle on the cheek. "Listen, I know how tough this is. Let me know if there's anything I can do."

She was gone almost before Marcelle realized she meant to leave. Marcelle felt oddly cheated. She had hoped Skip was settling in for a long, leisurely visit.

She'd wanted to talk to her about the black woman, at

least. Obviously she wasn't the murderer, but she wondered what Skip had learned about her.

She made herself a cup of tea, trying to distract herself with thoughts of the woman scorned, but Skip had triggered something and she couldn't run away from it. She knew, deep down, that she didn't really believe Henry. The baby had been brought home. How else could she have had such strong feelings of loathing for her? She had them still. The jealousy was almost unbearable, and the more strongly she felt it, the more frightened she became, the more her mind churned, able only to reach the same conclusion, again and again, no matter how hard she tried to wriggle out of the net. She, Marcelle, had killed her.

Surely it was the only explanation. Like Tolliver's suicide, it would explain so much. It would explain what she considered the great mystery of her childhood—why she had always been an outsider in her own family, ignored by her mother, despised by her brother. Her father had done what he could, but it must have been hard for him, trying to be compassionate toward the little girl who had killed his daughter.

How had she done it? she wondered. Had she smothered the baby? Dropped her? She had absolutely no memory of it.

But a strange thing happened. As she sat, trying to harden herself, to make herself flinty enough to face her crime, she was engulfed by waves of sadness, not for herself but for the baby. For a tiny innocent child not more than a few days old with so much danger in her life. Marcelle began to cry again, but the feelings only intensified and turned to panic, the panic directed full force toward André. He was only four, and there was danger in his world too.

When she had stopped sniffling and felt she was calm enough not to frighten him, she went into his room. Toys littered the floor like a lumpy rug. In the center was André, butt on his feet in a variation of the crawling position, coloring and singing to himself. He could amuse himself for hours this way, and she liked to think it showed artistic or musical talent, maybe both—certainly an incipient interest in the arts.

"André? Hi, darlin', what are you coloring?"

"Ti-Baby." The page showed a puppy playing with a ball, but André was making circles with a gold crayon, seemingly not even trying to stay within the lines.

"Ti-Baby? I thought you were Ti-Baby. Ma-Mère calls you that, doesn't she?"

"Umm-hmm."

"Well, the doggie can't be Ti-Baby, can he?"

"Uh-huh. He is. That's his name."

"But you're Ti-Baby."

"Puppy's Ti-Baby."

Oh, God, this poor child. He's gotten so little attention lately, he thinks he has to give some to himself. He's given the dog his own name so he can color it and pretend he's getting nurturing.

"André, darlin', you know who thinks you're Ti-Baby? Mommy does. You're Mommy's Ti-Baby, aren't you, sweetheart?"

"Um-hmm."

He didn't look up, just selected another crayon and made more scribbles. To her horror, it was a purple crayon. She had heard somewhere that children who colored with purple were depressed.

"Darlin', are you feeling sad about Poppy?"

"Uh-uh."

"But, baby, it's only natural to feel sad about something like that."

"I'm not sad when I color, Mommy."

"Oh, I know, baby. We all do things to make us forget other things. Mommy does all the time. André, darlin'?"

"Umm."

"Mommy's feeling sad. Could you give Mommy a hug?"

"Okay."

He looked up, walked on his knees the few inches over to

her, and offered his tiny embrace. Marcelle held him tight.
"Oh, darlin', that feels so good." He started to pull away, as
if preoccupied, eager to get back to his coloring. But Marcelle didn't think it was that—she thought he was smashing
down his feelings the way she did; what a horrid thing to
learn at such an early age.

I won't let that happen to my child.

"Now Mommy'll give *you* a hug." She tried to pull him
back, but he resisted.

"No!"

"No? André needs a hug just like anybody else."

"No!" He was fighting her now. She hung on to his wrist,
but he had begun to flail about, sending crayons about the
already cluttered little room.

"Why not, baby? How 'bout just a little hug? A little hug
for André?"

"No!" He was crying now, and struggling as if for his life.
"Leave me alone!"

Why had he gotten so upset at the simple prospect of a
hug from his mother? Perhaps he had been given unwelcome
ones, caresses that terrified him. Fear turned her belly to ice.
"André. André, darlin', did someone give you a hug you
didn't want? Did someone hurt you, André?"

"No! No! No! Nooooo! Nooooo! Nooooo!" He kept wailing
the word over and over. She let him go and watched him roll
about the floor, beating on it in his misery. She knew he
would beat her too if she got in his way.

As she watched him cry and flail, knowing there was nothing she could do, that the tantrum would have to run its
course, her mind slipped back to the place it had been trying
to get to for the past hour, the blackest, darkest pit there
was, the one she had been trying to pretend didn't exist.

If she had killed her sister, and didn't remember it, why
not her father as well?

But that was impossible—she had been making love with
Jo Jo Lawrence while Tolliver killed him.

Tolliver didn't do it. Tolliver couldn't have. Skip was right. Marcelle *would* have noticed if he was in love with Bitty. He could have seen Marcelle slip out of the Boston Club, and slip back in; he could have taken the rap for her, to protect the family.

Could she have slipped out and then back in? No! She couldn't have. She had been with Jo Jo. And yet, despite what she had told Skip, she could only remember going upstairs with him, and later, leaving him sleeping. Perhaps they had been too drunk to make love, had both fallen asleep. Perhaps that was why Jo Jo had made that odd remark about nothing happening.

3

Skip glanced again at her watch. Twenty minutes of four, and after four there was no counter service at the Bureau of Vital Records. She could scribble out a request in the office if she could just get there on time. She would die of frustration, at the very least bust a gut (to quote Jimmy Dee) if she didn't make it.

She could barely keep her mind on her driving, her head was spinning so far out of control. No one had told her the name of the baby before. Marcelle had given it the French pronunciation—"Ay-Lynn."

A variation of "Lynn," "something like Lynn," Sheree Izaguirre had said.

Now she saw things in a way she never had before. Bitty must have borne the child—you couldn't fool a whole hospital. (Of course there was the outside chance she'd never gone to a hospital, merely said she did, but Skip could see no point in that.) So if Hélène were Bitty's child, she must have had a lover other than Tolliver. A black one. *Of course* the thing would be hushed up, the baby never brought home.

Skip thought she could see the fine hand of old Haygood Mayhew himself on this one—people had probably been paid off, the nurses in money, the doctors in special favors. (At least her father, not being an obstetrician, probably wasn't involved.)

And then Tolliver, best friend of the family, would have been sent to find the baby a home, and he would have inquired among his friends and relatives as to whether anyone knew a smart, reliable young black woman who needed money. And the deal would have been struck, the baby condemned to the frightening world of the Project.

Skip got to the bureau with five minutes to spare and noted with relief that the clerk was the same one who'd helped her before. "Hi, remember me—all those LaBelles we looked up?"

The clerk looked dubious.

Skip produced her I.D.: "Officer Langdon. Listen, I really had to rush to get here and didn't have time to type out a request. Could you give me some paper and let me write one out real quick?"

"Sorry. It has to be on police-department letterhead."

"Shit!" she shouted, not caring whom she offended. With a quick glance at the clock, she raced for the elevator, hoping the state registrar would be in his office. She found the more lowly the bureaucrat the more trouble he gave you, and she always went to the top if she could.

The man was there, and cooperative. Curious as well, once she told him what she wanted. In seven minutes she had what she needed: Hélène St. Amant was born to Bitty and (ostensibly) Chauncey St. Amant in 1968. No death certificate had been filed for her, not in 1968 or any other year.

Elated, congratulating herself on her fine detective work, she nearly lived up to her name and skipped back to her car. She could imagine the scenario exactly as she was sure it had happened. Bitty had grown up with a harsh patriarch, a controlling old buzzard whom she longed to escape. In hopes of leaving all that behind, she married the seemingly sweet and gentle Chauncey, who was ever so eager to win the fair maiden. But Chauncey had ambition—to become a younger version of Haygood Mayhew. As his true, repellent self surfaced, Bitty rebelled in as thorough a way as she knew how. Her lover had probably been a gardener or . . . no; not a servant. Bitty was one of the few women in her circle who knew black men socially. Her lover would almost certainly have been one of Chauncey's musical protégés, or perhaps not a protégé, maybe an equal. A man whom her husband admired, who could be waved tauntingly under his nose. Maybe John Hall Pigott himself.

But she hadn't counted on getting pregnant—or maybe that was part of the revenge, only Haygood and Chauncey wouldn't stand still for it. Once they saw the baby, they weren't about to live the rest of their days with Bitty's scandal. And so the patriarchy had triumphed after all and Bitty, her spirit completely broken, had turned to the socially acceptable pleasures of alcohol. It was okay to be a drunk in New Orleans, it was even admired, Skip sometimes felt, and anyway, there wasn't a damn thing either Chauncey or Haygood could do about it.

But poor, sacrificed little Hélène had grown up in the noxious environment that had turned her into a prostitute and a blackmailer who reappeared to bleed Chauncey in his moment of glory.

It was a gorgeous theory. Skip had the whole thing worked out, in intricate detail, by the time she got to her car. But as she headed home, she addressed herself to the questions it brought up.

How the hell did LaBelle find out her true identity? Even Jaree didn't know, if she hadn't lied.

Why had Tolliver picked this particular time—the moment of Hélène's reappearance—to kill Chauncey?

Where had LaBelle gone? Had someone paid her off after all, her part of the deal being to get out of town by sundown? If so, who had? Chauncey? Tolliver? Haygood? The disappearing act seemed too big a coincidence.

And if LaBelle was gone, truly gone, who had been harassing Skip? She thought she knew.

She parked and didn't even go in to change out of the damned brown shoes. She walked fast, almost running, toward the river side of the Quarter. And as she walked, it occurred to her to wonder for the first time why Marcelle had gotten so testy when she asked about Hélène.

4

He was reconsidering moving in with Bitty. If he did it, he'd at least have to keep the apartment so he'd have a refuge. He'd stayed with her last night and most of today, finally dropping her off for one of her "naps" before their dinner tonight. He'd found himself unbearably oppressed by the house and, face it, nearly at the end of his rope.

Today had been the worst by far. He found that he literally couldn't imagine life without Tolliver, knew now that his fantasy of living with Bitty had included Tolliver, had always included him, he just hadn't realized it. He was smoking a joint as if it was a cigarette, puffing nervously, just wanting to get as stoned as he could as fast as he could.

He thought when this was all over—if it ever was—he would go to AA. Knowing better, much better, he had fallen off the wagon once already with disastrous results. He knew better right now; he shouldn't be letting down his guard like this. But he couldn't help it. Honest to God he couldn't live another moment in the melancholy and misery the day had brought. He supposed that was the definition of an addiction, but he couldn't worry about it now. For today, he was getting stoned.

He was just starting to relax, to think he could face getting ready for Bitty, when someone pounded on his door. "Open up, Henry. I know you're in there."

Tubs Langdon. How the hell did she get in the downstairs door? A friendly neighbor must have arrived at the same time she had and helpfully let her in. But she was lying. She couldn't possibly know he was in there.

"Come on, Henry! The pot smoke's so thick out here half the neighborhood's getting stoned."

She was probably telling the truth—you probably could smell smoke from out there. Still, if he kept quiet—

"Goddamnit, don't you think I learned how to kick in a door at the police academy? You really want me to do that?"

He put out the joint, quickly flung up the windows, and opened the door. "All right, *officer*. You don't have to squeal and go 'oink.' A simple huff and puff, and I'm sure you could blow my house down."

She grabbed his shirt and backed him into the apartment, throwing him roughly onto the sofa. "Don't get me any madder than I already am."

Jesus. It was true what you saw on TV—cops really did assault you if they felt like it. And there were no witnesses. He could report what she'd done and she'd just deny it. The injustice of it infuriated him, reminded him of the time he'd mouthed off at a traffic cop, who'd threatened a few charges besides running a red light. And he'd known he had to shut up, that the First Amendment got temporarily suspended when you were nose to nose with an officer of the law.

He sat up, trying to recover a modicum of lost dignity, and gave his head a shake. "I'd ask you what I could do for you but my brains are too scrambled right now."

"You broke into my house, you little asshole. Twice! You ransacked it *and* you mugged me *and* you smeared that stupid blood on my front door *and* you slugged my boyfriend. Have you any idea how mad that makes me?" She moved closer to him, threatening, a dowdy harpy in a shapeless suit and hopeless shoes.

"Would you like to sit down?" he said.

"Talk, Henry."

"You're making me nervous."

"Gosh, I wouldn't want to do that." She sat.

Jesus, it felt good to have her out of his space. "I didn't slug your damn boyfriend," he said. "I didn't even know you had one."

"Steve Steinman. Big guy with a beard and film of the murder—the one you hit on Mardi Gras night. You listened in when Marcelle phoned me, and found out he was coming to my house."

"I don't know what you're talking about."

"Okay, let's talk about the other stuff."

"It's obvious, isn't it? I was trying to get you to butt out."

"Sure you weren't trying to kill me? Like you killed your father?"

"I didn't kill my father. Tolliver killed my father." Even to his own ears, he sounded whiny.

"It strikes me there's something slightly wrong with that theory, Henry boy. If Tolliver killed your father, what were you doing, oh, tearing up my apartment, for openers?"

"I told you. I did it to scare you."

She leaned toward him and hissed, "What were you looking for?" God, she was an ugly bitch.

"Would you mind giving me a little space? I talk better that way." An odd but beautiful thing was happening. The marijuana had done its work and taken the fear away. As long as she kept out of his immediate vicinity, he was okay. Not only okay, but calm. Clear-headed, able to see possible results and consequences without panicking. And then of course, there wasn't that much to lose anymore.

When she had leaned back, he said, "I wasn't looking for anything. I just wanted to spook you. The same with the gris-gris."

The tap on the head was another matter. He really had hoped to take her out of the case—not to kill her, just to put her on her ass for a few days. (But probably he shouldn't mention that part if she brought it up again.)

"What for, Henry? If you didn't kill your father, why'd you give a damn?"

"Because I guessed, that's why." He said it with all the frustration of having held it in for a long time. "I knew Tolliver did it." He spoke sadly, resignedly, and leaned back spent against the cushions. "Things had come to a head, you see."

"Go on."

"Look, what is this? Is this you and me having a private conversation, or what? Am I going to have to sign some kind of a statement?"

"You've already confessed to half a dozen crimes. I'd say I'm the one with the bargaining power, wouldn't you?"

"Not at all." He really couldn't believe how calm he felt. "I don't remember confessing to anything. That must have been your imagination, officer."

"Okay, for now it's just you and me talking. Whether you'll have to repeat it depends on what you say. Tell me about things coming to a head."

"Tolliver wasn't in love with my mother. He was my lover."

Skip blinked but didn't speak.

"My dad didn't care much for homosexual perverts. Did I ever mention that?" His voice was measured, not too bitter, he thought; rather more civilized than he really felt.

"You may have."

"He'd known for years that I was a homosexual and you'd think he'd have known Tolliver was—God knows everyone else did—but he always 'defended' him." He gave a short rueful snort. "That was his word—'defended.' Whenever the subject came up, Daddy 'defended' him. So I guess it was quite a shock when I told him Tolliver and I were planning to move in together." He didn't even care if his expression showed he had savored his father's reaction.

Skip said only, "How did he react?"

"Threw a fit, of course. Threatened everything he could threaten—to have me locked up, never to speak to either of us again, to disinherit me. The usual stuff."

"If it was the usual stuff, how had things come to a head?"

"He made threats about Mother. To have her locked up.

And he might have been able to pull it off. It scared me. And I don't scare easy either. I told Tolliver we should put off moving in together.

"And then Tolliver threw a fit. I've never seen him so mad. I've known Tolliver all my life. You know that, don't you?" A funny little memory popped out of nowhere, of Tolliver picking him up and swinging him around. He must have been about four at the time. Grief seized his throat and he was embarrassed to find that, before he could stop himself, he had gasped and moaned in front of Skip, temporarily losing the wonderful drug-induced cool.

"Are you all right?"

He swallowed until his throat opened again. "I was just remembering him, that's all. What I was going to say is that all our lives, my mother's and mine, Tolliver was there, to be the father and I guess in some ways, the husband that Chauncey couldn't be bothered being. You think I fell in love with a father figure? Okay. I admit it. Sometimes I think he's the only reason I'm still alive."

"Did your father abuse you? Or your mother?"

"He didn't beat us, if that's what you mean. Or he didn't beat her anyway. He worked out on me a couple of times. The main thing was, he just—" Henry searched for the right words, didn't find them. "He wasn't a father, that's all. Wasn't there. He never cared who I was or wanted me. I was just some potential ornament in the crown of the mighty King of Carnival. Only I never obliged him by turning into a miniature Chauncey. Therefore he had no use for me."

To his surprise, Skip said, "I can relate to that."

"And Bitty. Bitty was just a means to an end with him. He never wanted her, he wanted Haygood Mayhew for a father-in-law. The bastard." He kicked a small footstool across the room. "That bastard!" This time he yelled it.

"Tolliver knew all that—he lived through it. And, as if he hadn't, the poor man had to listen to the whole thing again, ad infinitum and ad nauseam. I can be rather tedious on the subject, you see."

"Oh?"

Condescending bitch. He hated her. "Anyway, to make a long story short, when Tolliver threw the temper tantrum, he threatened to kill Chauncey. I'm not kidding when I say I've never seen him so mad, but that's not the whole story. A weird thing was going on. He was having these really bad headaches and popping all these pills—I was really worried about him."

"What are you saying?"

"Let me finish, please. I don't know what was going on—or if anything was—but it wasn't like him to have a temper tantrum. And other things were strange. He'd get depressed for days, seemingly over nothing. He'd get mad at the slightest little thing. He'd forget things. I don't know if it was the drugs or what—"

"But in short he wasn't himself." She said it as if she'd been expecting this from him, of course he'd pull out that old saw.

"No, Miss Superior Attitude, he wasn't. But before you get too know-it-all about it, maybe you should remember he did kill my father and himself."

"I didn't mean anything. I was just asking."

"Look, I went to Tolliver. I confronted him."

"With killing your dad?"

"Yes." He spoke almost in a whisper, and tried to repeat it in a normal tone, but this time the words came out in a shout. "Yes! Yes, God help me I did, and I swear I'd die myself if I could just take it back. *I* killed him, do you realize that? *I* killed Tolliver!" To his surprise, tears poured out; he was crying for the first time.

"He didn't commit suicide, then?"

"Of course he did, stupid. Can't you hear what I'm telling you? I broke off the relationship—he killed my father, goddamnit! How were we supposed to live happily ever after with that one between us?" He was blubbering.

"Do you think that's what I wanted? Any of it? Beginning

with my dad . . . do you think I wanted that? Do you think I wanted you digging around in the muck? For a while after my dad died I couldn't feel anything. It was easier to be mad at you than at Tolliver, to admit to myself that he really did it. And I got kind of obsessive. All I wanted was for you to go away and leave us all in peace." He looked at her fat ugly face, now dark with pretended sympathy. He could feel the tears abating, his voice becoming clearer, close to normal. "That's why I tried to scare you. That was all I wanted."

"I see."

He didn't answer and for a while she said nothing else, just sat there doing what probably passed for thinking in that pachyderm brain of hers. "That was all you wanted?"

"Do you blame me?"

"Then why did you break into LaBelle's apartment?"

"LaBelle? The black woman you asked about? Who the hell is she, anyway?"

"Hélène," said Skip. "Your sister."

"Hélène? Hélène's dead. Marcelle . . ."

"Hélène is not dead. Hélène is a prostitute known as La-Belle Doucette, and she was seen at your father's house a few weeks before his death."

"You're crazy." He got up and started to pace, to range aimlessly about, the tension finally turning into body energy.

"You borrowed a car—or maybe stole it, I don't know—and you ransacked her apartment, looking for something. But you didn't find it because I interrupted you. So you later broke into my house looking for it—not very smart, Henry."

"I don't know what the hell you're talking about. I don't know any LaBelle and—"

"Are you going to deny it? I saw you, Henry. Twice."

"Shit, yes, I'm going to deny it." He stopped pacing and turned on her. "You didn't see me, Miss Bitch, because I wasn't there. I don't know what the fuck you're trying to pull, but my sister has been dead for twenty-one years, have you got that? If you want proof, just look at my poor wreck of a mother. Hélène is dead, and her death tore our family apart. Who the hell do you think you are, trying to stick your nose into old wounds and open them up again?"

"I'm sorry." For once she looked daunted. "But tell me something—what were you going to say about Marcelle?"

"Marcelle! I thought we were talking about Hélène. Which is it, goddamnit?" He moved closer to her, threatening for real now, his voice probably carrying out to the Moonwalk.

"You said 'Hélène is dead,' and then you said Marcelle's name. What were you going to tell me?"

"Shit, you idiot, I was just upset, that's all. I wasn't going to say a goddamn thing and you know it—you just won't let well enough alone, will you? You've got to twist the knife once it's in. It's true what they say, you know that? Cops *are* sadists, especially fat, ugly women cops with ankles that belong in a zoo."

She stood up. "You little darling, you."

"I've lost my father and my lover. Can't you leave me alone?"

"With pleasure. The same pleasure I get from leaving maggots alone."

"Bitch."

"Next time I come I'll bring insecticide."

As she took her hippo-bodymus heavily down the stairs, Henry quickly found the joint he'd put out and sucked as if it was oxygen. Why the hell had he mentioned Marcelle? Maybe a combination of the pot and the conversation he had had with her about Hélène. Fuck. Despite his early cool, he felt as if he'd blown it after all. He wanted nothing so much as a drink, followed by another three or four or eight. But he simply couldn't let down his guard again. The pot was bad enough. Booze just wasn't going to get it. He'd nearly blown it, breaking into her apartment Sunday morning. He couldn't afford to get that far out of control again. And anyway, he had to cook for his mother that night.

BITTY

She was sitting still, not a muscle moving, in her wing chair, still wearing the black dress she had worn to the Harmeyers'. The low hum of the TV came from the back of the house, confirming André's small, comforting, if somewhat zoned-out presence. TV seemed to put him in a sort of waking coma, but Marcelle wanted him away from her, saying he had been sick earlier but now was well enough to go out—she just worried he was still contagious. Bitty thought he still looked too sick to go out. Marcelle had brought him over because she didn't want her mother to be alone. (She hadn't been informed that Bitty was soon due at Henry's, of course, but she might have guessed, might have known Henry wouldn't leave her alone.)

No one would leave her alone. Everybody was so afraid for

poor Bitty and her terrible addiction. Didn't Marcelle realize the television dulled her child's senses every bit as much as Bitty's booze dulled hers? Who was Marcelle to get high and mighty? The pill was wearing off and Marcelle had gone to get her another one—anything to keep her sober, even if it had to be drugs.

Marcelle had no way of knowing that Bitty had her own reasons for staying sober today. She could do it when she wanted to, no one seemed to understand that, and today she had to, even though it was the worst day of her life, even though she would have loved nothing better than to spend it in an alcoholic coma, preferably with an IV hooked up to drip the merciful liquid into her arm. She liked that phrase— "merciful liquid."

That Tolliver was dead was nearly unbearable. That she had to stay sober—and the reason for it—was salt in the wound. She couldn't drink today—and maybe not for many days to come. She couldn't go out of control in any way, she'd have to stay alert as long as Henry was talking about jail. He'd pulled it out of his hat with no warning—and rather cruelly, she thought, though she understood what he was trying to do, and why, but it certainly hadn't had the effect he wanted. Except for the temporary one of keeping her sober, and sober she would stay because she must not let that happen, no matter how much it hurt.

Did she want to die? The question kept coming up. No, she didn't want to die. She knew that because she didn't dare. Because if she died there would be no one to help Henry, and Henry was still desperately important to her. Therefore she didn't want to die.

Marcelle brought the pill and sat down silently, in the other wing chair, apparently unable to think of anything to say. For now, Bitty could only be grateful. But she wanted to say something to Marcelle—she would, as soon as the drug took effect and she felt she could talk. Her face was unbearably tight. It would probably crack if she tried to speak now.

She must look awful, sitting there like that, back straight, tears running down her face. She hated being so pathetic in front of her daughter.

She was seeing Tolliver and Henry holding hands, Henry about two and a half feet tall, headed out to find an ice-cream cone, or maybe just taking a walk around the block. They played catch sometimes, and inside the house, they played go fishing and crazy eights and checkers and later on, chess. The two people she loved most in the world—good pals, hitting it off. Thank God for Tolliver in those years, or Henry would have had no daddy at all. Tolliver had seen that and had stepped in to do what he could. For her. For Bitty. And because he was a wonderful person. And because he loved Henry. She thought he had probably felt cheated out of having a son himself. But the thing had backfired or something; she wasn't really sure what you'd call it. She could see now that Henry must have been in love with Tolliver almost all his life.

The pill was working now. She took a deep breath, savoring the sensation of hardly feeling suicidal at all. Marcelle looked so miserable sitting across from her, like a mother outside a hospital room waiting for her child to come out of its coma. She was such a good girl. And she hadn't had it easy either. Chauncey had been erratic with her. At least Henry always knew where he stood with him. Sometimes, when he was tense, he yelled at Marcelle for no reason, just as he did at Henry.

And then there was the indisputable fact that he was—she hated to say it—he was seductive with her. Well, anyway, to her it seemed indisputable, but Chauncey called her sick when she brought it up. Bitty's own father had sometimes treated her like his girlfriend. She knew how bewildering it was and she had tried to tell Chauncey, but he called her crazy, as if he was an expert on the raising of children, when he hadn't read a line on the subject. Not a word, and she had read every book in the library. Chauncey just took it for granted that he knew everything there was to know, and his way of expressing that was simply to dispute her.

"Chauncey, that can be confusing for a little girl."

"Oh, Bitty," in a tone of utter condescension and deepest sarcasm.

"I know. It happened to me."

"She's not confused, Bitty." Angrily. "Are you crazy?"

"Chauncey, you don't know."

At this point he would laugh, a little condescending chuckle as if at himself, for getting into this web of irrationality in the first place. "It isn't confusing."

Just like that. As if it was received knowledge, like the Ten Commandments; and absolutely as sure of himself as Moses could ever have been. Setting himself up as some twentieth-century prophet of childhood. Maybe he thought that "Saint" in his name really meant something.

Still, it had to be something more than Chauncey's occasional flirtatiousness that had made Marcelle, in the end, so unhappy, so unsure of herself. What had happened to the little girl who could do anything? Bitty didn't know. She didn't understand Marcelle. To her, Marcelle seemed the picture of competence—a single mother with a lovely child. But Marcelle tried to talk to her sometimes. Bitty hated it, was made hugely uncomfortable by it—but she told her how she felt inside, how unable she was to decide things, even to know what there was to decide. Bitty didn't want to hear about it. This wasn't the Marcelle she knew.

But it must be true. If Marcelle said she was unhappy, she must be. Bitty wanted to do something for her, and she realized that right now she could. The drug was working and she could talk. She could tell her what had really happened in Covington, that she wouldn't have hurt poor Marcelle for anything.

She wondered if Marcelle would enjoy running an antique store or if she would sell Tolliver's. And she really couldn't help wondering why Tolliver had left his shop to her. To ask her about it seemed churlish, but somehow Bitty hadn't known they were that close. She and Henry were the ones who were close to him—Henry in love with him and Tolliver in love with her. Just like always. She knew that it was true because the note said so. There was no doubt, no question now. Despite the pill, thinking too much about that made her shaky.

Yes, Tolliver had loved her, but she had loved Chauncey. For so many, many years. With surprise, she realized she was actually ashamed of that now. Of loving her own husband and the father of her children. But she had, and who had Chauncey loved? No one, she thought bitterly. Himself. No one else.

He had given her baby away. Even now, she couldn't think of it without surprise. Given her baby away, her own flesh and blood, condemned her child to a life of poverty and misery, just to further his own political career. If she thought it monstrous to contemplate, that was nothing compared to seeing the reality of it. When she found out what Hélène had become, she wanted desperately to help her, would have done anything to undo what Chauncey had done—but Hélène didn't want help. She lived in another world, beyond help, beyond anything her mother could do for her. She closed her eyes and squeezed to erase the memory of her grown-up daughter rejecting her.

"Mother, are you all right?"

"My eyes hurt, that's all." She opened them.

"Crying," said Marcelle. "It's overrated. Burns the eyes and turns them red." She rummaged in her purse for a plastic vial of eye drops.

When Bitty handed it back to her, she said, "Marcelle, I want to tell you something. About that summer in Covington."

Was that fear in her eyes? Bitty tried to reassure her. "You know I wouldn't hurt you. Don't you?"

Marcelle stared at her lap. "Of course, Mother."

"I was so depressed that summer. I don't think I've ever been that depressed. Except now." She left unspoken the loss of her baby. "Marcelle, I guess I should say that I was drinking a lot that summer. I guess—I don't know, I was very short-tempered. And . . . ."

"And what, Mother?"

"And miserable. Things took on significance. Something that might be small another time was a big deal at the time. I'm sort of ashamed to say this, but all that really happened was that your father snapped at Henry."

She replayed it in her mind, knowing she would whitewash it a little for Marcelle but sparing herself nothing.

It was early evening. She and Ma-Mère were cleaning shrimp at the kitchen table while Marcelle played quietly in the living room, where Pa-Père was reading the paper.

Henry and Chauncey were standing together across the big, open kitchen, Henry trying to untangle a fishing line. Chauncey was watching, supervising, hovering like a vulture, it seemed to Bitty. Suddenly he reached out for the tangled line, grabbing impatiently, violently, but Henry pulled it away. Bitty gasped. "Let me do it," Chauncey ordered.

"Daddy!" Henry's voice was tragic. "I've almost got it."

"You've been working on it for twenty minutes. If you're going to do something, do it right."

He snatched it from the boy's small hands, leaving Henry with a shamed, stricken look that made Bitty want to kill.

Her composure disintegrated. Suddenly she hated Chauncey for everything he had done to her and to Henry and to Tolliver, and most of all to Hélène. The hatred crystallized in that moment, over Henry's molested fishing line.

"You don't deserve children!" she shouted as loud as she could, the only time she could remember yelling like that in her whole life. She had yelled in horror when she killed the rabbit, and probably she had screamed once or twice when something startled her but she had never simply gotten furious with someone and bellowed like a fishwife.

"Bitty!" Ma-Mère's voice was shocked.

Across the room, Chauncey turned toward her, surprised, probably not realizing she had it in her. She watched his face become a mask of concern. "Dollin', are you all right?" His voice was saccharine.

Bitty stood up, picked up the chair she was sitting in, and went for him. Tiny, quick Marcelle, frightened by the yelling, ran from the living room into her path and froze, too late sensing danger. She stood looking up at her mother with those plate-sized eyes. Bitty tried to step aside, but it was too late. She mowed her down with the chair.

By now, though, trying to avoid hitting her child, she had lost her own balance and she fell sideways to the right, missing Marcelle, at least not falling on her, and twisting her own ankle. As Marcelle had stood there, staring up at her, Bitty had yelled, "I hate you!" Not at Marcelle, but at Chauncey.

"Mother is that really what happened? You wouldn't lie to me?"

"Of course not, Marcelle."

"I remember it—I remember your saying 'I hate you!' I remember it so clearly. I thought you meant me."

"You poor child. Of course I didn't mean you."

"You really didn't?"

"Of course not. And I didn't really hate your father either." *Not till later.* "I was just upset."

"Did this happen before or after the baby died?"

Marcelle had brought up Hélène as if it was nothing. Bitty took it like a blow in the stomach. Looking down, she said, "After."

"After? Really?"

"Marcelle, that's what was wrong with me. Don't you understand? That's why I was so excitable." *So violent.*

341

"I didn't kill her."

Bitty wondered if she'd heard right. She didn't understand what Marcelle meant, but she felt suddenly too ill to try to fathom it.

"Mother, what is it?"

"I think I'd better lie down." Marcelle helped her to the sofa.

When Marcelle had said, "the baby," just the two words, that was all, the image had come—the ugly mark on Hélène's backside, like a fading bruise mark.

"Someone hit her," Chauncey had said. "They spanked her to make her breathe. They hurt her—nurse, look at this."

"Oh, that's not a bruise. It's a Mongolian spot, a kind of birthmark." She looked at Chauncey quizzically. "Are you French Algerian? Mediterranean?"

Chauncey didn't answer, only looked confused.

"You're not, are you, Mrs. St. Amant? It must be Mr. St. Amant?"

"Why do you ask?"

"I never saw a Caucasian baby with a Mongolian spot."

And then the accusations had started. He had examined Hélène every day, her skin and her hair, as if she were a doll, and after a month or so, both hair and skin had begun to change. Her father noticed too, and Chauncey told him what Bitty had done—what he *said* Bitty had done. She had cried and denied it and told them both what Ma-Mère had said, but they didn't hear and they wouldn't have cared if they had.

RECOVERY

I believe I truly hate the little bastard. What kind of attitude is that?
  Unprofessional.

Skip felt a little rueful about pushing Henry around, but
the hell of it was, she longed to do it again. She had to get a
grip on herself or she was going to end up the kind of cop
she told herself she'd never be.

Okay, count to ten. Burn some incense. Try to sit still.
She tried sometimes to meditate, but was usually so wildly
unsuccessful at it that she settled not even for sitting still,
simply for trying to. It helped with the adrenaline rushes that
were epidemic in her job, helped a little anyway, even
though she usually felt as if somebody'd just dropped a sack
of ants on her the second she assumed the lotus position. It
was so hard for her, so alien, that she took that as her clue: if

she could ever master this, then she could probably master her fate. But that was for later. She wasn't yet spiritually advanced enough for ten minutes of meditation. Five minutes of sitting reasonably still would have to do for the moment.

At the end of the five minutes—actually more like four and a half—she felt she could cope. She had already dumped her suit, panty hose and shoes, and was down to panties and bra. She got a Diet Coke and sat on her sofa, massaging feet that were bitterly protesting the walk back and forth across the Quarter in the damn heels.

Nothing was any better. The "meditation," if you could call it that, hadn't changed a thing. She still didn't believe a word that came out of Henry's mouth.

Hélène is dead. Marcelle . . .

Marcelle what?

He had spoken with passion and seemingly a lot of pain, but Henry was an actor. However, say she didn't know that—would that make his story any easier to believe? It might if she didn't know Tolliver—and Henry himself.

A passionate man given to histrionics might well have killed Chauncey for interfering in his romance, but Tolliver had always seemed so phlegmatic. (Which argued against his killing Chauncey for love of either mother or son.) Yet people did do things that were out of character.

There were other problems. If Tolliver was gay at all (which she doubted because Jimmy Dee didn't think he was), he was certainly secretive about it. Why, at age fifty-odd, should he suddenly decide to have a particular young man come live with him?

Of course he could have been in love with Henry all his life and it could finally have gotten to him, but that was the hardest of all to swallow. Okay, she was prejudiced—she couldn't stand the little bastard. But who could? Frankly, he just wasn't lovable.

Not to you maybe, but what if you'd seen him grow up, watched him go through all the tortures of childhood and adolescence—which must have been considerable in that household. You might have more compassion for him. You might see, not Henry the grown-up brat, but Henry the brave four-year-old struggling valiantly against vast and terrifying odds.

Forget it, only a mother could love him.

Well, all right, maybe a mother or an uncle. So for the sake of argument, say the elegant Tolliver really fell in love with the egregious Henry. How about this disinheriting business? Pretty baroque. Tolliver wasn't poor and exploitive, after Henry for his imagined future fortune. He was wealthy enough so that he and Henry could have lived perfectly comfortably without a dime of St. Amant money. (Besides which, there must be Mayhew money under Bitty's control.) And why should Tolliver leave a note saying he was in love with Bitty if he wasn't?

Looking at it with a more or less cool head (the sort you got from more or less sitting still), Henry had a much better motive than Tolliver. He was the one who had reason to hate Chauncey, and indeed to do him in for personal profit. And he was the one who had gone to truly astonishing lengths to get her off the case. What did she have that was scaring him? Some shard of unsuspected evidence, some overheard gobbet of conversation that could unravel the whole thing? Why the hell wouldn't it come into consciousness?

It would if I could sit still long enough to meditate.

If Henry had been attacking her, than it hadn't been La-Belle, which blew the notion that she had been in town all along.

Where on earth does she fit in? Okay. Really think about it. Did she kill Chauncey?

If so, she would have had to have a key to Tolliver's. Now there was a thought. Maybe she could have got one. As a prostitute, she always went to the trick's house or hotel—Calvin Hogue had been very specific about that, and so had Hinky Hebert. Perhaps she had serviced Tolliver and lifted a key.

But what was her motive? Revenge? She certainly had reason to get even. But it seemed to Skip that blackmail would be a better plan—why not cash in, better late than never, on what she'd missed out on? Sheree Izaguirre had seen Chauncey throw her out on her ear. Perhaps she had come into his office to blackmail him and he'd refused. And then she'd given it a second try at his house, where Marcelle saw her. He didn't pay and so she killed him.

No good. Exposure would have made much more sense and would probably have been more satisfying. And anyway, if LaBelle killed Chauncey, why on earth would Tolliver confess to it?

Hélène is dead. Marcelle . . .

Hold it, here. She was actually getting an idea.

Suppose Hélène did kill Chauncey, which caused Marcelle, who loved her father, to kill her, and Tolliver to kill himself to protect Marcelle. Perhaps, as a matter of fact, he was really in love with Marcelle, not Bitty or Henry at all.

Oh, that's too silly.

Maybe, but he sure as hell must have been in love with one of them, and offhand, Marcelle seemed the most palatable of the lot.

The longer Skip sat and waited to fall into a creative meditation, the more she became aware of her changing physical condition. The illness she had pleaded that morning was leaving her body as if she'd just bathed in the healing waters of Lourdes.

Tarantino and O'Rourke were both still in the office, having a last cup of coffee and chewing the fat about something—basketball, she thought.

"Look who it is," said Joe. "Surprise about Tolliver Albert, huh?"

"You aren't kidding. Hi, Frank."

He gave her a barely perceptible nod—not quite rude, but not civil either.

"It's okay if you don't want to talk to me. I know you're going through a hard time."

"What do you know, bitch?" He got up with a great scraping of his chair and left, not even saying good-bye to Joe.

Skip said, "I don't know why you wouldn't tell me the story on him. They all know it Uptown."

Joe shrugged his meaty shoulders. "He's a proud guy. What can I do you for?"

"It's written all over me, huh?"

He shrugged again. "Just a guess."

"Have we had any murders—or even suicides—of unidentified black females in the last week?"

"Negative."

"Damn!"

"Your mystery woman?"

"Well, she never came home. I thought I might as well see if maybe she couldn't walk."

"Can't help you, I'm afraid. We know everyone who bought it this week. Now last week, that might be another matter—"

"Can we check?"

He pulled out a folder, went through it, and handed her two pieces of paper. "Here you are. Jane and Jill Doe."

One had been found on the street a week or so ago, dead of a head injury, probably mugged. She was about sixty. The other had been pulled out of the river, strangled, about a month ago. The coroner estimated her age as somewhere between twenty and twenty-five.

"Shit."

"No luck?"

"Yeah, luck. The young one's somebody I better look at. You don't have her, do you?"

"Jill? No. I think Silverman and Schlosser got her. But they're gone for the day." He threw her another piece of paper. "Here's something might interest you."

347

Skip skimmed it quickly. It was the autopsy report on Tolliver. The cause of death had turned out to be the advertised drug overdose, but the coroner had found something else.

"His brain was spongy? Does this mean what I think it does?"

Tarantino nodded smugly. "Uh-huh. He was a walking dead man. The thing he had—Creutzfeldt-Jakob Disease, it's called—kills you in a few months. A year at the most. He knew he had it too—there's a drug called Klonopin they use to treat it. He was on it."

"Jesus. This doesn't seem to you to shed a new light on things?"

"You mean, like he had nothing to lose by checking out? So he might have done it to protect somebody else?"

"Something like that."

"Well, let me tell you a little about this disease. It's very rare, but not that difficult to diagnose. The less serious symptoms are strange little muscle twitches and another funny thing—an exaggerated startle reaction."

"A what?"

"You know, like you startle easily. Also anxiety, fatigue, headaches, weakness, dizziness, stiffness of the limbs—"

"Everything in the book."

"I was saving the best for last. The thing's a dementia, like Alzheimer's. The serious symptoms are memory loss, impaired judgment, personality change, and this thing that goes by a real technical name—'unusual behavior.'"

"Oh, shit."

"Yeah, like maybe you might dress up like Dolly Parton and shoot your best friend. Would you call that usual behavior? Duby's out of his mind with delight."

Skip said nothing.

"This was a very messy homicide, didn't you notice? One of the town's most prominent citizens mowed down on a city street. Not your average tavern stabbing. The brass wanted the thing to get unmessy real bad. And your friend Tolliver was gentleman enough to oblige."

"Tolliver or whoever killed him."

"Whoever killed him? Gimme a break. You know how many pills he took? Look at that thing again. About fifty, all different kinds. And there weren't any signs of force anywhere in his place. Uh-uh, babe. He did himself."

"I better get to the morgue. And thanks. It's really nice to have somebody treat me as if I might not be an ax murderer."

"Ahhh, Frank'll be fine. He just needs time, that's all."

Jill Doe had the light skin and red hair Skip was looking for, but it was hard to imagine she had ever been beautiful. She must have floated a few days before she'd been pulled out. She looked ugly—very ugly—but mostly she looked pathetic and sad and in an odd way, innocent, as dead people always did to Skip. Or the ones she saw in the morgue did, without their mortuary beauty makeovers. Whatever hardness or meanness LaBelle had learned in her meager life was unlearned, unimportant when life left the body. Now it was just a body—not bad, not good; not pretty, not ugly; not smart, not dumb, simply there, lying perfectly still.

Skip wanted to bring her back to life. She never saw a corpse that didn't make her feel that way. She wondered if that was sick.

She told a friendly coroner's deputy she thought she could ID the corpse, had him give her a set of prints and went back to the office, to Latent Prints. She left the set and went home, too edgy to sit and wait. She wanted to be alone to think.

They'd told her half an hour. She'd been home ten minutes—still had five to go—when Steve called.

"Hello, dawalin'."

"Hi."

"What's wrong? You sound so distant."

"I was thinking. What's up?"

"I just wanted to gossip. I was thinking about Marcelle . . ."

"Listen, could we talk later?"

"What's wrong?"

"Nothing." Without meaning to, she snapped the word out. "I'll call you back." She hung up.

Damn. She should have reacted sooner. She should have said she couldn't talk right at the start.

The phone rang again. "Hey, it's a match. Congratulations."

"Jill's LaBelle Doucette?"

"You got it. Good work."

Shitfire. Why hadn't she thought of it before? When someone doesn't come home for weeks, there's a good chance they're dead.

Oh, bullshit. She could have been in the Caribbean.

But she wasn't. She'd been lying on her slab for nearly a month, strangled to death by someone, Skip had a feeling, whom Skip had known all her life.

Hélène is dead. Marcelle . . .

Skip shivered. Surely not.

Okay, what did she know?

Hardly anything. Not even how LaBelle found out who she was. And she had known, because she told Sheree Izaguirre to tell Chauncey she was Hélène. Anyway, that explained how the St. Amants learned who she was. Chauncey could have told any or all of them—Henry, Marcelle, even Tolliver. (And Bitty, of course.)

But how did LaBelle find out?

Well, there was one thing. Jaree might not know what family she came from, but she did know it was a fancy one. LaBelle had no doubt asked all the questions other kids ask and had probably been let in on her sketchy heritage. Skip could see how her old-fashioned great-grandmother might even have made kind of a fairy story of it—*"So you know you better be proud, baby; 'cause tha's blue blood runs in them veins of yours.''*

Next thing you know—say, some ten years later, LaBelle starts telling the story around town to Hinky Hebert and her other clients, and one of them not only thinks the story rings a familiar bell, but, remembering Jaree, recognizes her last name. He might have asked a few discreet questions—her mother's name, the name of the family she used to work for—just to make sure.

There were three men in the case—Chauncey, Tolliver, and Henry. Which one was most likely? Henry was most assuredly gay—or at any rate a transvestite who claimed he was, and Skip was willing to bet he wasn't lying on that one. So that left Tolliver and Chauncey. Chauncey would never have told her who she was—it would have made him too vulnerable.

That left Tolliver. On the face of it, he seemed a good candidate. His sex life wasn't publicly known, and the call girl theory would explain a lot. But why the hell would Tolliver clue Hélène in on her identity? The idea was preposterous.

She paced. She couldn't meditate, and she didn't think a joint would help. Pacing didn't either. Frustrated, wanting a momentary distraction, she took a shower. And emerged, she later thought, purified. Along with the dust of a day that had been more like a ride on a roller coaster, the warm, prickly water had washed away everything she thought about the case.

Silently thanking Steve Steinman for what he had taught her, she hunted up a pencil and paper, took the phone off the hook, and settled back on her sofa, naked, wet hair dripping down her back.

She didn't know how long she stayed there; not long, she thought. The whole thing seemed to have turned itself upside down in a split second.

The important question now was who had killed LaBelle—and why. Only one answer made any sense.

She dialed Chauncey's mother.

After extended condolences, she popped her question: "Mrs. St. Amant, I hate to bother you, but I have to finish up the paperwork. I find we need one little thing for our records—Chauncey was adopted, wasn't he?"

"Why, yes. And you never saw a prettier baby either."

"Do you know who the biological parents were?"

"They never would tell us that—they didn't in those days, you know."

A LENTEN DINNER

"You were right, Henry. Hélène's dead."

"What the fuck do you want?" He had come out on his balcony to see who was there.

"We need to talk again. About why you broke into your sister's apartment."

"You got a warrant for my arrest?"

"This is an informal call, but don't press me, baby. I can have twenty cops here in twenty minutes."

He buzzed her in without another word. Upstairs, she found the apartment door unlocked as well, and Henry in the kitchen, tearing up salad greens. Skip could smell potatoes baking, and on the stove was a pot of milk. Henry didn't speak, made no move to greet her, simply continued attacking his Romaine. She made herself at home, taking time to notice that on a nearby counter was a cookbook open to oyster soup. "You're expecting someone."

Still, he didn't speak.

"Henry, I think you lied. I don't think Tolliver was your lover. His note said he was in love with your mother."

"He was protecting me—protecting all of us. This way there's no taint of the dread and ugly homosexuality."

"Frankly, I don't think Tolliver was a homosexual at all. I think he suffered from unrequited love, if you'll forgive an antiquated expression, and once in a while relieved an itchy libido with a prostitute."

Henry turned to stare at her, angry-eyed, but not speaking.

"I think he was in love with your mother, just like the note said, but I don't know if it was conscious or unconscious."

"Sigmund Freud rides again."

Unperturbed at the gibe, Skip reached over and helped herself to a bit of lettuce, which she chewed slowly, maddeningly, she hoped.

"Maybe he didn't realize he was waiting for her, it just kind of turned out that way. He watched her fall apart after her daughter 'died,' as the story went, but one day the daughter, who *he* never thought was dead, walked into his life, grown-up."

"Oh, brother."

"We're only supposing here. You don't have to buy it if you don't want to. I'm just telling you a story I might have made up or I might not have. Maybe he thought that if he returned Bitty's daughter to her, it could help her get well. So he told her he'd found Hélène. Or perhaps he told Hélène who her mother was, but I don't think so. I think he'd want to leave it in Bitty's hands. At any rate, the two of them got together."

"I don't believe what you're doing. You're like something out of a circus." He was looking at her in such amazement that Skip nearly lost her nerve.

"It's just a story, Henry. I was just trying to think what

could have happened to poor Bitty—after all, it's a pretty awful thing to lose a child. And what I was thinking of was that old saw about being careful what you wish for. I bet Bitty wished a million times to have her child back but when Hélène turned up, she was LaBelle—not the child Bitty wanted at all. I bet Bitty wanted to help her—to get her out of prostitution, to help her get a job, maybe to send her to college. I don't know what she offered exactly, but it was some kind of mothering, I'm pretty sure. Only LaBelle wouldn't want that—she'd have had no use for Bitty and the family that gave her away. I bet she hurt Bitty pretty badly, somehow or another. My guess is, she tried to shake her down. She asked for money not to tell Chauncey (who probably did know she'd been given away instead of died, but LaBelle wouldn't know that), or not to tell your grandfather or maybe the *Times-Picayune* about her existence. Or maybe she didn't even put it that way. Maybe she more or less demanded reparations—said Bitty owed it to her for the horrid life she'd had to lead."

"Go on."

"I think she had a blackmail tool—not a very effective one, but one with dramatic impact. All she had to do to get a copy of her birth certificate was write to the Bureau of Records. Once she knew her real name was Hélène St. Amant, she could do that. And I think she did. Have you ever heard that expression, 'the child is the father of the man'? You've lived it anyway. You've had to be your mother's parent in lots of ways, haven't you? Bitty turned to the one she always turned to when she needed help—you, Henry."

"You don't know what you're talking about."

"Oh, she probably told Tolliver too. First, I imagine. I don't know when all this happened. Weeks ago, probably. But you didn't get the copy of the birth certificate until Saturday, when I caught you at LaBelle's. It was taped to the back of a picture, wasn't it? Not that it proved anything, it just tied her to the St. Amants."

"Get out of here."

Insouciantly, Skip reached for another lettuce leaf. He grabbed her wrist: "Get out."

She saw that she had won, and the knowledge made her calm and a little smug. "You thought it was the only thing that could connect her with your precious family—you must have been pretty shocked to find the scrapbook. And then it turned out you had to leave in a hurry. But you came back to get it, didn't you? You really shouldn't have broken into a police officer's house, Henry. And certainly not twice. That sort of thing makes us really mad." Almost immediately, she realized she'd gone too far. She was being mean and bullying.

A paring knife sailed past her cheek.

She stepped toward him, but a plastic bowl of salad dressing splashed her face like a custard pie and dripped greasily onto her sweater. He bounced a jar of vitamins off her shoulder.

"Cunt!" He was way out of control. She made her voice silky and comforting, the voice you use for frightened toddlers.

"Henry, everything's okay. Nobody's going to hurt you."

He caught her eye for a moment, as if trying to decide whether to believe her, and stepped backward into the living room. He picked up the ottoman, holding it like a shield. Slowly, Skip followed, trying not to make any sudden moves. She braced herself, but when the leather lump slammed into her chest, it knocked her down. She was unhurt, popped up quickly. But it gave him time to grab a lamp.

Realizing there was nothing else to do, she rushed him and dived at his legs in a flying tackle that brought him down in a heap, unplugging the lamp. The room went dark as she wrestled him.

"Cunt!" screamed Henry. "Get off me, you bitch. I killed him, goddamnit; I killed him, you cunt. Leave me the hell alone or I'll kill you too. I swear to God I will."

Through his shouting, Skip was vaguely aware of a pounding on the door, but she had no time for that now. He was small, much smaller than she, but he was wriggling like a cat being bathed, and he was at least as slippery and bony. He was strong too. Maybe it was the fabled strength of the insane.

"Henry! What is it? Henry! Oh, God, what is it?"

It was Bitty's voice. For a moment he was distracted enough for Skip to pin an arm behind him.

"Mother! Mother! Get her off me!"

A light went on—Bitty had found the floor lamp. "Skip? Skippy, is that you?"

Skip didn't know what to say. She settled on, "He's upset."

Bitty knelt by them. Skip had Henry on his belly now, straddling him, twisting one arm behind him and holding the other. Bitty stroked his hair. "What's wrong, baby?"

"The bitch knows, Mother. She knows I killed Daddy. The bastard—he was going to cut my money off. He wouldn't leave me alone. He wouldn't leave Tolliver alone . . ." His voice was trailing off now, deteriorating to a toneless gibber.

"What are you saying?"

Without warning, he started shouting again. "I hated the bastard! I hated his guts! I hated his ass! I've wanted to kill him for years."

"But Tolliver—"

"He did it to cover for me, Mother. Don't you see?" He sounded like a sometime lunatic just back from the edge of madness, trying desperately to be rational.

"Officer Langdon," he said, "I confess to the murder of my father. Will you let me up please?"

Skip got off him and pulled him to his feet, still holding the arm behind him. She had cuffs in her purse. "Henry, you're under arrest," she said, very deliberately and quietly. "You have the right to remain silent . . ."

"Shut up!"

She turned in surprise. She hadn't thought Bitty had that much noise in her small frame.

"Let him go." Bitty was holding Skip's gun, fished from the purse.

The whole family was going nuts on her. Once again she spoke deliberately, trying not to frighten either mother or son. "I can't do that, Bitty."

"He didn't kill his father. I did."

"She's lying."

"Shut up, Henry. Promise to sit down, so Skippy can let you go."

"Mother, you can't protect me. Nobody's going to believe you did it—and I don't mean just because you didn't have a motive. Frankly, my dear, you drink too much to pull off something like that."

"Henry, it's no good." She threw the cuffs to Skip. "He's protecting me, you see. Put these on him and I'll tell you what happened."

"Oh, Mother, it's all right. I'll be good."

Skip said, "Why don't I believe that?"

"Because you're a stupid cunt!" He kicked backward at her shin but missed. In one smooth movement, Skip took the cuffs from Bitty and wrestled him into them. She would have pushed him roughly into a chair if Bitty hadn't been there, but out of deference to her teachers at McGehee's, she resisted the impulse. She waited until he had sat and then reached for the gun.

"Okay, Mrs. St. Amant, I'll listen."

Bitty sat down. "What if I told you Chauncey was black?"

Henry said, "Funny, he didn't look black."

"Maybe he was an eighth black—a sixteenth. Who knows? He thought it was enough to ruin his life if anyone knew."

Skip said, "I understand. I know about LaBelle."

"LaBelle?" Bitty sounded unconvinced that the word had come out of Skip's mouth.

"I know you gave birth to a black baby and gave her to a black woman to raise."

"How dare you say that! How could you know what it

means to be a mother? I did *not* do that, Skip Langdon. I did not give up my own child. No mother would do that.

"Chauncey did it. He didn't want anyone to know. He accused me . . . but how could you know Chauncey was her father? Even my own father never believed it."

"I made a lucky guess. I saw this kid—Estelle Villere's child—who looked white even though his parents were black—or what passes for black in New Orleans. And I remembered Marcelle told me how much Chauncey hated the word *bastard*. I was playing around with different ideas, trying to figure out why LaBelle was given away. And I thought, what if *Chauncey* was the father? If he'd been adopted, he might look white and still be 'black' enough for the genes to come out in one of his children. So I called his mother and asked her."

"You talked to his mother? But she doesn't know about the black . . . blood."

"I didn't tell her."

"Marcelle doesn't know either. We never told anyone Chauncey was adopted after Hélène was born—Chauncey couldn't stand the thought that anyone would find out the truth. He didn't know himself until she was born. And he never really accepted it, even though he had the same kind of birthmark she had, one that a lot of black kids have. That's how we found out. A cute little nurse put her hand on the baby's butt, where it was all blue, and said, 'Oh, a Mongolian spot; I never saw one on a white baby before.' And Chauncey turned pale. Ma-Mère said, 'Oh, Chauncey had one till he was three or four.' That was the only way you could tell, when Hélène was first born. She had such lovely silky red hair—did you know black babies don't look black?"

"No."

"They change after a few months, or even weeks. Hélène started changing almost right away. Chauncey made me keep her away from people—even his own parents. That's how I know he knew he was the father. They're racists, the St.

Amants. They hated Chauncey's musicians and they could never understand any of his civil rights positions." She looked pathetically at Skip, defending her dead husband. "But he was like that before Hélène was born. Even when he didn't know about himself. All that was genuine. He just couldn't—" She bit her lip, on the verge of tears. "He couldn't accept himself as black. It was okay for other people, just not for him."

Skip could imagine. What he had done was difficult enough if you were white—come up from nowhere, married a Mayhew, gone from there to become King of Carnival. No known black man could have done it—even a man who was one-sixteenth black, or whatever Chauncey was. To acknowledge his blackness was to give up life as he knew it. To die, in a sense. To throw everything away.

"I would have loved him no matter what. As long as I could have kept my baby."

Skip wondered about that.

"I thought there was no other way. I thought he wouldn't love me any more if I didn't do it."

"He talked you into giving her up?"

"I was sick. I had the flu and this awful headache—I was full of drugs. They had to bribe a few people—he and my father and Tolliver—but not as many as you'd think. They just put a notice in the paper saying she was dead and we'd had her cremated. No one questioned it. Everyone sent flowers. Later he said I agreed. Even Tolliver said I did, so I must have. But I wouldn't have—" She was wailing it, eyes pleading for belief. "I never, *never* would have, if I'd been in my right mind. All I remember was, we got in the car and Chauncey drove a few blocks, not very far, and Tolliver was waiting for us in his car. And Chauncey made me give her to him. And I did. I just handed her over. I thought I had to. They never told me who the family was—just that it was very nice and respectable."

Skip said, "I'm sorry."

"Then Tolliver found her—she was a prostitute, you

know—that's how he met her. She told me that, not him. When he found her, I felt alive again. Like I had a new lease on life. But she rejected me; my poor daughter rejected me because of what I did to her. And then she went to Chauncey's office and tried to blackmail him—he was about to be Rex and she knew it. But he wouldn't pay and so she came to the house. I saw her that time. I heard the whole thing, and I confronted Chauncey about it. He already knew I'd met with her—she told him the whole story—but he didn't even mention it to me. Can you imagine that?

"Anyway, he told me he'd take care of her and he went out one night and came back disheveled and got drunk and wouldn't talk, and couldn't sleep that night. And then a couple of days later I read in the paper that the police were trying to figure out the identity of a body they'd fished out of the river. And I knew she was Hélène. *I knew.*"

"Did you mention it to Chauncey?"

"Of course. I beat him up. I accused him of killing his own daughter and I climbed up on his chest and I beat him as hard as I could. He didn't deny it either. When he got tired of me beating him, he just pulled me off. It never even hurt him." Her shoulders sagged. "And he said it was for the best. That she was dead. And so I did what I'd been wanting to do for years."

"She didn't. I did." Henry's eyes were sullen and defiant.

"First I sobered up. Do you know how easy that is? Really easy. All you have to have is a good reason. You can stay sober for weeks if you have to. Of course the craving doesn't go away—the 'addiction,' as they insist on calling it nowadays—and you go back to it as soon as the threat, or whatever it is, is past—believe me, I know. But you can do it for a while. Make no mistake about it.

"In this case I didn't get sober because of a threat in my life. I had a mission." Her voice rose a little and for a minute tiny, fragile, usually unobtrusive Bitty convinced Skip that she was someone to be reckoned with. She remembered stories Marcelle had told her, stories about Bitty's resourcefulness when everyone else was falling apart, and she kicked herself for not remembering earlier. "I never felt better in my life either. I *lived* to kill my husband. I relished it. I thought when it was done I could live a normal life, that I would never drink again."

She looked at her lap. "It didn't turn out that way. The whole thing caved in as soon as he was dead. I turned to mush again, only it was suicidal mush this time."

"Mother!"

"Right now, I have only one thing to live for—Henry's life. I want to live to make sure that Henry doesn't suffer for what I did."

Skip said, "You're sober right now, aren't you?"

"And I will be as long as I have to be. Shall I go on?"

"Please."

"I expect I've already surprised you, and I'll do it again. I can shoot. I'll demonstrate if you like. My father taught me when I was a kid. I had to find the right weapon, of course, but that wasn't hard—Chauncey had an array to choose from—and I had to practice up. I took a selection to a firing range across the lake and figured out which one would work best, and then I kept practicing until I was as good as I ever was. The .44.40 was a large enough caliber to be accurate at the distance I needed, but not so huge it couldn't be managed by someone who's a pretty good shot. Henry's probably never shot a gun in his life, but plenty of witnesses will tell you I have.

"One thing I've kind of regretted, though. I put my costume together from bits and pieces I found here and there, but I couldn't really find the right wig anywhere." She turned to her son. "Except here, Henry. I shouldn't have taken it, should I? That's how you figured it out."

"Mother, don't be absurd."

"Because you already knew about your father killing your sister. You thought I didn't remember telling you, didn't you?

It was just before I decided to kill him—the last time I was drunk, I think. But I do remember; I didn't for a while, but I do now."

"Mother, I think you're drunk now. You never told me any such thing."

"I hid the whole outfit in a bag of peat moss at Tolliver's. The police have probably already put the rest of it together—how I just got the car, drove to Tolliver's, and drove back."

"How do you explain Tolliver's suicide?" asked Skip.

"He was ill. Did you know that?"

"The autopsy showed it."

"I told him Chauncey killed Hélène, back when I told Henry—I was in such a depression I'd probably have told you if I'd seen you that week—or your mother or the governor. And Tolliver told me it wasn't true, of course—that I was imagining things. After that, he noticed that I was sober for a while. So then I pretended to be more out of control than ever, and I'm afraid I really upset him. He kept saying things about a new life—that he'd get better, and I'd get sober." She wiped away tears.

"I think he was telling the truth when he wrote that note. He really was there for me every day, all my life. I guess, in the end, he figured out I killed Chauncey. Or maybe Henry told him."

"Mother!"

"And what he did was the most gallant thing I've ever heard of." Her eyes were shining like those of some medieval lady dreaming of her knight.

God! I'm going to throw up.

"He sacrificed his life for me."

In more than one way, baby.

And yet, sick as she thought it was, there was a piece of Skip that admired him for it.

Bitty came back from her romantic reverie and gave Skip a gaze so level there could be no doubt she was sober and possessed of a lot more strength than Skip would have guessed. "Are you going to arrest me, Skippy?"

It was the question Skip was pondering.

Henry said, "She's telling the truth."

"Of course I am."

"Except for one thing. It all went exactly the way she described it. I bet I still have the receipt for the wig. The only difference is that, at the risk of belaboring the point, *I* did it. I did it for her, you know." He was no longer the lunatic-on-the-brink, just a guy having a conversation with a woman he'd known all his life. "I knew she wanted him dead; if you want, Officer Freud, you could even say she did it through me. But I was the one who pulled the trigger. I wanted her to have a chance at life—without *him*."

Bitty laughed, an odd sound to Skip's ears. She realized that in all the time she'd known the St. Amants, she'd probably never once heard Bitty laugh. "Henry, it won't fly," said his mother.

"She's right." Despite Henry's ability as an actor, his words were as hollow as Bitty's were heartfelt. He hadn't killed Chauncey.

The question still stood: Was she going to arrest Bitty? The temptation simply to flee was almost overwhelming. If Chauncey had killed his own daughter, and Bitty had killed him, wasn't that justice? She wondered if she could leave right now and forget she ever heard any of this. But she was a cop. Justice and the law weren't the same thing. Yet somehow she couldn't see dragging Bitty Mayhew St. Amant, still in her elegant black dress, down to headquarters in handcuffs.

And there was another problem. Skip wasn't sure she could prove anything.

She said, "Mrs. St. Amant, can I trust you?"

"Trust me? You mean you don't believe me?"

"I do believe you. But I want to spare you as much as I can. I won't arrest you now if you'll promise to go to headquarters tomorrow and tell your story."

"But . . . I don't know anyone there." Her eyes brimmed. Moments ago the competent murderer, now she was once again the helpless socialite.

"Ask for Inspectors O'Rourke and Tarantino. They're the officers on the case."

"But I don't know them. Will you be there?" Her eyes pleaded.

"Of course. But if you don't come—by noon, say—I'll tell them the whole story myself. And there'll be lots of proof. Hélène's body, for one thing." She was being deliberately harsh. "And witnesses from the firing range. So don't think this is the end of it. I'm not arresting you tonight, but tomorrow's another day. Would you prefer to do it this way?"

Bitty's blue eyes were aghast. "I guess so."

"You promise you'll be there?"

She wet her lips. "I promise."

"See you tomorrow, then."

She removed Henry's handcuffs and left, bracing herself for a long wait in the night air. Given the crime rate in New Orleans, Henry would walk Bitty to her car, but she didn't know whether that would happen in minutes or hours. She huddled across the street, standing on one foot and then the other, cold and impatient, until a plan finally formed in her head, inspired by what she was looking at—the window Henry had left cracked earlier, when he cleared the house of the pot smoke. She'd have to leave her post and trust to luck for a few minutes, but this way would be much cleaner and more elegant than the alternative, which was conning her way in the downstairs door and kicking in Henry's.

She phoned Steve, told him to meet her immediately, and to bring a long rope.

Luck went her way. Bitty and Henry didn't come out for another hour. As soon as they were out of earshot, Steve threw the rope over the gallery rail, and Skip shinnied up. It was a struggle, but it hadn't been easy at the academy, either.

Henry might destroy the birth certificate—might have already—but it wouldn't do her any good to steal it. It wasn't evidence unless it was found in his apartment, not stolen from it. What she wanted might or might not be evidence—but no one would ever believe it had been taken from his apartment. That was the beauty of this little burglary. And the justice of it pleased her. Henry had twice invaded her home.

TUESDAY

She arrived promptly at eleven-fifty and asked not for O'Rourke and Tarantino, but for Skip, as Skip had known she would, because by this time she knew that Bitty knew the other two would be busy. They had been closeted with Henry since ten-thirty, taking his confession.

Skip got her a cup of coffee and sat her at Tarantino's desk, feeling she ought to have removed the snake poster for the occasion. As quickly as she could exit gracefully, she left, ostensibly for lunch, actually too tense to eat, too bewildered and disoriented to stick around headquarters; and far too angry to stay in the same room with Bitty.

She had spent the early-morning hours—from seven on—with Duby, Tarantino, and O'Rourke, one or two at a time, mostly being yelled at, now and then being patted on the head when one of them (never O'Rourke) actually remembered she had done a good job, however unorthodox. (They didn't know how unorthodox, and she was never going to tell them.)

When Henry showed up, she nearly lost it—nearly ran screaming into the street and disgraced her uniform, knowing what he was going to try to pull. She didn't think it would work—it certainly hadn't on her—but thinking wasn't doing her much good. Feelings were getting the upper hand and she felt as if someone was slowly shrinking her skin, making it tighter and tighter, like some shroudlike version of all-body thumb screws. Bitty's appearance only made things worse. What the fuck were these two up to? But she knew; she knew. Deep in her heart, goddamnit, she knew.

She found an empty office and used the phone, able, at last, to return Steve's call, to ask him if they had anything. She had found the film within thirty seconds of entering Henry's apartment, but Steve had long since returned the projector he'd rented at Mardi Gras, so they hadn't been able to view it.

Steve wasn't home. How dare he! But of course—he must have already left for her house.

She found him sitting on her front steps, film and freshly rented 16-millimeter projector in hand, shit-eating grin on face. She said, "What is it?"

"I *think*—I really think—we've got what you want."

Her knees buckled. What the hell did she want?

The film was exactly as advertised a week ago—perfect; gorgeous. Dolly playing the gun tricks, Dolly drawing, Dolly shooting—"and then nothing," as Steve had said then.

But that had been only the filmmaker in him talking. There was something; plenty of something. A collage, as the camera was jostled. First the bunting-covered balcony, then Dolly's face again. Then a piece of the wall, with just the blonde wig at the bottom of the picture, a back view—she had turned around. Then more wall, as the camera was pushed up. And that was it. But the proof was there.

Skip's stomach hurt. The last thing she felt like doing was eating, but she couldn't risk getting faint at a tense moment.

They walked together to the Quarter A&P, fast, trying to work off stress, and bought the makings for health-food shakes. This was far from her usual style, but she couldn't possibly get down anything solid.

She consumed hers absently, not really tasting it, just hoping it would do its work and see her through the afternoon.

Afterward she thought about making herself try to sit still for five minutes, but she knew it wasn't in the cards. Instead, she did some stretches. When she couldn't think of any other possible way to relieve tension that didn't involve sex or drugs, she and Steve went back to headquarters.

She had given him a rundown of the morning and together they'd worked out a plan. She put him in a borrowed office and went to find O'Rourke and Tarantino. The plan called for getting the lay of the land before firing the bombshell.

The stars were sitting at their desks, quietly doing paperwork as if nothing had happened.

Quiet. Too quiet, as they say in old movies.

"What's the story?"

O'Rourke didn't bother to look up.

Tarantino spread his arms. "He says he did it; she says she did it."

"So who did you believe?"

"Skip, listen, it's no good. We haven't got any proof."

She turned briefly toward the snake wall to hide her disappointment.

"You got the search warrant?"

"We searched his apartment, her house. And we found the birth certificate at his place. So what does that prove? We've only got that and the scrapbook to connect Doucette with the whole damn family. There's nothing at all to show St. Amant knocked her off."

"Tell me the truth, Joe—who the hell did it?"

"Did Doucette? How the hell should I know?"

"Did Chauncey!"

He made his goddamn expansive Italian gesture again. "Tolliver Albert—"

"Shit!" She put her hands in her pocket and kicked the desk, knowing she was acting like a child but also knowing no one would really mind. This wasn't IBM, and corporate behavior wasn't required. This was Stressout City; never had she felt it more than today.

"Sit down, Skip. Let's talk a minute." She sat. "Get you some coffee?"

She managed a tight little smile to acknowledge the kindness. "No thanks, Joe."

"We talked to the Harmeyers. They say Albert never told them whose baby it was."

"Surely they guessed."

"What are we gonna do? Beat it out of 'em with rubber hoses?"

Skip had the feeling of sliding into a dank, dark tunnel, one that would get darker the deeper she got, would twist and turn crazily, and would eventually drop her out into sunlight. When she landed, it would not be on her feet, and she would be covered in muck.

What was wrong with her? Wasn't this the best way?

But she did it. She shot her goddamn husband. And you're a cop.

He deserved it.

You're a cop! What are you here for?

Justice, maybe?

What's wrong with you?

"Look." Joe's voice was cajoling, almost begging, yet Skip knew he didn't want anything for himself. He was trying to get her to understand that they were backed into a corner. "Just because they both confessed doesn't mean a damn thing.

Suppose we charged one of them. Is he or she—let's say she—gonna get a lawyer? You bet. Just because she tried that little ploy of confessing to get her kid off the hook, is she going to go into court and plead guilty? Not real likely, kid."

"Ploy! She did it and you know it."

"That's not what her lawyer's gonna say. We don't have a case, baby."

"Yes, we do."

For the first time, O'Rourke deigned to acknowledge her presence. "Oh, we do, do we? When did you get to be a legal expert, sugar?"

"Don't call me sugar, asshole."

He repeated it, mimicking in a bratty falsetto.

This was getting her nowhere. "I've got a witness," she said.

"Oh, yeah? Why didn't you tell us before?"

"I didn't find out till half an hour ago."

"Oh, sure you didn't."

Tarantino looked very grave indeed. "Tell us about it, Skip." He pulled up a chair for her. "Here. Make yourself comfortable."

Even now, sitting down in the thumb-screw suit that currently passed for her skin, she felt a rush of affection for Tarantino and his old-fashioned courtesy.

"His name is Steve Steinman."

"Your boyfriend." O'Rourke's tone was still mocking, but at least he'd abandoned the falsetto.

"I don't deny it. If he weren't, he wouldn't have realized what he had. He filmed the shooting."

"What!" O'Rourke went red in the face.

Tarantino shouted, "Goddamn that sucker! What's the matter with him?"

Skip made placating, air-patting gestures. "Take it easy, fellows. As soon as he had it developed, he watched it once and didn't notice anything out of the ordinary."

O'Rourke roared. "It was still evidence, goddamnit! Why didn't he goddamn bring it in?"

"Oh, he did." Her adrenaline was kicking in. She could manage a pseudo-sweet condescending semi-smile. "To me." She knew she was being bitchy, but she told the story of how Cookie Lamoreaux had recommended her and only her, and she also told a lie. "I looked at it and saw nothing also."

Tarantino spoke. "I don't get it."

"Well, Steve and I were just having lunch and he reminded me about it—"

"How did he happen to think of it, Langdon?" asked O'Rourke.

"We weren't discussing the case, O'Rourke. I just told him we were having problems with it. And he asked if it would help to see the film again. Knowing what we know now, I suddenly realized it would."

Tarantino said, "We better look at it, Frank." To Skip: "Where's Steinman?"

He had already set up the room for viewing, closed the blinds, threaded the film onto the projector, and faced it toward the far wall, to serve as a screen.

After introductions were made, Skip noticed that Tarantino was nervous about something, but she couldn't figure out what. He cleared his throat. "Uh, Mr. Steinman. Would you mind waiting outside?"

"I beg your pardon?"

"This is kind of a delicate case . . ."

"But there's nothing on that film I haven't seen. This is crazy." He stared past the giant shoulders at Skip. Unsure what was going on, she shrugged but said, "Why don't you have some coffee, Steve? We'll call you back in a minute."

Sulkily, he showed Tarantino how to run the machine and then suffered his banishment. Tarantino ran the film.

When it was done, Skip thought the relief in the room hung as thick in the air as cigar smoke. Apparently O'Rourke and Tarantino hadn't seen what she and Steve had.

O'Rourke said, "Big deal. Where does that get us?"

Tarantino was more cautious. "I don't see anything."

"Go back to where she's doing the gun tricks."

Tarantino obliged, and held the frame. Skip said, "See that sconce on the wall behind her?"

"What the fuck is a sconce, Miss Uptown?"

"Let her talk, Frank. It's the flower pot thing."

Skip said, "It's still on the wall. We can measure its height, and we'll get Dolly's."

Tarantino said, "Wait a minute. I remember that thing. Seems to me it was up pretty high—about six feet or so. Albert was about six feet tall, wasn't he?"

"At least."

He drummed his fingers. Dolly's head was well below the sconce. "How tall's Henry?"

"About five six or seven, I think. But there's something else. Remember how Tolliver seemed puzzled about the bunting? Said he hadn't draped it and didn't know anything about it?"

No one said anything.

"The murderer took an extra precaution in case he—or she—was seen. He stood on something to disguise his height. And that's what the bunting was for—because otherwise you could have seen through the ironwork."

Tarantino said, "I'm startin' to remember something. Look at that thing, Frank. Remember, one of the plants was sittin' in a chair? I wondered about that."

"I did too," said Skip. "But it didn't occur to me until I looked at the film again that Dolly moved it so that she'd have room for something else—the thing she needed to stand on. I think I know what it was too."

"Son of a gun. So do I."

And she knew that Tarantino had done what she had on her lunch hour—brought the murder scene piece by piece back into his memory. Even if he hadn't, it wouldn't matter—they had the crime-lab photos. The pictures would show the little pile of clothes in the middle of the carpet and the holster draped across the needlepoint footstool that was jutting out at such a funny angle—as if someone had kicked it. Or moved it and returned it hurriedly, simply flinging it down, not bothering to place it properly.

"That little stool thing. I bet that was it. Let's see—it's about six inches high, so if Henry's five six . . ."

Skip interrupted. "Did you notice there's a difference in the distance at the end? When the camera jumps around?"

Quickly, Tarantino ran the film to the end. There were two shots—one with Dolly's masked face to the camera and the one at the end, showing the back of her head, which must have been taken after she stepped off the stool. The distance between her head and the sconce was blatantly apparent. It wasn't any six inches. It was more like a foot.

"Holy God!" said Tarantino. "I'll get Duby."

Duby was smoking. The atmosphere changed as soon as he walked in, got thicker in more ways than one.

"Look, lieutenant." Tarantino's voice was excited. "We got it. I swear. With the confession and this, we could do it, I'm not kiddin'. Look at the back of her head—jus' look at that—and look at that flower thing! No way it could have been Albert. And no way it was the kid. Dolly was about five feet tall. Period. It's right there in living color. And we got a five-foot suspect who just confessed."

Skip was mesmerized, staring as if it were the Mona Lisa instead of a scrap of a bewigged head. Before her eyes, it melted. She wheeled.

Duby looked at her apologetically. "Ash fell off my cigarette. I shouldn't have been standing so close. Goddamn, is there anything else we can use? Can't see a thing." He struck a match and held it to the film. "Shit!" He sounded as shocked as if it had really been an accident. "Sorry, guys." He left the room instantly, giving no one a chance to utter a syllable.

For a minute the three sat in the dark, in shock. Finally,

O'Rourke said, "Goddamn," and Tarantino turned on the light. Skip could not trust herself to say anything, for fear that she would make a complete ass of herself, would be sent babbling to a hospital. She could not really have seen what she thought she had. It was just not possible.

O'Rourke said, "You Uptown bitches run the whole fucking world, don't you?" shoved the projector onto the floor, and walked heavily out of the room.

Tarantino bent to pick up the machine. He spoke with his back to her, as if he couldn't bear to look at her face. "Mayhew was here this morning. Spent about an hour with Chief McDermott. He dropped by to see the D.A. as well. I heard he was over by the mayor too."

"Haygood?"

"Her old man. Whatever his name is."

She fled, hoping she could keep back the tears till she was out of the building. As she tore through the detective bureau, Steve shouted her name.

"Ask *them* for your film," she shouted back.

"Where are you going?"

"I'll be right back." That was so he wouldn't follow her. Ignoring the elevator, she ran down the two flights to the first floor, as if pursued by all the demons of hell instead of only her personal ones.

She would have run all the way home if it hadn't been for traffic lights and for the fact that she was wearing her uniform. She settled for walking fast.

I ought to be glad Bitty's going scot-free. Glad she killed the sonofabitch and glad she got away with it.

Part of her was glad. But her premonition had come true. She was covered in slime. Bitty was not innocent, not of Chauncey's death and not of LaBelle's exile.

She handed that baby to Tolliver. She admitted it. She sent that child to a life of poverty as surely as Chauncey did. Where does she get off blaming him for everything that happened for the next twenty-one years?

She was furious at the system and furious that Haygood

Mayhew could manipulate it and furious that it hadn't worked. And that she was part of it and was covered in slime; part of the system and part of a conspiracy to let someone get away with murder. She didn't think she could have felt more guilty or remorseful if she had pulled the trigger herself.

The phone was ringing as she entered. Knowing it was Steve, she waited for his message before she unplugged it. Even as she listened, she was ripping off her uniform, sending buttons flying and rolling on the threadbare carpet. She tore off her underwear as well, tied her hair in a scarf, tignon-fashion, and threw on a flannel nightshirt. Barefoot, she carried the pile into the courtyard and set fire to it, grateful Jimmy Dee wasn't home to shout witticisms from his windows. Later she would worry about cleaning up the mess in the yard, and about whether to get a new uniform or a new career. Later she would see Steve, and she would cry.

Now she threw the rest of the incense he had brought onto the fire. As she watched it burn, she sat with legs crossed, perfectly still, almost meditating. It occurred to her that there was nothing like a severe shock to still the brain. If you had good reason not to think, you didn't. Or, put another way, there were things that happened that made thinking seem trivial.

When sandalwood no longer scented the almost-spring air, and when no trace of blue remained, she threw the scarf and nightshirt onto the blaze and ran naked into the house, hoping she met no one on the stairs. From her window she watched the fire die. As the last ember winked itself out, she stepped into the shower.